There Abideth Hope

Cover designed by The Magic Quill Graphics
Editing Services from Above the Pages

There Abideth Hope is a work of fiction. Names, characters, places, and incidents either are products of the author's imagination or are used fictitiously. Any resemblance to actual persons, living or dead, events is entirely coincidental.

Printed in the United States of America

First Printing: Dec 2014
CreateSpace Independent Publishing Platform
10 9 8 7 6 5 4 3 2

ISBN-13 978-1-7329237-1-3

Dedicated to my Lord Jesus Christ who has given me the ability to write and guided me through the story.

Acknowledgements

My thanks to all listed on this page for their contribution to the details of this story with professional information, critiques, support, and so much more. I am ever so grateful.

Author, Alan J. O'Reilly

Deputies John and Joanna Wilson, Escambia County Sheriff's Department

Duane Martinez, U.S. Navy (Ret.)

Ron "RJ" Miller, U.S. Marines (Ret.)

Arnold C. Hauswald, U.S. Army (Ret.)

Many serving at NAS Pensacola

Faye Hamilton, RN

Drs. Martin & Plunkett

ACFW Scribes Critique Group

And the many members of the Christian Writers & Readers Facebook Group Forum for their encouragement.

Be of good courage, and he shall strengthen your heart, all ye that hope in the lord.
Psalm 31:35

—KING JAMES AUTHORIZED VERSION 1611

There Abideth Hope

Sharon K Connell

Chapter One

May 2003

University of Illinois, Chicago Campus

Lynne Temple's frame hit the wrestling mat on the gym floor. "Oomph!" She gasped for air as she leaped to her feet, resuming her fighting stance, arms extended, semi-flexed, gloved fists ready. "Bring it on, Jimmy Boy." She squared off against her muscular opponent.

She and Jim circled each other a few feet apart. Her eyes locked onto his, tracking every slight movement.

He grinned. "Gotta watch that leg sweep, Sis. It'll take down the best of them, especially when the kicker's got the extra reach, like me."

Lynne set her jaw and narrowed her eyes. At six feet, three inches, he towered over her. Why couldn't she have been a little taller than five feet eight? She'd have bruises on bruises after this bout.

Although three and four years her senior, her brothers, Jeff and Jim, had always treated her as their equal. Too bad her brothers couldn't get home on leave from the Marine Corps more often to help with her training.

Thump

"Oww! At least there's not a dust cloud filling our nostrils like there used to be when we sparred in the barn back home." One of these days, she'd get the better of him. "Remember the ballet lessons Mom insisted on for poise when I was in high school?"

Jim snickered. "Yeah. But they helped with balance and endurance."

"Strengthened my bones too. Good thing, the way you guys tossed me around in that barn. But I loved it."

He let out a bark of a laugh. "We never could get Mom to see how these exercises build character. But I'm glad you kept up with it. After seeing some of the guys who hang around campus, you may need these skills."

Lynne's shoulders and thighs throbbed from repeated collisions with the floor, but she resumed her position. "Come on, Big Brother. What are you waiting for? Afraid of your little sissy?" That should get him riled.

Her mind ventured back to a Midwestern summer day when the heat had turned the barn into a sauna. She and Jim had jabbed, kicked, blocked, and lunged. Sweat streamed down her face and drenched her gloves and rubberized sparring helmet as she'd weaved and parried. Black and blue marks on her body were common back then. Not so much anymore.

Lynne dodged another leg sweep. "Ha! Missed." And Mom...dear

Mom. She'd had a stern admonition for them when they got back to the house.

"You know, Jim? Should've brought a change of clothes to the barn out there on the farm. We could've jumped in the pond out back to clean up after we finished with our bouts. Mom would've never known."

"Yeah, right. Keep telling yourself that, Lynnie. You know Mom." He winked.

"Okay, Sis. Pivot, high kick, left, right, again, again, recover. Now balance, spin, round kick, left, right, again, again, recover. Jab, jab, left, right, again, again. That's it. You're doing great."

"You'd think I was trying out for a tournament." She bent her frame, hands on her thighs, catching her breath.

"Awesome." He gave her a high-five. "Let's quit and go through cooldown exercises."

Lynne's limbs felt like hunks of lead. Her insteps ached, and her muscles burned with fatigue, but she made it through the cooldown and collapsed on the mat. "I can't move a finger."

Jim reached out his arm, grabbed her by the wrist, and pulled her up as if she were a feather.

"Thanks. I sure love it when you and Jeff take time to visit me on your leaves."

"We do too. Hey…remember the day Dad stuck up for us when Mom got all upset over our fighting? Just before you left for Chicago."

"How could I forget the way her jaw dropped when we walked in covered in straw bits and dirt? She said you'd beat permanent black and blue welts into me one of these days. Then it was my turn for a tongue lashing. 'Lynnie, just look at you. Anyone would think you'd been caught in your father's combine.' Boy, was she upset that time."

Lynne mirrored Jim's grin. She reached into her backpack and pulled out a shiny red apple. "Mom worries too much." Lynne sunk her teeth into the fruit.

Jim stole the apple from between her teeth. "She's a mom."

"Hey, Stinker, get your own." Lynne tried to snatch it back as he held it high over her head. "Gimme that."

"Nope." He stuck his tongue out at her. "That day was when Dad reminded Mom you had your heart set on becoming a nurse, and that meant school in the big city. He said the training we gave you might help you out in a jam someday."

"Dad just didn't want to alarm Mom, but he was right. Although nothing's ever happened here on campus, even though it sure isn't as quiet as living in Kewanee, Illinois."

With a pounce like a puma, Lynne launched a successful grab at the apple before Jim could take another bite. She eyed the enormous hole in the fruit and grimaced at him, then reached into her backpack for a second apple and handed it to her brother.

"Thanks, Squirt." He tapped the back of her head. "Another year of this training and you'll be able to take on any guy in my outfit."

She took a bite of her apple. Take on any guy? "Jim, do you think Mom's accepted my decision to have a career in the Navy? I'm still not ready to settle down like I know she'd rather I did. Haven't met anyone I'm serious about yet. You think there's something wrong with me?"

Her brother picked up his gym bag and cocked his head at her. "Not a thing wrong with you. I, for one, am glad you haven't met Mr. Right. Jeff and I wouldn't be able to give him a thorough checking out the way things are right now with us overseas most of the time." He chuckled. "Nothing's wrong with you. I saw the way the guys eyed my gorgeous, hazel-eyed sister today."

He ruffled her short brown hair. "Look, not every girl gets married and starts a family right out of high school, or even college. You do what you think is right, okay? Just like you always do."

The siblings headed for the exit. "The Naval Reserve Officer Training Corps here at the university has been great. I'm excited about finishing next spring. I've prayed about it, and God's given me peace. With Dad having been a Navy Corpsman, I knew he understood."

Jim nodded. "They both stand by your decision." He turned to her. "Just before I left to spend the day with you, Mom hugged me and said, 'God's kept you and your brother in His hand all this time. I guess He can take care of Lynnie too.' It's just hard on her."

"Thanks for telling me that, Jim. Serving is something I have to do. After I pass my exams and finish my last year, which won't be easy-peasy." She passed through the door Jim held open. "This year at school has been the fun part. New friendships, studying together, pizza parties. And I've been close enough to go home often. It's been a real adventure. Good memories. Not a sour note among them, so far."

That night, Lynne stood from the table in the campus library and shoved her study sheets into her backpack. Boy, time sure had flown by. Exams on the horizon. She pulled on her windbreaker, slipped the backpack over her shoulders, glanced out the window into the darkness, and then at her watch. Twenty after eight. Dr. Lindstrom should be working late in his office in the Medical Sciences Building, as usual. But the security guard would lock the main entrance doors precisely at eight thirty to go on his rounds…also as usual. She whispered, "Just this one time, please be late, Walter." She rushed out of the library.

The evening was unusually warm as Lynne jogged along the path from the library to the medical building in darkness except for an occasional street light. Sweat prickled her forehead. By the time she got back to the dorm, she'd need another shower.

A rustling noise made her stop. What was that? She searched the deserted street scanning the few cars in the parking lot beyond the building and one further down past the Medical Sciences Building. An orange tabby bounded out of the bushes next to her and ran across the street.

Lynne let go of the breath she'd held. Why was she so jumpy? Couldn't have anything to do with exams so close and not being ready, could it?

She resumed her jog. Her sweet country-bred mom would have a heart attack if she knew her little girl was jogging alone this late in the city, even if it was on campus.

She hated to bother Dr. Lindstrom this late but needed clarification on his tutorial that only he could provide. Finals were next week. She needed an answer now.

After she bounded up the steps to the glass double doors, Lynne let out a sigh of relief at the sight of Walter still at his desk in his well-pressed guard uniform. Behind him, the wall clock's minute hand moved to the eight forty-five position.

She waved her arm over her head, then pressed her face to the glass and tapped her nail on the metal doorframe. Walter ran a hand over his receding ginger hair as he looked toward her. A smile spread over his ruddy features. He stood and strode toward the doors, reaching for the keys on his belt.

He unlocked the door, and Lynne breezed through. "Hi, Walter." She grinned at him. "Is Dr. Lindstrom still here? I have an important question to ask him about his lecture."

The thickset, middle-aged guard relocked the doors. "Yes, Miss Temple. Only one here apart from us. He told me earlier he had business to attend to."

"Lucky for me. And I was lucky you hadn't started your rounds yet."

Walter pulled his mouth to one side. "Yup. Well, I was reading and lost track of time. But it's always quiet around here. Nothing ever happens. A few minutes one way or t'other makes little difference." He chuckled.

With a nod, Lynne headed for the stairwell. "Thanks for letting me in. I'll take the stairs." Good old Walter, always so obliging to us students, unlike the rest of the guards.

"Figured you would." The man laughed.

She bypassed the stairwell at the front of the building, which displayed a sign saying the stairs were under repair. Too bad, it opened in the hall next to Dr. Lindstrom's office. Lynne continued to the back of the building, swept through the door, and ran up the steps two at a time.

On the landing before the fourth floor, she paused to wipe away a film of perspiration from her forehead and catch her breath. Then she continued up the last set of stairs, opened the metal door, and stepped into the space between staff offices and the elevators.

Halfway down the hall, empty worktables and chairs, used by students during the day, took on a whole new life in the semi-darkness. A tingle snaked up the back of Lynne's neck. She scooted past the eerie section.

Recessed ceiling lights illuminated the elevator doors and reception area on the left. Beyond the receptionist's desk, racks of magazines and periodicals ran along the wall.

The hall plunged into darkness as she reached the far corner. She turned to her left and entered another hall of staff offices. Soft white light streamed through the glass door of Dr. Lindstrom's office and lit a small section of the carpeted hallway. At the end of the corridor, the stairwell exit sign cast a red glow.

When Lynne reached the office about twenty feet short of the stairwell under repair, she gazed through the glass. The doctor sat at his desk, eyes focused on his computer screen. Half-glasses perched on the bridge of his aquiline nose. Long bony fingers tapped on the keyboard.

Had her visit come at an inopportune time? Judging by his furrowed brows, something troubled him. Well, she wouldn't keep him long. In and out. That's all. Lynne knocked on the wooden doorframe.

The professor looked up and beckoned her in. "How can I help you, Miss Temple?"

Not a glimmer of a smile, and his brows remained pinched. What had him so upset?

Lynne laid her backpack on the floor near the desk and crouched to unzip the flap. "Sir, I'm sorry to bother you so late, but I need a clarification on a statement you made today in class." She pulled a file out of the bag and glanced at him.

Before she could say another word, he shook his head. "I'm sorry, but I haven't time to go into it. It'll have to wait. I have an important meeting in a couple of minutes. My visitor should have been here already." He checked his watch. "I really can't help you right now. Come back first thing tomorrow morning. I'll be happy to answer your questions then." The man rounded his desk.

She shoved the file back in the bag, zipped her pack, and stood with it dangling from her arm. His hand trembled as he showed her the door. "Are you okay, Dr. Lindstrom? You don't look well."

"Huh? Oh. No. I'm okay. Well, perhaps a cold coming on. I'll be fine."

Lynne headed for the door. "Okay. I'll come back tomorrow morning." She looped the strap over one shoulder. Her professor followed her to the door.

Once in the hallway, she glanced back at him. "Are you sure you're okay, Sir?"

"Yes. Yes. Thank you. I'm fine. I'll see you tomorrow." Dr. Lindstrom closed the door and rushed back to his desk.

Odd. Lynne retraced her steps through the darkened hall, shaking her head. That wasn't like Dr. Lindstrom at all.

After she turned the corner and neared the elevators, she glimpsed the current issue of the medical student's newsletter in the rack by the receptionist's desk. She'd receive a copy in her mailbox tomorrow, but as long as it was here and so was she, she could scan her favorite section. Maybe the doctor's meeting would only take a minute or two. After that, he might have time to discuss the question. The student paper was always good for a laugh. She could use one after her long morning of classes and an afternoon of sparring with her brother.

Lynne grabbed the paper, placed her pack next to the chair, and settled in beside the receptionist's desk. As she perused the lead article, the faint swishing of a door sounded from the hall she'd left. Must be Dr. Lindstrom's guest. Odd that he came up the stairs instead of the elevator.

Chapter Two

Johnson glowered and listened to the ring on the other end of his cell phone. A shaky voice answered. "Hello...Dr. Lindstrom speaking."

"Good evening, my dear doctor. I understand we still have a problem. Did you read the lovely email I sent you a few minutes ago? You never replied to the one from this afternoon."

"Yes, that terse email is on my computer screen as we speak. I can't keep giving the agency a clean bill of health, Mr. Johnson. The Department of Children and Family Services is asking questions. They want to interview the children and their adoptive parents. I received a second request from them today. They'll find out the parents are fakes! What am I going to do?"

"Let me deal with child welfare, Harold. You'd best keep in mind how I can ruin your reputation in a heartbeat." Heat ran up Johnson's neck. He clenched his teeth and took a deep breath. "Keep filing the reports as you have been. That's what we pay you for, remember?"

"Look, Johnson, I can't do it. Blackmail won't work anymore. I'll take my chances. Find someone else." The doctor's voice rose. "If I go to jail because of this, I won't go alone."

While Dr. Lindstrom continued his complaints, Johnson pressed mute on his cell. He turned to the man with a shaven head and granite-like features sitting next to him in the car. "Cathcart, get in there with Epstein. He should be on the fourth floor already. Tell him to retrieve all the paperwork from the doc. Take this." Johnson pulled a plastic bag from the glove compartment. "Make sure everything looks right."

"Understood." The man with icy blue eyes slipped out of the car and entered the rear of the Medical Sciences Building.

Johnson deactivated the mute feature on his phone. "All right, Lindstrom. Mr. Epstein should be there any minute with those documents I told you he was bringing. Just give him the rest of your paperwork, and we'll find a replacement for you."

"Good. I'll have everything ready."

"Fine." Johnson disconnected the call and snorted. "You'll be replaced all right."

The stairwell door opened and closed again. Lynne peered down the hallway toward the sound. The doctor must have meant visitors, not visitor. Who could they be…and, now that she thought about it, why had both used the stairwell under repair instead of the elevator?

Wouldn't Walter have directed them to the elevator or, at least, had them use the other stairs? Did he even know they were in the building? But he'd have to know, or how had they gotten in with the doors locked?

Lynne left the chair and tiptoed to the second hall. A mammoth planter housing an overgrown indoor palm in a shallow alcove at the corner screened her as two men in dark suits huddled under the red light at the stairwell door. Lynne hushed her breathing.

The glow over them distorted their features. Devilish. Thank God darkness cloaked her hiding place. A shiver ran through her, and she bit her bottom lip. What kind of business would they have with her professor?

As they came closer to the whitish glow of Dr. Lindstrom's office, the heavyset man with short-cropped salt and pepper hair, a prominent chin, and slightly curved nose, glanced at his watch. In his other hand, he carried a dark briefcase. He spoke in a low tone, but his words traveled right to Lynne along the smooth corridor walls. "Fifty minutes for the guard to complete his rounds." He turned to his broad-shouldered companion. "He starts on the tenth floor, so it'll be at least thirty minutes before he gets here. That gives us plenty of time."

Lynne narrowed her eyes. Plenty of time…for what? Obviously, these men were familiar with the medical building and Walter's routine.

The bald man nodded as he handed something to the other. "I took care of the security camera after the boss sent me to help you. Are you sure there's no one else in the building, Epstein?"

The man called Epstein opened the briefcase and placed the object inside. "I've had it under surveillance all day, except for the few minutes it took me to fix the door lock. Everyone but the doc and guard has left the building."

Lynne shook her head. Why watch this building? He must not have seen her come in. Fixed the door lock?

"Let's go, Cathcart." They entered Dr. Lindstrom's office.

When the office door clicked shut, Lynne inched her way along the carpet. Should she find Walter and report this? Report what? Maybe I'm just imagining something's wrong.

From the hall, Lynne peered through the edge of the glass door. Dr. Lindstrom rose as the man called Epstein placed his briefcase on the desk behind the computer screen and flipped it open. The doctor lowered himself into his chair. Cathcart stood at the far side of the desk. Her professor craned his neck, looking toward the case, but Epstein closed the lid.

Drat. Can't hear them. If she opened the door just a crack—

Lynne pulled downward on the door handle until the latch released. Without a sound, she pushed until a narrow gap of light showed.

Epstein lifted the briefcase lid again and took out a manila folder. He placed it on the desk in front of Dr. Lindstrom, who peered at the file and then at his visitor.

The professor's brows pinched together. "What's this?"

"It's an empty folder for you to put the rest of Mr. Johnson's paperwork in. He wants it all back." The stocky man gave half a smile.

Dr. Lindstrom opened a locked file cabinet next to the desk and lifted out a large, fat white envelope. The man named Cathcart stepped behind him. Her professor placed the envelope inside the manila folder. "I've done everything Johnson has asked of me. Now I need him to straighten out the mess I'm in."

Epstein smirked. "Don't worry. We'll take care of everything." He returned the folder to his briefcase and glanced at Cathcart, who had slid on surgical gloves.

Lynne gasped. Her heartbeat went into overdrive as Cathcart stepped behind Dr. Lindstrom and seized his throat in a chokehold.

Her mouth dropped open. "Uh—" Nothing else would come out.

Her vocal cords seemed paralyzed. Before she could get her wits together, it was over. The professor fell to the floor.

The two men hefted Dr. Lindstrom's lifeless form into an upright position in his office chair. Cathcart picked up the doctor's glasses and replaced them on his face. They then rearranged the body, so it slumped over the desk.

Epstein pulled on a pair of surgical gloves and removed a syringe from a plastic bag he took from the briefcase. He shoved the needle into the unconscious man's bare left arm.

Tears welled in Lynne's eyes. She'd done nothing. But what could she have done? If she'd tried to intervene, they could have killed her too. She chewed her bottom lip and swiped at the tears.

Manipulating the fingers and thumb of the doctor's right hand around the syringe, Epstein made it look as if Dr. Lindstrom had injected himself.

She had to leave. Call the authorities. Wait! Now what's he doing?

The heavyset man took a flash drive from the briefcase and plugged it into her professor's computer. After a few keystrokes, he smiled at Cathcart. "That virus ought to do the trick. Nothing to tie him to us."

As she rose from her crouched position outside the door, dizziness overcame Lynne. She leaned on the doorframe. She'd better get out of there and go to the police.

From inside the office, she heard Cathcart say, "What was that noise?"

Then Epstein's voice. "What noise?"

"Thought I heard something."

Thank God she'd pulled her head away from the door. She flew down the hall, rounded the corner, and ducked behind the plant. She hadn't had time to pull the door closed again.

The two men stepped into the hall and stared at the stairwell door and then toward Lynne's darkened hiding place. Cathcart pulled a gun from inside his jacket. He pointed to the office door. "I closed it when we went in."

She held her breath.

Epstein faced the dark corridor. "I don't see anything. Do you? I think you're hearing things." He turned to Cathcart. "Quit being so jumpy. You probably didn't close the door all the way."

"That plant…near the end of the hall." Cathcart pointed his gun toward Lynne. "The leaves moved."

She froze.

The heavyset man gazed upward. "It's just the vent blowing. Let's get done and get out of here. That guard will be here before long." They reentered Dr. Lindstrom's office.

After a deep breath, Lynne backed against the wall. She had to get to the stairwell.

The office door opened again, and the men stepped into the hallway. "I still think we should check that hall, Epstein. What if someone was there?"

Lynne crept to the reception desk, snatched her pack, and hurried to the stairwell door. *Please don't make a sound.*

"I heard a door open."

Cathcart's words reached Lynne's ears before the door eased shut. They must have come into the second hall. She hurtled the steps to the third-floor landing just as the door opened above her.

Was this a nightmare? Lynne trembled. Her mouth was like

sandpaper. Her heart pounded, and sweat prickled her scalp. She flattened herself against the wall next to the doorway. Did she dare open it? Would they hear it?

Her vision blurred. Her knees buckled. She couldn't faint now. Not now. She had to get out of there.

Footfalls neared the edge of the stairs. "Come on, Cathcart. Let's go. Your imagination is running wild. You sure you're not losing your nerve?"

"Well, someone may have been there, but they're gone now. Let's grab our stuff and check outside."

The upstairs door closed. Lynne fled down the stairwell in a headlong flight to the first floor. At the bottom, she dashed into the foyer and listened, alert for any sound of elevator movement. None. *Thank You, God. Please help me get out of here without them seeing me.*

She sprinted to the double doors of the foyer entrance and hit the emergency push bar. No alarm sounded. Her pulse raced as she descended the stairs. The cool night air hit her face.

Lynne reached into her backpack for her cell to call 911. *Drat.* Must have left it at the library. *Security.* She had to get to the guard on duty in the library. Report what she saw. But would it still be open? She bolted across the street and then glanced at her watch. Almost nine thirty. Should still be open.

A large group of students sauntered in her direction. They laughed as if at a party. *If they only knew.* Lynne took in a sharp breath. She'd forgotten Walter. He was still in the building somewhere.

Doubled over, she tried to clear her mind. There was nothing she could do about him now. She had to get help.

The students passed in front of her headed toward the library. She knew those two in the back. Lynne slipped in next to them. Forcing a smile, she followed along as they neared the medical building's wing.

As they approached the wing, Lynne glanced toward the rear door. She gulped. The two assailants stood outside and surveyed the street. Had they seen her leave the building…join the group?

The man called Epstein shrugged and lit a cigarette as she and her companions passed. The other man glared in their direction.

Lynne turned her head toward the student beside her as if listening to what he said. Would those men snatch her from the group? Had she put them all in danger?

A second later, Epstein and Cathcart walked past the group. Like two cockroaches running from the light. She shuddered. She'd never forget those faces.

The path to the library skirted a faculty building and small parking lot. As they passed the building, Lynne glimpsed a huge man in a light gray suit with an open-necked white shirt. He leaned on the driver's side door of a late model BMW. Another sinister figure. Or was she seeing threats everywhere now?

The streetlight reflected off the shiny Illinois license plate. The letter-number sequence stuck in Lynne's mind. As did the imposing frame of the man. He turned and rested gorilla-like arms on the top of the car, watching the group pass. The man's hair appeared to be light brown, cropped short, in a scraggy crew cut. His bulging eyes were dark and cold. His jaw heavy, thick. *What a Goliath.*

Why had she taken in his features? He hadn't killed Dr. Lindstrom. Yet, something about him—

The man turned his eyes toward the medical building and the two killers who had come back to the rear entrance. A chill ran through Lynne.

The group walked past the faculty building. Lynne looked behind her. The two murderers, the BMW, and Goliath were gone. She stopped, and the other students continued without her. She surveyed the area. No sign of the killers.

Lynne yanked on the pen clipped to the neck of her sweatshirt and scribbled the license plate number onto her left wrist. Mom's scolding voice entered her thoughts. "It's not ladylike to write on your hand, Dear." If she weren't so scared, she'd laugh.

Where had those men gone? Were the three of them together? *Are they searching for me?*

Chapter Three

$\mathcal{A}$s Lynne approached the library, two security guards with unfamiliar faces pushed their way through the glass front door. Her skin prickled. She'd go to the police station not far away instead. She'd have to tell them anyway.

Lynne ran across campus, down tree-lined streets, and past half-lit apartment buildings and open lots, a can of pepper spray clutched in her hand. A gray BMW whizzed by. Maybe the killers and that big man? Had they seen her? Two more blocks.

She stepped up her pace. Her legs voiced their complaint as the station came into view.

Sirens screamed, and flashing lights rocketed around the corner headed toward the Medical Sciences Building.

She hurried through the doors to the front desk. A heavy-built, silver-haired officer looked up. "Can I help you?"

Lynne doubled over, hands on her legs. "Yeah." She panted and let the backpack fall to the floor as she leaned on the wall and pulled in a deep breath. "I've seen a murder." She took another breath. "Two men had a syringe."

Sparkles danced in her vision, and she clung to the counter, sucking in air. "I ran here…to get help. Walter's still…in the building."

"Calm yourself, young lady. Let's take it slow."

"I just saw two police cars…heading that way."

The officer grabbed a notepad and pen. "Why don't you start with your name and address?"

Lynne's pulse raced. "Lynne Temple." She shuddered. Dizziness crept in again. She lost her balance and slid onto the floor.

He rushed to her side, then helped her stand and escorted her to a chair in the waiting area. The officer brought a paper cup of water from the cooler and handed it to her. "Here. Drink this. I'm Sergeant McGinty. I'll be right back." He sprinted through a door on the other side of the room.

Lynne lowered her head to her hands, elbows on her thighs. Then she glanced around the room. Alone. But in a safe place. She'd never been worried about being alone before now. Her heart pounded in a crazy rhythm.

A door opened across the room, and Sergeant McGinty returned to the front desk. A young woman in uniform carrying a clipboard came toward Lynne. "Miss Temple?"

Lynne nodded.

"I'm Officer Kim Travis." The slender, auburn-haired girl smiled and sat in the chair next to Lynne. "You witnessed a murder?"

"I didn't know what to do." Lynne wrung her hands.

"It's okay, Miss Temple. Was this at the Medical Sciences Building on campus?"

"Yeah."

Officer Travis nodded. "We received a call."

Lynne's eyes filled with tears. "From Walter? Is he okay? He's the guard."

"Yes, and he's fine."

She blinked, and the tears fell.

"The guard said it looked like the doctor committed suicide. You told Sergeant McGinty you saw two men with a syringe."

"I did." Lynne pulled a handful of tissues from her backpack and blew her nose. "Not suicide."

Kim made notes on the clipboard. "Let me get you through what we call witness processing. Sounds ominous, doesn't it? But don't worry. You're a person, not a pratie. Sorry, potato. Our process won't peel and package you." She grinned.

Lynne smiled. "You must be Irish."

"Sure am. You?"

"I am. On my mother's side."

"I'm Irish on me mathair's side too."

Lynne's heartbeat calmed. "I haven't heard a potato referred to as a pratie for a long time. Nor the word mathair instead of mother. It's what Mom called Gran."

Kim stood. "Well, now that the two of us have a comfortable connection, let's get a statement from you."

Lynne grabbed her pack from the floor and followed Kim across the waiting room to the counter. "Sarge, would you locate Detectives Helmer and Trent? I'll take Miss Temple back."

The sergeant nodded.

As they passed through the door into a long hall, Kim asked, "Where are you from, Miss Temple?"

"Please call me Lynne. Kewanee, Illinois."

"Really? Outside Decatur, myself. And you can call me Kim." She led Lynne into a green-walled room, with one rectangular table and two chairs on either side.

"Have a seat." Kim laid the clipboard on the table. "The detectives will join us shortly." She sat next to Lynne. "Tell me about your home in Kewanee. Haven't met anyone from that close to my hometown in a long time."

As Lynne spoke of the farm, a man and woman entered the room. Attired in a Navy blue suit and white blouse, with carefully groomed dark brown hair that hugged the back of her neck, the slim woman's smile reached to her brown eyes. She looked more like a secretary than a police officer. Probably in her mid-thirties.

"Miss Temple, I'm Lieutenant Jane Helmer." She turned to the man standing next to her. "This is Sergeant Loring Trent."

After Lynne shook hands with them, Sergeant Trent sat across from her. His athlete's muscular physique and rugged features reminded her of the cowboys in movies she'd watched as a teen. He also looked nothing like a police officer in his charcoal sports jacket, matching slacks, white shirt, and light blue tie. Probably in his late twenties. The pressure from his handshake remained.

What was she doing? She'd observed each of them as if she were a detective. Should she change her goal from nursing to law? At least the small fish symbol pinned to their lapels made her feel better.

Fellow believers. Tension flowed out of her taut muscles.

Detective Trent smiled. "Care for a cup of coffee? Or water?"

Lynne relaxed even more at the sound of his calm, deep voice. Just like her brothers' voices. "Coffee'd be nice." She glanced at Kim, who gazed at the man. That expression meant something beyond a work relationship.

Kim stood. "I'll leave you with the detectives. Here's my cell number." She wrote it in the lower corner of the paper on her clipboard, tore it off, and handed it to Lynne. "Let's get together and reminisce about home. I'm a farm girl too."

"Thanks, Officer Travis…Kim." *Lord, thank You for placing good people here to help me through this ordeal.*

"You're welcome. You're in good hands." Kim turned to the lady detective and handed her the clipboard. "This is what Lynne's told me so far."

At the door, Kim turned back. "Please call. We colleens need to stick together." She gave a thumbs-up. Lynne returned the sign with a smile, and Kim walked out as Trent eased past her in the doorway carrying two cups.

Trent put one cup in front of Lynne. "Hope black's okay. I forgot to ask."

"It's fine. It's how I drink mine."

He pulled out a recorder from the middle drawer of the table. "This is to make sure we get the details of your report correct."

Lieutenant Helmer nodded. "Shall we begin? May we call you Lynne?"

She nodded.

"And you can call me Jane."

The man raised his hand. "Loring here."

Lynne's breathing eased.

Loring folded his hands on the top of the table. "Give us as much information as you can remember. Please, take your time, and let us know when you need to take a break."

Lynne nodded again, and Loring started the recorder. He named the people present, gave the time, and that the case related to the death of Dr. Lindstrom.

While giving the details of what she saw, Lynne had to stop several times to mop away tears from her eyes. She explained the stairwell under construction. Her voice broke when she described the smirks on the faces of the killers. "Dr. Lindstrom dropped to the floor, and his glasses fell off."

Lynne gulped. "I can't understand why anyone would want to murder the doctor. He's always been so pleasant."

Jane touched Lynne's forearm. "Tell us every detail you can remember, no matter how unimportant it may seem."

After thinking for a moment, Lynne shook her head. "That's it. It's all I can remember."

"You did great." Loring turned off the machine. "Now we need sketches of the suspects." He and Jane stood.

Lynne took in another deep breath and rose. "Oh, wait! I almost forgot. It might be nothing, but you said everything."

Jane sat again. "Go ahead." She nodded for Loring to switch on the recorder.

"There was a man outside leaning against a BMW when I passed the faculty building." Lynne pulled her windbreaker sleeve up to reveal the license number on her wrist. "I guess I should have shown you this earlier."

Detective Trent snickered, pulled out his cell, and snapped a picture of her wrist. She tried not to laugh as her mother came to mind again.

Jane repeated the numbers. "This information may be key. Can you describe the man?"

"Yeah. He was huge and standing right under a streetlamp." She described his clothes. "Guess that won't help identify him. He was sinister-looking." She closed her eyes. "I can picture him. His arms reminded me of a gorilla, his hair light brown, short, a crew-cut style that looked like it had been licked by a cow. When he watched us go by, his eyes bulged. They were dark, like a dead man. His jaw thick and heavy. Middle-aged, maybe. Hard to say." She opened her eyes. "That's it."

"Good job, Lynne." Jane reached past Loring and turned off the recorder. She gathered it with the clipboard and headed for the door. "Let's get you to Kim. She doubles as our sketch artist in the evenings."

Loring got up and snickered. "The guys in forensics will roar when they see how you recorded the number. They do it all the time."

Jane's phone rang. "Helmer." She listened for a few seconds. "Yes, Captain, we've taken her statement. Doesn't sound like suicide, two assailants, a hypodermic placed to make it appear he took his own life." She paused. "Convincing, even with no note. The witness reports a third party may have been outside." She paused again.

"The witness came straight here from the scene. Nobody else knows what happened, apart from Sergeant McGinty, Officer Travis, Detective Trent, and me."

Lynne held up her index finger.

Jane raised her eyebrows. "Hold on, Sir. What is it, Lynne? Did you speak to someone else?"

"Walter knows I was there. The security guard let me in. I ran before I remembered him, so we didn't talk about this."

"Sir, the security guard at the scene knows Miss Temple was in the building but not that she saw the crime."

Jane nodded as she listened to the captain. "So, he thinks it's suicide." She glanced at Lynne. "The guard's been told we've checked on you, and you're fine." The detective repositioned the phone close to her mouth. "We'll have Officer Travis make sketches of the suspects, Sir."

When the call ended, Jane turned to Loring. "Won't get anything from Lindstrom's computer...at least, not right away thanks to a nasty virus. Someone shot out the security camera at the side entrance. The alarm system had been tampered with too. I'd say not a suicide. Forensics is collecting what evidence they can."

Lynne interrupted. "Excuse me. How is Walter?"

"Mr. Prescott is shaken, but fine. We won't tell him it wasn't a suicide for now."

Loring led them into the hall. "If anyone should ask you about tonight, say only that the police talked to you and took a statement. Nothing else. Not even to your family."

"I understand...I guess."

"We'll let the murderers think they got away with it. And you'll be safer if they don't know you saw them." He held up the paper where he had jotted down the license number. "I'll call in those plates, Jane." He strode through the corridor and disappeared around the corner.

"Jane, Cathcart may have heard me in the building before I got away."

"But they didn't see you. And we want to make sure they don't find out about you, so everything has to remain hush-hush."

Lynne bit her lip and nodded.

They entered another hall. "You could be in a lot of danger if they learn you're a witness. Dr. Lindstrom has been a person of interest for some time."

Lynne whipped her head around to face the detective. "Why?"

"Child trafficking investigation."

"You must have the wrong man. Not Dr. Lindstrom."

"I'm afraid not, Lynne. It appears he provided fake medical clearances to bogus agencies."

"But he was a nice man. He never—" Lynne's stomach knotted.

"That's usually the way it goes. These people try to live exemplary lives…on the outside."

"I can't believe one of my professors could—" She bit her lip again.

"It's still a suspicion, but we're pretty sure. Spurious reports. Names that don't line up with children and their adoptive parents. Dr. Lindstrom was deep in debt, mostly from gambling. Unscrupulous people have radar when it comes to qualified professionals in debt. They use the information to their advantage."

Lynne lifted her hand and massaged her forehead. It fit the comments the three men had made in the office.

Jane led her into another hallway. "He may have wanted to get out before he got caught, so they eliminated him to keep him from talking."

Tears welled in Lynne's eyes again.

"These traffickers are experts. They kill possible witnesses."

Lynne pressed her lips together and fought back the tears.

Jane laid her hand on Lynne's shoulder. "I'm afraid Dr. Lindstrom isn't the first. But don't worry. We'll protect you."

When they reached the end of the hallway, a door opened, and Loring stepped out. He held it as Lynne entered the room. "Kim's ready. And those plates are interesting, Jane. We may have stumbled onto The Piper."

Chapter Four

The shocked look of dread on Jane's face sent a shudder through Lynne. "Who's The Piper?"

Jane led her to a seat next to Kim. "I'll explain later. Right now, let's work on those sketches."

Loring followed without a word. He sat at one of several unoccupied desks in the room. Lynne glanced at her watch. It was late, and she had studying to do. But this was more important.

Kim turned from her desk and smiled. She pointed to the chair next to the computer screen in front of her.

Lynne lowered herself to the seat. "I hope I can give you enough information."

After Jane handed the clipboard to her, Kim read the description and faced Lynne again. "These are good details. Give me a few minutes to enter the preliminary info, and then I'll ask you some questions."

As Kim tapped on the keyboard, Lynne glanced at Loring. He watched Kim intently with a smile that flirted on his lips. Lynne's brows rose. Were they or weren't they a couple? Neither wore a wedding ring.

A few minutes later, Kim turned to Lynne. "That didn't take as long as I expected. Let me explain these drawings. The point is to get a close enough resemblance to trigger the memory of a viewer about someone they've seen or know. It's not supposed to be an artist's portrait or photographed likeness. Now I'll ask you questions that hopefully trigger your memory about things you don't realize you saw."

Lynne let out a sigh. She rubbed her neck and rolled her head around to relax the muscles. "Okay."

"What did you do when you first entered the building? It helps to go through your actions one step at a time."

Closing her eyes, Lynne recalled her tap on the glass entry door to get Walter's attention. She told Kim every detail she could remember up to sitting at the reception desk and the sound of the door opening in the hallway outside Dr. Lindstrom's office. "After I heard the door open a second time, I peeked down the hall where the two men stood under the exit sign." She opened her eyes.

Kim typed furiously. "Now, describe the perpetrators?"

"Let's see." Lynne shut her eyes again. "Under six feet tall for the man called Epstein, and the one named Cathcart, six feet, three inches maybe." About the same as her brothers. "The men were both middle-aged. Late thirties, early forties." She went on describing minute details she had no idea she'd noticed about the killers. Then moved on to their attack on her professor and their emotionless expressions.

"Lynne, what's the one thing regarding the attacker that stood out to you?"

A chill ran through her. "I saw Cathcart's eyes when he looked up at Epstein before he grabbed the doctor. They were light blue, cold as ice."

"Good. That's good, Lynne." She made adjustments to his eyes and then turned the screen toward Lynne.

She pulled in a sharp breath. "That's him."

Kim worked on the other likeness, asking more questions. Then she started her sketch of the man outside, the one they called The Piper. When she finished, Lynne's jaw dropped open. The big man's eyes stared out at her, dark and muddy. "Yeah. It's him."

"This is the first time we've learned this much about his appearance." Loring leaned in closer to the screen. "Until now he's been a ghost. I can't help but wonder if other witnesses were too scared to describe him."

"The jaw." Jane pushed her head closer to the screen. "Is it that big?"

Lynne nodded. "Yeah, that big. He was massive."

After Kim retrieved copies of the sketches from the printer, she handed them to the detectives. Jane headed for the door. "I'll see that these are distributed."

The wall clock ticked in the sudden silence. Lynne glanced at her watch. After midnight already. She yawned. "Don't you people ever go home?"

Loring stared at the pictures still on Kim's screen. Then he grinned at Lynne. "This is our shift."

She examined the pictures the officer had drawn and whispered, "I'll never forget those faces."

Kim returned to the keyboard. She resumed her typing, and mug shots popped up on the two killers. "I thought I recognized them. Leo

Goldberg, age forty-one and John Price, age thirty-seven. Epstein and Cathcart are new aliases. Both from out of town, the Big Apple."

As he glared at the pictures, Loring's brows lowered. He faced Lynne. "Your testimony will be vital for us to convict them."

A murder trial? Lynne shivered as a chill ran through her. *I can do all things through Christ which strengtheneth me. Philippians four, thirteen.* So glad she'd memorized that verse before she left home. She could do this.

Jane returned to the room, sat down, and folded her arms.

Kim scrolled through a list of arrests on her screen. "These guys are real pros. Serious stuff too, including contract killings. But convictions only for minor offenses. Interesting. No mention of human trafficking. They're known associates and said to have connections in New York."

A grimace covered Loring's face. "They're sure to have a slick lawyer in their corner."

Kim twisted in her chair, draped an arm over the back, and scooted it to one side for the detectives to view the rest of the information. Jane and Loring rolled their chairs closer and perused the details.

Lynne covered her mouth and yawned again. "Sorry. It's been a long day."

"Circulate the details, Kim." Jane stood.

"Will do, Lieutenant." She turned to the screen and typed as if on a deadline. "You think they'll make a run for it?"

Loring placed a hand on her shoulder, and Kim smiled. He said, "They might. But they're clueless that we're on to them, or that we have a witness. We'll have to work hard and fast."

He removed his hand and faced Jane. "My money's on The Piper as the ringleader."

"Mine too," agreed Jane. "I know you're tired, Lynne, but let me explain why it's so important to keep quiet the fact that you witnessed the murder."

Loring rose from his seat. "I'll get us more coffee."

Jane motioned for Lynne to sit at an empty desk. "Child traffickers include facilitators. They're essential for ensnaring the victims who are often street kids, runaways, or from poor immigrant families with a lot of children."

"Kids no one will miss." Lynne shook her head. "At least not right away."

"Right. The facilitator, who may run the bogus agencies, has underlings working for him to abduct the kids and eliminate witnesses."

"And here Mom was only worried about muggings and—she had no idea." Lynne pursed her lips.

"Children who've tried to escape have met the same end as Dr. Lindstrom, I'm afraid."

Lynne closed her eyes, rested her elbows on the desk, and cradled her head on her clasped hands. Awful.

"These guys are ruthless. That's why we have to be sure no one finds out you're a witness."

Loring reentered the room, the aroma of freshly brewed coffee floating in with him. He set a cup on the desk in front of Lynne. Her eyes misted and stung as she reached for the drink. "I understand."

He sat next to her, his spicy cologne mingled with the scent of coffee.

"There are those higher up the chain," Jane continued. "But we're not sure how high the chain goes—yet. That's one reason nailing them can be tough."

Heat rose in Lynne's neck. How could human beings do this to one another?

Loring lowered his cup from his lips. "The Piper's one of the worst." His eyes narrowed, and his voice had an edge to it as he talked about the criminal.

After Lynne swallowed the last dregs of her coffee, she dropped the empty cup in a wastebasket beside her. "How did he get that name? Sounds like The Pied Piper of Hamelin?"

"It does, and...in a way, he is." Jane pulled an old newspaper clipping from a file cabinet and handed it to Lynne. "The news media gave him that tag. Someone had heard his real name was Hamelin. His ability to lure children–teens–was a legend. He's reveled in the name ever since. Even taunts the police with it. Police departments in several major cities have received letters or emails with an attached classic Pied Piper graphic. Our department received one not long ago. We were pretty sure he was in the area before, but with your statement, I for one no longer doubt it. So far, we haven't been able to find out where those emails come from."

Jane tilted her head. "That was probably more information than you wanted to hear, but you need to be careful."

"How is it you figured it was him from my description?"

"Mainly rumors from our snitches and those from other cities. Little bits and pieces of description. And that car was typical of those stolen in the areas where other tips have come in."

Loring pointed to Lynne's ink adorned wrist. "That license plate number belonged to a stolen BMW. That's the one constant with The Piper. He loves his BMWs. Until now, we had no idea precisely what he looked like. Only his closest associates, whoever they may be, could identify him. We still don't know his true identity. Goldberg and Price have been involved in crimes where we suspected a connection with The Piper. But they've played dumb each time. Probably scared."

"Surely, The Piper's build sets him apart." Lynne's voice trembled. "He's so big."

Jane shook her head. "Not necessarily. There are thousands like him in the criminal realm. Or, after seeing that sketch, almost like him. No one has ever described his jaw that way, nor his eyes. Too frightened, I suppose." She glanced at her watch. "Time to call it a night. We'll be in touch, Lynne."

The detectives stood and walked Lynne to the door. "Loring, drive our witness home."

"Be glad to escort the lady."

Lynne caught a sudden flinch of Kim's head. Jealousy? The last thing Lynne wanted to do was give Kim anything to worry about. "Kim, I'll give you a call, okay? I graduate next year, and then it's off to the Navy Nurse Corps. But I'd like to keep in touch even then." That should ease her mind. She had no designs on Sergeant Loring Trent.

Kim spun in the desk chair and smiled. "Please do."

"Thank you, Jane." Lynne picked up her backpack and slung it over her shoulder. It seemed to weigh a ton. That dorm bed sounded so comforting. But would she be able to sleep?

Lynne walked in front of Loring to the front entrance of her dorm. She drew her key from a side pocket on her backpack and inserted it

into the lock. When the door creaked opened, she returned the key to the backpack and faced him. Should she say something? Mom never liked it when she tried matchmaking back home, but he and Kim obviously had something going. "Thanks for the escort, Detective."

"Loring, please. It doesn't seem like we just met for the first time tonight."

She had to say something to discourage any interest he had in her. Although, he was the most handsome—

"And driving you home was my pleasure."

With one hand still on the door handle, backpack dangling from her other hand, she turned away. "Loring, you do know Kim likes you, don't you?" She faced him again. "I'm sorry, that's none of my business."

"Don't worry. You're not the first person to point it out." His brows furrowed. "And I'm more than interested in Kim, but we're trying to keep things professional at work."

He clamped his lips together. "I wasn't hitting on you if that's what you thought. I didn't mean for it to sound that way." One side of his lips hiked up. "I'd just like for us to be friends." Loring chuckled and raised his brows. "Guess I'll remove the foot from my mouth now and say goodnight. You'll hear from us soon."

"Thanks, Loring. I'd like to have you and Kim as friends."

"Good. And remember. We'll look after you. You can count on us."

She nodded and hurried through the door. When it clicked shut behind her, Lynne leaned against it. After she heard a car door slam, she peeked out the window at the side of the doorframe and watched as Loring's car drove away. She'd always thought she could take care of herself, but it was a relief to have someone else watch over her.

The wind picked up outside. Tree limbs waved and made shadows skitter across the walkway. Lynne shuddered. What a horrible experience she'd had. Was it the last? Would the police be able to keep her safe?

Chapter Five

"Lynne! Lynne! Wake up!"

She opened her eyes to find her roommate bending over her. In the background, the television blared out, "That's what we've been able to ascertain so far. Now to the weather."

Lynne squeezed her eyelids together. It couldn't be morning already. She glanced at her alarm clock and back to the ash blonde whose bangs hung in her eyes. "Amanda, I had another half hour to sleep."

"I know. I'm sorry. But—" Amanda's eyes misted. She chewed her lip. "It's Dr. Lindstrom. He killed himself last night."

Oh no. Here we go. What should she say? "What? Where did you hear that?"

"It's all over the news. I flipped the TV on while getting ready for my early class, and…and…they found him in his office. It's terrible." She pressed a hand to her chest.

She had to act surprised. Lynne blinked. "I can't believe it! What did they say?"

"They said it was an apparent suicide. Why would someone like Dr. Lindstrom kill himself, Lynne?" A tear trailed down her cheek.

"Why does anyone do such a thing?" Lynne's heart raced. She touched Amanda's shoulder. "Come on. Don't let it get to you. There's nothing you can do about it. And you have a class in twenty minutes." Tears sprang to Lynne's eyes as she thought about the doctor's murder. She wiped them away with her fingertips and swung her legs out of bed.

"You're right." Amanda took a deep breath, crossed the room, and picked up her backpack from her bed. "Sorry I woke you. You got in late last night. Where were you? You never stay out late."

"You'll be late for your class if you don't leave. We'll talk later, okay?" Maybe by then, she could think up an excuse. Amanda was never one to let anything drop.

"Check. Let's go out for pizza after classes tonight. Maybe it'll get our minds off this." She gestured toward the TV.

"It's a date. Now get!"

Her roommate rushed out the door with a wave. Lynne shook her head. How many of these encounters would she face before the ordeal was over? *Lord, I need Your help.* She didn't feel like running this morning, but maybe it would help her think. And wake up.

She washed up, pulled on her sweats, and headed to the kitchenette for a glass of water. The cell rang. "Hello?"

"Lynne, this is Jane. Thought I'd check with you this morning to see how you're holding up."

"I'm okay, but my roommate hit me first thing with the TV report of Dr. Lindstrom's suicide. It'll be a madhouse here at school. I'm so afraid someone will ask questions since he was one of my professors."

"Just stay calm. Let everyone else do the talking and act surprised."

"Don't worry. I won't say a word." Lynne stepped to the window and spotted a reporter with a microphone clutched in her hand, accompanied by a cameraman with his equipment on his shoulder. "The press is out there."

"Things will settle down soon. Reporters are bugging us for details too, but we're holding them off."

Lynne wedged the phone between her shoulder and ear while she tied the laces on her running shoes.

"We won't give out information about an ongoing case, but they keep asking for details of the suicide anyway. All they get from us is, 'No comment.'"

Lynne snatched the keys from her backpack and went out the door. Excited voices drifted up the stairwell from the first floor. "Sounds like everyone in the dorm has heard the news. This will be a strange day."

"Stay away from reporters if you can. If one approaches, and you can't dodge them, say you can't provide information you don't know. We've instructed Mr. Prescott not to speak with them either. Nor to anyone else, for that matter."

A long yawn escaped Lynne. "Sorry. My roommate woke me with the news half an hour before my alarm was to go off, and I had a fitful night's sleep. I couldn't get those faces out of my head."

"I understand. We're doing all we can to help you through this, Lynne. Just to be on the safe side, we'll provide discreet protection even though we don't anticipate any problems. And if the press or anyone else tries to pin you down for information, tell them you've got nothing to give them. If that doesn't work, we'll be around to step in."

"Thanks, Jane. It *is* comforting. Well, as much as it can be in this situation."

"Stick with your normal routine, but as a precaution, don't go anywhere alone or outside after dark."

"Oh, don't worry. I have no desire to be out in the dark now."

"It's good you're taking this seriously. Many people don't. Stay close to other students when you walk on campus. Oh, and only keep company with trusted acquaintances. Lock your door as soon as you walk in, and report any strangers to us right away, especially if someone takes an unusual interest in you. Any questions?"

"I don't think so. My roommate wants to go out for pizza tonight. But we'll be back before dark."

"That's fine. Remember, normal routine and stay around friends. I'm glad your room's on the second floor."

"Me too, considering." Lynne skipped down the stairs to the foyer and stepped outside. Reporters spoke with students at both ends of the building and out by the sidewalk. She sat on the stone door stoop to finish the call before she started her run.

"Sorry I put you on edge, but we want to make sure you stay safe. You don't walk around the campus in the evening as part of your routine, do you?"

"No, but on Monday, Tuesday, and Thursday I go to the library to study. I normally don't stay late. And there's church service on Wednesday night. A group of us students go together."

"Okay. Sergeant Trent and Officer Travis will shadow you back to the dorm on those evenings. They won't mind going to your church service. Undercover, of course."

"I'll enjoy seeing them again. Monday through Saturday mornings, I run in the park near our building. Usually only around the recreational area on the east side campus. But once in a while, I run to another nearby park. I planned to do that this morning. It's pretty deserted at this time."

"Kim and Loring are runners too. They'll have no problem joining you from a distance." Jane gave a lighthearted laugh. "They need to stay in shape anyway. And when they can't be your protection detail, another couple of officers who can blend in with the students will be there. You'll meet them beforehand."

"I appreciate that."

"You planned to run this morning?"

Lynne glanced at her feet. "Ah, yeah."

"I don't want you to go out on your own. I'll call Loring and Kim. Can you delay for half an hour?"

"I guess so." Lynne rose, turned to the door, and got out her keys. "I'll go back up and study. They won't come up to get me, will they? It would be strange if they did."

"No. They'll wait outside. Tell me where they should stand so you can see them when they arrive."

"Hang on." Lynne hurried back inside, ran up the stairs, and entered the dorm room. She gazed out the window. "There's a clump of trees across the street on the north side of my building. It has a bench in front. I'll come out and start my run when they get there. It'll be a short one today."

"Lynne, you may be a natural for police work. You sure you want to be a nurse?"

"Ma'am, I'm headed for the Navy." She chuckled. Jane had a way of making a person feel relaxed.

"Okay, then. I'll let you go and get those two over to your dorm." Jane disconnected the call.

Lynne rifled through her pack on the desk and pulled out the notes she'd been studying for finals. *I wonder what they'll do about Dr. Lindstrom's exam. Never did find the answer to the question I wanted to ask him.* She pressed her lips together and took a deep breath. Then she dragged a chair to the window and read her material, glancing up to check the bench outside after every few sentences.

Loring and Kim. They were so right for each other. Now if she could only find a special man for herself. Someone like Trent. But it couldn't be until after her tour of duty in the Navy.

She'd love to meet someone like Loring though.

Lynne settled into an easy pace on the trail. Kim and Trent followed behind, close enough to intervene in the event of trouble. *Thank You for the new friends, Lord.*

After several minutes of focusing on her route and breathing, the tension drained out of her body. She ran through her favorite section where the path inclined upward and then fell again as it curved gently around dense trees. The fragrance of roses floated in the air. She almost forgot her guardians were behind her. As she rounded the last bend, she glanced back. Loring and Kim had drawn nearer. She smiled. They wouldn't let her out of their sight.

As she passed groups of students, the bits and pieces of conversation she heard were about Dr. Lindstrom's suicide. Guess that was what she'd hear for days.

Outside the Medical Sciences Building, Lynne took a break. Walter Prescott came toward her. He must have taken the morning shift today.

The guard scanned the surrounding area before he stopped in front of Lynne. "Did the cops contact you, Miss Temple?" He spoke in a hushed tone. "I told them you'd gone up to talk to Doc Lindstrom last night. Worried me to death. I thought you might have found him after he did it."

"The professor was fine when I got there." Although he wasn't when she left. A twinge of guilt hit her. But she had to be evasive with the man per Jane's instructions. "The police contacted me. The officers took my statement."

"I gave them mine too. Boy, I'll tell ya though, it was a real shock, finding him dead. I reported the suicide right away. You must have been the last one to see the doc alive and then left the building before—"

"Yeah. I suppose I was." It was rude to interrupt, but what else could she do? She couldn't talk about this.

"I wonder what made him do it." Walter shook his head. "I can't figure out why Doc Lindstrom would want to commit suicide. But then, we shouldn't be discussing this, should we? I mean, the police don't want us to talk about it while they try to figure out why he did it."

"No, we shouldn't." *Thank You again, Lord.* Lynne glanced at her watch. "I'm sorry to rush, Walter, but I've got to get to class. Running late this morning."

"No problem. Take care of yourself, Miss Temple. At least this wasn't a murder. We don't have to worry about a killer running loose on the campus."

"You too, Walter." Didn't need to be reminded of that. But what could happen on campus with people milling around and officers following her?

After her run, Lynne showered and headed to her first class. She dodged microphones, passed teary-eyed classmates, and avoided faculty members. Did anyone besides Walter know she'd gone to see him? She hated the thought of being vague or outright lying to everyone.

Even the faculty wore stunned looks on their faces. Did hers show the stress she was under? Her fear?

After a week of finals, Lynne strolled to the student residence in a loose gaggle of other undergraduates. Before she reached her building, she pulled out her cell and hit the button for her parents' phone. "Hi, Mom. Thanks for praying. Last exam was a breeze."

"Oh, Lynnie, I'm so glad. Can't wait to see you. And guess what? Jeff will be here when you get home. He says he can't wait to see his baby sister."

"I'm happy he'll be on leave. Can we talk later tonight? A few of us are getting together for a finals party. Pizza and stuff."

"Of course, Dear. Have a good time. You deserve it."

"Give my love to Dad. Love you, Mom."

She disconnected and pressed Lieutenant Helmer's number. "Hi, Jane. Decided to check in before things got busy tonight. I think I aced my exams. We're having a small party here in the common room to celebrate."

"Sounds like fun. Congratulations on the finals. Before long, these days will be a memory."

Lynne breathed a sigh of relief. One of those memories she'd like to forget. "I plan to go home to Kewanee for a break. That's not a problem, is it?"

"I've no problem with it. Loring and Kim said they've detected no cause for worry since they've been tailing you. Go ahead and enjoy the time with your family. We're making progress on the case."

"That's good." But how long would it be before she got her life back?

"Just give me the details of your trip home when you have them so we can arrange your protection. Be careful. And call if anything unusual happens."

Be careful? What could happen in a little farm town like Kewanee if there's been no cause for worry?

Chapter Six

One week later in the early afternoon, Lynne boarded a Greyhound. She leaned back in her seat, pulled out her phone, and punched in her mother's number. "Hi, Mom. I'm on the bus. We'll leave any minute, so, I should be home before you know it."

After a short conversation, she hung up and yawned. She'd catch up on sleep when she got home…if the dreams let her. As the hum of the road filled her ears, her eyelids drooped.

When she woke up, familiar sights came into view. Rows of corn shined in the glow of the late afternoon sun. How she'd missed the peacefulness of her rural community. Acres of green fields and rich pastures with grazing cattle, tails swishing at flies. Farmhouses, tall silos, and barns brought on a homesick pang in her stomach. A vast panorama nestled beneath a blue sky dappled with fleecy white clouds. Tears welled in Lynne's eyes. *Almost home.* If only she'd never have to leave again. But then she couldn't join the Nursing Corps and serve her country as her brothers had.

She glanced at her watch and hit redial on the cell. Her mother answered on the second ring. "Hi, Mom. Who's picking me up in Ottawa? I should arrive in half an hour."

"Dad just told me he can't leave the grain elevator right now. And Jeff won't get in until this evening. I'll be late, but I'll be there. Just a moment."

A faint familiar voice came over the line. Sounded like Uncle Pratie with his lyrical Irish brogue.

Her mother came back on the line. "Lynnie, Patrick O'Brien stopped by. He said he'd pick you up. He has to check on an order in Ottawa anyway."

"That's wonderful. It'll be good to see him. Love you, Mom."

Lynne hung up, settled back in her seat, and closed her eyes. *Uncle Pratie.* He and Auntie Eri had been like family for as long as she remembered. She laughed. Odd how people acquired nicknames. All because he loved potatoes.

Farmland gave way to clusters of buildings and signs announcing the way to Starved Rock State Park. Moments later, passengers filed off the bus and collected their luggage. Lynne waited for the crowd to thin. It would take Uncle Pratie at least another half hour to get there.

The driver yanked the last bag from the storage area and handed it to Lynne. "You're traveling mighty light, Miss."

She smiled. "Just the necessities. Have to get used to it. I'll be in the military soon."

"Good for you. My son's in the Army."

As she moved to the sidewalk, a hearty voice hailed her. "Weeell, if it isn't young Lynnie Temple herself. Sure and you're a sight for sore eyes, lass."

"Uncle Pratie!" Her arms wrapped around his ample middle. Her pack fell to the ground, and he gave her a squeeze. When he let go, she backed up and gave him the once-over. "Same old Uncle Pratie. You got here faster than I expected."

"Weeell, ma lead foot was extra heavy. Besides, it was downhill." He laughed.

Lynne reached for her pack strap, but he caught it. "I'll take that, lass." He slung the bag onto one broad shoulder.

"How's Aunt Eri?"

"Fit as a fiddle, and twice as mean. I have a time keeping up with her, and that's a fact." His teasing, laughing, and way with words was a beautiful melody to Lynne's ears. "The truck's right o'er here." He led the way to a gleaming metallic silver Dodge pickup and opened the passenger door.

"Wow! This is *nice*. How long have you had it?"

"A month. Got one like that Texas Ranger fella on TV. The one that's always in car chases and kicking the bad guys into the middle of next week! More power to 'im, I say." He grinned.

Lynne laughed, but her eyes misted. She bit her lip. *Wish those Rangers would kick my bad guys into next week. No…into prison…forever.*

The expression on Uncle Pratie's face changed. His brows lowered. "Speaking of bad guys, heard ya had upheaval at the university. One of your professors."

She stared into sharp blue eyes. "How'd you know?"

"Retired from the Chicago Police Department, remember? That report in the papers didn't set right. Told the missus. She agreed. Suicide, nothing. Hope I didn't upset ya though."

"No. Not more than I've already been. It's just that—I saw it." She took in a sharp breath. Now she'd done it. She'd broken her word and said something she shouldn't have. How would she keep this from her family?

For several minutes, they drove through the countryside in silence. Lynne focused on the rustic sights. As if he'd read her mind, he patted her hand on the leather passenger seat. "Don't ya worry, lass. I'll not say anything. Neither will Eri."

"Are you still acquainted with officers in Chicago?" Lynne turned to him.

"Indeed. I've maintained a keen interest in my old stomping grounds. Ha! Sergeant McGinty at the University PD, right enough." He laughed. "He was a rookie when I left, mind you. And, Jane Helmer, or Jane Enderby as she was. She's as fine an officer as ya'd hope to meet. Her dad was one of the youngest officers to make precinct captain."

"That's good. How about Kim Travis and Loring Trent?"

His forehead furrowed as he mouthed the names. "Nope. Don't sound familiar. But if they're working with Jane, they'll be up to the mark, and that's a fact."

Lynne laid her head on the headrest mulling over the confidence he had in his old department. Had they changed? Sometimes cops turned bad. No. Jane, Loring, and Kim would be there for her. She breathed a sigh of relief.

Before turning down the dirt road to her parent's farm, Uncle Pratie pulled the truck onto the shoulder. "Lynnie, if your parents ask questions, tell them the police have an open investigation and asked you not to talk about it. Then your parents won't be pressin' for information. Best not to say yer a witness, since yer going back."

"Mom already called the day after the news came out. She was worried. I told her there was nothing I could tell her. Then I changed the subject."

"That was the truth, enough of it. It's what ya have to do. Tell me if they ask a'gin. I'll talk to them."

She nodded.

He pulled the vehicle across the road into the dirt drive that led to the farm. When he turned off the engine in the circle between the house and barn, her mother ran from the house with open arms. Her dad strode over from the barn. Lynne hardly had time to get out of the vehicle before they enveloped her in a three-way hug.

After her dad grabbed the weekender from the truck bed, he headed for the house. With her arm around Lynne's waist, her mother waved to Uncle Pratie. He tipped an imaginary hat, slid into the driver's seat, and headed toward home.

After another hug, Lynne and her mom strolled, arms linked, along the path to the house. "Oh, Lynnie, I'm so glad to have you home, away from that horrible incident at your school. Have you found out any more about the suicide?"

Oh no. "Mom, I can't talk right now."

"Sorry, Dear. You're tired after those exams and your trip back. Not to mention the stress of everything. I wasn't thinking. We want you to enjoy your time here. You're home, and that's what matters. Jeff will be here by tonight, and then we'll celebrate."

When they reached the porch, her mother stepped into the house, but Lynne sauntered to the porch swing. She took a deep breath and sat. If only she *could* forget the last couple of weeks, this time at home would be peaceful.

Gazing out the bedroom window toward the barn, Lynne smiled. Boy, what a relaxing week it had been with her family, away from the stress of…everything. If only Jim were home too.

She walked down the stairs and entered the living room. Her cell rang. When Jim's face came up on the phone display, Lynne let out a squeal. "Hey, you. This isn't as good as having you here, Big Brother, but it'll do in a pinch." She collapsed onto the couch.

"Yeah. Sure wish I was, but someone has to be out here saving the world." He laughed. "How'd you do on exams?"

"Great." Had he heard what happened at school? She hoped not.

"Awesome. Has Jeff been working with you on your martial arts? Or have you guys goofed off?" He snickered.

She sighed. "He's pushed me beyond endurance." She eyed Jeff as he came into the room, wiping his hands on a dishtowel. "At least when he isn't off with Nicole."

Lynne hopped off the couch as Jeff twisted the towel and grinned. "You escaped KP this time, but not for lunch, Squirt." He whipped the towel at her, and the tip snapped her buttocks.

"Yeow! Stinker!" She rubbed her bottom.

"What?"

"Not you, Jim…the other stinker. He snapped me with a wet dishtowel! I won't say where, but…I'll be very careful when I sit."

Jeff doubled over in laughter.

"Let me talk to my reprobate little brother. Take care of yourself, Stringbean."

Tears filled her eyes. "I will, Jim. You too." She handed the phone to Jeff and hurried to the bathroom to dry her tears. Wouldn't want to make Mom start crying. *Next year I'll be gone too.* Definitely a mixed blessing. She'd miss her family, but maybe she'd be able to forget about the past year.

The time at home had gone by much too fast for Lynne, but she had to get back to her routine and start the extra summer classes she'd signed up for. "Don't look so sad, Mom. I'll be back for a visit soon." Lynne handed her bag to the bus driver who stowed it in the luggage compartment of the Greyhound at the Ottawa bus station.

As she hugged her mother, movement at the corner of the building caught her eye. Her first week home, she'd seen that same man with wavy light brown hair leaning against the wall of a restaurant in Kewanee. Who was he? The person Jane assigned to watch over her? It had to be. Nothing had happened to her for the entire two weeks.

Her focus returned to her weeping mother. "Remember First Peter, five-seven, Mom. 'Casting all your care upon Him.' And you can call my cell whenever."

"I know, Honey. First Peter, five-seven." She wiped her eyes and smiled. "I taught you that verse when you were little. But I'll miss you."

Mom had become over-emotional since Jeff went back to duty last week. "I'll miss you too. Both of you."

Lynne wrapped her arms around her dad and squeezed. He kissed her on the forehead and then lifted her chin. "You remember everything your brothers taught you, okay?" He winked.

Self-defense? Had he the same instincts as Uncle Pratie?

"We'll be praying for you." Her father hugged her, then leaned in close to her ear and whispered, "Call me on my cell when you need to talk." He held her at arm's length. "Your last year, and an important one."

"I will, Dad."

With a final wave, she boarded the bus.

The vehicle moved through the countryside, but instead of enjoying the view, Lynne's thoughts drifted to the investigation of Dr. Lindstrom's death. Jane hadn't called once in the past two weeks. Uncle Pratie said not to worry. *"Jane would contact you if there was a need to. Mark ma words, lass."*

But as soon as Lynne stepped into her dorm room, she called Jane's number. No answer. She left a message.

Lynne tried Kim's phone. "Hi, Lynne. Back at school?"

"Good, you're there. Just got back. I tried Jane's number but got her voicemail. Is everything okay?"

"She may be in a meeting. We're getting close to an arrest. Then we'll ask you to come to the station to make an ID."

"Do you have any idea when?"

"Not yet, but it shouldn't be long."

Lynne's stomach tightened. She needed a more pleasant subject to dwell on. "How are things with you and Loring?"

"Good. Will you go back to your routine now that you're back?"

"I'd like to. Is that okay?"

"Sure. Loring and I plan to run as before." Kim giggled. "I need it."

"I doubt that, but it will be nice to run with you two again."

"To ease your mind, Lynne, there doesn't seem to be any chatter on the street about a witness."

"Thanks. That is a relief." She lay back on her bed, head propped against the pillows. "Twice, while back home, I noticed a man hanging around. Made me nervous after the second time. But then I realized he was probably sent to watch over me."

"Sounds right, but I'll ask Jane."

Lynne rose and opened the window to let fresh air into the room. The tree-lined paths across the street beckoned. Would it hurt to take a quick run on this peaceful afternoon? "Does everyone still believe Dr. Lindstrom committed suicide?"

"Publicly, yes. But among the criminal fraternity, no. Don't worry. There's no word out there connecting you with the case."

Best tell them about Uncle Pratie. "A friend of our family figured out what happened to Dr. Lindstrom."

"Here's Jane now. Why don't you tell her about your friend and the man you saw? But let's get together when you're settled. We can go out for pizza and girl-talk. And let us know if you see that guy hanging around at school."

"That's a date, and I will."

"Here's Jane."

"Hi, Lynne. Welcome back to the big city. Hope you had a good time."

"I did, thanks. A family friend I call Uncle Pratie guessed what happened to Dr. Lindstrom. He used to work for the Chicago Police Department and knows you and Sergeant McGinty."

Laughter came over the line. "Pratie O'Brien? He's a friend of yours? 'Weeell, sure an' it's a small world,' to quote the man."

Lynne stifled a chuckle. "He's more a part of my family. Anyway, he guessed it was a murder, not suicide. But he promised not to say anything."

"He's a good man. Good officer, he was."

"It was comforting having him around. He advised me what to say to Mom and Dad if they asked about the professor. But after the first day, they never brought up what happened at school." She leaned against the windowsill, gazing at the trees.

"I'm sure he gave you good advice. Nothing to worry about. We'll be in touch. And Loring and Kim will resume their watch over you."

"I'll plan to start my run again tomorrow morning." Best pass on one for tonight.

The call ended. Lynne sat in a chair by the window, still surveying the tree-lined street. Better not take a chance on running without Loring and Kim. She got up and unpacked her bag. *Oh drat!* She'd forgotten to mention the man at the bus stop. Kim would probably say something.

Lynne hung up the last item from her bag and peered out the window again. Would the Lord keep her safe through this entire ordeal, or test her faith? *I'd rather You tested me another way, Lord.*

Chapter Seven

*W*inter passed and with it a challenging semester of nightmares and waiting to hear from the Chicago Police Department about any progress in the case of Professor Lindstrom's murder case. Kim had explained things were not moving as fast as she had thought they would.

A warm spring breeze carrying the scent of lilacs demanded Lynne's attention as she sat in the common room of the dorm studying with classmates. Her last year at the university. What an adventure it had been.

Her cell chimed, and Jane's number popped into the screen. Lynne hurried outside and stopped under the budding trees next to the front entrance. She connected the call. "Hi, Jane. Haven't heard from you for some time."

"We've been busy. Pulled in the two suspects and plan to interrogate them. Can you come to the station to make an ID?"

Lynne's heart jumped into her throat as she glanced at her watch. Only a little past twelve. "Of course." A tremor went through her. Could one of them be The Piper?

"Can I send someone to pick you up?"

"No, I'll jog over. Shouldn't take very long." Lynne hung up before Jane could voice an objection. She strode out of the dorm toward the precinct. Her pulse quickened, and a sense of foreboding intensified with every footfall. *Father, help me get through this.*

Just inside the station door, she encountered Kim. "Hey, girl. You look like you need a bottle of water before I take you to Jane." She led Lynne through a hallway and into the kitchenette, snatched a water bottle from the refrigerator, and handed it to her.

Lynne twisted the cap off and took a drink. "Thanks. Forgot mine. Nervous when I left." Nervous? More like scared to death.

Kim took her to Jane, who smiled her greeting. "Thanks for coming in right away. Loring and I will interrogate the two suspects. You'll watch through here." She pointed to a dark glass window on one side of the room. "Kim will stay with you."

Lynne nodded and took a drink. "Is one of them The Piper?" Clammy sweat oozed from her forehead and hands.

"No. Don't worry." Kim laid her hand on Lynne's shoulder. "We haven't located him yet. But we will, eventually."

As Loring entered, Jane picked up a file from the table behind her. "Let's go, Sergeant." When the door closed behind them, Lynne released the breath she'd been holding. How could they remain so calm when facing cold-blooded killers?

"You okay?" Kim asked.

"Yeah. Okay." Lynne stared at the pitch-black window. A door opened on the other side of the darkened room, and a uniformed officer switched on the light. He escorted in the man she recognized as Cathcart and motioned for him to sit in a folding chair on the far side of a rectangular metal table.

Kim flicked a switch under the window. The scrape of the chair came through an overhead speaker as Cathcart pulled it back.

"That's Cathcart," Lynne whispered. "Or Price, you called him. The one who killed Dr. Lindstrom." Her head whipped toward Kim. "Did he hear me?"

Kim shook her head and touched the window. "Soundproof." Another man, portly and middle-aged with gray hair, followed Jane into the room. "Price's lawyer, Luther Dovecot of the Pemberton and Dovecot Law Firm."

With a smug expression, the attorney stepped to the table. Lynne grimaced. "He sure has an air of confidence."

"More like arrogance." Kim's lips pursed. "Lawyers don't come more expensive than him and his partner. And he's as slippery as a greased eel."

The killer's icy stare focused on the glass partition between the rooms. Lynne's heart thudded. Price and Dovecot both glared when Loring entered with a file.

Jane motioned for Dovecot to sit next to his client. The two detectives took their places on the opposite side of the table. Loring turned on a recorder and stared at Price. "State your name, please."

It felt as though ice crystals ran through Lynne's veins at the sound of the man's voice. The vision of Dr. Lindstrom's body crumpled on the floor burst into her mind. She shuddered.

Preliminaries completed, Dovecot slapped his hand on the table. "This is an injustice, to begin with, Lieutenant. Could you at least remove my client's handcuffs and ease his discomfort?"

"No." Jane's voice was hard. "Mr. Price, where were you on—"

The entire scene with Price and Cathcart played in Lynne's memory like a movie. She chewed her lip.

Loring spoke, snagging her attention. "Your client resisted arrest, Mr. Dovecot. He's continued to display hostility and a lack of cooperation."

Dovecot focused on Loring. "My client plans to lodge a complaint against you, Sergeant Trent. Excessive use of force during his arrest."

"Indeed." Loring smirked. Dovecot's gimlet eyes shot daggers at him.

Lynne raised a hand to her throat. "Takes a special person to do this job, doesn't it?"

"You're observing two experts." Kim's eyes focused on Loring. She smiled. "Price is edgy. Loring'll try to provoke him into incriminating himself. The lawyer will have a time keeping his client under control."

Lynne glanced at her. She longed to love a man the way Kim loved Loring.

"Well, Lieutenant. I hope this won't take long. My client has urgent business to attend to."

"So do we." Jane's words were clipped. She focused her gaze on Price, her mouth in a straight line. "I'll ask you again. Where were you on Thursday, May eighth, two thousand and three at nine p.m.?"

Dovecot nodded to Price, who smirked and turned to answer her. "That was the night I drove with my sister to New York so she could take care of a personal matter with her ex. I stayed with her all week."

"You've used a new alias, Jerome Cathcart." She opened the folder Loring had placed in front of her, perused the documents, and closed the folder. "You signed checks using that name, both here and in New York, but that was after the eighth of May."

"My client has a residence in New York City. He goes there often on business."

Jane turned her attention to the lawyer. "But your client didn't go to his *residence*." Her eyes met Price's. "We know you moved into a rundown part of town the following week—alone. Were you hiding?" She stretched her arms on the table and clasped her hands. "There's no official record of any name change for you. You also used fake identification to open a bank account, so you could lay low after the murder."

"I've done nothing wrong." Price glared.

Lynne's mouth dropped open. Nothing wrong?

"There seem to be discrepancies in your story, Price." Loring narrowed his eyes. "We have information that you were at the college the night Dr. Lindstrom was murdered."

The lawyer shot a quick look at Price.

"Okay, that shook up Dovecot." Kim grinned.

Jane leaned forward. "You were at the Medical Sciences Building before you left for New York."

"Not a coincidence, was it?" Loring glared at him.

Price tried to jump up, but Dovecot grabbed his shoulder and forced him back into the chair. The killer bared his teeth. "So what!"

"Your evidence against my client is weak. I insist you either charge Mr. Price or release him immediately."

This time, Jane ignored the lawyer. She tapped the file folder with a forefinger and shifted in her chair.

Price's face turned ashen. Dovecot glowered. "This is all mere insinuation, Lieutenant Helmer. The checks are one thing, but an unsubstantiated charge of murder is quite another. I'll file a complaint for police harassment of my client if this doesn't stop."

She kept her eyes on Price. "Mr. Goldberg will have no problem letting you go down for the crime alone."

Price bellowed as he leaped out of his chair. The uniformed officer who stood by the door lunged forward, grabbed the suspect, and shoved him back into the seat. Dovecot's eyes bulged.

"Got 'em." Kim's words were barely audible. "Dovecot underestimated Jane and Loring. Bet he wishes he'd never agreed to represent this loser."

Lynne's pulse pounded from Price's lunge at the detectives. She let out a relieved breath. Jane's earlier statement to the suspect struck her. "When Jane said Price was at the college, she meant what I told her, right?"

"Not just you. You're the witness to the murder, but you're not the only one who saw them around the building."

Loring stood. "John Price, you are under arrest for the murder of Dr. Harold Lindstrom. Officer, take him to his cell. But first, you might want to move the cuffs behind his back. He doesn't seem to like it here."

Dovecot rose from the chair, picked up his briefcase, and headed for the door.

"See you in court, Counselor," Loring remarked.

The lawyer spun and glared. "We'll see about that."

After the interrogation, Kim led Lynne back to Jane's office. Lynne took a seat next to the desk, but as soon as the detectives arrived, she jumped out of the chair. "You have another witness?" Her pulse continued to throb.

"There were others on the university grounds who saw Price and Goldberg outside the building, but only you saw the murder. The rest is circumstantial. But they don't know about your testimony."

Lynne pulled her lips to one side and returned to the chair. "What about the one you called The Piper?"

"So far, no one else saw him." Jane glimpsed her watch. "How's your schedule today, Lynne? Do you have another class?"

"No. Only a martial arts session at five."

The lieutenant's smile reached clear to her eyes. "Nurse's training and martial arts. You're a force to reckon with."

Loring grinned at her. A warm sensation traveled up Lynne's neck and into her face. "That was something back there in the room. Is it always like this with guilty suspects?"

"Not usually." He lowered himself into a chair in the corner. "We took advantage of Price's quick temper. The next guy won't be so easy."

Jane sighed and turned to Lynne. "Leo Goldberg. His lawyer, Radcliffe Pemberton, is the senior partner in their firm. Dovecot most likely will present the case at trial, but Pemberton will ride shotgun. It's how they work." She dropped the file she held onto the desk. Loring lifted another. Then she approached the office door. "Let's get this over with."

A sense of dread overcame Lynne. She followed Jane, Loring, and Kim out of the office. The four of them reentered the viewing room with the large window as an officer led Epstein and his lawyer into the other chamber.

"Humph." Loring glared. "Pemberton acts dignified, but he's slicker than his buddy Dovecot."

The detectives left the room. Kim joined Lynne at the window. "He's gotten some horrible people off."

Jane and Loring strode into the interrogation room. Lynne shuddered at the cruel, craggy features of the heavyset man who had downloaded a virus onto the doctor's computer. "It's him. Epstein…Goldberg."

Kim nodded. "They'll have a harder time with him than Price. He's as cold as ice."

Taking the chair next to Goldberg, Pemberton smirked. With thick grayish-white hair, an almost-white mustache, and impeccably dressed, he was impressive, except for his evil black eyes. *Wouldn't want to meet this one on a dark street. Or anywhere else.*

"This guy is loaded." Kim leaned on the edge of the window frame. "Part owner of a country club on the north side of town and has megabuck houses in Long Island, Cape Cod, Palm Springs, and Pensacola, Florida." She glanced at Lynne. "That we know of."

"Then why does he bother with the likes of Goldberg and Price?"

Kim's gaze turned sober. "Narcotics and human trafficking. Big bucks, with Mideast connections. Probably how he paid for all those houses. Though, no one's been able to prove it. Or that he's linked with The Piper, who no doubt foots the legal bills."

Loring dropped the file folder onto the table in front of Jane with a slap, reeling in Lynne's attention. Pemberton donned a pair of glasses, produced a file from his briefcase, and read the papers inside. Goldberg yawned.

"Okay, Pemberton. You've had your fun." Jane opened her file folder. "You've already reviewed the paperwork before you got here.

Stop the stall."

The lawyer put his papers away.

The same line of questions proceeded from Jane and Loring after they established Goldberg's use of the alias Albert Epstein. He responded to questions in a monotone. How could he stare straight ahead without blinking for so long? A chill went through Lynne.

"My client's precipitous departure from Chicago following the alleged murder of the unfortunate doctor was entirely coincidental." Pemberton mimicked Goldberg's stare.

Loring spoke softly. "Where first-degree murder and your client are concerned, nothing is coincidental."

"Mr. Goldberg has acknowledged certain irregularities in matters of identity and financial transactions, which were beyond his control."

"I'm sure." Loring grimaced.

The lawyer stared icily at him and continued. "However, trivial issues such as these are not grounds for interrogation on suspicion of first-degree murder. If you have witnesses who *allegedly* place my client at the scene of the crime, Lieutenant," he moved his frigid stare to Jane, "give me the details forthwith so I can check their credibility."

Jane placed both hands palms down on the table and rose. "You'd like that, wouldn't you? No. You'll receive the details in due time."

Lynne jumped. "Will she give him my name?"

"He'll only get what's necessary according to law."

Jane charged the stony-faced Goldberg, and the officer led him away.

Lynne took in a sharp breath.

After he snapped his briefcase shut, Pemberton rose to his full height and looked down his long, thin nose at the two detectives. "When my client is acquitted of these trumped-up charges, it will give me great satisfaction to see you relieved of your badges."

Jane raised an eyebrow and cocked her head. "You enjoy tying up loose ends, don't you? I seem to recall an investigative journalist for the Boston Globe who died eight years ago after he asked questions about a wingding in your Cape Cod mansion. It involved prominent D.C. dignitaries...and minors."

The fingers of Loring's right hand drummed on the tabletop. "The reporter's car plunged into a river. Right?"

Kim leaned her head next to Lynne's. "Drumming fingers is a pet peeve of Pemberton's."

The muscles in Pemberton's jaw twitched as he glared at Loring's fingers still tapping on the table. He snatched his briefcase and moved toward the door. "Accidents happen." He clasped the doorknob.

"The Massachusetts State Police didn't think it was an accident," Loring said to the man's back.

He turned the knob.

Jane added, "The arson investigators found traces of accelerant at the scene where fire destroyed this same journalist's computer and files in his motel room."

"Well, you detectives know much more about the case than I do." The lawyer's eyes narrowed as he opened the door a crack and glanced behind him. "You're venturing into dangerous ground, Sergeant. The outcome of a successful libel action could be damaging to your purse, not to mention your career." He opened the door. "Investigative journalism can be hazardous. Just like police work. I'm sure you both recall the tragic case of Holly Richmond."

Loring's eyes grew large. He leaned forward as if to spring on Pemberton, but Jane gripped his arm. Loring glared as the lawyer left the room.

"What was that about?" Lynne looked at Kim.

"One day, God willing, we'll have enough evidence to put this piece of work where he belongs."

"I mean, who is Holly Richmond?"

"Holly worked in drug enforcement. She and Loring were engaged. Two years ago, they worked on a case involving The Piper. Loring found her dead. Strangled."

Lynne sucked in air and prayed to hold back the tears in her wide eyes. *Is Holly the reason Loring doesn't respond to Kim?* Her heart broke for both of them.

"Enough sad stories." Kim turned to Lynne with moist eyes. "Jane told us former Officer O'Brien is your neighbor." Her blue eyes twinkled as they brimmed with tears. "Never met the man, but he's pretty much a legend around here."

If they couldn't keep one of their own safe from The Piper, how safe would she be once Pemberton found out she was a witness? Lynne's temples pounded.

Coffee dribbled into Lynne's cup in the police station's small kitchen. Was there anything more tantalizing than the aroma of fresh coffee? Her watch showed it was after two. She removed the cup from the coffee machine and followed Kim to Jane's office. How would she get through this ordeal? The police and detectives couldn't stay with her twenty-four hours a day. She pulled in an uneasy breath.

"I'll bet Radcliffe will hire goons to declare on their grandmothers' graves that Leo and John were playing pool in some beer joint the night of the murder." Kim opened Jane's office door, and they entered the room. "He'll want to convince the jury the witnesses saw men who only looked like his clients."

Before the door closed, Jane and Loring walked into the office. Jane sat at the desk. "Well, that's what we're up against." She quirked her mouth at Lynne.

He strode to the window. "Pemberton is up to his neck in this crime." Loring turned. "I'm sure of it." He glanced at Lynne.

She focused on Jane. "I didn't see the lawyer at the school that night."

"Don't worry about Pemberton." Jane shook her head. "The important thing is you identified Price and Goldberg. We'll take care of the lawyer."

"And what of the man you call The Piper?"

Loring dropped into the chair next to Lynne. "So far, zip, I'm afraid. He's skipped town. But we'll find him."

Jane stood. "We're done for this afternoon."

As Lynne tossed her empty cup into the wastebasket, Loring headed for the door. "I'll give you a ride home."

Another pained look flashed across Kim's face. Lynne rose and faced her. "Kim, will you drive me instead? I'd like to talk to you."

"Sorry, Lynne." Jane grabbed a knitted shawl from the corner coat tree and slung it over her shoulders. "You girls'll have to catch up later. We need Kim to draw more sketches in a few minutes. Another case we're working on."

A film of moisture came to Kim's eyes. She laid her hand on

Lynne's arm. "I'll see you soon." She left the room.

Lynne bit her lip and joined Loring at the door. His attention would be wonderful…if it weren't for Kim's feelings. Loring touched her elbow as she passed through the doorway, and a quiver skittered up her arm. This was not good. She couldn't fall for him…not at Kim's expense.

As Loring escorted Lynne to his car, Pemberton's verbal attack on him came to her mind. Kim's reaction to his suffering was so obvious. Loring had to get over Holly. Lynne glanced at him. "It must be so hard to lose someone the way you lost Holly. But, you can't love a ghost, Loring. You've got to move on."

He opened the passenger door for her. "Thank you for your concern, Lynne. Guess Kim told you about Holly."

"She did, and your pain hurts her. It's in her eyes."

"I think of Holly all the time." He shut the door, got behind the wheel, and drove out of the parking space into the evening rush-hour traffic.

"But she's gone, Loring. And Kim's here."

He didn't respond.

When he parked in front of the dorm, Lynne gripped the door handle. He softly touched her shoulder. "Lynne. You're here now too," he half smiled.

She faced him. Butterflies flew in her stomach. Her face warmed.

Chapter Eight

A semi-state of normalcy continued for Lynne. She hadn't talked much to Kim since the interrogations. Although her friends had resumed their runs with Lynne for her protection, Kim seemed withdrawn.

Lynne's mind turned to Loring. He cared about Kim. *"I'm more than interested in Kim, but we're trying to keep things professional at work."* Poor Kim. She must have guessed about his new interest. Lynne shook her head. She had to discourage him about his attraction to her. But if Kim asked her how she felt about Loring the next time they talked, she couldn't lie. She found herself just as much attracted to him. Maybe Kim would never ask.

A sigh escaped her as Lynne rounded the next bend. She turned and jogged backward a few steps to check on her companions. Ever since the interrogations, she hadn't seen Kim and Loring laugh with each other as they used to either. She faced forward. Her heart ached.

As she approached a gravel path through the wooded area that edged the university's recreational field, she glanced behind her again to see how close her friends might be. They were still out of sight, but they'd catch up. She continued her run.

Mixed emotions overwhelmed her with graduation approaching. She'd leave for service with the Nurse Corps. Even if she and Loring developed stronger romantic feelings, she'd been told long-distance relationships didn't work out so well. And the last thing she wanted was to hurt Kim. *Oh Lord, I'm so confused.*

Focus on something else. Jeff's unit was in Afghanistan. Would the Navy send her there too? They might since Jim was now stationed in the States. All three of them wouldn't be in harm's way. After her training to become an Ensign, it was up to God where He thought she could serve best.

Along another turn in the path, Lynne peeked behind her. Still no sign of Kim or Loring. What happened to them? Maybe one pulled a muscle. Still, wouldn't the other have kept following her? She slowed her pace.

As she loped along, the rich fragrance of roses filled the air. She loved this stretch through the recreation field with its row of pale pink bushes, especially on an early Saturday morning. Strange that no one else was running the path today.

In the distance, a group of students had a game of football going with her first-semester chemistry teacher, Mr. Davis, playing referee. A few of the guys lifted their heads as Lynne glided by. Was that a whistle? She chuckled and waved but kept her pace steady.

Leaving the grassy field, she entered a section where thick tree branches overhung the trail. Mottled sunlight made a blotchy pattern on the ground. Dense, shoulder-high bushes flanked either side of the path with the street at her left. A few parked cars dotted the avenue.

Lynne passed a long break in the bushes. A battered, dark-colored van sat parked by the curb, the driver hunched behind the steering wheel. The van's engine idled and sent black exhaust plumes out the tailpipe. His motor needed a complete overhaul and tune-up. Her dad and brothers had always kept their vehicles and farm machinery in tip-top condition.

As the bushes closed in again, two dumpy, medium height males, wearing faded jeans and sweatshirts leaped out at her. Lynne collided with them. The first man, bald and reeking of nicotine, lunged to grab her around the waist. His partner, dirty brown hair hanging over his ears, tried to slip what looked like a large pillowcase over her head.

She ducked. Then, with all her strength, she shot upward and rammed the heel of her hand against the bottom of Baldy's jaw. *Crack!* Blood trickled onto his thick lips. He staggered and let out a yelp of rage. Red spattered his sweatshirt.

To avoid a second attempt from the attacker with the pillowcase, Lynne ducked again. "Oh no you don't." Lynne twisted and pasted a tight fist to the side of his head. He stumbled back, then shook.

Once more, he reached for her. She turned and rammed her elbow into his stomach. As he bent forward, Lynne spun out of his grip. A second clenched fist struck his eye. Longhair reeled backward, clutching his midriff with one arm, while his other hand covered his eye.

Lynne stepped away from her opponents and slammed the returning Baldy with a lightning-fast roundhouse kick, sending him into the bushes. She then turned on Longhair with quick jabs to his face, neck, and chest. The would-be attackers fled through the shrubs toward the van. Curses soiled the fragrant air.

Adrenaline rushed through her. Should she pursue the enemy? No. Lynne hurdled over the lowest section of bushes on the field side and peered over the top as the van driver's door opened. A thickset man with a mop of dark hair stepped out. He glared in Lynne's direction and raised a handgun. She crouched and prepared to flee.

Rapid footsteps galloped on the turf behind her. *Oh, no! Not more of them.* Her heart pounded. Her pulse raced. She whipped around, ready to take on a new series of attacks.

But relief flooded her body when she recognized the guys who played football as she had passed the recreation field. The broad-shouldered chemistry teacher in the lead. *Thank You for sending the cavalry, Lord.*

The teacher skidded to a stop in front of her. "Are you okay?"

The rest of the guys clustered around, except for three of the largest who ran after the retreating van.

She gulped deep breaths, hands pressed to her hips, head down. "I'm…okay. Thanks, guys. How did…you know?"

Mr. Davis pointed at one of the young men striding toward them from the street. "Jerry over there missed a pass which bounced halfway here. When he caught up with the ball, he yelled back at us that some men had grabbed you. Guess you were too busy to notice," he added with a grin.

Lynne nodded. "I guess so." Her breathing slowed. "Sure am glad you fumbled the pass." She smiled at Jerry as he neared.

Kim's shout reached Lynne before her friend came into sight. Around the last bend, Kim sprinted toward her with Loring right behind. Both with pinched brows and labored breaths.

When he came to a stop, Loring examined the crowd of students, then searched the street at the sound of screeching tires in the distance. He returned his gaze to Lynne. "Are you okay?"

"Yeah. Thanks to my heroes here. They came to my rescue."

The teacher laughed. "Not that she needed rescuing, from what we saw. She sent those two packing."

Kim's eyes were round and wet. "Oh, Lynne. I'm so sorry.

Someone shot at us when we entered the wooded area along the path. Never saw who. We ducked behind a clump of bushes. Loring figured whoever it was planned to get you next, but every time we raised our heads, another shot went off. A bullet whizzed right by his ear."

"I didn't hear shots." A charge zinged up Lynne's neck as if she'd touched a bare electrical wire. She stared at Loring.

"Silencer." He laid his hand on her arm and shook his head. "We thought things had quieted down. We should have been more alert. Are you sure you're not hurt?"

The concern in his eyes melted Lynne's heart. *Stop looking at me like that.* She moved away from his touch.

"Obviously, this young lady can take care of herself." Mr. Davis grinned again. He eyed Loring, then Kim. "Are you students?"

"They're friends of mine." Lynne clutched Kim's arm. "Came to run with me this morning." *Hope that satisfies him.* Her legs wobbled.

The teacher grabbed both of her upper arms. "You'd better sit." He led her to a park bench on the other side of the bushes where the group had left their gym bags. One student pulled a plastic water bottle from his and handed it to Lynne.

"Thank you." She took a long drink.

Another student who had run after the van returned. "They're gone."

Mr. Davis rummaged in his bag while everyone else hovered nearby. He pulled out a cell. "I'm calling the police. We'll stay until they get here."

Loring reached over and stopped the teacher as he punched in the 9. "They're already here. I'm Sergeant Loring Trent from the Chicago Police Department." He motioned toward Kim as he pulled out his ID.

"This is Officer Kim Travis. We're good friends of Miss Temple. We'll take care of her and make the report."

Lynne sat in Jane's office, the plastic water bottle still clutched in her hands. The shock had worn off, and her eyes burned from restrained tears. She'd been afraid something like this would happen.

Loring paced from the door to the window and back. "They're the dumbest gang in Chicago. If The Piper found out about Lynne and hired them to get her, he must be desperate."

"Today's episode is the most daring thing they've ever tried." Kim turned to Loring.

"That's for sure." He glanced at Lynne with a smile. "You gave them a surprise. And their old rattletrap hitting the fire hydrant as they flew around the corner down the street was a stroke of luck. We got them."

Jane looked up from the report on her desk. "They've admitted to attempted kidnapping. Wanted to ransom you to The Piper. The van driver, no doubt, hoped for a big reward once they'd put word out they had you. But I doubt The Piper put them up to it. We also have them for assault with a deadly weapon for the attack on Kim and Loring. Two bullets were retrieved from the scene and match the shooter's gun."

Lynne sucked in a loud breath.

"Still, how they found out about you is a mystery. Someone who knows you're a witness has a big mouth. That means Hamelin might find out too. But he has two pressing priorities. Get outta Dodge, if he hasn't already, and set up business somewhere else. We don't know where he'll settle, but rumor says he's headed south. He'll probably concentrate his network there. Always a large number of homeless and vulnerable children."

Lynne bit her lip. "How did they know to attack me on the path this morning?"

Loring's brows furrowed. "The guy whose teeth broke when you hit him had a part-time job driving a roach coach on campus. He often parked near the field where you ran and had seen you run in the mornings. Somehow, he knew who you were. They must have hung around the park until you showed. Had part of their bunch keep us busy while the rest went after you. But they didn't count on the guys playing football. Nor your martial arts training."

She tried to smile at Loring's reference to the assailant's teeth, but couldn't. The murder. The Piper. The trial. These goons. And now the problem of her growing feelings for Loring, his for her, and how it affected Kim, her new friend. More tears edged her lower lids.

"We'll get him, Lynne." Jane's voice interrupted her thoughts. "You are not number one on Hamelin's agenda at the moment. I'm sure of that."

"I could be in the future though, right? Is there any hope he'll be caught?"

Jane took a deep breath. "Ever since we put out your description of him, he's gone into hiding. But we'll take more precautions with your protection."

"You must have a guardian angel watching over you." Kim's gaze traveled from Lynne to Loring.

Lynne fought her tears. *Let's hope so.*

Chapter Nine

L ynne gulped, though her throat was dry. Today, she'd have to face two killers. The year away from Illinois after graduation had flown by, but her service at Naval Air Station Pensacola hadn't taken away the nightmares about the murder she'd witnessed. Today, she'd testify in court that she saw Price and Goldberg kill Dr. Lindstrom. She prayed God would give her courage, and her heart would be strong enough.

Supported by her mother, Jim, his fiancée Darcy, and Uncle Pratie, her hands still trembled as she waited in the fifth-floor hallway of the Criminal Court Building. Across the hall, a sizable knot of sinister-looking men in suits cast glances at her and Darcy. *Those creeps!* Lynne adjusted her skirt, crossed her ankles, and turned away.

Next to Uncle Pratie stood her brother in dress blues. Both men glared at the mob. Uncle Pratie nodded toward the group of men as he bent over and spoke in his lyrical brogue. "Here to cheer for the accused. Hooligans, the bunch of 'em. I recognize a couple from when they were young, stealin' fruit and candy from stalls at the market. Didn't improve with age, and that's a fact."

He straightened. "Weeell, lass, see you inside. Don't be worryin' yourself. The State's Attorney's in your corner. Mark ma' words." At his wink, much of the tension flowed out of her body.

Lynne stood and gave Uncle Pratie a hug. "Thanks for being here."

Jim gave her a quick squeeze of the shoulders. "Knock 'em dead, Stringbean." He and the old Irishman strolled toward the courtroom doors.

After seating herself again and exchanging smiles with her mother and soon-to-be sister-in-law, Lynne bowed her head. *Please help Mom get through this. I know you've calmed her a lot since I told her I had to testify.* Her parents' strength had bolstered her since they found out she'd be the key witness. *In Jesus' name, Amen.* She opened her eyes and gazed down the hall toward the sound of footfalls on the marble stairs.

Her father rounded the corner and strode toward Lynne. When she rose, he wrapped his arms around her and spoke into her ear. "You can do this, Lynne. You're a daughter of the King. You have truth and God on your side. No matter what happens in there, He's with you, and I'm sure there's a legion of angels surrounding you."

Lynne nodded. The courtroom door swung open. The bailiff stepped out and approached her. "It's time. Follow me, Miss."

Her heart lurched. She hugged her mother and Darcy.

A woman dressed in a tailored black suit and white blouse exited the elevator and rushed toward Lynne. *Kim.*

Kim threw her arms around Lynne. "Sorry I'm late." She stepped back with a smile and laid a reassuring hand on Lynne's arm.

"I didn't expect you." A sense of relief flooded Lynne. Her friend was still there for her.

"I know we haven't kept in touch much lately. Work's been a bear.

But with all you've gone through, I wanted to be here for moral support."

"Thank you. Did Loring come with you?"

She pursed her lips. "No. He wasn't able to get away."

Lynne tried not to show her disappointment. Neither he nor Kim had emailed for a few weeks. The bailiff cleared his throat. Lynne took a deep breath and marched toward the wooden doors.

"The State calls Lynne Temple to the stand."

Lynne took the witness stand. As the bailiff swore her in, the men Uncle Pratie called hooligans ogled her from behind the defendants. A loud whistle pierced the silence.

The judge rapped his gavel. "Order!"

Mr. Andrews got up from the table and approached the witness stand as Lynne glanced up and caught her father's nod. Her mother, Darcy, and Kim had bowed their heads. They'd pray her through this.

The State's attorney guided Lynne through her testimony. He paused, glanced at the jury, and then back to Lynne. "Now, Miss Temple, when you looked down the hall, as you testified earlier, what, if anything, did you see?"

"The two men entered the door to Dr. Lindstrom's office."

"Are the men you saw in this room?"

"Yes, Sir."

"Point them out, please?"

She indicated the killers across the room at the defense table next to

Pemberton.

"Let the record show the witness identified Leo Goldberg and John Price as the men she saw on May eighth, two-thousand and three."

Mr. Andrews addressed Lynne again. "What happened next?"

"I crept down the hall and looked through the glass door into the room. Mr. Goldberg talked to the doctor for awhile. Mr. Price stepped behind Dr. Lindstrom and grabbed him by the throat. The doctor fell to the floor. They picked him up, sat him in his office chair, and shoved a hypodermic into his arm."

Tears welled in Lynne's eyes. She swiped at them.

"Which one strangled the doctor?"

She pointed. "That one, Mr. Price."

"And which of the men injected the hypodermic into his arm?"

"Mr. Goldberg."

Murmurs filled the room. Both killers' eyes sent shafts of ice through Lynne's body. The gavel struck the wood again. "I'll have the room cleared if these disturbances continue." The judge asked, "Do you have any further questions for this witness?"

"No, Your Honor." Mr. Andrews returned to his table.

"Mr. Pemberton, do you wish to cross-examine?"

He stood. "Yes, Your Honor."

Lynne clasped her hands behind the wooden rail. She fixed her gaze on Pemberton, and another frigid chill coursed down her spine. He'd do his best to shake her up. *Remember, the Lord is right here with you.*

Pemberton strode to the stand. She squeezed her hands harder. *Philippians four, thirteen. I can do all things through Christ which strengtheneth me.*

Dressed in an immaculate pinstripe suit, the big man towered over her, large and threatening. As she waited for him to speak, her hands grew clammy. Pemberton's lips lifted slightly on the right side of his mouth. The cold, dark-eyed stare seemed to penetrate her soul. She repeated the verse to herself.

He smiled, his gimlet eyes riveted to hers. "Now, Miss Temple. You wish us to believe you have provided an accurate description of what happened on the night Dr. Lindstrom died?"

"Yes, Sir, I have." She returned his stare, but her stomach plummeted like an elevator from the top floor of a skyscraper to the basement. She swallowed.

"And yet, you were in no position to see my client, Mr. Price,"—he gestured behind him with one hand to the sullen ogre next to his partner at the defense table—"vandalize university property while you were inside the building, were you?"

Mr. Andrews stood. "Objection, Your Honor! The question is irrelevant. She never stated she saw him van—"

"Yoouurr Honor. My clients are on trial for murder. I must do everything in my power to establish their innocence and integrity. The court has amended statements sworn to by each of my clients as to their whereabouts on the night of Dr. Lindstrom's tragic death."

Standing with his fists clenched and pressing down on the tabletop, Mr. Andrews opened his mouth, but the judge raised his hand and glared at defense counsel. "Mr. Pemberton, you will confine your arguments to points of law and facts in evidence. One more trick like that, and I'll fine you for contempt."

The judge then turned toward the jury box. "The jury will disregard the remark made by defense counsel. The objection is sustained. The defense may proceed with cross-examination."

Lynne shook her head. Pemberton was trying to discredit her as a reliable witness. She watched as Mr. Andrews took his seat, and she gave him a quick smile. *Price's innocence and integrity, my foot.*

Pemberton grinned at Lynne. She gritted her teeth and half listened to the attorney as he droned on in an obvious attempt at flattery to the court and impressing the jury with his words while he promenaded back and forth in front of the judge. Pemberton would face a higher court one day where the Judge of all mankind wouldn't be fooled.

The State's attorney jumped up. "Your Honor, is counsel cross-examining the witness at this time or making his closing argument?"

The judge exhaled sharply and frowned. "Counselor, proceed with your cross-examination. Or sit down."

Lynne pressed her lips together. Didn't sound as though he fooled this judge either. Pemberton gave Mr. Andrews a self-satisfied look as he once more crossed in front of the judge and neared the witness stand. Then he faced her with his piercing stare. Like a giant bird of prey, which made her the cornered mouse.

"How did Dr. Lindstrom seem when you spoke to him?"

Lynne glanced at Mr. Andrews. Pemberton stepped in front of her, blocking her line of sight. She recoiled. "I don't...understand the question, Sir."

The lawyer spread his hands in an expansive gesture. "Well...was he composed, pleased to see you, cheerful...or otherwise? How did his manner strike you?"

"Preoccupied." She tilted her head to the right. "He said to come back later."

"Ah." Pemberton steepled his fingertips, touching his thumbs to his upper chest, and stepped back from the witness. Then he leaned in toward her, too close for Lynne's comfort. "Were you in the habit of visiting Dr. Lindstrom in his office at that hour, Miss Temple?" He grinned.

"No. Usually earlier, if I needed to. I had an important question to ask that night. But many of my classmates visited—"

"I'm not interested in your classmates, young woman. It's your actions I question."

What was he insinuating?

Mr. Andrews slammed his pencil on the table. "Objection, Your Honor! Counsel is trying to intimidate the witness."

"Sustained. You will moderate your tone, Counselor." Murmurs arose from across the room again. The judge rapped his gavel once.

Father, please help me get through this. Lynne searched for her family across the rows of spectators. Her mother and Darcy were still praying. Dad, Jim, and Uncle Pratie shot daggers from their eyes at Pemberton.

The attorney backed away from her. He nodded at the judge, faced Lynne again, and spoke in a softer tone. "So you visited the doctor's office only on that occasion…after hours?"

"I did. I was studying in the library and needed a question answered before the exam. Many students visited the doctor late in the evening with questions. He always worked late in the Medical Sciences Building and didn't mind when we came by for help."

"Yes, yes." He spun and walked toward his clients. "Did you get good grades, Miss Temple?"

"Yes."

Pemberton turned and narrowed his eyes. The tip of his tongue showed in the corner of his lips. "I understand Dr. Lindstrom's class was a major one in your course of study. You desired a high grade in that subject for your future employment prospects. Didn't you?"

"Of course."

Mr. Andrews stood again. "Your Honor, where is this line of questioning going?"

The defending attorney raised his head smugly and addressed the judge. "I'm trying to establish Miss Temple's relationship with the doctor. Her reason for bringing accusations against my clients. Since she's the only witness who alleges my clients were in the building where the decedent died, I believe this is important."

"I'll allow it. Continue."

Both corners of Pemberton's lips curled upward as he fixed Lynne with a stare and fired several propositions at her in quick succession. Tears welled in her eyes at the insinuations. "Miss Temple, isn't it true Dr. Lindstrom told you not to come to his office late at night anymore when you arrived that night? Weren't there rumors?"

Lynne shook her head. "No. That's not—"

Mr. Andrews jumped up and screamed. "Objection. Hearsay. Your Honor. Seriously?"

"I withdraw the question. Miss Temple, didn't you leave the building and then return to the doctor's office to find he had, in fact, committed suicide because of your affair?"

"Enough. This is all unfounded speculation. Your Honor, he's badgering my witness. These questions assume facts not in evidence. Counsel is attempting to tarnish the reputation of this witness with absolutely no foundation. Total fabrication."

Pemberton ignored the State's attorney. "Miss Temple, didn't you threaten to expose your liaison with the doctor if he did not give you prior knowledge on the exam?"

Lynne gasped. "No. It's not true. I didn't." She glanced to the row where her family sat.

Mr. Andrews' voice grew louder. "Objection, Your Honor! Objection!"

The court burst into an uproar with cries of outrage on one side and approval from the other. At the back of the room, Pratie O'Brien jumped to his feet and pointed at the defense attorney. He bellowed, "You lying scoundrel." Jim joined him as her father put his arm around his wife.

The judge pounded his bench with the gavel. "Order! Order! Or I will have this courtroom cleared." The gavel slammed down one more time. "Both attorneys, please approach the bench."

Pemberton and Mr. Andrews stood in front of the judge whose eyes glared at Pemberton. The judge spoke in a quiet voice. Then they both took their seats.

"Objections sustained." The judge continued to glare at Pemberton. "Unless you can substantiate the accusation, Counselor?"

Lynne breathed a sigh of relief. Uncle Pratie and Jim sat but continued to glower at Pemberton. Her mother and Darcy wiped their eyes with tissues.

When the room quieted, Pemberton turned to the judge. "Your Honor. I have no desire to *slander* the witness. I'm simply establishing reasonable doubt about my clients being responsible for Dr. Lindstrom's death…considering there *is* only one witness." He glanced at Lynne.

Lynne sat up straighter and glared at Pemberton.

He flinched and stepped back as if suddenly afraid. Lynne recalled her father's words. *"You have truth and God on your side. No matter what happens in there, He's with you, and I'm sure there's a legion of angels surrounding you."*

Pemberton wet his lips and once again faced the judge. "If Miss Temple happened to find the doctor's body, in the manner I have described, regardless of what might earlier have passed between them, I can understand her subsequent action of running away. May I continue my cross-examination of the witness?"

"You may proceed." The judge leaned forward. "But, you will proceed with caution."

A hush fell over the courtroom. A calm engulfed Lynne as she caught Jim's eye. She could almost hear his thoughts. *"He's trying to knock you off balance, Sis. Stay focused, and keep your guard up. Remember what we taught you during those workouts in the barn."*

She smiled at Jim and braced herself. The lawyer's voice broke in. "How would you describe your relationship with the late Dr. Lindstrom, Miss Temple?"

"He was my professor," she answered coldly.

"You must have been very upset by the doctor's death, studying to be a nurse and virtually on the spot when he committed suicide, as your witness statement shows."

Mr. Andrews interrupted. "Your Honor, now counsel is assuming facts contrary to the evidence. Murder has been established beyond all doubt."

"Sustained. Mr. Pemberton, rephrase your question. And remember, there are sanctions if you continue in this manner. Phrase your questions with care."

Pemberton pulled his lips into a tight line. "Were you upset by the professor's death?"

What was Pemberton driving at now? She looked him in the eye. "Of course, I was upset."

"And you reported his death to the police right away?"

"I did."

The doors in the back of the room opened, and Loring slipped into the courtroom. After he handed an envelope to the State's Attorney, Loring took a seat next to Kim. What had he given to Mr. Andrews?

While the attorney read the papers he'd received, Lynne refocused on Pemberton.

"And to exonerate yourself from any blame for the doctor's death or lack of skills to save him, you implicated my clients in a tissue of lies."

The roar from both sides of the room was deafening. Again, the judge's gavel banged.

This time Lynne was ready with her answer. She sat erect, shoulders back. Her voice came out rock solid. "I told the police exactly what I saw."

Pemberton frowned at her from under his lashes and then flinched again. "I have no further questions." He plodded back to his table. Goldberg and Price glared at him as he lowered himself into the chair.

The judge addressed Mr. Andrews. "Do you have further questions for the witness, Counselor?"

"No, Your Honor. However, I would like to introduce an affidavit from another witness who isn't able to be in court today. I just received it."

As Mr. Andrews rose from his seat, the judge said, "The witness is dismissed."

Pemberton leaped to his feet. "Objection. Your Honor, this is hearsay." He shot daggers at the State's Attorney.

On her way to join her family, Lynne made eye contact with Loring who smiled at her. She returned his smile and sat next to her mother. Lynne exhaled a long, tired breath.

Mr. Andrews argued, "This witness is in the hospital, having suffered a stroke. Would the statement not be admitted as an exception to hearsay?"

The defense attorney took in a deep breath. "In that case, if *this witness* was well enough to make a statement, surely he's well enough to at least be deposed—at the hospital."

A buzz broke out among the spectators. The judge's gavel sounded.

Chapter Ten

*L*ynne's heartbeat soared into overdrive. Another witness? To the murder? Who?

The judge summoned the attorneys to the bench. During the murmuring among the three men, Lynne thought she overheard the name Walter Prescott.

Walter? Her mouth dropped opened. She leaned back in her seat. Walter had thought the doctor committed suicide. He'd never hinted anything else. But then, she hadn't either.

As the judge spoke, Mr. Pemberton shook his head. His clients sat, staring at their lawyer's back. The courtroom reminded her of a scene in a movie, a graveyard in the middle of a cold night. The stillness sent a shiver through her. Everyone's eyes were glued to the front.

She glanced at her hands, white and trembling. It must've been terrible for Walter, all those months. At least she had the police and Uncle Pratie to talk to. Silence prevailed in the courtroom, except for her heart pounding in her ears.

When Lynne raised her head, the defendants were scowling. Price turned and stared directly at her. She returned the glare. Would he burst into a rage as he had in the interrogation room? Lynne bit her lip. The same fear that gripped her in the Medical Sciences Building that night attacked again. She gritted her teeth and refused to let him intimidate her. *"Yea, though I walk through the valley of the shadow of death, I will fear no evil: for thou art with me;"*

How long had it been since she thanked her mother for all the time she'd spent forcing Lynne to memorize Bible verses? She reached over and squeezed her mother's hand.

Her mother turned her head and smiled. "Are you okay, Honey?"

The scene Lynne witnessed in the professor's office flashed in her mind. The hypodermic. Dr. Lindstrom's glasses. Her arms prickled. She'd been right there, watching him die. Her throat dried. Sparkles danced in front of her eyes. Everything became a foggy blur and went black.

When Lynne opened her eyes, her mother's arm was around her as they sat on a bench in the hall outside the courtroom. Her free hand wiped Lynne's forehead with a wet handkerchief. Darcy sat on the other side of the bench, her arm around Lynne's waist. Uncle Pratie, her father, and Jim stood peering at her with concern in their eyes.

Lynne blinked. "Wha…what happened?"

Her father squatted and took her hands. "You passed out, Sweetheart. Jim scooped you up and carried you out here." He lifted his hand to her cheek. "How do you feel?"

"I'm okay." Lynne rubbed her forehead. "Is it over?"

"Sure is, lass, at least for you." Uncle Pratie grinned. "Told ya that State's Attorney was on your side. And that Mr. Prescott will cinch those hoodlum's fate."

Her mother hugged Lynne. "Mr. Prescott is a godsend."

"He is, but what happened? Where's Kim? Loring?"

"Kim and Loring said they had to leave." Her mother wiped her brow again. "But they told us Mr. Andrews insisted they wouldn't need further testimony from you. And the defense attorney finally agreed. The judge has called for a continuance. Oh, and Kim said you should call her when you're feeling better. You've nothing to worry about anymore."

Her mother's eyes turned sad. "I suppose you'll head back to your unit now that the court has released you. Wish you had more time to spend with us."

"I have a few days of leave left. I'll come home first."

Her father squeezed her hands. "Good. It'll give you time to relax before you report back to NAS."

"And, in the meantime, we can think about good times and good things." Her mother hugged her. "Speaking of good things, those two detectives sure make a nice couple, don't they?"

A twinge shot through Lynne. "Yeah. They do." *I don't have to worry anymore. Not over Loring, Price, Goldberg, or The Piper. Not while I'm in the service.*

Late that afternoon, Lynne and her parents arrived at the farm in Kewanee. As she rested in her old bedroom with her eyes wide open, helplessness filled her. *Why, Lord? What more could I do? What am I to do now?* The trial was over for her. She needed to talk to Kim and find out more details about what happened.

Lynne rolled to the edge of the bed and planted her feet on the floor. She reached for her purse on the nightstand and retrieved her cell. Her hands still trembled as she found Kim's number in her contacts and punched the send button.

"Hi, Lynne. Are you better now? You scared us when you passed out in court."

"I'm okay now. A buildup of stress must have caused the blackout. I called to ask what happened. What's going to happen now?"

"I'm afraid I can't get into that at this moment. Hold on a second."

Loring's voice in the background sounded urgent. "We have to leave now."

Lynne's neck hairs bristled.

"Sorry, Lynne," Kim said. "We've had a few incidents tonight. I've got to go for now. Been on the run since we returned from court. When I get off, I'm going straight home and to bed, but I'll phone you tomorrow during my lunch break. Okay? We can talk then."

"Sure, that's fine. Say hi to everyone for me."

Kim disconnected the call.

Lynne slid the cell back into her purse. *Great.* Now she wouldn't find out until tomorrow. She needed to have patience. *"For whatsoever things were written aforetime were written for our learning, that we through patience and comfort of the scriptures might have hope." Romans 15:4* She chuckled. God always brought a verse to mind when she needed one. Whether she wanted it or not. Might as well accept the fact that God would make her learn patience the hard way…when she least wanted it. She quirked her mouth.

Since her mother wouldn't let her do anything in the kitchen to help with dinner, and she was too antsy to read her Bible, maybe she'd spend some time outside in the fresh air. But how would that help? She felt like she'd been thrown into limbo. It'd be good to get back to her unit. At least there the familiar routine would help her get back to normal.

Lynne plopped onto the bed, pulled on her running shoes, and rushed out of the bedroom.

As she reached the bottom step, her mother came out of the kitchen. "Mom, I'm going out for a little stroll."

"Okay, but don't go far because dinner's almost ready. Your father's in the barn. Tell him to clean up."

"Okay. Will do."

The screen door slammed shut behind her as she skipped down the porch stairs. She laughed. Now there was a sound she'd missed since she left home.

Lynne headed straight for the barn. It had been so long since she and her brothers sparred out there. Those sessions sure came in handy when she needed them. She'd do something special for her brothers to thank them, besides praying. Lately, petitions to keep Jeff out of harm's way during his tour in Afghanistan had filled her prayers. Would God bring him home from there soon?

Inside the barn, her father lifted a bale of straw and pitched it onto a corner pile. "Dad, Mom said to get ready for dinner. Is there something I can do out here to help you? She won't let me near the kitchen. And I need to keep busy."

Her father chuckled. "Not really. I'm done for the day." He turned and strode to her side while he brushed off pieces of straw from his shirt. As they walked back to the house, he put his arm around Lynne. "Wish you could stay longer, but I understand the Navy. And you'll be busy soon enough."

"Once a Corpsman, always a Corpsman. The Navy never really

leaves you, does it, Dad?"

"You can take the Corpsman out of the Navy…but you can never take the Navy out of the Corpsman."

"Yeah. I've heard that a time or two." She smiled at him, and he nodded. "Do you suppose Jeff will have to stay in Afghanistan much longer?"

"Can't rightly say, Sweetheart. Depends on how long they need his unit." He squeezed her. "Now don't you worry about Jeff. God's watching out for him. You need to get on with your life. Forget this court stuff too."

He was right. No sense fretting over things that might not happen. But that was easier said than done.

The next morning, Lynne woke up with a jerk. Her cell rang. Kim's tone. The clock showed seven a.m. Lynne grabbed the phone and answered. "Kim, what's wrong?"

"Nothing's wrong, silly. Thought I'd return your call this morning and fill you in before I left for work. Is everything okay?"

The sound of a coffee maker gurgling out its last drops came through the phone. Lynne took in a deep breath and exhaled. "The call startled me, that's all. I was still asleep."

"Oh, I'm sorry. I thought everyone on the farm would be up and at'em already. Should've realized you might sleep in after the turmoil of court yesterday."

"It's okay. I'm glad you phoned. So, what happened after I passed out?"

Kim's soft giggle came through the phone. "It was something to behold. Sorry you missed it. You were with us up until Pemberton said they should depose the witness. Right?"

"Yeah, I heard that. I remember the judge saying something to the attorneys. My mind wandered to poor Walter and how horrible it must have been to keep his secret all those months. The courtroom was deathly quiet. Then I started to shake, and my pulse and heart raced. I could hardly breathe. Price stared at me. His glare was so penetrating I feared he'd go berserk. I started to pray, but everything turned dark."

"Wow. The way you swooned onto your mother's shoulder must've petrified your family. And Price did go berserk. Called Pemberton a weasel. More like he screamed it at him. Accused him of being incompetent. Then Price jumped out of his chair to go after him."

"Passing out was a new thing for me. I've never fainted before. What happened next?"

"Price was restrained by the officers in court. The attorneys continued to argue back and forth, and then the judge declared a continuance to allow time for Mr. Prescott's deposition, as soon as his doctor gives the okay. The trial will resume after that. The court released you from having to give further testimony, under the circumstances."

"Mom told me. But what happens now?"

"Pemberton will have his say in court. Then the jury deliberates and gives their verdict. I can guarantee these guys are headed to prison."

"Good news to my ears. But, what about The Piper?"

"Still nothing on him. But, hey. You're off to the Navy again, girl. Don't let him spoil what's ahead for you. Who knows what wonders you'll see? You're off to see the world. Isn't that what they say happens when you join the Navy?"

Lynne laughed. Off to see the world. Was everything else finally behind her? Did that include Loring's feelings for her?

Chapter Eleven

W ithin a week of her return to Naval Air Station Pensacola, Lynne's unit had received orders to deploy to the Middle East. She found herself in a field hospital thirty miles from an area of major conflict in Afghanistan. Her adrenaline pumped. She was up for the task, but this wasn't exactly what she had in mind when she thought she'd be off to see the world. Yet, she knew it was always a possibility. After all, she chose to be a Navy nurse.

Dressed in combat boots and camouflage fatigues while small arms fire sounded in the distance, Lynne tossed a used syringe into the sharps container. The sounds of battle raged around them but scarcely registered anymore after she and her nurse friends had worked relentlessly for months.

"Hey, Lynnz!" A plastic water bottle from a fellow Navy nurse came flying through the air to Lynne.

"Thanks. My lips are like sandpaper."

Lynne had become Lynnz to all her fellow nurses and other peers in the military. Funny, how the nickname others chose for her had become so endearing. No wonder Uncle Pratie kept his Army moniker.

She finished cleaning and dressing a young man's deep shrapnel wounds as he clung to life on the stretcher. Poor kid couldn't be more than eighteen years old. Hopefully, he'd make it to nineteen. Victims from insurgents' bullets, roadside bombs, artillery, rocket and mortar attacks, and who knew what. Not to mention the everyday accidents and illness in their hostile environment. She spun to face a nurse with short-cropped, strawberry-blonde hair who worked on another wounded Marine.

Lynne's shoulders slumped as she willed tears to remain in her eyes. "Samantha, I'm not sure I can stand watching another injured Marine hauled through the tent door. Each time, it terrifies me. I'm scared to death I'll see Jeff's face on the next one. How much more of this can I take?"

"I know what you mean, Lynnz." Sam kept working. "Though I don't have a brother in the Marines like you, I worry about the fellas we've gotten close to. We get a steady stream of wounded through here. Not sure how I'd react if one of them showed up on a stretcher." Sam finished inserting an IV and hooked the bag to the stand.

When relieved, the girls dragged themselves to the mess tent where they collapsed at a corner table. "What a long day. But cheer up, Lynnz. Scuttlebutt has it we'll return home soon."

"Yeah, I've heard it before. And yet, here we are." She didn't mean to be so down. Probably just the influx of casualties for the day. When had she last read her Bible? She always found solace there. She'd make time tonight. "Let's have a Bible study tonight?"

Sam's dark brown, bloodshot eyes gazed back. "Now you're talking, girl."

The next dawn, Lynne stood in line with the rest of her unit waiting to board one of a line of Humvees parked nose-to-tail along the rutted highway. "Sam, do you know what's up?"

"I heard they're fixin' to move us up to a battle zone where our ground forces are slugging it out with entrenched insurgents."

A new nurse named Tammy stopped next to Lynne. She pulled her shirt away from her skin and back again to fan herself. "No way," she whispered. "Me, a rancher's daughter from San Antonio, Texas, and I've never known heat as intense as this."

"Yeah." Lynne chuckled. "Hotter than I remember any Illinois summer too, even in July." They stowed their kits in the rear of the vehicle. "Careful you don't touch bare metal. It'll scorch your skin."

"The sun's done that already." Tammy pressed an index finger to the middle of her forearm. When she removed it, a reddish glow covered her arm everywhere except for the oval indentation left by her fingertip.

The two squeezed themselves into the twin seats of the passenger compartment with a pile of equipment next to them. Sam hopped into the front. The driver took off. Tammy flirted with him nervously while Lynne closed her eyes. She hated these drives. Would they get through this deployment, or would she or some of her fellow nurses never make it home?

After setting up base, Lynne, Sam, and Tammy sipped coffee sheltered in the mess tent. Lynne rose and fastened the tent flap against an abrupt gust of wind and sand. "Gotta love this weather. Never a dull moment out here. One minute you're being roasted. The next, sandblasted." She refilled her cup and sat back down with the other two nurses.

Sam smiled at her. "Lynnz, were you serious about getting out of the Navy when we return to the States?"

"Absolutely!"

"What will you do next?"

"I want a job in a civilian hospital." A loud burst of gunfire sounded in the distance. She cocked her head in its direction. "Somewhere quiet. I dream of taking care of patients who aren't blown to bits and pieces and don't have to be sewn back together." She grimaced. "Sorry, guys. I'm just tired." She lowered her head to her folded arms on the table.

At a soft touch, Lynne raised her head. Tammy withdrew her hand. "I've only been here a few weeks, and I feel that way already. I hope you get your dream when you're ready for discharge."

Sam nodded. "I hope we all do." She pressed her lips together and gazed at Lynne. "Right now, we need rest while we can get it."

Lynne stood and nodded. "You're right."

The three headed for the door and pushed their way through a blast of wind. The sand stung the exposed part of Lynne's body and niggled its way into her clothing. She clenched her jaw, biting down on grit as she grabbed the wispy Tammy on one side. Sam held onto her other arm. Inside their tent, they stripped off their outer clothing, brushed the sand to the floor, and dropped to their cots.

As she lay in the dark, Lynne thought about her last trip home. When would she see it again? She'd never be the same. She had to stop thinking such depressing thoughts and be an example to others. *But Lord, it's so hard out here. Give me strength.*

The end of Lynne's tour of duty drew near. It was time to put in for her discharge. She and Sam had made it through the Afghanistan experience and were now back in Sam's hometown of Pensacola at NAS. But should she go back to Kewanee when she got out? Home?

She stood on the Pensacola pier, as she did often when she had time off, watching the seagulls dive for fish in the emerald green waters of the Gulf. The last few months of service here had been wonderful. But the thought of having to go back overseas in the future made her decision easy. Sam's time was up too. She'd be out by next month and planned to get a job at a local hospital.

Such a faithful friend and support all these months. Even in her worst moments. Especially when Tammy died from a sniper bullet the week before they returned to the States. Would she ever get that memory out of her mind? Dark brown curls brushing against Lynne's arms as she held Tammy. Her light brown eyes that held a look of unbelief, large as silver dollars until they closed forever. Lynne's heart wrenched all over again.

"Hey, Lynnz."

Lynne jumped. She brushed the tears from her cheeks before Sam reached her. Then she turned. "What's up?"

"I had a moment of genius on my way back from applying for work at the local hospital. Why don't you stay here in Pensacola with me after your discharge? You're an excellent nurse. I'm sure you could get a job at the hospital where I'll be working…if I get the position. Wouldn't that be super? We could even room together, if you like." They turned to face the water and leaned on the rail.

Stay in Pensacola? The breeze picked up strands of Lynne's hair and tickled her nose as she gazed out over the white breakers. She loved it here. A smile spread across her lips as she turned to Sam. "It's a great idea. And they'd be crazy not to hire you." *A new adventure.*

With arms linked together and laughing, they strolled off the pier. "Sam…we could be embarking on the fulfillment of our dreams. Full steam ahead for the nursing sisters at arms." *And leave behind sorrow and bad memories.*

The next morning Lynne spoke to her commanding officer.

He leaned back in his chair behind the desk. "I don't suppose I can persuade you to re-up."

"No, Sir." Tammy's last gasp for breath flashed before her eyes. "I can't do—I need to get on with my life."

He shook his head as he prepared the paperwork for her discharge. "Can't help but wonder if you've met a young surfer who's swept you off your feet, Lieutenant." He grinned.

"No, Sir. Not yet." Lynne's lips lifted into half a smile as heat rose from her neck to her face. If only there was someone. Loring hadn't written in so long, but Kim had. Nothing had changed in their relationship, apparently.

"Well, I'll be happy to recommend you wherever you apply." He stood. His pale blue eyes sparkled under white eyebrows. "We're losing two of our best nurses in you and Lieutenant Rease. You've both served well."

"Thank you, Sir." Her commanding officer dismissed her, and she went in search of Sam.

Hope we both get jobs at the same hospital. It'd be hard not going home to family, but having Sam around would make things easier. As she marched across the parade grounds, she chuckled to herself. Sam hadn't found that surfer yet, either. Perhaps they'd both find a couple of handsome doctors and fall madly in love. She took a deep breath. First things first. She had to call and tell her family after dinner tonight. Lynne bit her lip.

"Mom, please don't fret. I know you expected me to come home, but Pensacola is my home now. I've felt that way from my first assignment here."

"But Lynnie, it's so far away." Her mother sniffled.

"Not really. And oh, the places I can show you here when you come for vacation. You'll love it."

Her dad hadn't said a word since they'd put the phone on speaker. "Dad, aren't you going to say anything?"

"What can I say, Sweetheart? You're a grown woman. You have your own life to live. I've been to Pensacola, and I agree. It's beautiful. It's also peaceful. I understand."

"Thanks, Dad." Lynne pressed a hand to her chest. Her parents had always wanted what made her happy. To avoid worrying Mom, she'd told only her dad about her fears in Afghanistan. She didn't dare tell her brothers. They would blame themselves for encouraging her to serve.

"Not to change the subject, but I'm so glad Jeff's back in the States now. That's a big relief."

"Oh, Lynnie. It's a blessing to have you and the boys out of that horrible place. You've no idea."

Yeah, she did. Maybe she'd not had as much anxiety as her mother while both she and her brother were serving overseas. But still.

Her mother's tone changed. "Well, I guess we'll get used to you being a Florida girl. And it will be a nice place to vacation. But you'd *better* plan to visit your old home too."

"Don't worry, Mom. Even Pensacola isn't as laid-back as Kewanee. Being a nurse in a civilian hospital is still work, and I'll need to get away from time to time."

After the call ended, she tried to phone Jim but got his voicemail. She'd try later. He and Darcy were probably up to their earlobes in preparations for the grand appearance of her soon-expected nephew.

Jim was so fortunate to have someone like Darcy to love and vice versa. When would her turn come? *Stop it.* She couldn't worry about that right now. She had plans to make.

Lynne headed for the pier, her favorite spot to think. Her mind drifted to Loring. She sighed. Would she ever see him again?

As she stared out over the Gulf, lost in thought, Sam bounded onto the wooden planks. "Lynnz! You won't believe it." Lynne continued to gaze at the water as Sam sprinted across the weathered boards toward her. "I got it. I got the job."

"That's wonderful, Sam. I'm happy for you. At least your dream is coming true."

"And guess what?"

"You fell in love with one of the doctors?"

After slapping Lynne on the shoulder, Sam burst into laughter. "Not yet, but you never know." She leaned on the railing. "The head nurse mentioned there were two nursing positions open on the same floor. When I told her about you, she said you should apply. Isn't that perfect?"

This was too good to be true. They'd be working together. *Lord, that's more than I ever expected. Thank You.* "That is perfect. As long as they hire me."

"Hey, girl. With our CO sending his recommendation, you're a cinch to be hired." Sam snapped her fingers. "What do you say we stretch out on the sand before dinnertime? The breeze is so cool and relaxing. We're without a care in the world now. Discharges coming, new jobs in my quiet home town, working together—say, what are the chances we'll get the same shift?"

"Let's not get our hopes up too high. I'm thrilled at the thought of working in the same hospital. It'll be hard not to go back home, plus leaving the Navy and its familiarity to become a civilian."

"We can at least pray for the same shift. Can't we?" The smile on Sam's face traveled all the way to her eyes and thrilled Lynne to her toes.

They left the pier and shuffled through the white, sugary sand down to the last dune before the color turned a light tan in the pounding waves. Lynne stretched out on the warm sand, clasped her hands behind her head, and gazed at the white whipped-cream clouds scooting by. This was the life. This setting reminded her of ones she'd seen often in romantic movies. The only thing she needed now was romance.

She propped herself on her elbows and spotted three male surfers heading out into the water. Was the CO right? Was the love of her life one of them? She watched as they jumped onto their boards and stroked through the breakers to catch the right wave.

Her eyes closed as she took a deep breath of salty air and listened to the waves crashing to the shore. What a carefree life she was about to begin. Her phone conversation with Kim flashed in her mind. *"...what about The Piper?"* *"Still nothing on him."* Lynne flinched. She'd forget about him soon.

Chapter Twelve

*L*ynne approached the nursing station on the north wing of the hospital's fourth floor where she and Sam had been working since they were discharged. The halls had never been as quiet as they were that morning. "Hey, Sam."

Sam dropped the metal tray of paper medicine cups she was about to fill and distribute to the patients. The clatter echoed from the smooth wall behind the back counter. She turned. "You scared me to death, Lynnz. Don't do that." Her glare changed to laughter as she straightened the pill cups. "Why are you so out of breath?"

"Decided to take the stairs instead of waiting for the elevator. Today promises to be a busy day with visitors, so don't get used to this silence. Dr. Meredith asked me to take these to the ER for him." She waved a stack of forms at Sam. "I'll be back in a few minutes."

"You don't fool me. It's time for rounds, and you're avoiding your favorite patient." Sam grimaced.

"You mean the one who proposes every time I enter the room? I might consider the handsome gentleman's offer if he were fifty years younger." She snickered and flapped the papers in the air once more as she headed back to the stairwell.

As she skipped down the stairs, she thought about Loring. *Will he ever call again, or have he and Kim decided to get serious?*

When Lynne entered the emergency room, paramedics clamored through the entrance doors from outside. A young woman lay on the stretcher, blood caked in her wheat-colored hair.

Right behind the paramedics strode the new doctor she'd met recently, yelling orders. Even with his dark, wavy hair disheveled, as if he'd tried to pull it out, Lynne was struck by his extraordinary good looks. His green eyes glistened as though he held back tears.

The man had always been polite, although aloof. Too bad. With the slightest encouragement, she'd have fallen for him in a flash. But his demeanor in the hospital had been one of strictly business—until now.

She clutched his arm. "Dr. McLeod, they have this. Let them do their jobs. You should go to the desk and give them what information you can on the patient. Sorry, but you're not the doctor today."

"But I—"

He was distraught and not thinking. "Not this time, Doctor." Lynne accompanied him to the admission desk.

"Are you working in the ER today?"

"No. I had to drop something off and walked right into all the commotion. I heard you telling them what happened to her. Are you okay? You're covered with blood."

"It's Kathryn's. I don't know." His furrowed brows and intense eyes said this was no ordinary patient. "It's Miss Kendall's blood. She works in our office. I need to stay with her."

That's where she'd seen the patient's face. She sometimes brought things in from Dr. Hartley's office where Dr. McLeod worked.

She'd never seen him without a suit and lab coat. He must have been with the woman when she was injured. So much blood.

After giving the information about Miss Kendall the triage nurse needed, he retreated to the waiting room.

Lynne stopped at the admitting desk and dropped off the documents she'd brought downstairs. She then poked her head in to watch the nurses attend the injured woman. The head trauma looked as severe as any she'd seen in Afghanistan. She shuddered. But chances of survival were so much better here.

As she entered the waiting room, the distraught doctor sat alone on the other side of the room, his head in his hands. She should talk to him for a few minutes. It might calm him.

"Dr. McLeod, like I said when you came in, the staff will take good care of the patient. Are you okay? Your hands are shaking." She sat next to him.

"Tired and hungry. That's all." He gazed at her. "I've had nothing to eat since yesterday morning when I left Minnesota. Kathryn's lost so much blood." He stared at the door where they'd taken the woman from his office. "I did the best I could. Thank God I was there."

He's really a mess. "Let me get you something to eat. I'll be right back."

Lynne grabbed a water bottle from the ER supply room and brought it to Dr. McLeod. Then she hurried to the nearest nursing station on the second floor to get one of the sandwiches they kept on hand for their patients.

She rushed to the on-duty nurse. "Meryl, would it be okay if I took a sandwich to a doctor downstairs in the ER? He came in with a critical patient and needs something to eat."

Meryl handed her the sandwich, a pack of cookies, and a cup of coffee. "This should do it."

"Thanks." Lynne ran back downstairs to the ER waiting room. As she handed the food to the doctor and set the coffee on the table beside him, a man sitting next to Dr. McLeod wrote something in a small notebook. He looked up at her.

"May I get you some coffee?" She smiled.

"No thanks, I won't be here long. Just taking a statement." He went back to his notes.

He must be with the police. What had happened to Miss Kendall?

Dr. McLeod gazed at Lynne with a blank stare, then looked at the food she'd placed in his hands. He blinked. "Thank you."

She smiled. "Go ahead and eat. It'll make you feel better."

"I doubt it. But thanks."

When Lynne turned to leave, she spotted another young man about the same age as Dr. McLeod, an identical anxiety-ridden expression on his otherwise good-looking face. Elbows pressed into his thighs and chin resting on his fists, the newcomer glared at Dr. McLeod, who sat several feet away.

He must be here because of Miss Kendall. His gray eyes narrowed and darkened, giving his complexion a pale appearance. He ran his hand through wavy, light brown hair and leaned forward in the seat as if his life depended on what the doctor said to the other man.

Lynne caught Dr. McLeod's faltering words. "When I saw him standing over her with that grin, I ran and grabbed the depraved—"

She shouldn't be eavesdropping, no matter how curious she was. Lynne stepped closer to the sandy-haired man. He couldn't have meant this man. She sat next to the troubled visitor. "Are you here with Dr. McLeod?"

He didn't look up. "Sort of."

"May I get you a cup of coffee?"

He gazed at her. "Thank you, but I'll be fine."

Both Dr. McLeod and this young man acted as if Miss Kendall was special to them. A rivalry maybe? How sad. She sighed. *Please let her pull through this. They must care for her deeply. Will I ever know love like that?*

Loring Trent's face flashed in her mind.

Days later, Lynne responded to a patient's buzzer. She entered Kathryn Kendall's room, which rivaled a florist shop. "What a big smile after such trauma, Kathy. And look at this room. How cheerful." She smiled. Praise God Dr. McLeod had stopped an assault on the woman.

"Did your two special visitors come by today already?" Kathy was so fortunate to have both the doctor and Mr. Livingston vying for her attention. But the doctor had won the prize with his proposal. Yet, Mr. Livingston continued to visit. *Not your business, Lynne.*

"Jacob and Nick were both here early to check on me."

"They seem to get along very well, even though Dr. McLeod's the one who won your hand."

"They do now. Nick was my late brother's roommate in school. He's been like a brother to me ever since mine died in Afghanistan."

Lynne's heart twinged.

"I was never in love with Nick, and when he finally accepted it, he and Jacob became friends. Both of them told me how kind you were in the ER." Kathy leaned over and lifted a white rosebud from the bouquet in a vase next to her bed. "Please take one of these. As a thank you for taking such good care of all of us."

Lynne smiled all the way back to the desk. She retrieved a bud vase from a bottom drawer in the file cabinet and placed the rosebud in it. After she filled the vase with water, she sat down to make her notes. Dr. McLeod and Nick Livingston had both spent so much time at the hospital. She pulled her lips to one side. If only she could have such devotion from a man someday.

When the whirring of the elevator stopped at their floor, she glanced at the doors. They opened, and Nick Livingston stepped out, linebacker physique and all. As he neared the nursing station, her pulse quickened. "Can I help you, Sir?"

She'd be happy to help him with anything. He smiled, and goosebumps ran over her arms. *Stop looking at him as if he were a juicy steak.*

He made a point of inspecting her name tag. Then his eyes latched onto hers. A patient's call button interrupted the moment. *Oh drat!* Sam was with a patient. Lynne switched off the buzzer and rose. "Excuse me. I'll be right back."

To her surprise, Nick fell into step with her as she hurried down the hall. "I wanted to ask…Kathy, ah…Miss Kendall, seems to be improving, but I wonder if you'd tell me how she's really doing."

Lynne glanced at him as they strode through the hallway. "Dr. Smith is very pleased with Miss Kendall's progress. But that's as much as I can tell you."

"Thank you." He checked his watch. "Guess I'll say a quick hello. Have to make a fast visit today. Preparing for my youth group's Bible study at church tonight."

They arrived at Kathy's room. "Have a good meeting, Mr. Livingston." Wish she could spend more time talking to this sweet guy. Kathy had told her he was a youth pastor. Nice. After he ducked into her room, Lynne continued on her way to check the other patient.

When she returned to the desk, Sam glanced up. "Time for rounds." She got to her feet just as a patient call button activated.

Lynne grinned at her. "It's the surfer again. You go. I think he's sweet on you. I'll start rounds."

Sam stood. Her grin screamed mischief. "Do you think the sandy-haired friend of Miss Kendall's keeps coming just to visit her? Or…do you think he comes to talk to you?"

"What?"

"I'm very observant. He has that special gleam in his eye every time he's near you."

"On your way, *Samantha*." Lynne pointed toward the surfer's room and smiled.

Sam snickered and spun to leave.

The following day, Nick stepped off the elevator, and his pulse soared into overdrive as Lynne's smiling face greeted him. He couldn't stop a grin from spreading across his lips. He strode to the nursing station, rested his forearms across the chest-high counter, and gazed into her beautiful hazel eyes. "Are you working by yourself today, Miss Temple?"

"No, Sam's checking on a patient. And you can call me Lynne. How are you today?"

"And I'm Nick. I'm much better now with Kathy on the mend. I worried about her, but I guess I don't have to anymore. Not since Jacob has taken over."

Lynne tilted her head and wrinkled her brows. Had she guessed his feelings for Kathy when she first saw him in the ER? But things had changed since he realized how much Jacob loved Kathy...and vice versa. It was as if God had moved Lynne Temple into his path to show him he hadn't been *in love* with Kathy at all.

"Kathy told me she'd be discharged soon. She also told me how well you've taken care of her." Was she blushing?

Lynne lowered her gaze to the patient files on the desk. "She's been a real trooper."

"I guess I'd better go check on her." Nick grinned and turned from the desk.

Another patient's buzzer went off. Lynne flipped the switch and came around the counter. She fell into step with him, much to his pleasure.

"Have you known Kathy long?"

"Ever since college. I was her brother's roommate."

"She told me. I was sorry to hear she lost him in the war. I thought maybe you knew her before then."

Her lips curved into another smile. She was the loveliest woman he'd ever seen, aside from Kathy. A never-felt-before sensation stirred. His arms ached to hold her. But he'd just met her. How could this be?

Lynne stopped walking. She pointed behind Nick. "Weren't you going to visit Kathy?"

He turned and chuckled. He'd passed Kathy's room while his mind was on Lynne. "Guess I lost track of the doors."

Lynne tittered and picked up her pace through the hall. He backed up until he was even with Kathy's room but kept his eyes on Lynne and her shapely figure, evident even in scrubs.

As she rounded the corner to enter the next hall, she glanced back and smiled. Her silky, chestnut hair curled inward at her jawline and swung as she turned. Then she was gone. "Wow!" he whispered.

Nick faced Kathy's room and found her watching him with a grin. A giggle escaped her. He stepped to the bed and gave her a hug. "Heard that, did you?"

"Oh, yes. Made me very happy. Jacob and I've been praying for you to find someone. I found out today that Lynne is a Christian. She was in here earlier talking to me. When I mentioned you, she perked up."

"You wouldn't be trying your hand at matchmaking, would you?"

Kathy laughed. "You could use a little matchmaking. But I don't think I need to. I saw the way you looked at her."

After a short visit, Nick returned to his truck. He'd have to find another reason to visit the hospital if Kathy was discharged. He didn't want to come on too boldly with Lynne. What could he do? Too soon to ask her out. Was Kathy right about her being interested? Hard to believe a beautiful woman like Lynne was unattached. If she wasn't, then what?

Chapter Thirteen

*A*fter a fitful night's sleep, Nick stared out his third-floor apartment window as the sun rose. Pensacola's downtown streetlights shone over streets wet from heavy dew. In the distance, the waters of the Gulf shimmered.

As he gazed, he spoke aloud. "God, what should I do about the feelings I've developed for Lynne…in such a short time? She's so—" He shook his head and smiled. She must have a legion of admirers. For all he knew, she could be in a serious relationship. Another rejection isn't what he needed in his life right now. He drew in a long breath. "But I can't control these emotions."

He strode back to his desk and sunk into the chair. Elbows on the desk, he cradled his head in his hands. He'd ask Lynne out. If she was seeing someone else, she'd tell him, and that would be that.

After he'd prepared the lesson for next Sunday's teen class, Nick drove to the hospital. How could she have captured his heart so fast?

Every red light along the way conspired to keep him from his destination. Murphy's Law was in play with these lights. The last one caught him again. He glared from behind the steering wheel. "Hurry up."

The glowing orb, with its curved crack in the lower part of the lens, grinned at him as it merrily swayed back and forth over the intersection. When it turned green, Nick stepped on the gas. "Finally."

He sighed as he pulled into the parking lot. What if she was off today? At least he'd get an update on Kathy's release while he was here. Maybe she knew Lynne's schedule.

When Nick stepped off the elevator, Lynne sat in her usual place at the nursing station. He headed across the tiled floor toward her but paused when her coworker sashayed around the corner and stood at the desk. He veered off toward a nearby bulletin board and pretended to peruse items stapled there while his focus remained across the hall.

Lord, please make the other nurse go away. His brows furrowed as he rubbed the back of his neck. Why was he so nervous? You'd think he'd never asked a girl out before. But Lynne was no girl, and he hadn't asked anyone other than Kathy on a date in years. Cold feet. That's what he had.

As Nick stared without reading the plethora of documents on the corkboard in front of him, the other nurse's softly spoken words reached his ears. "He must be psyching himself up for something." She giggled.

"Shhh. He'll hear you," Lynne countered.

"Lynnz, with Kathy being discharged later today, I can guess what that *something* is."

Nick glanced at the station. Lynne turned and smiled at the other nurse. He raised his brows. She must expect him to talk to her. Could she have sensed his attraction to her during their brief conversation yesterday?

The second nurse returned to a normal voice. "One of us needs to disappear, and it ain't you, Sister." She stepped away from the counter. "Why don't I start rounds?"

"That's a good idea, Sam. Why don't you?" A slight bit of sarcasm edged her voice.

Nick chuckled as Lynne's eyes narrowed at Sam.

As soon as Sam sauntered away with a grin on her face, Nick took a deep breath and approached.

Lynne peered up at him. "Good morning, Nick. Here to see Kathy before she leaves today?"

A tingle surged through him. "Yes." *Don't get flustered now.* "But before I do, I want to tell you how grateful everyone is for the care you've given her." *Birdbrain.* He'd told her that already. He had to pull himself together. Was she trying to hide a snicker?

"You're all very welcome."

Nick fidgeted with a pen on the counter for a second. *Spit it out.* He'd never been this nervous asking someone out before. "Um…Miss Temple—"

"Mr. Livingston, Sir, call me Lynne, remember?" She pointed to her nametag.

"Lynne. Of course. And I'm Nick, not Sir, or Mr. Livingston. Well, actually I am, although I don't have a name tag." Had he lost his mind? What a winner.

Lynne pressed her lips together.

Nick clamped his jaw tight. "I promise you, I'm not the idiot I sound like at present." She'd never go out with him now. "What I'm trying to do is ask you out to dinner—as my way of saying thank you for being so kind to all of us."

Now he'd blown any chance for a date. He searched the area to see if anyone else had heard his bumbling. Did he really sound as dumb as he thought he did?

Lynne rose, entwined her fingers, and rested her forearms on the counter. "I'd love to, Nick. Thank you."

"Excuse me?"

"I'd love to go out with you, Nick. When?"

His mouth opened and snapped shut before he grinned. Not the response he expected. He'd better make it right away before she had time to change her mind. But he had a counseling session with a teen from the youth group. "Tomorrow night? I'd ask for tonight, but I have an appointment."

"Sounds good."

"Ah…fantastic. Tomorrow night. Say six?"

"Six is fine. I'll look forward to it."

"Wonderful. Guess I'll go see Kathy now." He turned to the corridor.

Lynne's melodious voice called after him. "Oh, Ni-ick."

He spun.

She jotted something on a notepad on the top of the counter, then held it out to him. "You'll need my address and phone number." Her eyes twinkled, reflecting the overhead lights.

Heat radiated through his neck and down his chest. He returned to the station and placed the note inside his wallet. "Thank you. Obviously, I haven't done this for a long time. But I'll get better at it." What was he talking about? A giggle escaped her lips, and he grimaced. *Just go see Kathy, now that you've made a complete fool of yourself.* He hurried off, hoping she wouldn't change her mind.

Lynne kept her eyes on Nick until he entered Kathy's room. At the desk, she fell back into her chair and laughed to herself until tears came to her eyes. Could he have been any sweeter?

Sam waltzed in from the other side of the hall a few minutes later. "Rounds are finished. You owe me one." She leaned her hip against the side of the desk and folded her arms in front of her. A quirky smile formed on her lips. "Well?"

"Well, what?"

"What happened?" Sam swatted Lynne on the shoulder. "You're like a feline trying to hide a canary under its paw. He asked you out, didn't he?"

Lynne nodded. "I wish you could've seen him. He was so cute and nervous. As a matter of fact, he did ask…eventually. Wasn't sure he'd ever get to it, though. He was adorable."

"I knew it. I just knew it. After all this time, Lynnz has been conquered. I thought you'd never accept a date from anyone again."

"Nick didn't come across bold, pushy, or cocky. He was a gentleman. Exactly the way I wanted to be asked. Not assuming, like the other guys. As if I'd fall at their feet because they deemed me worthy of going out with them. Nick had the right approach. A little shy. But I loved it."

Sam's eyes lit up. "You need to tell me the details at lunch. And you're going where?"

Lynne narrowed her eyes. "Haven't you got some work to do?" A patient buzzer sounded. "I'll get that." She jumped from her seat and scooted down the hall to the patient's room.

"We'll pick this up later, Miss Temple," Sam called after her. Giggles trailed Lynne, followed by Sam's sing-song voice in a Welsh melody. "Lynne's fine-ly a-a-gre-eed to go o-out on a da-ate…"

As she shook her head, Lynne suppressed a giggle. *Oh, I'm sure we will, Sam. You never let go until you've heard the entire story.* What an eventful day so far. What would tomorrow night bring?

That afternoon, Lynne and Sam ate lunch in the hospital cafeteria. "Nick said he hadn't asked anyone out for a long time. That's why he was nervous."

"But where are you going for dinner, girl? And when?"

Lynne shrugged. "Tomorrow night. No clue as to where, yet. I asked as he left so I'd know what to wear, but he said he'd call before I left the hospital today."

"This is so exciting, Lynnz. You have a date with a guy, and he's not even a doctor. As if it would've killed you to go out with one."

As the memory of Dr. Lindstrom's body collapsed on the floor flashed before her eyes, Lynne's head reeled. She rubbed her forehead.

"Lynnz? What's wrong?"

"Nothing—an old memory I thought was long gone." She couldn't rid herself of the vision for the remainder of her lunch break.

With pinched brows, Sam glanced at her. "You've hardly said more than a few words since I mentioned you not dating the doctors. You'll feel better if you talk about whatever's bothering you. Is it something from Afghanistan? Something that happened over there?"

Lynne gulped. "No, something when I was still at the university."

"It's not good to keep stuff in. Tell me. If you're free to talk about it, that is."

"I am now."

During the rest of their lunch and on the way back to 4-North, Lynne explained how she'd witnessed Dr. Lindstrom's murder and what transpired at the trial.

"Wow, Lynnz. I had no idea you'd been through such a horrible experience. You never mentioned it when we served together. How could you keep it inside all that time?"

"I guess I've tried to bury it. Thought I did…until now."

"So, what happened to Walter? The other witness?"

"He gave his deposition, and the court convicted the killers. Walter was shocked to learn I'd seen the murder. Such a nice man. Sort of a much older version of Nick, really. Thoughtful and kind." Lynne chuckled. "I was so relieved when Kim told me Walter recovered completely from his stroke."

After they relieved the nurse covering for them, Sam tossed her empty coffee cup into the trashcan and turned to Lynne. "Didn't you have to go into witness protection or something?"

Lynne shook her head. "They offered, but I declined since I was in the Navy." She dropped her cup in the trash on top of Sam's. "Thanks for coaxing me to tell you. I do feel better now. After my concern for Walter having kept the murder to himself all those months, here I did the same thing. You sure are a blessing, Sam." Lynne wrapped her arms around her friend and squeezed her shoulders.

"Hey, girl. What's a roomie for. I don't want you to mope around the apartment and make me moody too." Sam laughed and hugged her back. "But, Lynnz. What about the guy they called The Piper?"

"From what Kim last told me, he's gone underground. Nothing about him has surfaced. Maybe it never will." *I can only hope.*

Chapter Fourteen

"I like your dress. I mean. It's nice on you." Nick gritted his teeth and grimaced as Lynne strolled up to him in her apartment building's lobby. *Really dumb, Livingston.* Obviously, he'd left his brain at home.

His gaze roamed from the rounded neckline of her Navy blue dress with short flowing sleeves to her shapely legs below the flared skirt. Then down to the matching heeled sandals. His pulse increased, and a surge of heat filled his neck.

"Thank you. Is it appropriate for wherever we're going? You said 'sort of dressy' but never said where you're taking me."

"It's perfect!" Whew! She wasn't offended by the once-over he'd given her. He gulped. No wonder the right words eluded him. She was so beautiful.

He reached for the dark blue shawl Lynne had draped over her arm. "Allow me. The breeze is on the cooler side tonight. Hope that hurricane the weatherman reported stays in the Atlantic. Far away from us."

She turned her back to him, and he wrapped the shawl around her shoulders. He breathed in the scent of roses. Definitely would be one his favorite fragrances from now on.

Lynne grasped the shawl and tossed one loose end across her shoulder. "Thank you, again."

"You're welcome." The flush of warmth flowing up his neck grew more intense. He acted like a schoolboy on his first date. He'd blow any chance of a relationship with her if he didn't stop.

They headed for the lobby door. "I think you'll enjoy the place I picked out. Russo's Roman Forum. It's a new Italian restaurant on the beach. I recently found it and was pleased with the menu."

"I was too." She glanced at him as they made their way to his white Ford Ranger. "I've been there once."

"So have I." She might think he'd taken other women there. "With friends from church."

As they reached his truck, Lynne smiled. "I went with people from church too. Sam's church."

So she attended church with a guy. His brows pinched. Were they a couple? "Sam? Is he a *special* friend of yours?"

She slid into the passenger seat. "He? No. Sam's the nurse I work with. Samantha." Lynne tilted her head and peered up at him. "You've met her. Long, wavy strawberry-blonde hair, five feet two?"

Nick chuckled. "Oh...*that* Sam." What a relief. Forgot her name was Sam. He jogged around the front of the Ford and jumped in.

"Kathy told me you were in the Navy." The engine roared to life, and Nick pulled away from the curb.

"I was. Reserves now." She looked around at the interior of the vehicle. "Always wanted a truck. Used to drive my brother's on the farm."

"Then you don't mind going out to dinner in this? I should have asked before."

"Not at all. It's in immaculate condition. My dad and brothers would be impressed."

Hmmm, brothers. Hope they weren't the overprotective type. Shouldn't dwell on that now. He was nervous enough as it was.

"What made you join the Navy? Is Lynne Temple your full name?"

Lynne laughed. "My full name is Lynne Bridget Temple. But please don't call me Bridget. Never was fond of it. My two siblings call me Sis or Stringbean…" she peeked at him from under thick, dark lashes, "…because I was a skinny teenager. Mom, most of her friends, and the neighbors back home all use Lynnie. And my Nurse Corps coworkers branded me Lynnz. Dad prefers Lynne. Enough to choose from?"

Nick chuckled. "Why Lynnz?"

"When I first joined, one nurse thought my name was Lindsey. She dubbed me Lynnz for short. By the time I got *her* straightened out, I had become Lynnz to everyone, so I gave up."

"Too bad they got your name wrong. People are sensitive when it comes to their names." Nick turned his focus to the heavy evening traffic as he navigated Three Mile Bridge over Pensacola Bay.

"It's okay. We all had them. Sam still calls me Lynnz. She and I served together in the same unit in Afghanistan and here in Pensacola. Mom doesn't care for the name much because *'it's too tomboyish,'* she says. But I've grown to like it. You can choose whichever."

"I choose Lynne." They stopped for the light on the other side of the bridge. He glanced at her.

"And you're okay with Nick, instead of Nicholas?" Her brows

raised.

"Definitely! Only my uncle calls me Nicholas…when I'm in trouble, which hasn't been for quite a few years now." He smirked. "My aunt and uncle raised me."

Lynne nodded but didn't ask why.

The light changed, and he drove on. "During dinner, I'd like to hear more about your time in the service. Sounds interesting."

"It had its moments. Some good, some bad." Her voice saddened and sounded as if her thoughts had drifted to someplace far away.

Better change the subject. Probably had more bad moments than good. "And you have brothers?"

"Yeah, two of the best, Jim and Jeff. Both known as 'Stinker,' as the occasion demands." She glanced back at Nick, her demeanor more cheerful. "Which it often does."

Nick grinned. A couple of guys he'd no doubt get along with. "Wish I had a brother…or a sister. Being an only child is the pits!"

Nick pulled the truck in front of the waterfront restaurant. He hopped out and hurried to the passenger door, but when he got there, she stood outside the truck. She closed the door and turned to him. "What?"

"Nothing. I was going to open the door for you."

"Oooh. Well…um…sorry, Nick. Guess I've been taking care of myself for so long, I've become independent. The Marines and Navy Corpsmen didn't open the Humvee doors for us." A smile spread across her face. "That was our job, they were fond of telling us, like wearing our own pack and carrying our own weapon." She shrugged.

As he shook his head, Nick offered his arm, and she took it. What a wonderful sense of humor.

A gentle breeze from the water ruffled her hair. A model...posed for a windswept look. His heart skipped a beat.

They entered the restaurant, and the aroma of garlic and spices filled his senses. The hostess wrote Nick's name on her list of waiting customers. Nick motioned for Lynne to have a seat on the bench next to the hostess podium. He wanted to learn everything he could about Lynne. "You didn't tell me how you wound up in the Navy."

"My father was a Navy Seal Corpsman. I wanted to be a nurse. Jim and Jeff, both Marines, were already serving, so I joined them. Hence, Navy nurse."

"It must please your mom and dad."

"In a way. Dad more so than Mom. But, they'd rather I had stayed in Illinois. They also wish I came back home when I discharged."

Nick closed his eyes for a moment. *Thanks for keeping her in Pensacola, Lord.*

The hostess led the way to a table and placed menus in front of them.

Lynne perused the menu while she talked. "Okay, Nick. Now it's your turn. How did you wind up a minister?"

"I'll give you my life's story after we've ordered. I'm hungry." He'd limit it to the good parts of his life. No sense bringing up how his mother dropped him on her sister's doorstep when he was only five so she could join her truck-driver boyfriend. Or that he'd never known his dad. Probably better off anyway. His aunt and uncle had raised him right.

A dark-haired, middle-aged waitress approached. She turned to Lynne first. "Are you ready to order?"

"I'll have the Fettuccini Alfredo and house salad."

The woman scribbled down the order and then turned to Nick.

"Spaghetti and meatballs for me."

When the waitress left, Nick launched into his college years. "Right after my graduation from college, Uncle John said he'd soon need help with the youth group at the church he pastors. The couple who ran the department was being transferred to California. Marines. When they say you go, you go. Well, you know that."

"Yeah. Tell me about it." Lynne cinched the side of her mouth.

"My uncle asked if I'd consider the position of youth pastor."

Her silky hair framed a flawless face, and hazel eyes twinkled in the light from the flickering candle on their table. He could get lost in those eyes. He grinned. "Where all did the Navy send you?"

Her lips parted. "Oh no you don't, mister. You haven't finished your story yet."

With a shrug of the shoulders, he chuckled. "I'm sure yours is more interesting."

"I'll be the judge of that. Now, come on. Proceed."

"There's not much more to it. The young people at our church are a full-time job now. I enjoyed working with them so much that Uncle John sent me to Bible school here in town. Classes were at night. It helped me in so many ways, not just to learn the Bible."

Lynne smiled. "There's more to your story."

Nick raised both hands in the air, then leaned back gazing at her. He clasped his hands and laid them on the red tablecloth. "Okay, what do you want to know?"

"Why don't you back up to college?" She pinched her lips for a moment.

He winced. She must have painful memories from her college days. Should he ask? He might be able to help.

But before he could say anything, their food arrived. Nick's mouth watered as he took a deep whiff of the Italian sauce, steeped with garlic and herbs. The large white plate piled with steamy, delicious-looking pasta under the sauce invited him to taste.

He licked his lips and rested his hand palm up on the table. Lynne placed her hand in his, they bowed their heads, and Nick asked the blessing for their meal.

As they ate, Nick explained his relationship with his university roommate, Chris Kendall, and talked about their life in college. "Chris was the best friend I'd ever had. We did everything together. We even worked together at a local fast-food restaurant."

"Kathy told me he died in service. It pained me to hear that." Her brows wrinkled.

"Yes. That's when I got closer to Kathy. But Chris was a real character. Loved to play practical jokes on me."

Lynne's happy expression returned. "Such as?"

"Okay. This one will give you a good laugh. The sheriff's office had arranged a fundraiser. They allowed ridiculous charges to be made against friends or relatives for which they were arrested and would have to pay fines. Chris had me arrested right in the middle of my shift at work. I don't remember the trumped-up charge, but the deputy hauled me off to the makeshift jail set up in the mall's food court. For my bail, I had to raise five hundred dollars, all of which went to charity, of course. They set up phones inside this jail so we could make calls and plead with our friends and relatives to supply the bail money, explaining it was for charity." Nick laughed so hard tears came to his eyes, then he caught his breath.

"That prank hasn't come to mind for a long time."

She covered her mouth with the napkin and bent forward. Her shoulders quivered while she laughed.

"It took me three hours to get half the pledges I needed."

Nick shook his head. "My good-natured boss had conspired with Chris and made himself scarce the day the deputy walked in. Then my boss came strolling into the mall with a stern face, and I thought I was fired. When I explained, he asked how much money I still needed to get out of jail. He stuck a hand in his pocket and pulled out the entire five hundred dollars in a single roll of bills."

Lynne continued to chortle. He loved to see her laugh. She fanned herself and took a drink of water.

"I asked him how he had found out what happened, but he turned on his heel. I didn't find out he knew about the setup until the next day. When I asked why he delayed in springing me, he said, 'Didn't want you to miss the fun.' I could've killed Chris." Nick snickered, but after a few seconds became serious. "Then Chris had to go and join the Marines after we graduated...and get himself killed."

The joy disappeared from Lynne's face. "That must have been almost as horrible for you as it was for Kathy."

Again Nick winced. He must have reminded her of one of those bad moments from Afghanistan.

"It was hard, but the Lord helped both of us work through it. I had to be strong for Kathy. It helped me understand the pain others experience when they lose a loved one. Like a few of the kids in our church have. Parents, family members, relatives, and even close friends have died in the war."

The server refilled their glasses and handed them dessert menus.

Lynne sighed. "I shouldn't eat a dessert after that Alfredo sauce, but—" She pressed her lips together. "I love cannoli."

Nick smiled. "We'll have the cannoli." He handed the dessert menu back to the waitress.

"Nick, you are detrimental to my waistline." Lynne tittered.

"Fair ladies need to indulge once in a while. Besides, I want our first date to be a memorable one."

"First date?"

"Yes, well…I wasn't entirely honest about my reason for asking you out. It wasn't to say thank you for being so kind to all of us. I knew when Kathy was discharged, I'd have no excuse to visit the hospital every day, so I had to do something. Since I'd just met you, I wasn't sure how to ask for a date without seeming pushy. It's been years since I asked a lady I haven't known for some time out. Made me nervous. Saying thanks was the first excuse I thought of."

Lynne's lips slowly curved upward at the corners. "It was the perfect way to ask me."

"I sounded like a fool." He rolled his eyes. "But thanks." He took a drink of water. "Do you go to church in Pensacola?"

"The NAS chapel when I can, and I've been to Sam's church a few times, but I don't consider either *my* church. Neither is as cozy as my little home church in Kewanee, Illinois."

The server returned with their desserts and placed them on the table. Nick took a bite of cannoli.

Lynne closed her eyes as she munched on hers, then swallowed. "Mmm, wonderful."

They finished eating, and Nick placed his napkin on the empty plate. "You haven't been to our church yet. I would have noticed. May

I invite you for Sunday's service? I'd be happy to pick you up and bring you home again."

"I'd love to come."

The waitress placed the bill on the table next to Nick. He slid his credit card into the holder. "What do you say to a stroll around the shops on the boardwalk? We could enjoy more of that nice breeze we got a taste of on the way in." And he could postpone the end of this evening.

Still haven't asked her if she's seeing anyone else.

Chapter Fifteen

$\mathcal{L}$ynne glanced at Nick in the moonlight as they strolled past the specialty shops on Quietwater Beach boardwalk. "Too bad the stores are closed at this hour." She grinned. "But you, being a guy, probably aren't interested in shopping." She laughed. And what a guy. What would it be like to have him hold her? Her heart fluttered.

Nick chuckled. "I wouldn't mind too much in present company. But right now, I'm enjoying the quiet evening since so few people are around at this hour." He pointed out a souvenir shop display window. "The teens in my Sunday school class have mentioned the treasures they've found here."

As they inspected the display, Lynne pointed to a yellow, purple, and white fan-shaped shell with dark lines running through it. "The beautiful designs God placed in these shells are amazing, aren't they?"

He stood behind her and peered over her shoulder. "They are. That one's a Calico Scallop. The scallops are my favorite with their variety of colors." He pointed to a spiral shell. "But look at the stripes on that Lightning Whelk."

She glanced at him. "You know your shells."

"I've spent my entire life here on the Gulf. Shell hunting was one of my favorite pastimes when I was a kid."

A short distance away, the laughter of young people filled the air.

Lynne moved to the end of the building to look at a display of larger shells. Nick followed. A group of teens rounded the corner at a full run. The boy in the lead bumped into Lynne and shoved her backward into Nick. He pulled Lynne into the doorway of the souvenir shop and wrapped his arms around her. A tingle charged through her.

As Nick and Lynne watched with their mouths open, the group ran to the parking lot without a word of apology.

Still holding Lynne, Nick called after them. "I saw you, Jesse. We'll discuss this at a later date." His voice lowered. "If you ever show up at church again." He shook his head and turned to Lynne. "Are you all right?"

Sunset had darkened his gray eyes, but they reflected the light of lamps on the boardwalk. She could dive into those pools and never come out. "Yeah, I think so." She didn't move, enjoying his closeness. His aromatic cologne reminded her of cedar trees in the woods and new leather. "Thanks for the rescue."

"You're welcome." Slowly he released her.

She needed to thank Jesse one day. Too bad the moment ended so soon.

Nick quirked his mouth. "You've had a close-up encounter with some of Pensacola's ill-mannered youth, I'm afraid. Sorry."

Lynne shrugged. "No doubt they have relatives in Illinois. I've run into a similar bunch there." She tittered. "Hope I didn't hit you too hard." At least her fleeting fantasy from a moment ago came to pass. She'd found out what it was like to have Nick's arms around her. She smiled.

"When I play football with the youth group, I'm hit a lot harder." He grinned.

They stepped out of the doorway and resumed their walk. When Nick offered his arm, she slid her hand through the crook. His fingers covered hers. "Shall we take a short walk along the shore before I drive you home?"

Drive me home? She didn't want the night to end. "I'd like that. The moon always looks so beautiful on the water."

They ambled down the wooden stairs of the boardwalk to the beach. At the bottom, Lynne removed her sandals and wiggled her bare toes in the soft, sugary sand. Not a soul could be seen in either direction. The only sound, waves crashing on shore. She took his offered arm again as they made their way toward the water.

When they reached the wet sand, Lynne closed her eyes and drew in a deep breath of the salty Gulf air. The breeze whipped hair into her face. She flinched as the strands came near her eyes.

"You're sure you didn't get hurt when those kids shoved you?"

She opened her eyes, tucked her hair behind her ears, and gazed at him. His brows wrinkled. "Not at all. Like you, I've had my share of impacts. My brothers taught me martial arts until I left for college. And when they visited me there, we'd go through sessions at the gym. Boot camp toughened me up as well."

"Hmmm." He grinned. "I'd better be careful not to get on your wrong side."

In a flash, she spun away from him, brought her left leg up, straightened it, and gave him a soft tap with her foot in the solar plexus. Nick recoiled and doubled over as he laughed. He straightened and brushed the sand off his shirt.

They continued their stroll, dodging lazy waves that rolled up onto the beach after their initial crash to the sand. When Nick stopped to capture a sand dollar from a retreating wave, Lynne lifted her eyes to the millions of stars above them. A few seconds later, the glorious expanse of lights faded as a cloud moved in and blocked the twinkling sky. Tiny drops of rain fell.

Nick grabbed Lynne's hand, and they raced back to the truck. "These storms come up fast and sometimes are pretty strong."

The downpour began as soon as they closed the doors of the vehicle. Lynne brushed wet sand off her feet. "I think I brought half the beach in here with me. Sorry I've made such a mess."

"Don't worry. No harm done." He handed her the sand dollar from the beach, started the engine, and drove away from the Gulf.

On the way to her apartment, Lynne glanced at him. The evening had gone well. At least until the cloudburst. Very well, indeed. Especially the part where he held her in his arms. *Lord. I really like him.* She hadn't felt such peace and contentment with anyone in far too long. He'd laughed when she told him about her martial arts training, but was she too independent and tomboyish for a minister?

Nick parked the truck in front of Lynne's apartment building. What an amazing woman. Beautiful, smart, sure of herself, and what a sense of humor. But after her exciting life in the Navy, could she fall in love with someone like him? A home-grown boy not interested in leaving Pensacola to see the world as she had?

He slid out of the driver's seat and hurried to the passenger door. She'd waited for him to open it for her. *Hmmm.* He pulled the handle and held out his hand to her.

Shivers sprinted up his arm at her touch. It had been so hard to let her go at the boardwalk after the teens left. What would she have thought if he continued to hold her for no other reason than because he wanted to? It took every ounce of his willpower not to kiss her. And yet, they'd just recently met.

When they entered the lobby of the apartment building, Lynne faced him with a smile. "What a wonderful evening, Nick. Thank you."

"Even though a herd of ruffians almost trampled you?" He raised his brows.

She laughed and took a deep breath. "That wasn't so bad. A hero rescued me."

His heart pounded.

Her lashes lowered. "The kids weren't that bad. Teens out to have a good time. Although they could have stopped and said they were sorry." She looked back into his eyes. "Young people their age aren't generally known to have good manners unless it's drummed into them by their parents."

"That's true. And Jesse, for one, has had that part of his education neglected for a long time. His is a sad story. He came to church with some friends for a while, but we haven't seen him in some time now. He's never home when I try to visit. We can only pray for him."

At the elevator, Lynne pressed the button. "I'll pray for Jesse. And that he shows up for church tomorrow."

The whirring noise from the elevator stopped, and the door opened. While Lynne entered the car, Nick put his hand against the rubberized bumper on the edge of the door to keep it open. He stepped in behind her and pressed the button for the second floor. He'd ask her out again before he left. Hopefully, he wouldn't make such a disaster of it, this time. Although, she seemed to like the way he asked before. Had she just been kind?

When the car stopped and they stepped into the hall, Nick cleared his throat. They reached her door, and she gazed up at him.

"Lynne? Would you consider going out with me again…soon?"

Her brows rose. "Of course, but—" She blinked.

"But what?"

"Maybe I misunderstood you in the restaurant. Please forgive me if I assumed."

What had he done now? Said something to mislead her? He thought he told Lynne he didn't invite her to dinner to thank her for her kindness. "Misunderstood what?"

"Well, I thought you had invited me to church tomorrow. I'm sorry if—"

"You're right. I did ask you. And I can't even blame my forgetfulness on a senior moment the way my uncle does. I'm the sorry one." He chuckled. *Nick, you blockhead!* "And you accepted my invitation." He exhaled. "*Again,* I feel like such a fool."

She laid her hand on his arm. "You're no fool, Nick. You've had a lot going on in your life recently…and…well…it happens. Do you still want me to go to church with you?"

He glanced at her hand, warm against his skin. "Always." His mouth dropped open. "I mean, yes. I'll pick you up at nine thirty. If you want to come to Sunday school, that is."

She nodded. "I would." She reached into her purse and pulled out her keys, then unlocked the door. "Thanks again for dinner and the stroll. See you tomorrow morning."

"Nine thirty. Goodnight." His heart sank as the slate-gray door closed with a click. He still hadn't asked if she was dating anyone else. He should have brought up the subject this evening.

Nick headed back to the elevator. She'd mesmerized him all evening. Their conversation had flowed so well. But then, she flinched when she mentioned college. Why? What had caused the pain in her eyes?

Lynne leaned her shoulder and head against the closed door. She could sense Nick on the other side. He'd forgotten he asked her to church, but it was understandable with the trauma he'd gone through with Kathy. Dr. McLeod proposing to Kathy must have added more. Was he still carrying a torch for her?

As she pushed herself off the door, Loring's face materialized in her thoughts. He was still doing the same thing with Holly. *Poor Kim.*

Her feelings for Nick were so different from those she had felt for Loring. His face faded, and another thought wedged its way into her mind. Had they heard any news about The Piper? Surely Kim would have called if they had. The thought of ever seeing that grotesque face again sent a chill through her.

Great. Just what she wanted to dwell on after one of the best evenings of her life.

Chapter Sixteen

The next morning, Nick stepped out the door of his apartment to pick up Lynne for Sunday school and church. He'd been ready to leave more than an hour ago, thrilled that she wanted to go to church with him.

As he drove through Pensacola to her apartment building, the lights seemed to be in his favor this time. Good sign. But he'd get to her place way before nine thirty. Still, better to be early than late.

He pulled up in front of the red brick apartment building at ten minutes after nine. Should he go in now or wait in the truck? She might not be ready. Oh well. If she wasn't ready, he'd sit in the lobby.

Nick strode through the front doors and rang the bell. A second later, Lynne's voice came through the intercom. "Hello?"

"Hi. It's me. I'm early. Shall I wait for you down here?"

"I'll be right there."

Nick smiled and sat on the bench near the elevator. The familiar whirring noise started. When it stopped, Lynne stepped out of the car wearing an off-white lace suit which, like the dress she wore Saturday night, showed off her figure much better than the scrubs he'd seen her in most of the time. His heart stirred. Her toeless beige shoes matched the purse hanging on a fine chain from her right shoulder. Tucked under her left arm was a large black Bible.

On the way to church, Lynne's signature perfume filled the truck. Nick's pulse pounded.

"Nick, do you think Jesse will show up today?"

"I'm praying so. Not so I can chew him out but to explain why he needs to spend time with Christians. That bunch he ran with last night is the same group he's been in trouble with before. I hope I can talk to him."

When they arrived at the church, Nick escorted Lynne to a seat in the main auditorium. "I have to teach the teen class, but I'll be back for the service. My uncle teaches the adult class. You'll enjoy his lesson."

Lynne slid into the pew, seated herself, and glanced up at Nick. "I'm sure I will." She smiled sweetly at him.

Nick hurried through the back of the auditorium, into the hall, and headed for his classroom in the ancillary building. He needed to take his mind off Lynne and get it on the lesson. *Lord, I'm relying on You for help here.*

After church, Lynne and Nick joined his aunt and uncle for Sunday dinner at their home in rural Pace on the north side of Escambia Bay. When they finished, Nick and his uncle stayed in the dining room deep in a Bible discussion. Lynne joined Gwen Marshall in the kitchen to clean up. "Thank you for the dinner invitation. Fried chicken is my absolute favorite. Something I've never gotten the hang of preparing the right way, I'm afraid."

"It's not that hard, Dear. I'd be happy to show you how I fix it sometime when you're free."

"Thank you." Mrs. Marshall was as elegant a lady as her husband was a wonderful teacher and preacher. "Mom tried to teach me how, but I guess back then I wasn't a very good home ec student." She peeked at her hostess. "Too busy sparring with my brothers."

The preacher's wife chuckled. "Well, the way I do it is so easy I even taught Nick how to make fried chicken. If he can learn, so can you."

Nick had mentioned the Marshalls raised him. But he'd said nothing of his parents. Maybe it was a painful subject. He'd tell her when he was ready.

After they loaded the dishwasher, Mrs. Marshall closed the door and pressed start. "While the men are talking sermon notes, how about a fresh cup of coffee?"

"I'd love one." Lynne wiped the spattered water from the counter with a dishtowel and then sat at the kitchen table. "Nick told me how he came to be the youth pastor. That's quite a calling."

"It is, and we're so happy with his work." The pastor's wife set a tray with two steaming cups, the sugar bowl, and creamer on the table, then joined Lynne. "Now, tell me about your adventures in the Navy. Nick told us that before you joined the hospital staff, you served as a Navy nurse. That must have been some undertaking."

"I suppose so, but I loved what I was doing. That is until I'd seen my fill of broken bodies in Afghanistan. At that point, I wanted to come home to the States and find a civilian nursing job. I have admiration for any nurse, male, or female, who serves in the trenches and continues to do it. But it wasn't for me."

Mrs. Marshall touched Lynne's arm. "I can only imagine how hard it was. But God's fulfilled your desire to continue nursing, and, from what Nick told us, we're blessed to have you in Pensacola."

"Thank you. I feel blessed to be here. I fell in love with this place from my first day at NAS."

"He said you're from Illinois."

"I am. Kewanee. Less than two hundred miles west of Chicago. My parents own a farm." She sipped her coffee.

"He also said you graduated from college in Chicago. What a busy place. We attended a conference there once. Oh my, the traffic."

Lynne laughed. "It *is* a very busy place." She hoped Nick's aunt wouldn't ask more about her life on campus. The memories were best put far from her. And she'd had such a hard time forgetting.

"So, are you still in the service? In reserves? I thought I heard Nick mention it at dinner."

"Yes, Ma'am. In reserves at present, but he was asking after my brother in the Marines. My brothers joined the Marines within a year of each other. Jim is out now, but Jeff is still serving."

When they finished their coffee, they joined the men in the living room.

Nick stood as they entered the room. "Lynne, shall we take a walk? The weather is more accommodating today. Blue sky as far as you can see."

"After that big dinner, a walk sounds perfect."

As they strolled the country lane, away from the Marshalls' home, Lynne lifted her face to the gentle breeze. She gazed up at the tree limbs which made a tunnel effect over the blacktop. "This would make a worthy calendar photo."

Once again, Nick offered his arm as they walked. She laid her hand on his forearm. The hair, bleached by the Florida sun, showed golden highlights in the sunlight and tickled her hand. She stifled a giggle. "This road is almost the same as the one that leads to my parents' home. Except for those funny-looking pines and the flowering bushes and trees everywhere. Do they always bloom at this time of the year?"

He glanced at her and grinned. "You're not in Kansas anymore, Dorothy." Nick laughed.

"*Illinois*. There *is* a difference, you know." Lynne quirked her mouth at him.

"Oh, I'm sure there is. And to answer your question, the crepe myrtle tree and oleander bushes always seem to be in bloom. Never paid much attention. Guess I take some things for granted. I've never wanted to live anywhere else. And we call those 'funny-looking pines' Longleaf Pines. I've always thought they were neat with the tufts at the branch tips."

Lynne envied the contentment evident in his voice and eyes. She'd felt the same growing up on the farm in Illinois. Until the terrible events at the end of her second year in college. She sighed. Would they *always* threaten her peace of mind? Even here, in this laid-back part of the country?

Nick stopped, faced her, and placed his hands on her shoulders. "What are you thinking about? Hope you don't mind my asking, but you wore that same troubled expression when college came up in our conversation on our first date. I didn't want to ask that night, but if you care to talk, I'm a good listener. That pained countenance you're wearing doesn't belong on such a pretty lady."

Pretty lady. Lynne smiled but looked away.

Nick lifted her chin with his index finger. His brows furrowed and held a worried expression. "Lynne, is something wrong?"

Her gaze dropped to the rutted road. Should she tell him? She'd told Sam, and it helped. Nick was a minister. He'd tell her to pray and give her Bible passages to help rid her of these images in her head. But she already knew all the verses, and they didn't help. *Did she want to tell him? Not now. Another time?* After they'd known each other longer. Then she'd confide in him. Explain the fear that plagued her. Fear that she hadn't seen the last of the man who ordered her professor's murder five years ago.

"No. Nothing's wrong." Although her heart pounded, she smiled and continued to walk. Nick took her hand, stayed by her side, and said nothing.

If only Kim would say The Piper was behind bars the next time she called. She'd have no more fear. After the murder, it had been rumored The Piper moved his operations to the South. What if he showed up here? Would he come after her? If she told Nick about the murder, he'd want her to tell the entire story. What if that fiend found out? He might come after Nick. No. She couldn't tell Nick. Not until they locked The Piper up for good.

Chapter Seventeen

*L*ynne stepped out of the hospital's 4-North elevator on Monday morning. Whew! I'm so glad there's no chaos here, unlike the emergency room. "Sam, what's going on today? Just passed the ER, and I've never seen it so busy in there."

"Have a seat. I'll fill you in on what Steph from four-west heard from Derek Appleby in radiology while you were on break."

As she sat, Lynne stashed her purse in the desk drawer and locked it.

Sam took a big gulp of coffee. "Earlier this morning, there was an interstate pileup. The paramedics brought several of the injured people here. After that, the emergency room filled up with victims from an overturned tourist bus."

"Are you pulling my leg?"

"Not kidding. It's been pandemonium in the ER. But that's not all. A man injured in a machinery malfunction at the paper mill also came in. Add to that some teens who overdosed at a liquor and drug-fueled rave party last night into the wee hours of this morning."

Lynne shook her head. "What were those kids thinking? Don't they realize what they're doing to their bodies and brains?"

"Tell me 'bout it. It's sad." She puckered her lips. "They brought the teens to *our* floor."

"This should be interesting." Lynne sighed.

Sam cried out, "Nooo! Not the computers." She grimaced as she turned to Lynne. "Now *they're* down. Can you believe this day? And we still have more than half our shift to go. Monday morning at its finest."

The nursing station phone rang, and Lynne grabbed the receiver. "Four-north, Lynne Temple speaking."

"Hi, pretty lady."

Lynne's insides tingled. "Nick. Good morning." She glanced over to Sam, whose brows almost reached her strawberry-blonde hairline.

"Thought I'd call and—"

"Ya-hooo. Prince Charming to the rescue." Sam winked at Lynne and moved away from the desk as a patient's buzzer light glowed.

"Excuse me a moment, Nick." Lynne stifled a laugh and rested the receiver on the desk. She crumpled a blank inventory form into a tight paper wad and threw it at Sam. The paper ball hit her in the back of the head.

"Yeowch!" Sam kept walking as she rubbed her head and giggled.

Lynne picked up the receiver again. "Sorry, Nick. What were you saying before Slick Sammy interrupted?"

"What was that about?"

"Nothing but Sam's tomfoolery. You were saying?"

"I thought you might enjoy dinner on a yacht. Having served in the Navy, you don't get seasick, do you?"

"No, I don't." Lynne felt her brows pushing together as she tried to imagine Nick on a yacht. "You own a yacht?"

"Me? On a pastor's salary? No way." He chuckled. "A friend from church owns it. Actually, his family does. Long story. In short, it's near a hundred years old, but they turned it into a restaurant. It's moored at the bay. I called earlier and made a reservation for tonight."

"That sounds wonderful, Nick." *Imagine. Lynne Temple, dining on a yacht.* "What does one wear for dinner on a yacht?"

"I'll wear a suit. I'm sure you'll figure out what to wear. Something more formal than the other night, I guess. I've never been there myself."

Hmmm, more dressy than what she'd worn for their first date. She had that pale yellow dress with sparkly things on the edges of the sleeves that might be appropriate. She'd ask Sam if it would do. "Okay. I have something in mind."

"Can you be ready at five?"

"Aye aye, Sir."

As Lynne hung up, Sam returned to the station. She pulled a chair next to Lynne and rested her cheek in her hand, elbow propped on the desk. "Okay, Miss Temple, how did it go? Saturday night, I mean. I want every detail since you've been avoiding the subject all weekend."

The patients' call buttons remained silent. Why couldn't someone need her now? Sam would not be put off any longer. "Uh, yeah." Lynne shuffled files in front of her. "It went okay."

Sam shot upright in the seat and folded her arms across her midriff. Her eyes bored holes into Lynne. "And what does that mean?"

"What?"

"You know very well what."

"No, I don't."

"You're avoiding the issue, lady."

"I am not!" Suppressing a smile, Lynne peeked at Sam, then burst out laughing. "Okay, pest. But don't think I'll tell you *every* detail of *every* date I go on. I don't drill you like this after you've been out with one of your hunks."

Sam giggled. "But this is a new venue for you, Lynnz. I need to keep up with how you handle things."

"Better than I've handled things from my past, I can tell you." Her heart lurched. No matter what she did, no matter what she said, everything seemed to bring her thoughts back to the murder.

At five, the doorbell rang. Lynne pressed the intercom. "Hello?"

"It's me. I'm here. And right on time."

"You are. Come on up."

Lynne rushed to the oval free-standing mirror in her bedroom and checked her tea-length, pale yellow dress. As she twirled, the elbow-length sleeves flared out and sparkled. She'd lived in khaki for too long. This style suited her better.

She tucked strands of hair behind her ear, fastened a glittery gold barrette in place, and draped a white lace shawl over her arm. In the living room, she finished lacing her gold sandals and grabbed her matching clutch bag.

A knock came to the door. She opened it, and Nick stepped inside, handsome in his tailored dark brown suit. She smiled. The slightest bit of curly golden hair peeked out from his cream-colored shirt worn open at the neck. Heat flooded her neck. She focused on his black shoes, polished to a shine worthy of an admiral. Probably could see her reflection in them.

"Oh. Forgot something." She hurried back to the bedroom. After two sprays of rose perfume to her neck, she reentered the living room.

His sparkling eyes widened. "You, lady, are a vision of loveliness, and that fragrance you're wearing is nothing short of heavenly." He shook his head, and his lips formed a silent whistle.

Was he serious? No one had ever complimented her that way. What a charmer. Warmth from her neck flowed into her cheeks.

"And you, Sir...I mean, you look—" She pressed her mouth shut. She'd never been at a loss for words before. She grinned. "Very handsome."

"Thank you. Well, I guess we'd better get moving if we're to make our reservation."

As they rounded a corner, Lynne's eyes popped. A large vessel, which she guessed to be well beyond one hundred feet, occupied the entire space at the end of a long pier. An elaborate sign designated it, 'The Yacht.'

Nick parked the truck and opened the passenger door for her. "Isn't she a beaut?"

"I'll say. Like something out of an old movie. How many people will she hold?"

"Near one hundred, according to Zack. After they bought it, his dad had the vessel restored but decided it wouldn't work in their business. They run fishing charters aside from being fishermen. You know, take people out on fishing trips. So he had it converted into a restaurant with a décor consistent with the Roaring Twenties, the era when the ship was built. They restricted the dining area to the enclosed top deck. More intimate. A friend of Mr. Adams had years of experience in food service, as well as in commercial fishing, so they gave the management over to him."

As they strolled to the vessel, magenta-colored strings of lights swayed in the wind on the back deck. Water lapped at the poles supporting the rustic wooden wharf. A mixture of aromas filled the air.

When they reached the wide-timbered ramp with its rope railing that led upward into the yacht, a splash sounded. Lynne's head whipped around. "Wait!" she stretched her neck, searching for whatever caused the noise in the bay. "Did someone fall into the water?"

"Where?" Nick peered into the dusky bay.

"*Look.* It's dolphins. And only a few feet away. I've never seen any in the wild."

"We see them here all the time. Guess they don't cavort around the lakes and streams in Kansas, do they, Dorothy? Oh, sorry, *Il-li-nois.*" He snickered.

After a playful dig in his ribs from her elbow, she moved closer to the edge of the dock to follow the bobbing marine mammals. "That was your first warning, Popeye. I want a closer look at those critters."

The ripples turned into shades of coral in the orange-red setting sun as the creatures splashed and played. Lynne leaned over the water, fascinated by one dolphin who swam under the dock. She took a step closer to a post, and the heel of her sandal lodged itself in the gap between the planks. She lost her footing and fell forward toward the water.

Nick grasped her arm with both hands and pulled her to his chest. He enfolded her in his arms. "Whew! That was a close one. Are you okay?"

Her heart beat triple-time as he led her away from the pier's edge. He unwrapped his arms but held onto her elbow.

"Yeah. Thanks." As she held onto his shoulder, she lifted a foot behind her to check the two-inch heel of her sandal. "Yeah. I'm okay. Heel's intact." She lowered her foot to the plank and smiled at him. "What a relief."

"You came within a gnat's eyebrow of swimming with those dolphins, and you're worried about your heel?"

"Hey. Do you have even the slightest idea what these heels cost? On nurse's pay?"

Nick laughed, and she joined him.

"But seriously. Thank you again for the rescue, big guy. You're getting pretty good at this."

"Miss Temple, do you solemnly promise never to scare me like that again?"

"Nooo. But how often do you really think I'll need rescuing?" Lynne chortled.

As they continued up the ramp to the floating restaurant, Lynne's gaze drifted to a large boat docked at the pier closer to shore. She stopped. A huge, dark figure skulked up the gangplank of the vessel. She froze. Her pulse raced. *No*. It couldn't be him.

Nick turned to her. "Now what? Is your heel stuck again?" He grinned.

"No. Nothing. It's—"

"It's what?"

Lynne pointed to the boat where the figure had disappeared below. "That vessel over there. Is that a shrimp boat? The one with those poles sticking up and out."

"Yes. Why?"

"Just wondering. And they go fishing at night? Right about now. Right? When the sun sets."

"That's right. Zack says it's the only time he and his dad go shrimping. What's wrong?"

"Oh, it's nothing—a fleeting thought. I'm curious. Silly really." Her mind must be playing tricks on her. Too many flashbacks. It was only a fisherman getting ready to go out. Not The Piper. *It's only your imagination working overtime. That's all.*

She smiled at Nick, and they made their way up the ramp. But her pulse kept up the race.

Chapter Eighteen

S eated at a table on the enclosed deck of The Yacht, Nick ordered dinner for Lynne and himself. After handing the menu to the waiter, he gazed into her glistening hazel eyes. "I've been meaning to ask, but the time never seemed right. And it seems a bit strange now that we've seen each other every day for the last three. But, you're not dating anyone else, are you?" He prayed she'd say no. "I mean, I would have thought you'd already be spoken for." He braced himself for an answer he didn't want to hear.

"No." She smiled. "Since I settled here, I've been asked out a few times. But rock concerts, lounges, and wild parties are not my idea of a pleasant evening. Thanks to Sam and her pre-arranged bail-out calls, I managed to skip out on dates without too much trouble. Guess word got around that I'm one of those *Christians*." She chortled.

"Sam says most of the doctors at work are dweebs, except for Dr. McLeod. He's always been too intense for my taste, even if he were free. And Dr. Smith's okay, apart from when he's losing his mind, as he puts it." She laughed. "His words, not mine. But neither of them ever asked me out, and now Dr. McLeod is engaged." She winced.

Nick nodded and exhaled his relief. But would she have preferred

Jacob's company to his? Was that a flinch? "If that reaction was because you thought my feelings are hurt, don't worry. Remember, I realized I wasn't in love with Kathy. She and Jacob were meant for one another as far as I'm concerned."

"I did wonder if it upset you. You were so distraught when she was brought into the ER." Lynne glanced through the window to where the shrimp boats were heading out for the evening.

The waiter arrived and placed an appetizer plate of lobster fingers with butter sauce in the middle of the table. Nick asked the blessing. When he finished praying, he pushed the platter toward her. "Help yourself. A couple of my friends said the food here at The Yacht is the best in town."

Lynne tasted a lobster finger and closed her eyes. "This is fabulous."

Nick tried the lobster. "This is good. By the way, Kathy told me how good Jacob, Dr. McLeod, has been with the children who have had hospital stays. She said he's a modern-day Pied Piper."

A pained expression flickered across Lynne's face and disappeared in an instant. What was that all about? What had he done? "Lynne. Did I say something I shouldn't have?"

"No. Of course not."

"But you sure had a strange look on your face when I mentioned Jacob."

"Oh, that." She waved her hand as if erasing a chalkboard. "I bit my tongue."

Did she? Had she and Jacob been together before he proposed to Kathy? No. Couldn't be. She said they hadn't dated. *Change the subject.*

"Next time you talk to your mother, I hope you'll tell her about the gallant gentleman who saved your life twice in less than four days." He bounced his eyebrows.

"I've already told her about you." Lynne's lips curved into a mischievous smile. "She called me Sunday night and asked why I hadn't phoned her over the weekend as usual. I had to fess up. But if you think I'll tell my fretful mother I almost stepped off a pier to swim with oversized fish, you've got another think coming, Sir Galahad."

He snickered. "So, what did you tell her?" He'd love to have been a third party to their conversation.

Lynne dropped her gaze and blushed. "Wouldn't you like to know?" She took another bite of lobster.

By the time they'd finished dinner, the sun had set in an array of purple, red, and coral hues. The two strolled to the end of the parking lot. Lynne gazed out across the bay at the twinkling lights on fishing boats. Gorgeous. "This is a perfect evening, Nick. Could we venture to the water?" Anything to extend the evening.

"I'd love to, but why don't we drive out to the beach and walk along the Gulf. It'll be a lot quieter there."

"That's a great idea."

"It's settled then." He guided her back to the truck, and they headed for Pensacola Beach.

Nick parked the vehicle in a lot on the Gulf side of Santa Rosa Sound near a sign that read Gulf Islands National Seashore. He removed his shoes and tossed them behind the driver's seat. His socks followed close behind.

He hustled out of the truck while Lynne slipped off her sandals and tucked her clutch bag beneath the seat. After opening the passenger door, he held out his hand to her.

They stepped onto a sandy path that led to the Gulf. As she held onto Nick's arm, she glanced around both sides of the mounds. Sea oats rustled and waved in the breeze. "This is so picturesque. Wish I'd brought my camera."

"There'll be plenty of chances to take pictures." He grinned. "I'll make sure of it."

When they'd crossed the dunes to the beach, Nick straightened his arm and took her hand. "With the tide coming in, this stretch of sand has diminished from our last walk." They shuffled through several yards of soft dry sand up to the edge of the water and watched the iridescent silver-topped breakers.

Lynne danced into a retreating wave and lifted the skirt of her dress just enough to keep it from getting wet. "The surf seems stronger than it was the other day."

Nick rolled up his pant legs, joined her on the wet sand, and slipped his arm around her shoulders. "Probably because of the storm passing by Puerto Rico right now. It's a big one and affects our weather. But according to the weatherman, we don't have to worry. At least not yet. Shall we walk along the shore a ways?" He removed his arm from her shoulder and reclaimed her hand.

In between the scudding clouds, the moon peeked at them from an indigo sky and then disappeared for a moment before making an encore appearance. They laughed and splashed along the beachfront, then listened to waves as they curled and dashed onto shore.

A few steps later, Lynne's right foot slid down a depression in the sand. "Whoa!"

Nick caught her before she fell into the pool of swirling water that had dragged the sand out and formed a sharp, cliff-like ledge. He pulled her away. "Girl, how many times do I have to save you tonight?" He laughed as she clung to his arms.

Lynne caught her breath and then doubled over with laughter. "Hope you're not keeping track. I'll owe you my life before long." She wouldn't mind that at all. And he'd do a terrific job of taking care of her, no doubt.

They resumed their walk with Nick's arm around her waist.

"Lynne, how did you take to college life in Chicago?"

Oh no. Why did this have to come up now? She paused. Tears rushed into her eyes. "I'm sorry, Nick. Something happened. The memory keeps coming up every time someone mentions college. It's—"

"Let's go back to the truck."

Her tears flowed as they made their way across the sand dunes and parking lot. He opened the passenger door and helped her into the seat. Then he tilted his head and gazed at her. "Lynne, please tell me what's wrong."

She grabbed her shawl from the back seat and sobbed into it.

After he jumped into the driver's seat, Nick took her hand in his. "Let's pray."

"Please. I thought I was past this crying but—"

"It's okay." He bowed his head. "Dear Lord, thank You for the beautiful evening You gave us. But now we need Your help. Please take away Lynne's sorrow. Help her find peace."

The sincerity and concern in his voice captured her heart. Her sobs quieted.

"Lord, if there's anything I can do to help her, please show me. If she needs to talk, please give her the words. In Christ's name, Amen."

Lynne searched Nick's eyes. She could trust him. She had to tell him. He'd help her. "I want to tell you, but I'm afraid for you."

Nick held both her hands. He'd be patient and wait for her to begin.

Lynne took in a deep breath and focused on his eyes. "I'm not sure where to start."

"Whatever it is, you can tell me. Start anywhere."

She shook her head. "I saw a murder. And this evening, I thought I saw the man responsible outside the restaurant."

"A murder? While you attended college in Chicago?"

Lynne nodded in jerky movements. He squeezed her hands.

"One of my professors, Dr. Lindstrom." Her gaze switched from his face to the darkness outside, back again, and once more to the window. She shivered. "Can we go somewhere…where it's not so dark and secluded?"

She was scared. Nick let go of her hands and started the engine. He pulled out of the parking place and headed back to Pensacola.

As they left the island behind, Lynne's sniffling stopped. Nick glanced at her and then back to the road. *Lord, please don't let there be a traffic tie-up.*

"It happened the year before I graduated. I needed a question answered for the upcoming finals, so I visited the professor's office."

Nick reached out his right hand and grasped hers. A block later, he pulled into a fast-food parking lot. He turned off the engine. "Is this okay? Enough light?"

She nodded.

"Go ahead." He turned sideways to face her and took both hands in his. They were like ice. Her eyes sparkled with unshed tears. "You went to the professor's office. Then what?"

Lynne tightened her grip on his hands and squeezed her eyes shut. "He told me someone was meeting him, and I should come back the next morning. I figured his appointment might not take too long, and then I could get my question answered, so I waited in the next hall and read. That's when I heard someone enter the hall where his office was located."

Her face contorted as she finished telling him why she peeked into the doctor's office, the gruesome details of the murder, and her narrow escape.

"Lynne, I'm so sorry. What an ordeal." He let go of one hand and wiped a tear from her cheek with his fingers. "You're shaking. Let's have some coffee. This place is open through the night." He made a visual sweep of the empty parking lot. "And right now, no customers."

"Coffee sounds good."

Nick got out and hurried to open her door. They stepped inside the burger-joint, and he ordered coffee. "Do you want anything else?"

"Are you kidding? I ate so much I'll still be stuffed by breakfast."

When she smiled, his heart swelled. Even with a burden, her spirit soared. What a girl. "Coffee will be enough for me too. Why don't you grab a table over there?" He motioned toward an empty area with no windows on the side of the building.

Nick paid for the coffee, then found Lynne in a booth at the back of the secluded section. He dropped down beside her and placed a steaming cup of brew in front of her.

"Black. You remembered from the restaurant." A soft giggle came from her lips.

"Black, strong, and fresh. I learned to like it that way in college. It always turned cold by the time I drank it. We only had powdered creamer, and you can't get that stuff to dissolve no matter how much you stir when you try for a warm-up."

A big grin spread across Lynne's face. "I learned in the Navy."

"I'm glad you're smiling again. Do you want to pass on the rest of your story for tonight?"

She gazed into the black liquid. "No. Now that I've told you the first part, I feel better." She looked into his eyes. "I could use your prayers, and I'm sure you have a good connection with the Father."

"Thanks, but I'm sure you do too. Okay. Let's hear the rest. The burden is always easier when two share the load."

"I like that. Thanks, Nick." She reached over and placed her hand on top of his as he held the cup.

He let go of the cup and took her hand. Lynne told the rest of the story through the trial and her departure for her tour of duty in Afghanistan.

Lord, she's had such a hard time of it these past few years. Help me be there for her in any way I can. Not just because of my desire to spend time with her.

When she stopped to sip her coffee, Nick picked up her free hand and kissed the back of it. "You've really been through it. But what about that guy you said you saw tonight?"

"We were on the ramp to the restaurant when I saw this really large man run into a boat docked near shore. He appeared to be the same build as the guy I saw on the street the night of Dr. Lindstrom's murder. The detectives knew him as The Piper. Mine was the first real description of him they'd had. When I saw that man tonight, icicles shot through my heart. But then you said the fishermen took their shrimp boats out at night, so it must have been my imagination."

"Right, probably was." Or had he found her? *Lord, I hope it was only a fisherman.*

Chapter Nineteen

Returning from lunch on Tuesday, Lynne stepped off the 4-North elevator to find Sam in conversation with their neighbor friend, Escambia County Deputy, Teri Coleraine. "Teri, what brings you here? Is everything okay at our apartment complex?"

The female officer with reddish-gold hair smiled and opened her mouth, but Sam spoke first. "She's not here for a social call. *Deputy Coleraine* is here to talk to those kids admitted yesterday."

"I have questions for them, Lynne. And one of you will have to accompany me since my partner is out today." She glanced from Lynne to Sam.

Lynne held up her hand. "I'll go. Let me call someone to cover the desk while Sam takes her lunch break." She reached for the receiver. "This'll only take a minute."

Teri nodded.

"It's okay, Lynne. I'll stay 'til you get back. You go with Teri." Sam covered Lynne's hand and pushed the receiver back into the cradle.

"No. You take your lunch break. You've been running since we arrived this morning."

Sam grimaced. "Once a sergeant, always a sergeant." She muttered, giggled, and lifted her purse out of a desk drawer.

"Lieutenant JG, if you please." Lynne laughed and picked up the receiver. "And you know there are no sergeants in the Navy, Smarty."

Teri snickered. "You two never stop, do you?"

After a gentle push from Lynne, Sam rounded the end of the counter. Lynne pressed the number for 4-West. Stephanie answered right away.

"Hey, Steph." "Can you spare someone from your station for…hold on." She raised her brows at Teri. "How long do you think you'll need?"

"I'll have to speak to all four. Might only take half an hour if they cooperate."

Lynne gave her a thumbs-up. "I have to be away from the desk for half an hour at least. A sheriff's deputy is here to interview patients on our floor, and Sam just left on her lunch break."

"Sure. Things are quiet here on our wing. Melissa's been nursing a cup of coffee forever, and we're caught up with our work. I'll be right there."

"That's great. I owe you guys." Lynne hung up and turned to Teri. "She'll be right here. No partner with you today, huh?"

"No. We're shorthanded at the station. Some kind of virus running through the ranks."

"So what's going on with these kids? Why is this overdose incident getting so much attention?"

"Can't tell you too much. Ongoing investigation. But the detectives found powder traces from something new when they checked the rave site." Teri sighed. "We had the powder analyzed. It has us worried. We need to find out from these kids where they got it. Possibly get a lead on the suppliers."

Lynne's heart ached. Such troubled kids. And from her experience yesterday with a couple of them on their floor, not cooperative. "Hope you get to the bottom of it."

"We all do. According to the lab, this stuff makes the victim languid and passive so they'll submit to anything. The kids have no idea what they're doing, though fully conscious. Really bad stuff."

"Worse than Rohypnol or Ketamine?" Lynne's brows knit.

Teri nodded. "More hypnotic. Much more. Absorbed by the metabolism so fast it's hard to detect."

Stephanie Madden came around the corner. "Here I am."

"Steph, this is Deputy Coleraine."

Teri extended her right hand to Steph. "Nice to meet you."

Lynne grabbed the patients' charts. "Page me if you need to."

As she and Teri started down the hall, Teri checked her notepad. "The first on my list is Jesse Kovacs. I've dealt with him before in Juvie Hall. Somewhat belligerent. Has he given you any trouble?"

"No, but he's been too sick since he came in. And I've *dealt* with him before too, in a way. Wasn't very polite on the day we *bumped* into each other at the boardwalk." Lynne's lips curled into a smile. She still hadn't thanked him for pushing her into Nick's arms. Maybe before his discharge.

"Jesse's not a bad kid. It's only recently that he's gotten in trouble with the law…since he turned fifteen. Has a hard home life. He lives with his mother who's a chronic alcoholic, and his little sister lives with the dad and step-mother."

As they peered into Jesse's room, the freckle-faced youth ignored them, his skin pale, as though he hadn't seen the sun for a long time. Short, bristly dark hair, pulled into spikes on top of his head and flattened on each side from lying in bed, resembled a porcupine with a Mohawk. Next to his bed, several bags of fluids hung from softly humming pumps, the tubing gathered together at an IV in his arm.

When they entered the room, Teri stood just inside the door while Lynne checked over the instruments that monitored the teen's condition. "How do you feel, Jesse?"

The boy said nothing, and his lackluster eyes didn't move. But when Teri stepped closer, he narrowed them. "Who's she?"

"Hello, Jess." Teri's voice brightened. "I'm Deputy Coleraine. I need to ask you some questions about that rave party." She pulled a chair next to the bed, seated herself, and removed her dark green sheriff's ball cap, placing it on her knee.

Jesse sneered. "I've got nothin' to say."

"Well, I've got plenty to say to you, Mr. Kovacs. You're facing time for possession with intent to sell if you don't cooperate. If you help us, we can help you."

The boy turned away and frowned at Lynne. "Where's my ma? I wanna go home." He kicked off the sheet and swung his legs over the side of the bed.

Lynne darted to his side and pressed on his shoulder to make him lie back on the pillow. She checked his tubing. "Hold still, young man. Let me make sure you haven't done any damage."

The teen dropped his gaze to his hands on top of the sheet Lynne threw back over him. She checked his pulse. Good thing he hadn't pulled anything loose. She shook her head. "You can't leave until Dr. Smith says you can." Lynne turned away from the bedside.

"Who are you, the drill sergeant?" Jesse scowled at her and crossed his arms over his heaving chest.

Lynne spun and gave him a stern expression. *Again with the sergeant.* She nodded at Teri.

She returned the nod. "We contacted your mother. You may as well give yourself a break by answering my questions."

"What do ya wanna know?"

Lynne kept watch on Jesse while Teri placed her ball cap on the vacant chair beside her and pulled a small black notebook and pen from her shirt pocket. "Tell me who was dealing that night."

"I don't know. A lotta guys. I couldn't see who they were. It was dark."

Teri leaned forward, tapping the notebook on her knee. "Jesse, you have a five-year-old sister. Name of Amber. Lives with your dad and step-mother, right?" Teri's gaze shot to Lynne and then back to the boy who glared at the deputy. "Do you want her to wind up in here, with a bunch of tubes sticking out of her? Or worse? Laid out in the morgue? If you keep up what you're doing, she'll follow. You're her big brother. If we don't get these dealers off the streets, they'll find her even if she doesn't follow what you do."

His eyes widened. "No!"

Lynne jumped at his response. Despite his recklessness, Jesse obviously loved his little sister. But would he cooperate to protect her? She hoped so. He pushed his legs to the edge of the bed again. Lynne eased him back onto the pillow, but he continued to push against her hand.

"Look, Jesse. If you don't calm down, I'll put restraints on you. Dr. Smith will order it." Hopefully, that would make him stay still. "The best way to make sure this doesn't happen to your sister is to answer Deputy Coleraine's questions."

He stopped struggling, and tears sprang to his eyes.

Teri poised her pen. "Names, Jesse. Give me names."

The teenager mumbled the names of several dealers he knew, and Teri wrote them down. She glanced at Lynne. "No surprise. Usual suspects." She turned back to him. "But they're not the guys who gave you this, are they?" From her shirt pocket, she retrieved a packet three-quarters full of white crystals and held it up to him.

Jesse gaped at the bag as if the tiny parcel drew him like a sorcerer.

"Who gave you this?" Teri demanded.

The spell broke. "I...I don't know anything about that." He squirmed in the bed.

"That's funny. The paramedics said it dropped from your pocket at the scene. They turned it over to us." She leaned closer. "Now, who gave it to you?"

"I don't know."

Teri sighed and replaced the envelope in her pocket. "This isn't simple angel dust. It's seriously high octane. The reason you're here and nearly put you on a slab. So again, I'll ask you. Who gave it to you?"

"I told you I don't *know*. Just some guy. Never saw 'im before. Some Yankee maybe, by the sound of 'im."

Lynne stared at Jesse. Tears welled in his eyes. *He's scared.*

Teri tapped the notebook with her pen. "I think you can tell me more. What'd he look like?"

As Jesse shook, he shrugged his thin shoulders. "He was a big guy. Hulkin' big. His arms and shoulders like a gorilla. Those big hands of his could snap you in two." The tears fell. Jesse's lips and chin trembled.

A chill rushed up Lynne's spine.

Teri kept prompting him for information. "Go on, Jess. It's okay. You're safe now. We'll protect you."

"He had a big, wide face, with a thick jaw. Short beard, mustache, black hair…no…yeah, or really dark brown. And cut short."

"Is that it, Jesse?"

"Yeah."

"That's good. But how was he dressed?"

"Like us. T-shirt, jeans, gym shoes."

"What did he say to you? Did you hear anyone call him by name?"

Lynne stepped forward to adjust his pillow. The hair on her neck bristled. It had to be The Piper. The chill in her spine skittered down her arms.

Jesse's brows furrowed. "That's the weird part. The guy said he was doin' market research. He said if I wanted any more of that stuff he gave me to ask for Hamelin. He was weird."

Lynne spun away from Jesse and crashed into the bed table. The plastic water pitcher and cup flew onto the floor. Teri rounded the end of the bed, helped her pick them up, and placed everything back on the table. Lynne bolted to the bathroom for a towel and mopped up the water and ice.

"Lynne, are you okay? Sit down."

"I'm okay. I'll be okay."

After giving her a keen look, Teri returned to the chair at the side of the bed. "Okay, Jesse. You were saying."

"I'm not positive that's the name I heard. His voice was so low. The whole time he had this weird grin like he was half-crazy. Gave me the creeps. The rest of the teens said the same thing."

Teri rose from the chair. "Thank you for cooperating, Jesse. Officer Delaney, our sketch artist, will stop by to draw a picture of this Hamelin character from your description." Teri placed her cap on her head. "In the meantime, get some rest and listen to the nurses and doctor."

Lynne's stomach did cartwheels as she replaced the tray, water pitcher, and cup, then followed Teri to the door.

As they walked back to the nursing station, Teri glanced at Lynne. "You doing okay?"

"Yeah. No. Actually, no." Lynne bit her lip.

Teri laid her hand on Lynne's arm. "I thought you were going to faint when Jesse mentioned Hamelin."

They neared the nursing station. Lynne whispered, "I have an idea who he is. His description. The name Hamelin fits. The Chicago detectives said they knew him as The Piper."

"Who? What detectives?"

When they arrived at the nursing station, it was empty. "Steph must be with a patient. We can sit here until she gets back. I wouldn't want her to overhear what I have to say."

With a nod, Teri sat at the desk. "Go ahead. Then we'll talk to the other teens on your floor."

Lynne took a seat next to Teri and explained what had happened at the Chicago campus and the following trial. Just as she finished, Stephanie returned, and Sam stepped off the elevator.

"Thanks for covering for us, Steph. If you need a favor, call."

She waved and headed back to 4-West. "Anytime."

As Sam dropped her purse in the desk drawer, Teri joined Lynne on the other side of the counter. "I guess we'd better finish the interviews, even though you've identified the scumbag."

Sam lowered her brows. "What's going on now?"

"I'll tell you after Teri's done." Lynne followed the deputy.

They strode through the hall to the next teenager's room. "Teri, will I have to make a statement, even though the Chicago police have mine and the information from the trial?"

Teri shook her head. "We'll contact Chicago."

As they drew near the next room, Lynne slowed her steps and stopped. "Jesse said Hamelin told him he was doing market research. Does that mean he's using kids as guinea pigs?"

"That may be only part of it. Morning cleanup crews or dog walkers find kids collapsed at a scene or still wandering around stoned out of their mind long after the party's over. But sometimes, the kids and the dealers disappear without a trace. We do what we can to find out where these raves are happening ahead of time, but it's hard. They keep them secret. Still, it's about all we can do. For now."

They entered the next teen's room, and while Teri interviewed the girl, Lynne checked her. What if she ran into that monster before the authorities caught up with him? Her pulse raced. How could this be happening?

Chapter Twenty

Wednesday morning, Lynne led the petite Escambia County Sheriff's Office sketch artist, Officer Caitlyn Delaney, to Jesse Kovacs' room. As the dark-haired, hazel-eyed officer stepped in, his mouth dropped open. Lynne stifled a laugh. This officer didn't appear any older than the boy. *He's smitten.*

While Jesse ogled her, Cat completed a drawing from his description. He verified the image as the man who called himself Hamelin at the rave.

When the officer held up the picture for Lynne to see, her blood ran cold. "That's him." Lynne's saliva dried as though her teeth were made of cotton. "He's grown a beard and mustache, and darkened his hair color, but it's him. The Piper. I'm sure."

"Okay. Thank you, both."

As they left Jesse's room, Cat turned to Lynne. "If you'll accompany me, I'll take this to the other teens for their confirmation. Back at the station, I'll run the sketch through the national database and contact the Chicago Police Department and Feds."

Lynne sighed. Would the drawing do any more good than her

description had five years ago? *And now he's here...right here in Pensacola. God help us.*

An hour before their shift was over, the desk phone rang. "Four-north, Lynne Temple speaking."

"Hi, it's Tracy. I've got a problem, and I'm hoping you can help me. My husband's been running a high temperature. He's really sick. I called his GP who wants to see him first thing in the morning, but I don't want to leave him alone tonight. He's been throwing up something horrible, so I won't make my eleven to seven shift. Could you cover for me? Oh...excuse me. He's calling for me. Be right back."

Great. As if her day hadn't been bad enough. But this might work out. She probably wouldn't hear from Nick tonight anyway with him out of town as a guest preacher in Gulfport. And Sam had a date, leaving *poor Lynne* all alone in an empty apartment to dwell on The Piper.

"I'm back, Lynne. So, can you cover?"

"No problem, Tracy. I'll be happy to take your shift. Doubles are my specialty." She pretended to laugh. "I'll rest when I get home this afternoon. It's been quiet on the floor today, except for Sam's jabbering. I'm sure it will be tonight too. Take care of your husband."

"Lynne, you're a lifesaver. Thanks."

As Lynne hung up, Sam zipped around the corner. "My what? Jabbering, you say?"

"You have the ears of a...I have no idea, but you've got them." Lynne rose and wrinkled her nose at Sam. "That was Tracy on the phone. She can't make her shift, so I'll pull a double from eleven tonight to three tomorrow afternoon. I'll go to bed as soon as I get to the apartment."

"You're *too* good, Lynnz. That's why people love you. But it's also why everyone counts on you to cover for them."

Sam checked supplies for the next shift, then sat next to Lynne at the desk. "Tell you what. You have to eat before you crash tonight. Why don't we stop for fast-food on the way home, so we don't have to take time to make dinner? We'll use the drive-through and be home in no time."

"Now you're talking. How about some of those chicken sandwiches and fries?" Lynne patted Sam's arm. "We have salad fixing's in the fridge from the other night."

With her fists on her hips, Sam narrowed her eyes at Lynne. "Will you never learn to talk like a southern girl? Fixins, girl, *fixins.*" She burst into laughter.

Lynne shook her head. She'd have to keep her mind on Sam. That way she'd laugh her way through the first half of the double, and Sam would keep her awake for their regular shift with her banter.

Lips pulled to one side, Sam sighed. "Not too sure I'm interested in this guy I'm going out with tonight. He was nice enough when I met him at church, but he said he's taking me to a car race, of all things. Not my kind of first date."

"Hey, it could be worse. At least it's not a bar or some of the other places dates have taken me." Such as the noisy lounge. One of her first dates in Pensacola.

Her thoughts traveled to the rave parties and the four teens who came so near death over the weekend. How many more would The Piper victimize before they found him?

After her three a.m. break, Lynne returned to the nursing station.

Lauren Greer, Tracy's shift coworker, smiled. "Be back in a few minutes. I need a restroom break." She headed for the ladies' room.

As she yawned, Lynne stretched her arms into the air, then dropped into the desk chair. What a quiet night. She'd never get used to this.

With his head down almost to the edge of the laundry bin in front of him, a burly, blond-haired Environmental Services employee ambled past the nursing station. A creepy vibe snaked through Lynne, and she frowned. The graveyard shift. Not only because of the quiet but any noise or movement spooked a body. She shook her head as she focused back on the historical romance she'd brought to help keep her awake.

Lauren strolled to the station and eased herself into the chair next to Lynne. "Odd to have someone from ES walking the halls at this hour. Where was he going?"

"I thought they were around all the time, even in the wee hours of the morning. Yesterday, ES cleaned up one of the rooms under renovation. Maybe he left something and went back for it." She shrugged.

Lynne reached for her coffee. "Lauren, I know you love working at this hour, but I'm so glad we're near the end of the shift. It's too quiet. I'll never want to work these hours on a regular basis."

"Is there any wonder they call it the graveyard shift?" Lauren winked one of her deep brown eyes and giggled. She yawned and leaned back in the chair. "Some nights, it's quiet as a tomb in here." She stretched her tanned arms and flexed her fingers as if trying to awaken them, then flipped Lynne's book to view the title. "Gives you plenty of time to read." She giggled again.

A quick glance at her watch told Lynne it was time for rounds. "Do you want to take the next tour of rooms, or shall I?"

"I'll go." Lauren pushed a stray lock of her fluffy black hair off her forehead and reached for a patient's clipboard. "Back in a few."

Couldn't have asked for better coworkers than Lauren or Sam. Or any of the other nurses on four-north for that matter. Even shorthanded as their floor had been on all three shifts, the hospital was still a fantastic place to work.

She picked up her novel and ventured back into the story. After only one chapter, a patient's monitor alarm sounded.

Beep, beep, beep

"Jesse's room?" Lynne jumped out of the chair. What had gone wrong? Lynne grabbed the phone and pressed the intercom. "*Code blue, code blue, code blue. Four-north, room four-six-five.*"

She sprinted through the hall as the alarm continued to relay its message through the corridors.

A fast-moving shadow rounded the far corner of the hall as Lynne neared the boy's door. She burst in. *Comatose.* She inspected the readouts. *He's flatlining. But why?*

Lynne reached for the CPR kit on the wall as she lowered the head of the bed and removed Jesse's pillow with her other hand. The kit was missing. Her heart raced. No time to lose. She tilted his head back and gave him two deep breaths and then checked for a pulse. None. She began hard and fast chest compressions. *God, please let them get here in time.* That CPR kit had been there earlier.

From the hallway, the sound of a crash cart rushed over the tiled floor. A second later, the team burst into the room. Lynne stepped away.

As the efficient team worked, she spotted a red mark on Jesse's arm. What caused that? Her brows knit.

With pinched lips, a male nurse from the team grabbed a mask from the cart and placed it over Jesse's face. He glanced at Lynne, who shook her head. "The mask over his bed was missing when I came in."

Dr. Kenner whipped his head around to look at her.

"We may have had an intruder, Doctor. I saw someone duck around the corner into the east wing as I arrived."

When the readouts showed a consistent heartbeat, Dr. Kenner stepped up to Lynne. "That was a close one. We'll have him transferred to ICU until we know he's stable." The rest of the team rolled the cart out of the room. One nurse sat next to Jesse's bed.

"Dr. Kenner? Check that spot on the inside of the boy's left arm. What caused it?"

The doctor lifted the sheet and checked the boy's arm. "I don't like this. We'd better get a blood sample. Looks like he may have been injected with something."

He straightened his long, lanky frame and fixed his eyes on Lynne. "You performed manual CPR?" The doctor wrinkled his forehead as he gazed at her.

Lynne nodded. "What could I do? I wasn't going to let him die if I could prevent it."

Dr. Kenner took a breath and blew it out slowly. "I'll contact security. They can handle calling the authorities."

The two of them left the room and headed for the nursing station.

When Lynne reached the desk, Lauren's mouth gaped. "I'll explain everything in a minute. First, I need to run to the supply room for a CPR kit." She handed Jesse's chart to Dr. Kenner and headed for the elevator.

As the elevator descended, Lynne pulled her cell from the side pocket of her scrubs and hit the button to call Nick. She'd probably wake him, but she needed to hear his calming voice. It rang a few times and went to voicemail. He'd have turned it off for the service. Probably forgot to turn it back on.

The shadowy figure came to mind. Hairs on Lynne's neck rose. That person was the same build as The Piper. Her heart thumped as the elevator jolted to a stop, and the doors opened. *Hope I'm wrong.*

When Lynne arrived at the station with the replacement equipment, the floor was quiet again. She held up the CPR kit. "Let me secure this in Jesse's room, and then I'll fill you in. Everything okay here?"

Lauren's questioning eyes stared at her. "Fine. A couple of patients woke up and asked what was going on. I got them settled. Told them it was a false alarm."

"That's what I'd have done." Lynne smiled. "No sense upsetting them. Back in a sec." She hastened to Jesse's room and replaced the unit on the wall behind the ER nurse.

Lynne returned to the station just as Dr. Kenner stepped off the elevator. "I was on my way to the cafeteria and thought I'd let you know the sheriff's office will send someone over. Thought you'd have changed shifts by now. Didn't check the time."

"Thanks, Doctor. Sam should be here to relieve Lauren in half an hour. I'm pulling a double."

He nodded, hurried to the elevator, and pressed the button.

Lynne took a seat as the doctor entered the car and the doors closed.

Lauren's dark brown eyes widened. "What happened tonight? Is the Kovacs boy okay? Why's the sheriff's office sending someone over?"

"Precaution." Lynne took a deep breath. Easy for her to tell someone else. What about her own nerves? "I'm not sure what happened, but something suspicious is going on here tonight. An intruder may have caused Jesse Kovacs' cardiac arrest. I'm sure the authorities will investigate." But she'd bet it was Hamelin.

Lynne took another deep breath. Was her mind playing games again? Maybe it had nothing to do with him. But that'd be a big maybe. She'd have to tell whoever the sheriff's department sent over about that ES employee.

Half an hour later, Sam relieved Lauren. "Lynnz, what's going on? Lauren looked as if she'd seen a ghost, and you're beyond worn out. Graveyard's supposed to be a nice quiet shift. Wasn't it?"

Lynne rolled her eyes. "You won't believe what we've been through this morning."

As Sam stowed her purse in the desk drawer, Lynne filled her in on the events of the morning. "I've aged ten years in the last three hours."

"Are you saying this Hamelin somehow found out Jesse was here and tried to kill him?" Sam's jaw dropped. "He thinks Jesse will identify him, not knowing he's already done that. Oh, brother."

"Wouldn't surprise me. But it's pure speculation on my part."

The elevator whirred to a stop. A security guard stepped off the car and approached the nursing station. "They sent me to guard a patient's room." He handed Lynne a note.

Sam read over her shoulder, then raised her hands palms up. "I thought you said the sheriff's office was sending someone over."

"That's what I thought. I should call them. Seems to me they'd want one of their own men on duty." She turned to the guard. "No offense to you."

His monotone voice replied, "None taken."

She rubbed her forehead. "Teri had told us they're as shorthanded as we are...remember?"

Sam nodded and rounded the station counter. "Come on. I'll take you to the room." The middle-aged man followed Sam into the hall.

Minutes later, Sam returned. "Well, he sure was thrilled to be here."

Another uniformed security guard got off the elevator and walked up to the desk holding a CPR mask wrapped in plastic. "I found this in an empty laundry cart right by an emergency exit. After last night's incident, my supervisor thought we should hand it over to a deputy." He searched the nursing station area. "Are they here yet?"

Sam took the bag and placed it on the shelf behind her. "No. We'll hold it for them."

The guard nodded and strode back to the elevator.

Lynne picked up the phone and dialed the sheriff's office. "Strange night." A few rings later, dispatch answered, and Lynne explained the call. "Are you sending a deputy over? We have evidence to turn in."

"We'll get an officer over there as fast as we can."

Lynne replaced the receiver. Would The Piper try again if he found out Jesse survived? Would the hospital security guard be of any help?

I wish Nick's phone wasn't turned off.

Chapter Twenty-One

Lynne set her tray on a table in the corner of the hospital cafeteria, lowered herself into the chair, and took a sip of soda, savoring the aroma from her freshly grilled cheeseburger and french fries. "I'm glad you called, Teri. I've been anxious to hear what's going on."

Deputy Coleraine sat in the chair across from her. "We're still trying to track down Hamelin. Or The Piper. Whatever he calls himself right now. We've been in touch with both the Chicago PD and the Feds. He's dabbling in more than drugs. They're pretty sure he's involved in several murders from Chicago to Florida, but can't catch up with him. He's a sly one, and into worse things now."

"What could be more terrible than using kids as guinea pigs for his drug operation?" Lynne took another drink. "What else is he involved in?"

"Selling those same kids to the highest bidder." Teri's eyes narrowed, and a flinty appearance covered her face with her lips flattened, nostrils flared.

"Child trafficking?" Lynne ground her teeth. *Slimeball!*

"He might be filling orders for gangs both stateside and overseas.

That's the theory, anyway." Teri took a bite of her hamburger, chewed, and swallowed. "A lot of money changes hands in these deals. If Hamelin's involved, it's not surprising he'd want to eliminate potential witnesses like Jesse, and the others."

Lynne bit into her burger.

"Everyone wants this guy nailed. I talked to your friends, Agents Trent and Travis. They'll be in Florida soon to help us. Not sure how much of this I should tell you, but I want you to be on guard. We still don't know if he's aware that you're here in Pensacola."

A chill ran through Lynne. Pensacola had been a paradise to her since her discharge. Especially now that she'd met and fallen in love with Nick. *Why, Lord? Why did You allow the fiend to come here?* Her appetite had vanished. She rewrapped her cheeseburger, stuffed it and the fries back in the bag, and leaned back in the seat.

In the four years since she'd seen them, Kim and Loring still had not become a couple, according to Kim's last email. "You said Loring and Kim are coming to Pensacola?"

Teri nodded as she swallowed a mouthful of french fries. "Their boss assigned them to the case since they have prior experience with him from their time in the Chicago Police Department. Well, as much experience as anyone can have with such an elusive character."

Lynne smiled. "Kim and I keep in touch as often as we can. She told me Loring had left the police department to join the FBI. And not long after, Kim got a job with them. But I didn't know they were working together." Why hadn't she said anything?

"He's a smart operator, this Hamelin guy. Agent Trent said he might have an inside man in the legal system who has enabled him to avoid capture. There's a big investigation going on in all departments now." She sipped her sweet tea.

"Do you think there's a security leak here at the hospital?" Lynne sipped her soda. "Someone who gave out the names of the kids who were admitted?"

"Possibly. Wouldn't surprise me if he has someone planted here. All the more reason to get Jesse and the other kids who identified Hamelin into witness protection." Teri chewed her lip for a moment. "We'll arrange it as soon as they're cleared to leave the hospital. Meanwhile, we'll keep them under twenty-four-hour guard."

"Glad your guys came not too long after our guard did. I wasn't too sure what was happening when hospital security showed up instead of an officer. The man sure wasn't thrilled with his assignment."

"Well, it wasn't for long. We sent over the first available officer. Our shorthanded situation has created all kinds of problems." Teri stared into Lynne's eyes. "Are you sure you don't want protection too? With you at the hospital and the possibility of Hamelin having a mole, you could be in danger."

Lynne stood and gathered her unfinished lunch. She gulped down the last of her drink and picked up her tray. "I'll be okay, Teri. God's watching over me. Besides, you have deputies on duty now." And with her and Sam praying every chance they got, she'd be okay. *Right, Lord?*

When Lynne returned to her station, she drew close to Sam behind the counter. After a glance around to see if anyone was within earshot, Lynne spoke in a hushed voice. "Since we work together, I thought you should know it may have been The Piper I saw the other night dressed as an ES employee."

She pulled Sam into a chair at the desk and seated herself. "I can't say much, but be on the lookout for anyone who doesn't belong.

Hospital employees. We have no control over the patients' visitors, but if anyone acts strange—"

Sam's eyes rounded as though she'd seen a scary scene in a horror movie. "You really think he'd come back?"

Lynne shrugged. "Teri told me to be careful, so I'm telling you."

"Check." Sam pulled in a deep breath. "We know pretty much everyone who works and comes through from ES during the day, the doctors, nurses, techs. Easy enough to call security and check if someone new shows up." She fiddled nervously with a pencil.

Lynne laid her hand atop Sam's and the pencil. "I didn't mean to upset you about this. Just thought it'd be a good idea for you to be aware." She rolled the chair toward a low file cabinet and extracted a supply checklist. "Speaking of watching...do you remember my mentioning Loring and Kim who worked in the Chicago Police Department when my professor was murdered?"

"Sure. What about them?"

"Kim's kept in touch with me. She told me they both switched from the police department to the FBI and are working together. Teri said their boss assigned them to investigate—" Lynne pressed her lips together. Had she said too much?

"Investigate what? The rave parties?"

"Well, in a manner of speaking. I'm not sure of all the details." Better leave it at that. "At any rate, Loring and Kim are arriving in Pensacola." One corner of Lynne's lips lifted. "Oh, drat! I forgot to ask when. Whenever they get here, it'll be nice to see them again, despite the circumstances."

"Lynnz, you should call Nick and tell him what's going on. With the two of you so close now and spending so much time together, he should be careful too."

"You're right. I've tried to reach him, but his phone's been off. He must have forgotten to turn it back on after he preached Wednesday night. I'll try again." She opened the desk drawer, grabbed her phone, and punched Nick's number. The phone rang twice.

"You've reached Nick Livingston. I'm unable to answer the call at this time, but if you leave your name, phone number, and a brief message, I'll get back to you."

"Nope, still not answering." Her number would show up in the missed calls, so no sense leaving a message. Lynne disconnected the call and glanced at Sam.

Her brows rose. "Still off?"

Lynne nodded. A gnawing in the pit of her stomach made her wince. "It rang, and I got voicemail." Why hadn't he answered? She understood having the phone off while he preached each night at the revival meetings, but why now? Sleeping maybe? She chewed her bottom lip.

Five minutes later, she called again. "Nick, it's Lynne. Please call me when you get this message."

After a busy afternoon on their floor, things quieted in the halls. The elevator doors shut behind a handful of visitors.

Lynne stretched and turned to Sam. "So far, so good. No strange happenings and no suspicious people walking the halls."

A patient call glowed and buzzed. As Sam rose to answer it, she pulled her lips to one side. "You were saying about it being quiet? This week's been something." She rounded the end of the counter. "Almost like a mystery movie without the popcorn." She took off down the corridor.

Lynne drained the last of her cold coffee, dropped the empty cup into the wastebasket, and glowered at the phone on the desk, willing it to ring. She needed to hear Nick's voice.

A few minutes later, Sam returned from the patient's room. "The little angel only wanted a drink and couldn't reach the water carafe. Bless her heart." She rolled her eyes. "When I gave her *the look*, she said, 'Isn't this what you get paid for?' With a saint's forbearance, I ignored the comment and gave her the water." Sam grimaced and turned her head slightly. She looked at Lynne out of the corners of her eyes.

After slipping into the small kitchen behind the nursing station, Sam came back with two steaming cups of coffee. She handed one to Lynne and reclaimed her seat.

"Thanks, Sam."

Lynne nodded, reached for her cup, and took a sip. She gazed out the floor-to-ceiling windows in front of the nursing station. Clouds gathered and flew by the fourth floor as if in a race. Would Nick get caught in the predicted storm on his way back from Mississippi?

The elevator doors opened again. Sam grinned. "Here's our relief, right on time."

The two evening shift nurses dumped their purses on the back counter. Lynne and Sam gathered their belongings, filled in the new arrivals on the patient transfers about to take place that evening, and left.

When the elevator stopped on the first floor, they exited and passed through the cafeteria to the rear parking lot. As they stepped out of the building, they spotted Teri coming up the sidewalk with a young man in uniform. Sam's eyes widened.

"Down girl." *Hmmm.* Tall and male. Sam's type. Lynne stifled a snicker.

As he drew near, his smile traveled all the way to his gray-green eyes. His short-sleeved, dark green uniform showed off muscular arms with a chest to match. Yep. Sam's type for sure.

The officers stopped in front of them. Teri smiled. "Lynne, Sam, this is Deputy Russ Highland. On your way home?"

Sam's mouth moved, but no words came out. Lynne choked back another laugh. "We are. Nice to meet you, Deputy Highland." She held out her hand, and he took it in his, but his eyes were on the short strawberry-blonde beside her.

"Please, call me Russ. Teri told me you're friends." He let go of Lynne's hand and thrust his toward Sam. She pushed her hand toward him so fast she rammed his fingers.

"Ouch!" He laughed.

Slow down, Rebel-girl. Lynne fought for control of the laughter bubbling up inside her. Had she acted so nervous when she first met Nick? *You are one smitten kitten, Sam Rease.* And she definitely made a favorable impression on Deputy Highland. "Where are you from, Russ? I didn't detect a southern accent."

"Canton, Ohio." He turned his charming beam on Lynne. "I take it you're not from here either."

"Not me. Illinois born and raised."

"Good to meet another Northerner."

Sam blinked as if she'd suddenly awakened from a dream. "What brought you to Florida?" A rosy shade of pink filled her cheeks. She glanced at Lynne and back to Russ.

His attention returned to Sam. "I was in the Ohio State Highway Patrol, but when my dad retired a few months ago, he moved here. So,

I put in for a transfer since I was the only family member still in the north."

Russ chuckled as he faced Teri. "With an A-Okay recommendation from this incumbent officer—" Russ continued to gaze at Teri. "—transferring here wasn't hard."

Sam's shoulders slumped.

He bumped Teri with his elbow. "Was it, Cousin Teri?"

She chortled. "The chief recognized a good lawman when he read your credentials. I had little to do with it."

Sam's eyes gleamed again.

Lynne had to cover her mouth to contain her laughter. *So they're related.* Rebel-girl lucked out. If her emotions had a voice, the entire hospital would hear hooting and hollering for joy. The laugh finally broke through.

Sam gave her a warning glare as if she heard Lynne's thoughts.

Still holding Sam's hand, Russ grinned and let it go. "I've seen you before. A few weeks back, you were in the visiting choir, which sang at my cousin's church."

"Oh."

Sam's cheeks glowed in a deeper hue, and Lynne's brows rose. She couldn't believe it. Sam Rease. Speechless and blushing.

"I was in uniform and stayed in the back. Sorry I didn't have time to meet you then. Had to duck out early for work."

"Like now, Russ." Teri tugged at his arm. She inclined her head toward the building.

He nodded then turned back to Sam. "Nice meeting you both."

The deputies headed for the hospital side entrance, but before he reached the door, Russ spun, walked backward, and waved. He then whirled and caught up to Teri.

Lynne bit one side of her bottom lip. She'd have fun with this. Payback time, for all Sam's teasing about Nick. "One thing's for sure, Miss Rease. Old *Depperity* Highland has given you an eleven plus on a scale from one to ten."

They strolled through the parking lot toward Sam's car without a response from her. "You'd have won an Academy Award with the shy-little-me scene you performed." Lynne burst into laughter again.

Sam giggled. "I don't know what happened to me. It was like my dumb alter-ego took control."

When they reached Sam's red Mustang, she pulled the keys from her purse. The car door chirped as the locks clicked open, and she slid into the driver's seat. Lynne slipped in on the passenger side as Sam adjusted the rearview mirror.

"You think Russ is interested in me?"

"Duh. Only as much as a starving man over a juicy steak."

A vision of Nick gazing into her eyes filled Lynne's thoughts. She sighed and ran her hand over the dashboard of the new car. Time for a change of subject. "I need to get one of these. I'm due for my own transportation." But a truck would be fun too—one like Nick's.

Why hadn't he returned her call? She hadn't heard from him in almost three whole days. Had he decided her problems were too much for him?

Chapter Twenty-Two

ate Friday night, Nick returned to his motel room after the revival. He'd better check for messages before he retired. Had it been only three days? Seemed like he'd been away from Pensacola a lot longer. At least he'd finally found his phone in the supply room at the church. Must have left it there Thursday morning before the service when he volunteered to fetch the extra hymnals.

Nick stifled a yawn. He hadn't talked to Lynne once since he left Wednesday afternoon. Sure missed her smile and wit. He should have committed her phone number to memory. Now why hadn't he thought to call the hospital? Dumb. Really dumb.

He looked through the list of missed calls for the last two days as he tossed his keys and wallet on the motel dresser and kicked off his shoes. "Uncle John. Better see what he needed." Nick listened to the message while he prepared for bed. He smiled. That was wonderful. At least he wouldn't have to handle that teens' problem when he got home. *Thank you, Uncle.* All he wanted to do was see Lynne…and then get some rest.

As he checked for more numbers, he found Lynne's. Had she left a message? Nothing. "Nuts." It would've been nice to at least hear her voice. He scrolled through a few more. "Another from Lynne? And another." Both this afternoon. But only one message.

"Nick, it's Lynne. Please call me when you get this."

She sounded worried. Late or not, he'd better phone her. Nick hit the number he'd assigned to her cell. It rang a few times, but she didn't answer. He glanced at the clock. Eleven. If she was already asleep—a knot formed in his stomach and twisted as he waited for the signal to leave his message. "Lynne. I'm sorry I missed your calls. Didn't have my phone. Long story. Get back to me when you can." He hung up.

Lord, please give Lynne peace. Remove whatever made her sound so worried. Help her have a restful sleep. And Lord, help me not worry so I can sleep before I drive home tomorrow.

He'd phone her in the morning. Nick took a quick shower and got into bed.

Eyes still wide open after an hour, he scrambled out of bed. Might as well give up on sleep for now. He paced across the room. What had prompted Lynne's stressful tone? Could it have something to do with the dark figure she'd seen on their dinner date at The Yacht? He should drive home tonight.

Nick dressed and packed his things. When he was ready to walk out the door, his eyelids grew heavy. He'd never make it back without rest. He set his travel alarm for four a.m., dropped his slacks and shirt on the bedside chair, and eased into bed. "Lord, keep Lynne safe." His eyes closed.

Bleep, bleep, bleep.

Nick turned off the alarm. After splashing cold water on his face, he grabbed his cell. What was he thinking? Too early to call. She'd still be asleep. And what if it wasn't urgent? If she had to work this Saturday, she'd need her rest. He'd wait until six. He reset the alarm and plopped his head back on the pillow.

Bleep, bleep, bleep

Nick jumped from the bed and slapped the alarm clock. "Man." Thought he set it for six, not six thirty. She'd be on her way to work now.

He grabbed his cell and phoned her. The phone rang six times and then went to voicemail. "Lynne, please don't be upset with me for not returning your calls. It's a long story. I'll save it for when I get back to town in a couple of hours. If you have time, please phone. I'll be on the road, but I can pull over." He ended the message.

Gathering his bag, Bible, and cell, Nick rushed out of the motel room door. He pitched his bag into the back of the truck, set his Bible on the passenger seat, and slid behind the steering wheel. Lynne's tone of voice in the message niggled at him. Maybe it was nothing, but he'd be a lot happier after he spoke to her.

Lynne stepped out of the shower and snagged a towel from the rack. She wrapped it around her and pulled out another to dry her hair.

Sam's voice came through the bathroom door. "Hey, Lynnz. Your phone was ringing on the coffee table. When I peeked at the screen, Nick's picture was there with his glorious smile."

"Drat. Why didn't you answer it?" Her heartbeat skipped. First time he called in almost four days, and she missed it. She yanked the bathroom door open and hurried into the bedroom. Throwing the towels over the edge of the hamper, she flipped her robe on and rushed to her phone. "Sam, you beat all."

"Well, I didn't want to assume. Besides, you can phone him back."

Lynne shook her head and punched Nick's number. As it rang, she glanced at Sam, who ate a bowl of cereal. Her feet waved back and forth on top of the coffee table, her eyes glued to the weather on TV. "Sorry, Sam. Guess I'm rattled."

She nodded as one eyebrow rose. Then giggled. "I noticed."

"Voicemail again." Lynne pulled in a deep breath and blew it out between her lips. "What's going on?" Sam shrugged and shoved a spoonful of cereal into her mouth.

Phone in hand, Lynne returned to the bedroom. He was supposed to be back today. She'd try again in a minute. *Nick, please answer.* When she laid the phone on the dresser, she saw the message icon flashing. She tapped the button to connect with voicemail and listened to the first message. Another sigh of relief escaped her. But why hadn't he answered? She listened to the second message and disconnected, setting the phone on the dresser. Would he call her back? *Wouldn't you know I'd leave my phone in the living room last night and miss his call? That was really dumb, Lynne.*

After pulling on a Chicago Bears T-shirt and worn jeans, she sat on the end of the bed to don her socks and shoes. The cell rang. Lynne lunged for it and tingled when the smile she adored appeared on the screen. "Nick. I'm so glad to hear your voice. Are you home yet?"

"Hi there, pretty lady. I'm en route. Should be home in an hour."

"No wonder you didn't answer."

"Right. Had to pull over. I hate it when people talk on their phones while they're driving."

"Yeah. Not a good idea. Too distracting. Why don't you get home and then call me?"

"Sounds like a plan. Are you at work?"

"No. Sam and I both have the weekend off for a change."

"Your voice sounded stressed when I listened to your message. Are you okay?"

"I am now. I'll tell you everything when you get home."

"Okay. Talk to you then."

Tears sprang to Lynne's eyes. He was okay. She sure had missed him. "Sam, I'm going out for a run around the apartment complex. Back in a few."

Half an hour later, Lynne freshened up and then ate from a bowl of her favorite oat cereal at the kitchen table. "The weather's still nice out there. Hasn't taken a turn for the worse despite the predictions."

Sam sat across from her. "I know. Weathermen don't know everything." She sipped on her coffee. "They said the storm has stalled."

"At least it's not a hurricane."

"Yes, Ma'am. We can be grateful for that. Bet it'll blow itself out."

Lynne finished her breakfast and brought the bowl and silverware to the sink. As she washed the bowl, her cell rang again. She glanced at the wall clock. Too early to be Nick. *Lord, please don't let it be work. I really need this day off.* She dried her hands and hurried to pick up the phone. Nick's smile greeted her from the screen.

"Nick! Thought you'd wait until you got home."

"I am home. Just pulled up, but I'm hungry. Can you join me for breakfast?"

Her pulse raced. "Just finished mine, but I'll be happy to keep you company."

"Super! Let me dump my things in the house, and I'll pick you up in say twenty minutes."

"Wonderful."

As she hung up, her heart thumped. Guess he didn't think her problems were so bad after all. She couldn't wait to see him.

Sam grinned. "Well, I'm glad he's back, so you'll calm down." She giggled. "I'm headed to my parents' for the morning. See ya later." She snatched her purse and sailed out the door.

The minutes dragged. With Sam gone, the apartment grew too quiet. And she was too antsy to read. She flipped on the TV and half paid attention to the talk show. How boring. A news segment broke into the program's regular chatter. A homicide in the downtown area overnight? Lynne's pulse raced.

Had The Piper been involved? She switched off the TV. A glance at her watch showed more than half an hour had passed since Nick's call. Where was he?

The doorbell rang, and Lynne sprang to the intercom. "Hello?"

"It's me. Sorry I'm late."

"Come on up." She pressed the buzzer. Another lungful of relieved air passed through her lips. As she waited at the open door, her pulse quieted.

Nick's smile sent butterflies loose in her stomach. "I was wondering when you'd get here."

"Sorry about that. Zack phoned just as I got in the truck. He wondered if we'd go boating with him tomorrow afternoon. Said he needed downtime on the Gulf with his friends."

"What fun."

"Let's talk it over while I eat. I'm famished."

She caught a whiff of his woodsy aftershave.

"Let's run over to the diner on Scenic Highway."

While Nick drove the few blocks toward Escambia Bay, Lynne's thoughts strayed to the events of the past few days. She pinched her lips.

"What is it, Lynne? Same thing that bothered you when you left the message on my phone?"

"Yeah. Something terrible happened at the hospital while you were away." Lynne's voice quavered.

Nick's brows knit. "Shall I pull over?"

Lynne wanted to throw herself into his arms and cry the tension out of her system. She nodded.

High over Escambia Bay on Scenic Highway, Nick pulled the truck into the parking lot at Bay Bluffs Park. They strolled to the covered observation platform and gazed out over the twenty feet drop from the wooden deck to the bay below them.

"What's going on?" He took her hand in his and led her to a wooden bench.

"There was an attempted murder at the hospital early Thursday morning while I was covering the graveyard shift."

Nick's brows lowered. "What happened? Are you okay?"

"I am, but one of those kids from the rave almost died. It was Jesse, Nick." When she explained, Nick took her into his arms.

"Nick, it might have been The Piper. Teri told me to be careful."

She leaned back and looked into his eyes bordered by curly blond lashes. He pulled her closer. While he pressed his cheek against her hair, she nestled her head on his shoulder.

"Man, Lynne. What a night. I figured there had to be a reason you were on my mind for the entire revival. Aside from your beauty, that is."

She wanted to laugh, but tears fell instead. Lynne slid her arms around his waist.

For several minutes, neither spoke. "Lynne, prayer is what we need now. Then we'll get something to eat."

They bowed their heads. "Lord, You know what's happening here. We're counting on You to keep Lynne safe and to protect those kids who've gone astray. We ask that You help the authorities find this guy and get him off the streets before more kids get hurt or worse. In Christ's name, Amen."

A heavy breath escaped Nick as he scrambled to his feet and pulled Lynne up from the bench "Now let's get something to eat before I pass out. We can discuss that boat outing of Zack's during the meal."

"Wait a minute. You didn't tell me why you didn't return my calls."

He snickered. "Oh, yeah. It was like this." He gave her the quick version of the lost cell incident as they drove to the diner.

At the Scenic Café, Nick ordered eggs, bacon, and toast. Lynne decided on a cinnamon roll with her coffee. While they waited, Nick described what Zack had in mind for a boating party. "A little fishing, swimming, and a trip past Fort Pickens. For all his introvert tendencies, Zack is great when it comes to giving the history of Pensacola to anyone who'll listen. Do you think some of your nurse friends might want to go?"

"Are you kidding? Sam for one. How many did he want us to

invite?"

"He didn't say, but I think three to five others would be fun. Can you think of a gal to pair up with Zack? He's a bit on the shy side and has dated little over the years I've known him. Zack's a loner. That's why he left the inviting to me." Nick grinned. "We've been pals for a long time."

The server placed their food in front of them, and after taking Lynne's hand in his, Nick bowed his head to pray. When he finished, he said, "Now I'm passing the *inviting* to you. I only care if we're there." He gave her one of his toothy grins.

By the time they neared her apartment after breakfast, Lynne had a good idea who she'd ask. "I'll talk to everyone this afternoon and see who's free."

"Terrific. Let me know who's coming when I pick you up for dinner tonight. I think you need a night out to relax."

Her heart danced. "Sounds good to me. What time?"

He parked the truck in front of her apartment, and they headed to the entrance. "Six okay with you? We'll make it casual tonight. Steaks or something."

After he'd seen her to her door, she listened to him running down the staircase, taking two steps at a time from the sound of it. How she'd wanted him to kiss her. But she had to be patient.

Lynne rushed to the living room window to watch him leave. When he reached the truck, he waved, hopped into the cab, and pulled away.

Before she turned from the window, a big man stepped from the shadow of a large tree a few yards back from where Nick had parked. The man slipped behind the wheel of a silver sedan and pulled away in the direction Nick had taken. Her stomach churned. "The Piper?" A flashback from the University Medical Sciences Building filled her mind.

Chapter Twenty-Three

Lynne paced her apartment. "It's him!" she screamed into the phone when Nick answered on his way home. "It's The Piper!"

"Hold on, Lynne. Let me pull over."

"No!" The cell made a clunking noise. Lynne chewed her bottom lip while she waited.

"Okay, now what's this about The Piper?"

"Don't stop anywhere." Lynne's heart raced. "I saw him from the window as you left. You need to drive to the sheriff's office."

"What? Why? Are you all right?"

"I'm fine, but you're not. I'm sure it was The Piper who followed you when you left. He got into a silver car like the one he had on campus."

"I don't see any silver car, and I'm almost home. Let me get there, and I'll call you as soon as I pull into the driveway?"

"I wish you'd go to the sheriff's instead." She kept pacing.

"If someone follows me, I will. I promise. In the meantime, phone the sheriff's office and tell them what you saw."

"I will." She took a deep breath. "But call me right away when you get home."

"I promise."

The line disconnected as Lynne peered into the street from her window. She pulled up Teri's number and hit send.

"Hello."

"Teri, are you at work?"

"Lynne? No, I'm upstairs. What's wrong?"

After taking another deep breath, Lynne blurted out her fears. Before Teri could say anything, call waiting signaled. "Hold on." Lynne pressed the button to shift to the other caller. "Nick, is that you?"

"Yes, I'm unlocking my door now...stepping into the house. There's still no silver car in sight, none on the street, and before you even ask, no one's tampered with my door. Did you reach Teri?"

A door click came through the phone. "I've got her on the other line. I asked her to hold. Let me tell her you're home. Please don't answer the door for anyone."

"Ooo-kay."

Lynne connected to Teri again. "Nick's home, and he says no one followed him. Am I crazy?"

"Try to relax. Did you get a tag number?"

Exhausted from tension, Lynne dropped into the armchair in the living room. "No, I'm sorry. The car was too far away when it pulled out. But the man was leaning on a big silver car. The same way he did in Chicago. And he got in the vehicle and pulled out after Nick. I thought for sure it was him." Lynne twisted her hair as she rose and paced the living room again.

"Don't worry. Is Sam there with you?"

"No. She's visiting her parents."

"To be on the safe side, I'm coming down to stay with you, and I'll phone Russ. He's on duty today. I'll ask him to swing by Nick's place and make sure no one's lurking around."

"Thank you. Nick's still on the line. I'll tell him Russ will come by."

"Good. Be downstairs in a sec."

Lynne drummed her fingers on the windowsill after she switched over to Nick. "Teri's sending Russ, Deputy Highland, over to your place. He's Teri's cousin. The deputy I told you we met yesterday. The one Sam almost swooned over." She gulped in a breath. "I was terrified when that car pulled out after you."

"Kind of nice having someone care that much. I know you were scared. I could tell. So, is Teri with you?"

"No—oh, that'll be her knocking now. Hold on." Lynne laid the cell on the coffee table.

The sound of faint knocking came through Nick's cell, followed by the rattle of a door chain. Then silence. The hair on his neck bristled. A door clicked shut, and hurried footsteps neared the phone.

"Teri's here with me."

He rubbed the back of his neck. "Good." A knock came to his door, and Nick jumped. *Man!* She had him rattled. "There's someone at my door now."

"Must be Russ. I'm sorry if I overreacted."

Nick headed for the front door. "I understand. Let me answer." He peeked through the scope and then swung the door open. "You must be Deputy Highland. Come on in." He put the phone to his ear. "Lynne, the deputy's here. I'll call you after he leaves."

"Okay. Teri wants to check around here too."

Nick slid the cell onto the coffee table. "Did you see a silver car out there when you drove up?" He held his hand out for Russ to sit on the couch.

"No, but several on the way. It's a popular color. Deputy Coleraine told me what Miss Temple said, but when I drove around the block, I found nothing."

The two men took seats on either end of the sofa. "Lynne told me that you're Teri's cousin. May I call you Russ?"

"Please do."

"Call me Nick." The men shook hands. "I think the attempted murder at the hospital has shaken Lynne more than she'll admit. But I guess it's better to be cautious, considering what she's been through."

Russ scribbled on his notepad and tucked it into his shirt pocket. "I'd say so. After Teri and I ran into Lynne and Sam leaving the hospital yesterday, Teri told me what Lynne witnessed a few years ago. She may be reacting to things that remind her of then too."

Nick nodded. "Why would he follow me? He doesn't know me."

"Right. I'd better go."

The men stepped to the front door. "Hey, Russ. Are you working tomorrow?"

"Nope. Finally have a day off. Why?"

"Any plans?"

While she waited for Teri to check outside for anything suspicious, Lynne made a pot of coffee and placed two cups on the glass-top kitchen table. Her stomach still hadn't recovered from the nosedive it took when she thought she saw Hamelin.

Teri returned, and Lynne led her to the kitchen. She pushed a steaming mug in front of her friend. After sitting down across from the deputy, Lynne took a sip of her coffee. "No one out there?"

"Not anyone who didn't belong. If it was Hamelin you saw, he hasn't returned. How well did you see this man?"

The wooden chair screeched as Lynne shifted on the padded seat.

She wrapped her fingers around her cup. "He was too far away. It was his size and the silver car. I overreacted." She'd been seeing ghosts. Dwelling too much on the sleazy Hamelin.

Teri smiled. "It's understandable. I'd have thought the same thing. And I'm a cop." She giggled.

Leaning back in the chair, Lynne gave her a hesitant nod. "Thanks." She bit her lip. She needed to get her mind off that fiend. "So, what's happened with the rave teens?"

After a sip, Teri threw her arm over the back of the chair and crossed her legs. "We've got Jesse and the others settled in. The Victim Advocacy Department is working with them. Oh, Jesse said to thank you again for saving his life. There's hope for that boy. First bit of gratitude I've ever heard out of him."

"He's welcome. As you would say, 'Just doing my job.' This might be God's plan to straighten him out."

"Right. Those kids are pretty scared right now. I'm hoping they'll consider the direction they've been headed."

They sat in silence for a few seconds. Lynne retrieved the pot from the coffeemaker and poured them both refills. "Teri, I forgot to ask you. Is there any word on when Kim and Loring will arrive? Agents Travis and Trent?"

"No. Our contact at the bureau says they're still on a previous assignment, but they've planned for replacements."

Kim and Loring working together—imagine that. Lynne couldn't wait to find out if their relationship had progressed outside of work. "It'll be good to see them again after all these years."

As Lynne lowered the mug from her lips, the watch on her arm clinked on the table. She glanced at the time. "Oh dear. I'd better get my chores done before Sam gets back. She's a stickler for getting the house cleaned on the weekend. And it's *my* weekend. You know how she loves to needle me about anything she can."

Teri chortled and rose. "You two act like sisters. Well, I'd better get busy too. Give me a jingle if anything comes up." She laid her hand on Lynne's arm. "And try to relax."

"Sorry I made such a fuss over nothing."

While Nick jotted down the address and instructions to get to Zack's bayside residence for the boat party, Russ's stomach grumbled. Nick's brows rose. Better offer this public servant some food. Nick handed the directions to Russ and grinned. "A little hungry there, officer?"

Russ gave him a crooked smile. "Sorry. I skipped breakfast this morning. The alarm went off, I hit it, and fell back asleep." He chuckled. "Fortunately, I woke up an hour later, so I wasn't late for work. I've been running ever since. Not even time for coffee."

Nick laughed. "When's your lunch break?"

"I plan to call it in now. I'm starved."

"Join me here. We can discuss tomorrow while we eat. Just had breakfast before all this happened, but I'm hungry again."

"Sounds good." Russ phoned dispatch. "Officer Highland here. No suspicious activity. Am I clear to take a lunch break?"

Russ dropped the cell back into its pouch and grinned. "I'm clear."

Nick led him to the kitchen, opened the refrigerator, and pulled out a selection of cold cuts, cheeses, and condiments. He grabbed a loaf of bread from a plastic container in the pantry, plates from the cabinet, and an assortment of cutlery from the drawers and piled everything on the table.

Straddling the seat he pulled out, Russ laid his cap on the next chair. "You always keep this much food handy? I mean, you're single, right?"

A bag of chips plopped onto the table as Nick juggled a roll of paper towels, glasses, and cans of soda. "I don't like to cook. So, if I don't feel like eating out, I have sandwiches. Besides, I did my weekly shopping Wednesday before I left town. I'll get some ice."

Nick filled the glasses with ice cubes, and the two built their sandwiches. While they ate, Nick explained Zack's plans. "He's an introvert, so he left the details to Lynne and me. He loves people but doesn't socialize well. I almost fell over when he suggested this party."

Russ took a big bite of his sandwich and shoved a couple of chips into his mouth with it. After a sip of cola, he nodded. "I had a reclusive friend in high school. Great at talking up a storm with me, but around other people he'd clam up. I'll look forward to meeting Zack."

He took another drink. "Ahhh...will Lynne's friend Sam be there?"

Nick suppressed a laugh. "I'm sure she will. Took a fancy to her, did you?"

"She's really something. I don't know what it was about her, but something clicked when we met yesterday. She's been on my mind ever since. I planned to ask her for a date soon."

"Lynne said Sam's off tomorrow, and I'm sure she's told her about the party."

When they'd finished their lunch, Russ rose from the table and donned his cap. "Thanks for lunch. See ya tomorrow."

After Nick closed the apartment door, he called Lynne. "Lynne, I invited Teri's cousin to the outing tomorrow."

"That's great. I talked to Sam. First thing out of her mouth was a request to invite Russ."

Nick snickered. "Funny. Russ asked if Sam would be there. The conversation centered on her. But then it turned to what you've been going through."

"I *thought* my ears were burning."

"Heeey. Actually, Russ told me Teri was concerned about your safety after that incident at the hospital. When I told him I planned to take you out for dinner tonight, he suggested I keep you away from public places for the time being. At least until they find Hamelin's whereabouts."

"That makes sense. So, dinner's off."

"No way. I still want to treat you to dinner, just not out. Russ recommended the two of us eat in. I can stop for ribs and sides, and we can have dinner at your place."

Lynne didn't answer. Was she uncomfortable with the idea? "Sam will be there, won't she? I'll get enough for three."

"No. Sam won't come home until later tonight. Her mom asked her to stay for dinner."

Better set her mind at ease. "If you don't want to be alone with me at the apartment, I understand. What if we bring dinner to my aunt and uncle's place?"

"Nick, I've no problem with dinner at the apartment. It just took me by surprise. It's a wonderful idea. And we are adults. Besides, Sam never stays out late if she can avoid it."

"Okay. Are ribs good for you? What kind of sides?"

While he scribbled a list of food to order from the local barbecue, Nick smiled. He'd dreamt of having a quiet evening with Lynne, only the two of them. But didn't think it would be this soon. Things sure had happened fast between them. "What do you want to drink with the ribs?"

"We have diet cola, sweet tea, and ginger ale in the house. Is that enough? And I can make coffee later to go with ice cream and chocolate syrup."

"All righty then. The lady knows the way to my heart." He laughed. "It'll be a little later than we planned before I get there. I want to drop by Russ's and pick up a movie he said he'd let us watch if we took his advice. One of those made-for-TV family flicks. It sounded good. Something about a mystery in a bakery."

"Oooo…I love mysteries."

He'd have to become more mysterious then. "I have calls to make now, but I should be able to leave around four and get to your place by six thirty, or seven. That's not too late, is it?"

"Sounds good. Over dinner, I'll tell you who else I've invited to the outing tomorrow."

"Catch ya later." Nick hung up.

A few minutes before seven, Nick pulled the truck to a stop in front of Lynne's apartment building. He tucked the movie under his arm, gathered the bags of food, and headed for the entrance. When he glanced at Lynne's apartment window, he stopped short. Dark. *"What?"*

He raced into the foyer and rang her doorbell.

Chapter Twenty-Four

The door buzzer sounded. Nick waited for Lynne to speak. Nothing. He yanked the door open before the buzzer quit. Why didn't she say anything? Nick sprinted up the stairway to Lynne's second-floor apartment and pressed his ear against the door. She usually asked who was there before buzzing him in downstairs. Something wasn't right. The hair on his neck rose. He raised his fist to knock, but before he could, the door creaked open.

Lynne stepped into the opening. "Hi. You're here."

"Hi?" His gaze traveled from her half-opened eyes to her hair. A tangled mess as if she'd awakened from a night's sleep. "Are you okay?"

"A little groggy. Why?"

He peeked inside. The lights in the apartment were off, except for the one over the stove in the kitchen. "Why are you in the dark? When I glanced at your window from the sidewalk, it was pitch-black.

Scared the tar out of me. What's going on?"

Lynne turned and surveyed the living room as though she hadn't noticed. "Oh. *Oh.* Sorry, Nick. Come in." She switched on a nearby lamp. "After I talked to you, I took an aspirin for a throbbing headache and must have fallen asleep." She blinked repeatedly.

Before she could shut the door behind him, Lynne's knees buckled, and she lost her balance. Nick dropped the bags of takeout he held and caught her halfway to the floor. He scooped her up in his arms and carried her to the couch. Once he'd lowered her to the sofa, he laid his hand on her forehead. "Temps normal, I think." Her eyes looked strange. "Lynne…Lynne?" Her lashes fluttered and closed. Would aspirin cause this? Now what should he do?

He rushed to pick up the bags of food and DVD from the floor and shut the door with his foot. If only he knew Sam's cell number. He brought the food and movie into the kitchen and dumped them on the table, grabbed a glass from the dish drainer, and filled it with water. Then he rushed to Lynne's side. Should he call nine-one-one?

As he lifted her head up, he touched the glass to her lips. "Drink this. That's it. Come on. A little more."

Her eyes opened again. "What happened?"

"You passed out. Are you sure it was only aspirin you took?"

"Yeah. The bottle's on the bathroom sink. Oooh…I'm so woozy."

After lowering her head and setting the glass on a coaster, Nick strode to the bathroom and picked up the open plastic bottle. Antihistamine. It could have put her to sleep. He took the bottle to Lynne and showed it to her. "You took this, not aspirin."

She sat up and wagged her head a couple of times. "My head hurt so much, I saw double. I grabbed what I thought was the aspirin bottle from the medicine chest. Didn't remember Sam's allergy meds were in there. Oh, brother. Now I've ruined our evening." She grimaced. "Please don't tell Sam. I'd never live this down with her, my being a nurse and all. I never take medicine for anything."

Nick sat next to her on the couch and took her in his arms. "You didn't ruin the evening. And I won't tell Sam. But I'll tell you, it made my hair stand on end to see your apartment in the dark when I arrived after what we went through this afternoon." He brushed stray hairs from her face. "How's your head now?"

"The headache's gone. Guess I needed the rest too. The attack at the hospital this week has had me so stressed. Then the guy earlier today who I could have sworn was The Piper. And everything in between." She leaned back and smiled at him. "I'm glad we're having a nice quiet dinner here tonight."

He stroked her cheek with the back of his hand and smiled. "Me too. Think you can eat something?"

She nodded.

"Where do I find plates and utensils? I'll get the table ready. You may still be a bit unsteady on your feet." He rose and headed for the kitchen.

"Thanks. Plates over the dishwasher. Utensils in the top drawer, right side of the fridge."

Several minutes later, Lynne had freshened up, and they sat at the kitchen table enjoying ribs, corn on the cob, and fries. "Nick, this food is fantastic. The sweet, smoky aroma made my mouth water while you got it ready. We need to do this again." She stole one of the largest ribs from his plate.

"Heeey. We will, but next time I'll make it a double order for you. Wait! Did you mean have ribs again…or me doing the work?" He laughed. He'd be a mess after eating these. How'd she stay so clean? "Doesn't matter. I'm game for both. Now, who did you invite to the boat trip tomorrow besides Sam?"

Lynne let out a soft snicker. "Because you told me Zack was somewhat of an introvert, I called Melissa to see if she was off tomorrow. She's one of the single nurses working on four-west. She's off and was thrilled. I thought she'd be a perfect match for him. Shy, pretty, and also a southerner. Hope he goes for tiny because she is. Couldn't be over five feet."

"Ha!" A bit of cola spurted out of Nick's mouth. "Sorry." He wiped his chin. "Every girl Zack's ever noticed has been a featherweight. But he never got up the nerve to ask any out. This will be good for him." He eyed Lynne. "Pretty, huh?" He made an hourglass shape with his hands and wiggled his brows.

She smacked his arm. "Short, curly, blonde hair with the lightest blue eyes I've ever seen. Petite and sweet."

"Perfect. Well, that makes six of us. Did you invite anyone else?"

"I checked with a couple other nurses, but they were working. On a hunch, I phoned Steph, even though I thought she might be working since Melissa was off. She's on four-west too. Turns out their boss scheduled both of them off for tomorrow. The bad news is, she asked if she could bring Derek Appleby. Apparently, they've been dating."

Nick shrugged. "What's wrong with that? We needed another guy to round out the couples."

Lynne took in a deep breath and let it out slowly. "Something about him bothers me. But I can't put my finger on why."

After dinner, Lynne gripped the side of the table as she rose. "Good. Sea legs are back. I'll clean the kitchen while you get the movie ready. The control for the player is in the magazine rack next to the couch." Time for him to relax after such a busy day. Not to mention her scaring him half to death…twice.

"I'll help you first."

"No, Sir. *You. Living room. Now.* This will only take a couple of minutes."

"Wow. I haven't seen this bossy side of you." He spun and strode to the doorway as he snickered.

Had she seemed bossy? Is that why Sam keeps calling her sergeant? She'd have to work on that. Too much of the Lieutenant JG left in her system. Lynne called after him. "You wouldn't know where to put things in here." Lame excuse. "Besides, you need to relax. You've been on the go since early this morning." And half the time worried about her.

Lynne finished in the kitchen and joined Nick.

Just as Nick was about to start the movie, Sam waltzed through the front door. She stopped dead in her tracks. "Well, look at you two. Isn't this a domestic scene?" She winked and made an exaggeration of eyeing him from head to toe as he sank deeper into the couch and put his hands behind his head. His long legs stretched out in front of him. "Comfortable, Nick?"

He chuckled. "Yes, thank you."

Lynne's neck grew warm. She glared at Sam. There were days when she could just slap that girl. "We just finished dinner. It was suggested I avoid public places for the time being while that criminal is on the loose. Nick brought over a movie, one of Russ's. You're welcome to join us. *If* you can behave yourself."

"Who, me?" Sam dropped her purse and the stuffed plastic bag she'd brought in with her onto an armchair and perched on the edge. "I'll be good. Where's Russ?"

Nick gave Lynne a cockeyed grin and nod. "Russ isn't here. Only one of his DVDs."

With her hand over her mouth, Lynne tried not to laugh. "If you're hungry, there are leftover ribs and fries on the counter."

Sam pinched her lips together. "Better not. Already ate too much of Mom's cooking, as usual." She jumped up, entered the kitchen, and came back with a tumbler in her hand. What appeared to be a french fry disappeared into her mouth. Ice clinked against the glass as she moved the bag and her purse onto the floor and reinstalled herself in the armchair.

"Mom sent over these T-shirts for us to try on." Sam pointed to the plastic bag on the floor. "She spotted them at the church bazaar last week. They have nautical terms on them." She tossed the bag onto the floor next to Lynne's end of the couch.

"That was sweet of her." Lynne peeked into the bag.

Sam took a sip of tea. "Before we watch the movie, tell me who's coming tomorrow to the outing. Did you ask Russ?"

As a stifled laugh sounded from the other end of the couch, Lynne gazed at Sam. "Nick invited him. Not to worry."

"Thanks. He's such a nice guy."

Nick's brows rose. "And how would you know, Miss Rease? From what Lynne said, you've only met him once." He chuckled. "Love at first sight?"

Sam giggled and batted her eyelashes. "And who else is going?"

Nick put his cola on the end table. "Lynne found a couple of your hospital coworkers who were off. Ah…Melissa and Steph. Right?" He turned to Lynne.

She placed a coaster under his glass. "Right. Melissa and Steph were both scheduled off for tomorrow."

With her brows lowered, Sam pinned her eyes to Lynne's. "That makes three fellas to four gals?"

Lynne grimaced. "No. Steph asked if Derek from radiology could come. She's been dating him."

"Oh, that's right. Now there's a strange couple." Sam's frown matched Lynne's assessment of the match.

Nick took another drink of soda and swallowed. "Why's that?"

After she blew a big puff of air through her lips, Sam leaned back in the chair. Lynne's brows rose, and she held her hand out for Sam to explain.

"Steph loves opera and classical music, like Derek, from what she's told me. They're even well-matched in appearance. Attractive, dark hair, dark eyes, near the same height and age, but—" Sam quirked her mouth.

"But what?" Nick wrinkled his forehead.

"Steph's from Tallahassee. Derek's a Yankee if I ever heard one. Steph is a church-goer, although I'm not totally sure she's saved. But Derek told one of the other x-ray techs Christians are a bunch of pansies and Bible-thumpers. It's the mismatch of the century."

Sam took a long sip of her sweet tea and set the sweating glass on a coaster next to her. "Oh, and Steph is refined and has a good sense of humor. Not the case with Derek. That's my own experience from listening to him, by the way. Plus, he flirts with every female he sees." She pursed her lips.

Nick glanced at Lynne. "Is that what bothered you about him?"

"No, something else." She turned to Sam. "Does Steph realize he's such a flirt?"

"Not sure. But she's probably as far gone as y—"

"Let's get this movie started before it gets any later." Lynne popped up from the couch. "Shall we?" She glowered at Sam.

Nick snickered behind her and pressed the play button.

After the movie ended, Nick, Lynne, and Sam sat at the kitchen table, eating vanilla ice cream with fresh strawberries and chocolate syrup. He glanced at Lynne. The evening went by too fast.

When his bowl was empty, he yawned and checked the wall clock. "It's close to midnight." He strode to the living room, took the DVD out of the machine, and placed it in the case. "Time for me to get home."

As Nick held open the front door for Lynne, he peered into the living room where Sam sat on the chair, pulling clothing from the plastic bag on the floor. The urge to pull Lynne into his arms would have to wait. If Sam saw them, she'd be merciless. He gazed into Lynne's hazel eyes, traced a delicate wing-shaped eyebrow with his finger, and then took her hands in his. "It's been fun tonight. Thanks for letting me have dinner here with you."

"I'm glad you suggested it."

They headed for the staircase.

"You never told me why Derek bothers you."

With knit brows, she shook her head. "Like I said, I'm not sure. But it may be because he's a player in my book…a scoundrel, as my mom would say."

"Not a very high opinion of him, huh?"

"No. He not only flirts, he also gets too physical with every female he gets near, or so I've been told. Although he's good-looking, I think of him as a weasel, a lowlife. I sure hope Steph doesn't get hurt."

"Maybe he's settled on her as the right one for him and will change." He grinned.

A deep shade of pink rose in her cheeks. "Sam did say Steph and Derek have dated for a few weeks, but when he was on our floor yesterday, the way he stared at *me* sent chills up my back."

They descended the stairs. "He'd better keep his eyes *off* you from now on."

Lynne smiled. Her head dropped forward.

She's so pretty when she blushes. Halfway down the stairs, Nick turned to face her. He laid his hands on her shoulders and kissed her forehead. "Tomorrow will be an interesting day. I'll pick you up for church. Then we'll see what this Derek is made of at the party."

Chapter Twenty-Five

$\mathcal{S}$ unday afternoon, Lynne had just changed into a pair of dark jeans and a powder blue T-shirt when the doorbell rang. She pulled her hair back and clipped it with a white barrette, then rushed to the intercom. "Hello?"

"Hey, it's me again. Ready for the party?"

"Come on up." She buzzed him in and donned a Chicago Cubs baseball cap. After his knock, she swung it open. "Sure didn't take you long to change from church duds, Mr. Livingston."

"Eager to get this party going and be with my gorgeous Navy girl again." He winked.

"I was with you the entire morning at breakfast and church." She laughed. "Or are you referring to some other Navy girl?"

"*Never!*"

They left the apartment and descended the stairwell as if they were two teenagers racing to be first. At the bottom, Lynne swung a small, dark blue backpack hanging from her elbow into her arms. "I brought a lined windbreaker. Wasn't sure what the temp would be on the water, especially toward evening with this storm still threatening. It's been out in the Caribbean a long time. Why did it have to move north of Cuba now? Hope it stays put and doesn't cause rough waters until our party is over—at least."

"Right. I've been watching it on the news. We've had enough bad storms lately, and I hope this one dies before it comes any closer. I feel for the people in Cuba."

Nick held the entrance door open for Lynne. As she passed, he glimpsed the message on her T-shirt. He smirked. "Wore that for me, did you?"

She stopped on the sidewalk and peered at the words that proclaimed "I get a kick out of you" in sparkling white letters. "Not exactly." She tightened her lips into a straight line, then snickered. "It's from a kickboxing tournament I was in a few years ago."

"Oh." The corners of Nick's lips drooped.

Lynne gave him a smirky smile. "But…I *do* get a kick out of you."

"Excellent!" He grinned as they continued on to the truck.

When they reached the end of the sidewalk, Lynne gazed down the street in both directions. What…or who was she searching for? She had to stop looking for trouble everywhere.

Nick opened the passenger door for her, and she hopped into the truck. He sprinted around the back end, stopping to check the street in both directions. Was he looking for the silver car too?

He jumped in behind the steering wheel. "We should ask for the Lord to bless the trip before we take off. And for His protection."

"Good idea."

Nick took her hand in his and prayed for safety during the boat trip, the ride there, and back. He released her hand and pulled away from the curb.

Lynne bit her lip and added her own silent request to the prayer. She'd be very pleased if that Piper character stayed away from them. She glanced into the truck bed. "Nick, don't we need some fishing poles for this excursion? We're not going to just ride around in the boat, are we?"

"Don't need a thing. Zack said he has everything we need onboard. Wait until you get a load of this dinghy. I'm taking you first-class, Sweetie."

There it was. The first term of endearment he'd used for her. Lynne's heart skipped into a dance. She'd always remember it. This would be a great day, and no Piper would ruin it for her.

Nick pulled the truck into a gravel driveway at the west end of Bayou Grande. The sun glowed overhead, matching his disposition. What a perfect day. And he'd make sure Lynne relaxed out on the water.

Zack jogged along the pathway beside the house to meet them. "Hey, ole' buddy."

Nick hopped out of the truck, grabbed his friend's hand, and shook it. Zack waited a few feet away while Nick strode to the passenger side and opened the door for Lynne.

As she slid to the gravel driveway, Lynne whispered to him. "Nimble, muscular, young, and handsome…in a rustic sort of way. Perfect for Melissa."

Nick's attention zoomed to Zack in his faded blue jeans, blue and black checkered, long-sleeved shirt rolled partway up his well-developed forearms. *Hope Lynne's not drawn to muscle-bound men.* He gazed at her. *If so, what's she doing with me?* He sure wasn't a lightweight, but not a heavyweight either.

When they approached Zack, his frayed, salt-stained cap showing the symbol of the U. S. Navy Blue Angels flight demonstration squadron came off in a flash. His friend held the hat with both hands in front of him, twisting the bill so much that the five Hornet aircraft represented on the side were near unrecognizable. Tufts of black hair stuck out in every direction as if he'd been through a gale. "Zack, may I introduce you to my date, Lynne Temple? Lynne, this is Captain Zechariah Adams."

He held out his hand, and she took it. Zack's blue eyes twinkled in his sunburned rugged face as he smiled. Nick bit the inside of his lip. Maybe this boat outing wasn't such a good idea, after all.

Lynne returned his smile with a gorgeous one of her own. "You remind me of the hospital corpsmen I served with. I can picture you shinnying up and down rigging lines…agile as a monkey, I'll bet."

They shook hands, and Zack's neck darkened to a deeper shade of sunburn. He laughed. "Sure nice to meet you, after listening to this old man gab about you so much. And yes, Ma'am—I can shinny with the best of them."

"Wonderful to meet you too, Zack. A fan of the Navy's Blue Angels, I see." She nodded toward the cap.

"Since I was born."

"Okay, *old buddy*. You can let go of *my* girl's hand now." Nick took Lynne's hand out of his friend's grip and wrapped his fingers around hers.

Zack grinned, and with a broad sweep of his brawny arm, gestured toward the path along the side of the house. "This way, Ma'am." He led them toward the dock. "The boat ought to be ready. Dad stocked it for the day with poles and everything else he thought we might want." He turned to Lynne. "Come meet him."

As the three of them rounded the back corner of the house, Nick and Zack waved at the hulking man on deck. Nick glanced at Lynne. Her eyes were huge. She gripped his hand harder as if she'd seen a ghost.

"It can't be." Lynne gulped in a deep breath and stared at Nick as the huge man ran from the deck toward the back of the house. Her heart pounded.

"What's wrong?" His gaze traveled from her to Zack and then to the man disappearing around the corner. He closed his eyes for a second and put his arm around her. "It's okay. That's Seth Adams, Zack's dad. Not who you think it is. I should have mentioned his size to you."

As they drew closer, Lynne shook her head. She had to stop reacting that way to every big man. What a fool. She glanced at Nick.

"I'm sorry. It's just—"

"I know. It's all right. It's a trauma that will take time to get over. Today, you're to relax and have a good time with friends. That's an order, Navy Girl."

"Aye aye, Sir." He was precisely what she needed in her life— someone who could understand her and make her laugh at herself. She gave him a crisp salute and darted along the flagstone path to the pier. Nick followed close behind.

Already onboard, Zack reached his hand out to Lynne as she approached the edge of the dock. She latched onto his arm, and he hoisted her aboard. "Great vessel, Captain. Sixty feet?"

"Sixty-five. Familiar with boats. Nice."

Nick jumped aboard and grimaced. "*My* girl…is a Navy girl. Comes with the territory."

With lowered brows, Lynne tilted her head to gaze into Nick's eyes as Zack climbed a ladder to the boat's steering cockpit overhead. She whispered, "What are you doing, Nick? You two aren't going to have a wrestling match over me, are you?"

He pursed his lips and shook his head. "Sorry. Overreacting. I guess it was that assessment you gave my buddy when you first saw him. 'Muscular, handsome.'"

She slipped her arm through his and squeezed it to her. "Nick. I was thinking of Melissa's reactions. Zack's not my type. Not who I'm interested in." She lifted her brow.

"Thanks." Nick planted a kiss on her forehead.

A sudden roar pierced the air overhead. Lynne jumped into Nick's arms. She jerked her head up. A jet left a trail of white and gray vapor. Nick held her tight, and she smiled sheepishly as the roar faded to an indistinct rumble. She exhaled. "Flight from NAS. Afterburner. Even though I was stationed there, they still startle me." Her heart beat double-time.

Nick's arm remained wrapped around her shoulders. "As Paul said, 'Be careful for nothing.' And 'nothing' means 'nothing,' by the way. Even Navy girls can get their hearts jumpstarted by those things, it would seem." He laughed and removed his arm.

She wished he had left it there.

From the steering cockpit, Zack called out, "I've lost count of the number of times one of those F-Eighteen birds has almost given me a heart attack while I've been trying to land a strike or take a nap. Scatters the fish every which way to boot. Hopefully, none will pass over while you're fishing today."

He descended the ladder. "A bunch of us charter boat owners discussed a petition to send to the Secretary of the Navy. We'd like them to put silencers on those birds. At least UFOs are quiet." Zack dropped the last third of the way to the deck and landed with a thump.

Lynne gaped at Nick.

Zack straightened. "Yep. Seen them out here too."

Was he serious? Overseas, Sam had mentioned people claimed to have seen UFOs here in Pensacola. Thought she was kidding.

The sound of wheels on gravel drifted to the water. Nick hopped off the boat. "Must be Russ." Lynne took his hand, and he helped her onto the dock. They loped up the pathway and around the house just as

Russ slid out of a blue Ford Ranger. Sam waved from the passenger seat.

"What do you know?" Lynne bumped Nick's upper arm with her shoulder. "I was wondering why she wasn't home after church. Russ sure didn't waste any time."

Nick chuckled. "He told me he'd wrangle her phone number out of his cousin."

Lynne tilted her head in the direction of the Adams's long driveway. "And there's Steph, Derek, and Melissa."

A gleaming silver Maserati convertible pulled off the gravel onto the grass. Steph waved as she popped out of the passenger side. Derek peered into the rearview mirror, ran a comb through his hair, and then exited.

Nick leaned toward Lynne. "That's a brand new sports car. Bet it set him back a bundle. Doing more than okay for a hospital x-ray tech, isn't he?"

She blinked and shrugged. "Must have money coming in from somewhere else."

As Zack reached Nick, he whispered, "Where is she?"

"In the back seat of the Maserati." Nick took Lynne's hand, and they hurried to the car while Steph engaged in a heated discussion with Derek several feet away.

Lynne reached out her hand to Melissa. "Come meet Zack." *She looks terrified. Wonder why.* After a little coaxing, Melissa stepped out of the back seat. Lynne leaned toward her and whispered, "Stay with Nick and me until you're comfortable around him."

Melissa nodded.

"Hi, I'm Nick." He held his hand out to Melissa. "I'm the one you've heard horror stories about from Lynne." He chuckled.

Lynne smacked his arm. "Pay no attention to him, Melissa." When she waved Zack over, he joined them. "This is Zack Adams. He's the captain of the boat, and the one who had us invite you."

Zack grinned and extended his hand to Melissa. "I'm glad you could make it."

As he held her small hand, her face turned a light pink. "Thank you for including me. I've never been on such a large boat before."

"Then I'll have to give you a tour…if that's okay with you." While his eyes fixed on Melissa, Zack's neck returned to a red glow.

Lynne beamed. Perfect match.

Behind them, Steph and Derek grew quiet and joined the group. Steph introduced her date to Nick, Zack, and Russ, who bored holes into Derek with his eyes.

Lynne pursed her lips. Easy to understand why Steph was drawn to him. Handsome enough, but what was with that scowl. They must have had a fight on the way here. That would explain the strain on Melissa's face. And what was with the glare Russ gave him?

"Nice to meet you, Derek." Nick offered his hand.

"Likewise."

Derek shook hands with Zack, but then he grabbed Steph's arm and led her away from the group without a word to Russ. He kept his eyes on Derek all the way to the back of the house.

How rude of Derek. Did these two know each other? Russ glanced at Sam and smiled, but it didn't reach his eyes.

Maybe it was nothing. Lynne sighed. A disagreement they'd straighten out during the day. But there was something strange about Derek. Had Russ felt it too?

Chapter Twenty-Six

$\mathcal{L}$ ynne glared until Derek and Steph disappeared behind the back of the house. What could Steph see in the man?

"Let's step inside for a few minutes." Zack led the way. "Mom has sandwiches, brownies, and all kinds of stuff for the trip. Besides, she'll want to meet everyone she doesn't know and tease the rest." He stopped on the back porch and called. "Derek. Steph. Join us."

In the kitchen, Mrs. Adams packed a plastic bag full of cookies, zipped it shut, and added it to a pile of other bags on the table.

"Mom, you know Nick."

Nick gave her a quick hug and turned to Lynne. "This is Lynne Temple."

"Nice to meet you, Lynne. And who are the rest of your friends, Zack?"

"Deputy Russ Highland, Sam…ah, Rease, Melissa Holbrook,

Steph, and Derek." He turned to them and squinted his eyes as if trying to recall something. "Sorry, can't remember your last names."

"That's okay, Russ. I'm bad at names too." Steph held her hand out to Mrs. Adams. "Steph Madden." Zack's mother smiled and shook the offered hand. "And this is my boyfriend, Derek Appleby."

Derek gave her a simple nod of the head.

"Welcome to our home. All of you."

Mr. Adams stepped into the room. Zack's Irish setter followed wagging her tail like it was trying to put out a brush fire. Lynne reached down and scratched the dog's ears. "What a beauty you are."

"Here, Tess." The dog ran to Zack and jumped up, her paws almost reaching her master's chest. "She's a sweetheart." Zack pointed to the floor, and Tess dropped, turned, and faced Derek. The hair bristled across her shoulders. A low guttural growl followed as she lowered her head.

Zack slapped his leg. "Tess. That's no way to treat a guest." The dog stopped and sat at his feet, eyes glued to the stranger. Zack ruffled her hair. "Go lie down."

As Tess trotted out of the room, Mr. Adams's brows lowered. He stared at Zack for a second and then turned to face Lynne. "USN Women's Kickboxing Tournament, huh? I read the back of your shirt. You are one impressive little lady. If you land a king mackerel today, we'll get you one with the title King Mackerel Queen."

"I'll do my best, Sir." She smiled. Nothing to fear from this gentle giant.

"This is a *fishing* trip?" Derek frowned. "I thought this was a party."

Zack raised a hand. "It will be, but we'll have time for angling too." He picked up the largest cooler. "Time's a-wasting, folks."

His mom placed cookie packs into a soft cooler and handed it to Lynne. Melissa grabbed another soft cooler. Nick hoisted a hard cooler onto his shoulder. The others picked up the remaining bags as Zack backed out of the kitchen, pinning the screen door open with his body. While everyone else followed the path to the pier, Lynne and Nick waited for Zack on the back porch.

Before Zack stepped away from the door, Lynne overheard his father say, "Better keep an eye on Derek. You know Tess only growls when something's wrong."

Zack nodded.

Lynne glanced at Derek's retreating back.

When they reached the dock, Zack held out his hand to help Melissa onboard as Nick helped Lynne. Then Zack let go of Melissa to help the other girls into the boat. He peeked at Melissa, who stood by his side, a glow on her face. "Mom raised me to be a gentleman." He saluted the men still on the dock. "But you fellas are on your own."

Clamping her lips tightly, Lynne stifled a laugh.

When everyone was on deck, Nick pulled Lynne to the side. "I have a bad feeling about Derek. Something's not right with that guy. You saw the way he watched Russ, didn't you?"

"I did. Like a moonshiner facing a revenuer. I'm afraid this won't work out well for Steph."

Nick sat next to Lynne in the stern. He'd never been this comfortable with any woman before, or as happy.

Zack led Melissa up to the steering cockpit. "Time to get underway."

Derek cast quick looks at Russ whose focus seemed to be on Sam. Nick's eyes narrowed. That Derek character best not start anything with the deputy, no matter what their past relationship.

From the bridge, Zack's voice boomed. "Since some of you are from other parts of the country, *Yankee-land*—" Giggles and chuckles broke out below. "We'll head to Fort Pickens. Should be a good place to drop anchor for refreshments."

While Zack steered the vessel from Bayou Grande into Pensacola Bay and headed for the pass just beyond Fort Barrancas on the north and Fort Pickens to the south, Nick monitored Derek.

Another call came from above. "Hey, everyone. Moby Dick's cousin on the port bow."

A dark form broke the water a few yards to the left. Nick followed Lynne to the bow with the group. She knelt on the seat, hands shielding her eyes from the sun as they searched the water in the direction Zack had pointed.

The boat lurched to starboard. "Whoa!" Lynne pitched forward. As she held onto the railing with both hands, her body hung halfway over the side. Nick caught her by the shoulders and pulled her back. She landed in his lap. With his right hand, he latched onto the low handrail in a viselike grip and wrapped his left arm around her.

She gulped air, her eyes big as saucers, while Zack brought the boat to a stop.

As the vessel bobbed up and down with the waves, Nick let go of the railing and moved his hand to her arm.

Lynne blew out a long breath. "Wow…thanks, Nick."

"You're welcome." He'd enjoy rescuing her like that anytime, as long as he could keep her from falling in and his heart didn't speed up any faster.

As a deep shade of red flowed into Lynne's face, she popped up from Nick's lap and spun to face him. "Sorry."

He pulled her onto the seat. As he smiled, he laid a hand on her shoulder. "It's okay. And you're welcome for yet another save from a swim with the fish."

"Everybody okay?" Zack peered over the rail.

Lynne waved. "We're fine. Just shaken."

Nick's brows furrowed. "Fine?" He gazed back at Zack. "Hey, Captain Hook. Lynne almost dove in."

Zack's eyes rounded. "Sorry, man. A small whale swam into our path. I would've hit it if I hadn't come about. A calf with the cow, I think."

"Cow? Where?" Lynne shouted. She twisted her neck to search the water. The others followed.

"Cow is a mother whale. But they're gone now."

Lynne glanced at Nick's hand. "I'm okay."

He grinned. "I'm getting used to keeping you dry."

Zack pointed to the starboard side. "There they are."

The calf edged closer to the boat and swam alongside the hull. Lynne knelt on the cushion. The cow swam a few feet away. Holding onto the railing, Lynne leaned way over the edge and touched the calf. Nick seized her waist and pulled her back.

She turned and dug an elbow in his ribs. "He's not Jaws."

"Lady, why are you determined to give me a heart attack? First it's dolphins and now whales. You're worse than the kids in my youth group."

"Well, next time you tangle with them, think how easy it will be by comparison." Lynne pinched her lips together as the rest of the group laughed.

When the calf cleared the boat, Zack increased their speed. "If you're finished bonding with whales and sparring with one another, can we continue to quieter water and dig out our food? All this excitement makes me hungry."

As they stood, the boat lurched again, and Lynne fell against Nick. "I've lost my sea legs."

He snickered. That was okay by him as long as he was close by to catch her. "If you can get them back, we'll join Zack up there." He pointed to the canopy-covered cockpit.

When they'd reached the upper deck, Lynne stood between Nick and Zack. "I didn't know there were whales in the Gulf."

"We see them on occasion. One broke surface right beside a

friend's catamaran last week. His girlfriend was sailing with him." Zack guffawed. "Scared her half to death. She'd been reclining on the edge, letting the spray hit her fingers when she caught the dark shape surface in her peripheral vision."

Melissa's eyes widened. "Honest? That'd scare me too."

Zack nodded and brought the craft to a stop, weighed the anchor, and got out the fishing equipment and harnesses.

"Would you get out the soft drinks from the cooler in the back of the boat, Nick? We'll eat while I tell everyone a little about Fort Pickens."

Lynne passed around plates and napkins, ham sandwiches, bags of chips, cookies, and brownies, while Nick handed out soft drinks.

Zack took a few bites of his sandwich and pointed to the distant shore. "Geronimo was a prisoner at Fort Pickens over there in the eighteen-eighties, along with others of the *Cheer-a-cowwa* Apache tribe. That's spelled C-h-i-r-i-c-a-h-u-a for those taking notes." He chuckled. "The fort, built in the early eighteen-hundreds, along with Fort Barrancas on the mainland," he pointed north, "defended Pensacola Bay until the nineteen forties."

Everyone stood. "We'll take a run through the pass later so you can see it better."

The group reseated themselves.

"The federals had held on to Pickens, but the Rebs occupied Barrancas. They fired at each other across the bay. However, with the distance between them, they couldn't do each other any damage."

"That's it?" Derek narrowed his eyes at Zack.

"Yep. All that work simply to build two tourist attractions. Now, who's up for fishing?"

Lynne raised her hand and nudged Nick. "You, Big Guy?"

"I think I'll sit this one out. It'll be fun to watch you though." He winked. It was always fun to watch her.

Secured in the boat's fighting chair, Lynne concentrated on her line. Within minutes, a strike yanked her arms forward, but she clung to the pole, leaning until she was almost bent in two.

Nick steadied her from behind, his hands once more on her shoulders. "A king mackerel. Look at him jump." The fragrance from her shampoo intoxicated him as the wind whipped her locks back and forth. His heart leaped almost as much as the fish.

For what seemed like forever, and with assists from Nick and Zack, in turn, Lynne fought the fish, but at last brought the giant mackerel close enough to the boat for Zack to gaff it. As the mackerel landed on the deck, Lynne let out a sigh of relief. Nick slid his arm around her shoulder. "Nice job, Navy Girl."

Zack fought with the flopping fish on deck. "Nice isn't the word for it. Lynne, I think you just landed *King* king mackerel."

"I thought for sure I was going in the water this time, despite the harness." She grinned.

Nick caught Lynne's gaze and held it for a few seconds.

"*Hey*. A little help here, buddy." Zack hung onto the wriggling mackerel.

Russ and Nick both jumped in to help wrestle the fish into a large cooler at the rear of the boat. When they rose, Nick stared at Derek who stretched his legs out with his back against the rail and yawned.

Nick beamed at the overjoyed look on Lynne's face after their brief tour of Fort Pickens. "I take it you liked the fort."

"I've always been fascinated with forts." She faced Zack. "Thanks for showing us around."

Zack saluted. "Setting a course toward my favorite fishing spot now."

A few minutes later, Russ took a turn in the fighting chair.

After Lynne volunteered to pass out refreshments, Nick bent to help her collect some cans from the cooler. "Let me carry those." *What a girl. She jumps in to help without waiting to be asked.*

"Care for a cola, Derek?" Lynne held one out to him.

"Is there something stronger in that chest?" He lifted one side of his mouth into a smirk.

"Soft drinks only."

"Give me a ginger ale."

She switched cans and handed him the ginger ale.

He popped the top. "Say, Lynne. You're not from around here, are you? Steph said she thought Chicago."

Nick stepped to Lynne's side. "You're not from here either, are you?"

"No." Derek rose from the seat and moved to the bow of the boat.

Lynne's eyebrows rose. "Why do I sense you interrupted a pending interrogation?"

"Not sure, but I don't care for the way he's been eyeing you."

An hour later, Nick found Derek asleep on the cushions in the bow. *Hard work watching others wrestle a mackerel, isn't it?* He left him and returned to the stern, where he stepped up behind Lynne and whispered, "Wonder why Derek came to this *boring* party?"

She shrugged and turned her attention to Steph, who was now fighting with her own fish from the chair. "Maybe after this trip, she'll realize she doesn't need him in her life."

Later, Melissa took the chair. Zack harnessed her and stood by her side. "Have you done any deep-sea fishing?"

"A little."

He handed the petite woman a pole. "I'll be here in case you need help."

In record time, Melissa landed a large red snapper. Zack's mouth dropped open. The slim, blue-eyed, curly-haired blonde unhooked the catch, dropped it in the cooler, and slotted her rod in its holder.

"Wow. Just—*wow*." Zack closed his mouth. "Who would have guessed?"

She giggled.

Nick leaned close to Lynne. "Is this the same shy nurse you've been working with?" He stifled a laugh.

Lynne peered up at Nick. "Is *this* the same introverted fisherman you described?"

For the rest of the afternoon into the evening, everyone took turns in the fishing chair except for Derek.

Zack guided the yacht out in the Gulf, through the pass into the bay, the bayou, and finally the slip. The sun dipped low in the west, casting a coral glow over the shimmering Gulf waters as they docked. Clouds in shades of purple and blue touched the horizon.

After the group settled in the bow, Nick gave thanks to God for a beautiful day, the stalled storm, and their safety on the water. When he opened his eyes, he found Derek glaring at him. Nick pinned him with a stare of his own, and Derek changed his focus to Steph. What was his problem?

Nick cleared his throat. "Zack asked me to give a short devotional before we break up tonight. When's the last time you gave thanks to the Creator? Check out that beautiful sky." He raised his hand to the heavens. "Even with bad weather on the horizon, the Master Artist has painted a more beautiful picture than any human could. Can you deny there's a God when you observe such beauty? My Father created that."

Heads nodded. Derek's remained still.

After a short time of discussion and more refreshments on the boat, the guests made their way onto the dock. Zack secured the dock lines. Nick gave him a hand and then asked Lynne, "Didn't you say you brought your camera?"

"Oh yeah." She slapped her forehead. "I've missed a whole day of great pictures. Guess I'm not much of a photographer." She dug the camera out of her bag. "Hey, guys. Do you mind standing in front of Zack's boat for a group pic?"

Melissa pointed to the cooler Zack set on the dock. "Can we show off our catches?"

"Great idea." Zack reached in for Melissa's huge red snapper, pulled it out, and handed it to her. "Anyone else want theirs?"

Mr. Adams neared the group. "*You* got one of those?"

"She sure did, Dad. This little lady's quite the angler."

His dad took the camera from Lynne's hand. "Allow me. You need to be in this too. Girls in front, men in back."

After the rest of the group waved off on holding their catch, Zack placed the open cooler in front of the group, then joined them. "Wait. I didn't get Lynne's king mackerel out of the deck cooler."

Lynne touched his arm. "Let's wait with that, Zack. It's so heavy. I don't think I could hold it up. We'll get a picture later."

"Okay, say cheese." Mr. Adams held the camera in front of him. "Derek, quit hiding behind Steph. Slide to her right. No need to be shy. This won't be going into the *Pensacola News Journal*."

From his position behind Lynne, Nick watched as Derek moved to the right and shifted his weight from one leg to the other. Why didn't he want his picture taken?

Chapter Twenty-Seven

$\mathscr{A}$fter the picture was taken, Derek grabbed Steph's arm. "Let's go." He had plans for tonight that didn't include this bunch.

Steph twisted away from his grasp. "Thanks for everything, Nick. Lynne, I'll see you at work tomorrow." She followed Derek at a leisurely pace.

When they were closer to the Maserati, Derek snatched her by the arm again. "Come on, Steph. Let's get out of here." So glad he didn't have to drive that simpleton Melissa. He had Zack to thank for offering her a ride home—although there wasn't much else to thank him for today.

As Steph eased into the passenger seat, Derek slid behind the wheel. He drove his sleek sports car toward her apartment. His cell rang, and he dug it out of the center console's storage compartment. "Hello."

"Did you get the information I wanted?"

The soft, deep voice on the other end never matched the image that rose in Derek's mind. The guy was a chameleon. One minute friendly and businesslike. But when crossed, his voice came across sharp as a chainsaw. "Yeah. I'll meet you later tonight, as directed." He disconnected.

Steph's head turned toward Derek. "Who was that?"

"Nobody important."

"So you'll just drop me off, right?"

"No." He smirked and increased the speed. "I'm looking forward to the rest of this evening, just the two of us."

She faced away. Wind whipped through the open window, tossing her cinnamon brown hair. The car filled with her exotic perfume. His pulse increased. He reached over and laid his hand on her neck.

"Derek, I'm exhausted from a day in the fresh air and sun. I'd rather just call it a night."

He yanked his hand back onto the steering wheel and clenched his teeth. It was that stupid preacher's doing. What had he said to her when he and Lynne took her below after the *sermon*? Derek glared at the road. Steph's red eyes when she had come back on deck came to mind. Had they convinced her she needed to be *saved*, as the Bible-thumper put it in his badgering talk. Devotional? Who needed a sermon after *that* poor excuse for a party?

The stoplight before Steph's apartment turned red, but Derek blew through it. He wouldn't bother with her again. She'd served her purpose. If that bunch of hypocrites hadn't seen her leave with him tonight, he'd—not worth the trouble it'd bring his way.

He jerked the car to a stop in front of her apartment building and let the engine idle, eyes glued to the dark night. "Good*night*."

Steph opened the door, stepped onto the sidewalk, and peered in at him. "Goodnight. Derek, we've taken our relationship in the wrong direction. After Nick's devotional tonight, I didn't need much to convince me I was a sinner. The minute I prayed and asked Jesus to come into my heart, my entire outlook on life changed. I don't want to displease God, and—"

"Shut the door."

"Please, Derek. Please consider what Nick said about your soul. Your—"

He stomped on the accelerator and screeched away from the curb. The passenger door closed with the thrust. *Stupid witch.* Who was she to preach at him? He'd had enough tonight from that Bible-thumper. Some party. *Soft* drinks. *Fish.* And a *lecture. The boss better be happy I endured it for the sake of his info.*

The breeze from the open window whispered through Lynne's hair as Nick drove to her apartment. She repositioned her barrettes to hold the loose strands. "Sure wish we knew what's up with Derek. I'm worried about Steph's relationship with him since she became a Christian tonight. He's not—" She wasn't sure exactly what was wrong, outside of his rudeness.

"I know what you mean." Nick turned the corner on her block and parked the truck. He shifted in the driver's seat and took her hand in his. "The way Russ eyed him the entire day can't be good. And it was strange that Derek didn't want his picture taken. They've crossed paths before, I'm sure."

Lynne smiled at him. "Care to come up for a cup of coffee? There's still ice cream in the freezer."

Nick jumped out of the truck without another word and hustled around the front to open her door. "With chocolate syrup?"

"Even whipped cream and a Maraschino cherry, if you'd like."

He rolled his eyes, groaned, and took her hand to help her out. "Could you make it decaf? I need to sleep tonight."

"Decaf ice cream?" She lifted a brow, and they laughed.

When they reached Lynne's apartment, Nick leaned against the wall while she dug out her keys and unlocked the door.

"Lynne, I'll give Russ a call tomorrow and see if he'll tell me about Derek. I want to find out why Russ seemed bothered by him. Something isn't right. Makes me nervous, since he works at the hospital."

She pushed the door open and flipped on the light. "Sam should be home soon. She may invite Russ up since the lights are on, and you can ask him tonight. I'd feel more comfortable knowing too."

A few minutes later, the aroma of freshly brewed coffee filled the apartment. Nick stepped up behind Lynne in the kitchen and laid his hands on her shoulders as she brought two mugs down from the cabinet over the coffeemaker. His body heat warmed her back.

"Mmm…is it done yet? Few things smell as good as coffee."

She chuckled. "Doesn't matter if it's regular or decaf either. Of course, chocolate comes close."

He slid his face next to hers, kissed her cheek, and turned her around. "I'll tell you what's even better." He wrapped his arms around her waist and pulled her to his chest. "You." He breathed in. Then he lowered his lips to hers.

So glad I wore that perfume he likes. The room spun. A tingle ran through Lynne's arms as she wrapped them around his neck. Butterflies burst into flight in her stomach. His lips were firm but warm. His muscular arms held her tight. She never wanted him to let go.

Sam's voice came to Lynne's ears. "Hey, you two. Don't you think you should lower the thermostat in here?"

Nick let go of Lynne. As he backed up, his face glowed red, and his eyes widened. "Uh oh." He murmured, "Did you hear her come in?"

Lynne mouthed, "No." She bit her lip. Her face had to be Christmas red. Still on her tiptoes, she gazed over his shoulder at Sam and Russ. They stood in the hall outside the open door, both with a big smile. *What did Sam do, put her key in stealth mode?*

Nick did an about-face and strode into the living room. "Just the man I wanted to talk to." He dragged Russ to the sofa while Sam made a beeline to the kitchen wearing an impish grin.

Lynne turned, tore off a paper towel, wet it in the sink, and pressed the cold surface to her face. *Lord, please don't let her say anything, or I may strangle her.*

Nick sat on one end of the couch and motioned for Russ to take a seat. How should he explain? Did he have to? Wasn't it natural for him and Lynne to show affection in their growing romance? Why even worry? It wasn't as if they were teenagers.

Russ took a deep breath and plopped himself onto the couch. "Sorry for the interruption. We saw your truck out front, so Sam asked me up for coffee."

"No problem. Only startled us, though we expected Sam home any minute. Glad you joined us." Nick sighed, then smiled. "I hope Sam will lay off Lynne. I wanted this to be a night she'd remember in a good way. Not one where she regrets our first kiss."

"First kiss? Great. Sam was hoping you two had something real going. She said Lynne's never had a steady boyfriend that she's aware of. That Lynne was waiting for the right guy to come along." Russ's brows rose as he glanced at Nick. "Looks like she found him."

"Thanks." Nick leaned forward with his elbows on his knees and peeked into the kitchen at Sam and Lynne. "Speaking of the right one, I think Steph's got the wrong man in Derek Appleby." He straightened. "You knew him before tonight. Right?"

Russ nodded and pursed his lips. "Steph's boyfriend and I *had* met, although he'd no doubt deny it. I kept tabs on Appleby today, as I've been doing almost since I got to Pensacola. When you invited me to that outing and then mentioned he'd be there, it was perfect. After his reaction to me, I'm certain it's the same guy from Ohio."

"You mean today was a stakeout?"

"No. You told me Sam would be there, and I jumped at the chance to be with her." He grinned.

"So, where did you meet Derek?" Nick leaned back on the couch, listening to the clatter of dishes still coming from the kitchen. "And why the surveillance?"

Russ shifted in his seat. "We have a lot of info on him, including his involvement with Stephanie Madden. Three years ago, I was with the Highway Patrol in Ohio. My partner and I pulled a guy over one night for a broken taillight. We thought it was routine, but when I approached the driver, I spotted a package sticking out from beneath the seat. I ordered him out of the car. It was drugs, bagged for distribution. When we searched the car, we discovered photos."

"You mean pornography?" Nick's eyes narrowed. He drew in a sharp breath and blew it out between his teeth.

"Mostly conventional stuff...but also pictures of children."

"That's sick. And you're sure it was Derek you stopped."

"Yep. He used a different name. Had a beard, mustache, sideburns, and bleached hair, but it was him."

Nick shook his head. Had Steph known? Surely not. She got saved tonight. "What happened to him back then?"

"We charged him with possession with intent to sell. Unfortunately, a slick lawyer got him off."

"What of the images in his car?"

Russ shook his head. "Unbelievable, but that lawyer—" He clamped his mouth shut and fire flashed in his eyes. "Big-time criminal lawyer from Chicago. Slick as a greased snake. Anyway, we struck out."

"One day, those crooked lawyers will have to answer for their actions." Nick glanced into the kitchen again. What were those two up to in there? He refocused on Russ. "They'll answer to a higher Judge than they've encountered here on earth."

"That's right. But thanks to the FBI and interdepartmental cooperation, we've kept Derek on the radar. When he moved and changed his name, we almost lost him. Then the boating party. I called my supervisor as soon as I could after you mentioned the name. It rang a bell as part of an alias he'd used in the past."

"Amazing that you ended up in the same place, just when you thought you'd lost him."

Russ chuckled. "Yeah. Well, that wasn't a coincidence. I worked with a few Christians in Ohio. We prayed we'd get wind of him again."

Laughter sounded in the kitchen. Nick peered in. Sam must not have teased Lynne after all. He caught the look Lynne sent his way and smiled back.

Russ lounged against the back of the couch. "Derek's up to no good, but we're not sure what…yet. My gut tells me it's something big."

Nick nodded. "That expensive sports car screams money. Probably from an income that won't appear on his tax return. From what Lynne's told me, his hospital pay wouldn't be enough to afford the Maserati he drives." His lips formed a tight, straight line as he pondered. "Did Derek have anything to do with the attempted murder of Jesse at the hospital?"

Russ shrugged. "We're trying to find out."

Lynne and Sam strolled into the room, each with a tray in her arms. Lynne set hers on the coffee table in front of Nick. "Okay, boys.

Enough guy talk."

"Right." Nick stared at the sundae dishes filled to the brim with ice cream, adorned with whipped cream and a fat cherry. "Now this is the way to have coffee."

Sam lowered her tray, which held mugs, spoons, a carafe, sugar bowl, and creamer, to the other end of the coffee table. She poured the hot, dark liquid into four mugs and handed one to each of them. Then she joined Russ on the couch. Lynne sat in an armchair on the other side of Nick.

After a sip of black coffee, Russ pressed his thumb and index finger together, signaling his approval. "Ooh…that's good."

When they finished their sundaes and coffee, Russ stood. "I'd better head out. On duty tomorrow. And I haven't figured out the drivers in this town, so I drive slower than normal."

Sam let out a soft snort. "Lynnz will be happy to give you her opinion of Pensacola drivers."

Lynne eyed Nick. "Now don't get upset with me, you being a southerner. Southern-belle-Sam's accepted my plausible theory."

With his hand held out to her, Nick tilted his head. "Let's have it, Navy Girl. I'm not thin-skinned."

"Okay. Even when I wasn't the one driving, I almost went nuts after I arrived at NAS and had to go to town on occasion. No one paid attention to the speed limit. They either crawled or flew down the roads. I asked the guys on base what the deal was. They had off-the-wall ideas. Then it occurred to me. There are only two kinds of drivers in Pensacola. The ones born and raised here—" she grinned at Sam, "who drive ten miles under the speed limit. And those who've been transplanted here from other parts of the country who drive ten miles over the limit, trying to get around the natives."

Nick rolled his eyes, and Russ gave her a thumbs-up.

"On that note, I'll leave and make my way home around both groups." Russ snickered. "Hopefully, in safety." He headed for the door. Sam followed.

Lynne waved before the couple stepped out the door. "Goodnight, Russ. Don't keep Sam downstairs too long. We have to be at work tomorrow too."

Nick helped Lynne to her feet. "This has been an evening I'll never forget." He kissed her fingers and turned to the door.

"One of the best evenings of my life." Color rose in her cheeks. "Oh, did you ask Russ about Derek?"

"He's no good, Lynne. Stay away from him."

Chapter Twenty-Eight

$\mathcal{A}$ month after the boating party, the ER admitted victims of a double-car crash to 4-North. Lynne returned to the nursing station after she'd checked on one of the teenage victims. She released a long sigh. "What a way to end a day of fun at a high school football game. At least no one died on the highway this time."

Sam shook her head. "They never learn no matter how many times they hear the warning or read the signs along the road, 'If you drink, don't drive.' What is it with people who think they're indestructible? Oh, I know. It happens to *others*. Not them. Right?" She hit her forehead with the palm of her hand. "I hope the judge throws the book at the driver who caused the havoc when he or she goes to court."

Lynne chuckled at Sam's indignation. The alcohol problem in the country wasn't the least bit funny, though. "Whoever caused this should lose their license permanently. But I guess the culprit will only get a fine and a slap on the wrist since there weren't any fatalities."

Sam rose from her seat, entered the kitchenette, and returned with a fresh cup of steaming coffee. As she sipped, a patient's call light flashed. "I'll get it."

As her friend headed for the hall, Lynne smiled and covered the rim of Sam's coffee with the cardboard back of a small note pad to keep it hot.

Upon her return, Sam plopped into the chair and grimaced.

Lynne's brows puckered. "What?"

"The other patient from the highway collision. You'll love this one. He said a flock of ducks flew in from the air vent, circled the room a few times, and then smashed into the walls and window. Then he pointed to what he thought were splat marks everywhere."

Lynne's jaw dropped, but just as quickly, she pressed her lips together to stifle her laughter.

A cockeyed grin formed on Sam's lips. "I called Dr. Smith. He'll come up and check on the patient. He said it might be a weird reaction to the pain medication the ER gave him. It's happened before. For the time being, I was able to quiet the patient. But only because the ducks flew out the door when I came in. So he said." She burst into giggles.

Lynne held her hand over her mouth. "We shouldn't laugh at this. It's not funny." She squeezed her eyelids shut. "But it's hilarious." She couldn't hold it in any longer and burst out laughing.

Sam grabbed Lynne's arm. "Did you hear about the patient who saw hundreds of snakes wrapped around the monument in Plaza Ferdinand downtown?" She hushed her voice. "Dr. Smith admitted the patient when he went berserk at the Mardi Gras parade this year. Gives me the willies."

"Yeah. He told me that one. But he thought drugs mixed with alcohol was responsible that time."

"If you indulge in that stuff, it'll bring a storm into your life." She sipped her coffee. "Speaking of storms, I listened to the weather report this morning while I helped a patient wash up. The squall, or gale, or whatever they called it, has moved into the Gulf but has almost blown itself out. Isn't that great? I thought the wind had stilled when we left for work. Guess we won't have to batten down the hatches for a hurricane after all."

Lynne grinned. *Thank You, Lord.* "You never mentioned hurricanes, tropical storms, gales, et cetera, et cetera, when you talked me into staying here in Pensacola after my discharge. Nor did you inform me of the huge bugs, snakes, and spiders you have here." She shivered. "But you couldn't know about the big *rat* that came to town."

Sam leaned forward and rested her forearms on the desk, eyes focused on Lynne. "It must be hard knowing The Piper's resurfaced, and he's probably been in this hospital…on *this* floor. Another kind of storm to weather."

"It is. Those memories of the past dredge themselves up every day." She glanced at Sam. "I find myself looking over my shoulder to make sure he's not following me."

After Sam drained her cup and pitched it into the trash, she patted Lynne's back. "With our friends and the church praying, not to mention the prayers of our families, the authorities will find this murderer soon. He's a sure cinch to be caught—even if forensics couldn't find anything useful from the CPR mask. It's only a matter of time, girl. Don't worry."

"I hope so." Lynne stared out the fourth-floor window to the blue sky. "God's in charge." He'd always taken care of her, and He would now. Her brows furrowed. *Won't He?*

That night, Derek drove to his favorite haunt in Gulf Breeze as a grin spread across his face. The pretty little thing he'd just left had been everything he'd hoped she'd be this evening. Even if he did have to leave her apartment before he'd had enough of her. And just out of her teens too. He laughed. He'd go back for more of her later. So unlike that loser, Steph.

The joy of his conquest faded as the image of Hamelin came to mind. When he'd told his boss the attack on Jesse in the hospital had failed, Hamelin's temper flared. And he exploded when Derek relayed the information that the cops now had the kid in protective custody at a safe house. Fortunately, he only spoke to the boss over the phone.

At least when he named Lynne Temple as the alert nurse who had saved the teen's life, it calmed the beast. Why? What made Temple so important to the man? Hamelin hadn't shown interest in any other female as far as he'd seen or heard.

Temple was definitely a looker. If she wasn't such a prude, he'd go for her.

Once inside the lounge, Derek ordered a drink and gravitated to an empty table in a secluded corner. He seated himself, took out his phone, and dialed. "Yeah, it's me. I checked their schedule. Temple will work her shift Monday morning, as usual, seven a.m."

"Good. It'll be nice and quiet. That'll be best. Can you get what I asked?"

Even calm, the guy's voice gave him a chill. "Already did. But why are you so interested in this particular nurse?"

"*Never mind.*"

Derek's skin crawled at the razor-sharp response. Not the first time he'd used it on him. "Okay, but—"

"Is there a problem?" The voice grew more menacing. "I don't like problems, Appleby."

"Nothing we can't handle, boss. It's just that one of Temple's friends is a local deputy. He's the one who pulled me over in Ohio the time you hired the lawyer to get me off. He was on that boat trip last month and recognized me. I've spotted him twice since then. The jerk's watching me."

"That's most unfortunate. Thanks for the information. I'll take care of the situation soon."

"Thanks." Should have told him right after that day on the boat.

"Appleby, get your mind on what I've asked you to do." The call disconnected.

A voluptuous red-haired waitress set Derek's beer in front of him. He ran a hand over her bare legs up to the tight black shorts she wore and ogled the revealing black lace, skin-tight top. He slipped her a generous tip. She winked at him and returned to the bar.

He dragged his focus from the sexy waitress and sipped his beer. The agents Hamelin had mentioned would have a big surprise when they neared Pensacola. *Travis and Trent*. Derek sneered as he gazed at the golden bubbles in his glass.

The information the FBI mole supplied to Hamelin had been well worth the money. From what the other guys in Hamelin's crew said, luck had followed the boss for a long time. Hopefully, it would continue. *With the kind of money Hamelin's paying me, I can quit my job as an x-ray tech.* But for now, he needed the cover.

Derek took a long swig and narrowed his eyes. Why had the agents flown into Jacksonville? The mole hadn't found out. Something about Hamelin? And why would they drive from there to Pensacola? A glitch in flights?

He gulped down another mouthful. If someone found out about the mole, the agents might have changed their plans at the last minute.

Just as well. Easier to knock them off in a car than on a plane. They'd have to cross long stretches of wetlands before they arrived in Pensacola. Isolated…nowhere to run. He couldn't ask for a better scenario to eliminate the agents.

Chapter Twenty-Nine

As Sam pulled her car into an empty spot Monday morning, Lynne glanced at her from the passenger seat. Sam insisted on parking in the front guest lot with that fiend Hamelin still on the loose. Didn't want to take a chance on a walk past the wooded area and through the less frequented path to work this early in the morning. She worried too much. "Sam, you've been treating me like a baby sister instead of a Navy-trained, adult nurse who worked with you all through our deployment in Afghanistan. The back lot is fine. It's as safe and patrolled as the front."

"Who says I parked here for you, girl?" Her lips rose on one side in a half smile.

After she shut the car door, Lynne glanced toward the entrance. A large man in a security guard uniform exited a Range Rover, and the vehicle sped away. She shuddered as the big man lumbered into the entrance.

She and Sam crossed the drive and entered the front waiting area right after the big man. With a flash across the sky and a loud clap of thunder, the clouds burst open. Lynne spun, her mouth open.

Sam patted her back. "Easy, girl. You're as jumpy as a frog. You're safe in the hospital now. And speaking of which, now that the teens are in witness protection, it's nice to have our halls free of security guards who made passes at us every day." She giggled.

"If you didn't encourage them, they wouldn't have."

While Lynne pressed the elevator button, Sam gave her a scathing look. "You're just like a baby sister."

Lynne chuckled. Odd. Where had that security guard we followed in go?

The door slid open. They rode the car up and exited on the fourth floor. The graveyard shift waited, purses in hand, as the girls trod across the space from the elevator to the station. Sam slipped into the kitchen while Lynne discussed patient notes with the night nurses before they left.

When Sam returned to the desk and sat behind the counter, she handed Lynne a cup of coffee. "Since you're making a list of supplies this morning, we need creamer. I'll pick up everything when I take my lunch break."

"Thanks."

The elevator door dinged open, and Deputy Coleraine stepped out. "Good morning, Lynne, Sam. Thought I'd pop up and tell you your friends Trent and Kim are on their way to Pensacola...at last. My supervisor informed me a few minutes ago. Hopefully, we'll get somewhere on this Piper case now that we'll have the FBI's help."

Lynne smiled. "That's great. I hope Loring and Kim find time to visit me, even though they'll be busy. But why didn't you just call my cell, Teri?"

"As I passed by the hospital, I saw Sam's Mustang in the front lot instead of where she normally parks. Thought I'd make sure you two were okay."

"Sam's got everyone on edge, and she's being a mother hen. Again. She thought it'd be safer for me to walk from the first rows of the front parking lot."

A grin accompanied Teri's nod. "By the way, my cousin Russ came into work last night on cloud nine, Sam. Even after the trauma of a rave party raid. Would that have something to do with you?"

The deputy's green eyes twinkled as Sam blushed and shrugged. "He's just a happy guy, I guess." She turned away. "I'll take the first tour of patients." She sauntered into the hall.

Lynne stifled a laugh. "It's fun to watch Russ and Sam together. Like teenagers in love for the first time. Sit down for a while, unless you have to leave."

"No, done for the day." She rounded the counter and pulled out the chair Sam had vacated.

Lynne brought Teri a cup of coffee from the kitchen. "Any news about this new storm that popped up so quickly out in the Gulf? It sure looks ugly out there again. We made it to work right before the downpour."

"The weather service expects it to become a tropical storm."

Thunder boomed outside the windows, and Lynne jumped. "Better than a hurricane, I guess."

A patient call light blinked. Lynne frowned. "That's an unoccupied room in the hall that's under renovation. That last thunder clap must have shaken something loose and bumped the patient buzzer. I'll check it out. Can you wait?" She glanced at Teri. "I'll be right back."

"Sure. I'm in no hurry. And the coffee's good."

"This'll just take a second." Lynne pushed her chair in.

"Why don't I go with you? We can talk along the way."

"No one but hospital personnel should enter those halls. Liability. And after all that's happened lately, I don't want our patients to see another sheriff's uniform in the hall. Could be due to a short too. If it is, I'll call maintenance. It's happened before. It's one reason they're redoing those rooms."

"Okay. I'll wait here." Teri leaned back in the chair.

Lynne stepped into the corridor as Sam returned from the other direction and took the seat next to the deputy. Teri's cell phone rang.

A plastic sheet hung over the door as Lynne approached the room. She pulled it aside just enough to peek in.

Materials for the renovation occupied one side of the room. On the other side, a larger plastic sheet covered the hole where a wall had been removed and the bathroom gutted. The single window in the room also had plastic taped over it in preparation for painting tomorrow. Dim light filtered through the plastic and from overhead fixtures at either end of the corridor outside the room.

She squinted and stared at the spot where a bed used to be, and then to the side wall where it now stood, covered with plastic. The cord and patient buzzer were gone. No one could have activated a call from this room. Must have been a short.

Lynne stiffened at the sound of running feet. She jolted to one side of the door and peered down the hallway. She let out a sigh. It was only Teri. But why?

After the deputy skidded to a stop at the doorway and yanked Lynne away from the door, she drew her gun and pressed an index finger to her lips. She motioned for Lynne to get behind her. "Stay close," she whispered. "Help is on its way."

"What?"

She held a palm up to Lynne.

A shiver skittered up Lynne's back as Teri stepped into the doorway.

Her friend scanned the room. She pushed Lynne back into the hallway and removed a flashlight from her belt. Again she whispered, "I can't send you back to the station because I've no idea where someone might hide in this hallway. We'll wait here until security comes. This might be a false alarm, but I told Sam to call both hospital security and nine-one-one."

"Teri, what's going on? I didn't see anyone. The cord and buzzer are both gone from the bed. I can't imagine why the light came on at the station unless it's a short."

"He's here. Hamelin. I sense it. As you left the nursing station, the nurse we questioned after the attempt on Jesse's life phoned. Stephanie Madden. I had told her to let me know if she remembered anything else. She said she was thinking about Derek Appleby last evening and got a strange feeling. She recalled his interest in the renovations in this hall and thought it odd. He told her he was just curious, but she said he acted strange, fidgety. We think he's involved with Hamelin."

Another set of feet pounded through the hallway. Lynne jerked toward the sound. "Oh, it's you, Jake."

The burly security guard narrowed his eyes. "Is everything okay?"

Teri hushed him. "Escort Miss Temple back to her station, stay alert, and stay with her when you get there."

"Yes, Ma'am."

Lynne turned to Teri. "But we can't leave you alone in here."

With the deputy's eyes still glued to the hallway, she whispered, "Being in the Navy doesn't mean you can handle this kind of situation. It's *my* job. Now go back to the station. When my backup arrives, direct them here."

She was right. This was not her arena, not a combat zone. Teri knew what she was doing. *God, please protect her.* Lynne headed back to the nursing station with Jake.

When they neared the desk, he glanced at her. "She'll be okay. This is what they're trained for."

Lynne's brows furrowed. "I hope…and pray so." Loring's dead fiancée came to mind.

Hamelin waited behind the large plastic sheet where he assumed they had removed a wall between the hospital room and a bathroom. Sheetrock panels were stacked in the space behind the plastic. His massive body barely fit between the plastic sheet tacked at the top of the opening and the stored three-feet-square panels of dusty gypsum and paper.

A quick rewire of the call button had been simple enough. He had hoped the blonde nurse he'd seen with Temple at the nursing station would respond to the call first. He could have dealt with his prey when the blonde failed to return, and Temple came to investigate. Blondie would have made a good addition to his shipment of teens. He could've at least had his revenge on Temple if that nosey cop hadn't shown up.

The officer slipped past the plastic on the doorway and shone her flashlight around the room. When she came to the second tacked plastic where Hamelin hid, she held it trained on the edge, her weapon steady in her right hand.

Hamelin tensed at the sight of the slim young woman in uniform as she approached the spot where he lurked. He continued to watch from a narrow opening between the wall and plastic sheet. This would be his lucky day, now that he thought about it. He'd dispose of one more cop and make his world a better place for business.

The officer took unhurried steps into the room. She moistened her lips. "Escambia County Deputy Sheriff. Come out with your hands up."

He waited behind the plastic as he fingered the razor-sharp edge of the Bowie knife held in his right hand. *So much quieter than a gun and silencer. Come on, sweetheart. A little closer.*

The officer's eyes were peeled on the covered aperture.

Hamelin lunged through the plastic to slam the knife into her. She lurched aside and swung the metal flashlight at him. It connected with his shoulder. He brought his left arm around and hit her full force in the side. The blow knocked her to the floor. She gasped. Her flashlight spun away into the middle of the room, along with her revolver.

A loose panel of sheetrock toppled onto her. Hamelin stomped his heavy boot onto the panel. She gasped again. He didn't have time to mess with her. Backup would be on the way. How had she known? Hamelin ran for the door and fled down the stairwell.

As he sped over the steps, a door crashed open above. She'd followed him.

Once he'd reached the ground floor, he tore past storage cabinets and laundry bins in a corridor. The cop wasn't that far behind him. He had to escape, but if he ran outside, she'd fire. No guarantee she'd have a bad aim either.

Near the end of the passage, he stopped in front of the outside door, weighing his options.

He turned to face the empty hall. From the door to his right, a wiry young man in brown scrubs stepped out. Hamelin whirled and pinioned the man in front of him with one brawny arm. As the deputy rushed in, Hamelin leaned back against the exit door. He grinned at her and raised his knife to the hostage's throat. The point pushed into the man's neck and blood trickled to his collar-bone.

The officer glowered. "Let him go and put down your weapon. He's done nothing to you."

Hamelin grinned wider as he tightened his grip on the captive and engaged the push bar on the door.

She advanced to within ten feet, her weapon pointed at Hamelin's face. The deputy glared and took another step. "Drop it."

A faint wail of sirens came from outside. Hamelin plunged his knife into the hostage's left shoulder and wrenched it out again. He shoved his victim into the cop, crashed backward through the doorway, and ran into the pelting rainstorm.

Chapter Thirty

After finding the room empty where she and Jake had left Teri, the plastic in a heap on the floor, and a piece of broken sheetrock where there had been none previously, Lynne raced to the stairwell. Jake was right behind her. She thought she'd heard a door bang against a wall as they waited for Teri at the nursing station. And then a second bang when they first entered the hall to look for her. "Teri must have gone after Hamelin."

The guard pushed through the door and peeked over the rail while Lynne picked up a pipe laying on the floor in the hall and joined him.

"There's no one there, Miss Temple. If they came this way, they're on a floor below us now."

"Jake, I'm going after Teri." She ran down one flight of stairs with Jake on her heels. On the third floor, she turned to him. "You've got to call this in. Go to the nurse's desk and alert your department, then find out where Teri's backup is."

He burst through the third-floor door, and Lynne continued her flight down the stairs. She hated to leave Sam alone, but she had to make sure Teri was okay. Where was her backup? Lynne paused to listen for any unusual sounds on each floor, then kept going.

When she reached ground level, a group of hospital employees and guests clustered around the front of the Environmental Services hallway several feet away. "What's going on?" Could it be Teri? Was she hurt?

An elderly woman pointed into the corridor. "Someone got stabbed."

Oh no. Not Teri. Lynne pushed her way through the onlookers.

Teri rolled a physical therapy tech off her onto his back. His brown scrubs bloody at the neck, with more blood oozing onto Teri's uniform. Her gun pointed to the ceiling.

Lynne ran to her side and knelt on the rain covered floor. Gusts of wind kept the exit door from closing.

The tech groaned.

As more waves of rain blew into the hall, Lynne pressed her hand over the man's wound. "Keep still." She pointed at another employee and yelled out, "You in the green scrubs. Call ER, now!"

"They're on their way," the girl in green answered.

Teri stood and faced the group gathered at the end of the hallway. "Are any of you a doctor?" She holstered her gun and then engaged her radio. "Intruder exited south side of the hospital. We think it was Hamelin. He stabbed an employee."

The clatter of gurney wheels entered the hall. "Out of the way." The emergency staff reached the injured man and examined the wound. They hoisted him onto the gurney and rushed him back down the hallway.

The deputy pulled her gun from the holster, slammed into the closing metal door, and ran out into the rain.

Lynne poked her head out the door. The rain had intensified, shooting thin, slanted silver rods to the ground. An occasional hailstone bounced off the pavement. Teri made it to the parking lot and rotated as if searching the grounds for signs of the attacker.

A uniformed officer ran from the outside cafeteria door to where Teri stood. A second patrol car arrived and cruised past, shining a spotlight around the campus. Teri and the officer returned to the building.

"Lynne, this is Sergeant Beckworth." She turned to the sergeant. "Sir, this is Lynne Temple. The young woman we believe The Piper planned to attack."

"We'll need to take your statement, Miss Temple." The three took the elevator to the fourth floor.

When they arrived, Sam stood behind the counter at the station. Her eyes grew wide. "What happened to you?" She grabbed Teri's hands. "You're covered with blood. Are you all right?"

"Apart from a few bruises, I'm fine. The blood's not mine. It's from a hospital employee Hamelin used as a hostage."

Sam's eyes widened even more. Her jaw dropped.

"The employee's in the ER now. Teri came face-to-face with The

Piper tonight. She and I need to wash up. Be right back." Lynne led Teri to the restroom.

After they washed up and returned to the nursing station, Lynne pulled a chair out and sat behind the desk. The sergeant took out his notebook, and Sam finally retook her seat.

Teri faced him, giving details of what had transpired after she sent Lynne back to her station. "When Hamelin pushed the wounded man into me, it knocked me to the ground. Fortunately, my gun didn't go off. He escaped out the door on the south side of the building."

The sergeant took Lynne's statement next and then stuffed the notebook in his pocket. "We'll set up more security here at the hospital until we catch this perp. He may still try to get to you, Miss Temple."

"I'm sure she was the intended target." Teri pursed her lips and clenched her fists as she leaned her elbows on the counter. "Hamelin could have used a sniper rifle, but he wants it up close and personal with you. He's a psycho with a Bowie knife. And he's out for revenge."

When Lynne bit her lip and shuddered, Sam put her arm around Lynne's back.

The sergeant glanced at Lynne and then Teri. "It's to our advantage you live in the same building, Coleraine. Keep the same hours as Miss Temple for now. Follow her to work, and make sure you're back here to follow her home again after her shift. I'll have the department shift schedules rearranged."

Sam grinned at Lynne. "That means you'll have a personal bodyguard for now."

Lynne leaned back in her chair. "I appreciate it, Teri. Sergeant."

She gazed out the fourth-floor windows and sighed. "This weather depresses me almost as much as my fear." She turned to the officers. "You'll get a lot of emergency calls because of the storm, won't you?"

"I'm afraid so." Teri nodded. "Flooded and washed out roads, accidents, power lines down. The winds are stronger than our last storm."

Sam pursed her lips. "When will Nick come back from his weekend camping trip with the teens, Lynnz?"

"He's supposed to be back tomorrow." *God, this isn't a test of my faith, is it?*

After her lunch break, Lynne's phone vibrated. She extracted it from her scrubs' pocket.

"Hi, Lynne, it's me."

"Nick. It's good to hear your voice. You called from the campsite?"

Sam poked her in the ribs. "You're blushing."

"No. We left before noon because of the weather forecast. I got home after the teens were picked up from church. This is some storm that popped up."

"I'll bet the teens were disappointed." She searched for something to throw at Sam, who fluttered her eyelashes and giggled.

"They had a great time until this morning. Yesterday, we went fishing. Told spooky stories last night, minus the campfire since the winds had already picked up. And we played board games inside the lodge this morning. They grumbled when I said we'd have to leave." He laughed. "Thanks for praying. I'll tell you about their antics on the trip when I pick you up after work."

"But Nick, aren't the roads already bad here?"

"I'm sure they're okay between my place and the hospital, and the hospital and your apartment."

"Oh, good. I'll call Teri and tell her she'll follow your truck instead of Sam's car tonight."

"Huh? Why would she follow my vehicle? That silver car didn't show up again, did it?"

Lynne bit her lip. "Not exactly. It's a long story. I'll tell you when you get here."

"Okay. Be there in three hours."

"Bye, Nick." *Love you.* Lynne's heart warmed at the thought of being with him again.

Sam pressed her lips together and gazed at Lynne. "Nick sure quickens your pulse rate."

"I'll save my comments for when *Dep-per-ty* Russ phones you at work next time. Remember, I don't get mad. *I* get even." Lynne chuckled and glanced at her watch. The next three hours would definitely drag by. She grimaced.

The desk phone rang. "Four-north, Lynne Temple speaking."

"Lynne, this is Teri. Something's happened to your friends, Agents Travis and Trent."

Lynne rushed to the ER and searched until she found the right cubicle. Loring lay stretched out on his back on the gurney, a large bandage on his forehead. "Loring? A friend of mine from the sheriff's department told me you were brought to the ER. She said your car took a nosedive into Escambia Bay? I thought you and Kim were flying in."

"There was a mix-up in the tickets. We flew into Jacksonville, checked in at the FBI office, and then rented a car. But we were ambushed on the road before we made it to Pensacola."

"What do you mean, ambushed? Where's Kim?"

"In Critical Care. They're admitting me too, but just for observation."

The privacy curtain swished back, and Steph stepped in. "Hi, Lynne. What are you doing here?"

"I heard my friends were here, so I came to find out if they were okay."

"They took Miss Travis to CCU. We'll admit Mr. Trent to your floor in a minute."

Lynne let out a sigh of relief. "Loring, I'll go back now. When you're settled in your room, buzz me at the nursing station."

"Thanks, Lynne. Please pray for Kim. She's in bad shape."

"I will. And I'll check on Kim." Lynne's brows pinched together. *Lord, take care of Kim.*

Lynne returned to the fourth floor and told Sam what Loring said while she called CCU. *Busy.* "I can't believe this day, Sam. What else can go wrong?"

"Don't say that, Lynnz. I'm not superstitious, but that's never a good thing to say. Tempting fate, you know."

"You're right. We've had enough happen already. And I've left you to do all our work so far. Thanks for understanding. I'll go on rounds. Can you keep trying CCU for me?"

"You betcha, girl. And talking to our patients may relieve your stress." Sam smiled and shooed Lynne away from the desk.

As Lynne finished rounds and came back to the station, Sam was hanging up the phone receiver. "Agent Trent's settled in room four sixty-seven. He's asking for you. He also asked after Agent Travis. I've tried to reach Critical Care, but their line is busy each time. I'll try again in a few minutes."

"Thanks, Sam. Do you mind if I check on Loring?"

"Not a bit. Other than your trauma, the floor's been quiet today." Sam picked up the receiver as Lynne headed for Loring's room.

When she entered, Loring had his eyes closed. Should I let him rest? She turned to leave.

"Lynne?"

She spun. "I was going to come back later."

"It's okay. I was praying for Kim. I'm so worried about her."

Lynne sat in the chair next to Loring's bed. "Sam's trying to get an update on her now. Can you tell me what happened?"

"Everything was fine on the drive from Jacksonville, until we neared the town called Crestview. We passed a rest area on Interstate Ten where I noticed a black Ford Taurus on the exit ramp a few feet from the parking lot. It was on the grass."

Lynne lowered her brows. "Strange place to stop."

"That's what I thought. After we passed it, I had a hunch. I watched in the rearview mirror. The Taurus sped onto the interstate right behind us, and for the next couple of miles, it stayed on our tail."

"Then what?"

"Nothing at first. I changed lanes. The Taurus did the same. Kim said we were better off going out of our way to lose whoever it was. She said it'd be too dangerous driving over the long bridge she'd pointed out earlier on the map she followed. If someone wanted to stop us, that'd be the place. So when I saw the next exit, we took it. They did too."

"When did this happen?"

"Early this morning."

Couldn't have been The Piper. He was in the hospital then. Lynne's top teeth clamped on her lip.

"Kim said we could take U.S. Route Ninety, so we turned there."

Lynne's pulse increased. "And then?"

"They followed. After a while, I noticed there was no traffic behind them. None from the other direction either. We knew something was up. She checked the map again and saw that we'd still have to cross a large section of waterway. I figured these dudes would pull something there."

"You mean over the rivers that empty into the north end of Escambia Bay?"

"I guess that's it. As soon as we saw the water, the black car rushed up in the left lane. Shot at us, but missed when I slammed on the brakes. I jammed the pedal to the floor and got ahead of them. They caught up and sideswiped us in a swampy area. Ran us off the pavement."

Lynne's hand covered her mouth.

"We plowed through a grassy shoulder and plunged into what looked like a bayou. A wave of water engulfed the front end of the car. Kim's airbag deployed, but mine didn't. My head hit the windshield."

"But you both made it out of the car."

"Yeah. It rested on the water like a houseboat. Then started to sink." He winced and raised his hand to the bandage on his head. "Kim pushed on the door, but it wouldn't budge with the force of the water up to the window frame. Thank God we could still open the windows. We pulled ourselves out and tumbled into the water. I trudged around in the mucky bottom to the back of the car as it sunk further, grabbed Kim's hand, and pulled her toward me."

"You're fortunate there were no alligators." Lynne took a deep breath and blew it out slowly.

"That was Kim's biggest fear. I was more worried about the two-legged predators at the moment."

"So did the car that ran you off the road keep going?"

"No. A car door slammed as we climbed up the embankment, and a burst of gunfire peppered the water around us. Kim collapsed. She slid back toward the water—" Loring turned to the doorway to see who stood there.

Chapter Thirty-One

r. Smith stepped into Loring's room. Lynne sat erect and pursed her lips. Why did he have to pick now to walk in?

"Hello, Mr. Trent. I'm Dr. Smith. Let's look at that bump on your head." He glanced at Lynne. "Miss Temple. Is the patient all right?"

"Seems to be. I stopped in to see Loring before starting rounds because he's a friend of mine. Do you want me to leave?"

"No. You're fine. I thought he might have passed out like he did when he came into the ER." He turned to his patient. "I have some routine questions. Won't take but a minute."

The physician examined Loring and received his answers. He smiled. "We'll keep you here overnight to make sure you have no problems from that blow to your head. But I want you to rest. Don't get out of bed except to use the restroom. You may experience dizziness again, so call for the nurse when you need to get up. If all is well tomorrow, you can be on your way."

"Thank you, Doctor."

The doctor turned, nodded to Lynne, and left the room.

Lynne shut the door and returned to the chair. "Finally. So what happened to Kim?"

His brows furrowed. "When she slid back toward the water, I grabbed her arm and pulled her up the slope. She'd lost consciousness. I heard one of them say, 'Got the chick.' He sounded a fair distance away, so I picked her up and hauled her into taller grass. They fired a couple more rounds in our general direction, but the bullets whizzed over the water."

"Praise God." Lynne shivered.

"Kim's forehead bled where a bullet had grazed near the temple. And blood oozed from her shoulder. I never prayed so hard in my life."

Lynne laid her hand on the edge of the bed. "I can only imagine."

"I tore off my shirt and pressed it into the wound in her shoulder, then used the strap from her purse to hold the shirt in place."

"What about the shooters? How did you get out of there and to the hospital?"

"Once I hid Kim in a thick stand of grasses closer to the highway, I crept to the road. Wasn't sure what to do since we'd lost our weapon in the water." He rubbed his forehead. "To make a long story short, they'd left the Taurus idling on the easement and had gone down to the water's edge."

A shudder surged through Lynne's body. She took a deep breath as if she were the one about to approach the shooters herself.

"They were crouched over. I ran down the slope and cannonballed into the taller one's back, sending him into the water. When the other guy turned, I slammed my fist into his jaw. He lost his footing and fell over a thick clump of grass behind him. His gun flew into the air. He must have thought I had a gun, because he leaped into the water to join his accomplice. I found his gun in the grass."

Lynne moved her hand to his arm. "Thank God, Loring."

He placed his hand over hers. "I fired off two shots to tell them I meant business even if I couldn't see him in the mist. Then the clouds opened up. I ran back to Kim, carried her to the Taurus, and took off."

As Lynne expelled the breath she'd held, she slumped back into the chair.

"When I drove over a high, curved bridge at the end of the waterway, there was a police car blocking traffic in the opposite direction. A deputy rushed out of the vehicle to wave me down, but something told me not to stop. As I hurtled past the roadblock, he yelled."

"You thought they were imposters?" She sat upright again.

"I didn't know what to believe. At the first intersection farther down the road, there was a gas station, so I pulled behind the building to keep the car hidden from the road. A startled young man behind the counter called nine-one-one for me."

"Is this what it's like to work for the FBI all the time?"

"Not really. This was as intense as it gets. The boy at the gas station also called the Pensacola FBI office. And after what seemed an eternity, we heard sirens headed our way. They pulled into the gas station."

"And the paramedics brought you here." Lynne leaned back in the chair and shook her head. "Has anyone told you anything about Kim's condition?"

"No. Except that she's in serious condition." His eyes misted. "Several things passed through my mind while I held Kim and sat in the car, waiting for the paramedics. One of them was what you'd said in Chicago. 'You can't love a ghost.' I told myself I'd tell her how I feel as soon as she regained consciousness."

Lynne stood. "She'll be okay, Loring. I'm sorry, but I have to get back to work now. I'm so glad you and Kim are here. At least you're okay despite your wounds, and I'm sure Kim will be too. She's in good hands. I'll see if I can get an update on her condition."

A tremor raced down Lynne's back. They'd gone to such an extreme to stop Loring and Kim from arriving. *Lord, for Loring's sake, let Kim be okay.*

"Boss, we have a problem." Derek gulped as he listened through the phone to the man's heavy breath. His Goliath of a boss had a mantra. *I don't like problems.*

"What?" The question blasted from the cell.

Derek gulped. "We ran the agents off the road. But—"

"But what?" he snarled.

Sweat seeped from Derek's armpits and forehead. Hamelin wasn't a guy you wanted to disappoint. "The agents escaped." The silence that followed was even worse than his razor-sharp tongue.

"What happened?"

Hamelin's bulging mud-brown eyes laced with blood red came to mind. Hopefully, he wouldn't have to see the hulk in person until the end of the week. Maybe he'd calm down by then. He hoped. "After we ran them off the road, their car hit the water. We were moving a hundred miles an hour, so by the time we stopped our vehicle and backed up to where they landed, they'd crawled onto the shore about fifty feet away from us. We hurried to the water and shot off a couple rounds."

"You were only fifty feet from them, and still they managed to get away?"

A crash passed through the earpiece. He'd thrown something. Derek's heartbeat raced. He was glad they were twenty miles apart. It could've been him Hamelin slammed around.

"Boss, somehow the guy slipped in behind us and got the drop." Derek rubbed his swollen jaw. "Forced us into one of those rivers. We lost our weapons when we fell into the drink. He started shooting. We were in the middle of the downpour, and they stole our car."

"Did they now?" The words were filled with sarcasm.

"Yeah...well, he took the keys when he snuck up on us." Stupid stunt to leave the car running.

The phone fell silent. "Boss?" Had he hung up?

"I'm here. How did they get past the rest of the crew? Weren't they at the west end of the bridge with a roadblock? Didn't they stop them?"

"The guys said the Taurus flew past them like a bullet. We had no idea which road they took after they passed Scenic Highway. And we figured the cops could show up any minute looking for the cruiser we stole, so we left."

"You bunch of—" A string of expletives flew. "You're useless!"

"Boss, he had the drop on us. The other guys didn't stop him." Yeah. He should buy that. It'd get *him* off the hook anyway. The only other person who could squeal on him was his partner, and he wouldn't dare since he's the one who left the car running. The agents would no doubt be dead before they could say a word to Hamelin.

I wonder what he'll do now.

Nick picked up Lynne at the hospital and drove to her apartment, Teri following close behind. Lynne sure has been quiet since she left her station. He reached over and took her hand in his. "I get the feeling something serious has happened. After that first smile you gave me when I stepped off the elevator, your expression has been one of the most tense I've ever seen."

"Nick, I planned to tell you when we were at the apartment. We had another incident at the hospital. A serious one. Plus, a couple of thugs attacked my friends Loring and Kim, the FBI agents from Chicago, on their way to Pensacola."

He pulled into a parking space and turned to her. "Who attacked your friends? No. Wait. Let's get upstairs, and then you can tell me what happened."

Lynne nodded, her expression somber.

Nick hurried to open the passenger door, and she slid out. As they walked up the sidewalk to the apartment building, she turned and waved to Teri, who also exited her vehicle.

Once inside Lynne's apartment, Nick sat on the couch and pulled Lynne down beside him. He lifted her chin with his index finger. "Do you need a few minutes to gather your thoughts?"

She nodded.

He took her hands in his. "Let's pray first. It'll help."

Lynne pressed her lips into a straight line and nodded again.

Nick bowed his head. "Lord, we need Your help. Thank You for keeping Lynne safe through whatever happened. Please calm her as only You can. In Your Holy name, I pray. Amen."

He smiled at her and ran his fingertips along her cheek. "Prayer's the best way to settle nerves." He leaned in to kiss her.

The deadbolt clunked out of the doorjamb, and Sam walked in. "Did I interrupt again?" She waved her hand as if to dismiss the question and closed the door. "Did you tell him?"

"Not yet."

Sam dropped her purse on the coffee table and headed to the kitchen. "While you talk, I'll get dinner started. You are staying for dinner, aren't you, Nick? Never mind. You are. Please make her relax?"

"I'll try." He smiled at her, then focused on Lynne. "I think Sam's the one who needs to chill out," he whispered.

Nick watched Lynne's lips try to form a smile that didn't quite make it. It dissolved into a sniff. "Now, start at the beginning."

For the next half hour, Lynne described Hamelin's intrusion into the hospital, how Teri foiled it, how The Piper wounded his hostage, and everything Loring had told her. Nick listened without interruption.

When she finished, Lynne leaned back against the arm he'd stretched behind her. His heart ached for her. *Lord, hasn't she gone through enough? Please let them get this guy.* "Better?" He hoped. Nick kissed her forehead.

"Thanks for listening. I feel better. Guess I needed to talk it out."

Nick pulled her closer with his outstretched arm.

Sam waltzed into the room. "Dinner's almost done. What do you two want to drink? And where is Russ? He said he'd come for dinner."

The doorbell rang, and Lynne jumped. "Man!"

Nick squeezed her shoulder with his free hand. "It's only Russ. Relax."

Lynne shook her head. "I'll try. Sure hope the authorities get a good lead on Hamelin and this nightmare ends soon."

Sam buzzed Russ up and peeked through the peephole while she waited. She opened the door before he knocked.

Nick let go of Lynne's shoulder. He rose from the couch as Russ stepped into the living room. "Glad you could join us tonight, Russ. Nice to have another male around, so I'm not the only one they pick on."

"Great to see you again." The officer clasped Nick's hand.

After she closed the door, Sam returned to the kitchen. "Lynnz, would you get out the drinks. I'm fixin' to set the spaghetti and salad on the table?" Sam opened the oven door, and the aroma of garlic bread filled the room.

Lynne entered the kitchen. "That bread smells so good. The whole meal looks fantastic. Thanks for cooking tonight."

"No problem, girl. You've had a rough time of it today. I'm sure my day's coming, and you'll have to play the mom." She giggled.

Nick joined the girls. "Let me get the glasses."

Lynne spun and the two-liter bottle of cola she'd taken from the refrigerator slipped from her grip. She gasped.

Nick caught the bottle before it hit the floor. "Good thing I hadn't taken those glasses out yet."

Russ chuckled as he came up behind Sam. "I'm afraid I'll have to eat and run tonight. A call came through before I arrived. I'm needed on a stakeout. Have to be there in an hour to relieve someone. Sorry to spoil the evening."

Sam's brows puckered. "Does this have something to do with Hamelin? Will you be in danger?"

Chapter Thirty-Two

$\mathcal{E}$arly Tuesday afternoon, the nursing station phone rang. She willed it to be good news for a change. She'd had enough bad to last the rest of her life. Scooping up the receiver, she said, "Four-north, Lynne Temple speaking."

"Dr. White here. I'm calling to tell you it's okay for Mr. Trent to visit his partner in the Critical Care unit. I thought it might help bring her around since she hasn't responded to anything else so far."

Lynne's heart filled with joy for Loring. Kim loved Loring. His voice could make the difference if anything would. "When should I bring him?"

"You can wheel him over now if you have time."

As she hung up, she smiled at Sam. "I'm taking Loring to see Kim. Shouldn't be gone too long."

"Wonderful. He'll be relieved. He asks about her every time I'm in his room. It's so sad." Sam shook her head. "So, she regained consciousness?"

"Not yet. Dr. White said they want Loring to talk to her. She might respond to his voice."

Sam nodded. "Lord willing, she will."

Lynne rolled out a wheelchair from the supply closet and headed to Loring's room.

As she pushed the chair through the doorway, his brows lowered. "A wheelchair?"

"Standard procedure, Sir. Of course, if you don't want to take a ride and visit Kim…" Lynne grinned.

His face lit up. "Let's do it." He pressed the button to raise the head of the bed.

"Now, don't stand until I'm ready for you." Lynne bent to raise the wheelchair footplates.

Loring sighed and swung his legs over the side. Before she could stop him, he stood. But only for a moment. All six feet of his athletic physique swayed to the left. "Whoa!"

Lynne caught him by the arms and shook her head. Just like a man. "What's this? A last-ditch effort to prove your macho independence? It's okay. I've got you, Superman." She helped him lower into the chair. "Easy now. Next time listen to the trained medical professional who knows what she's doing, okay? Looks like you'll be here for at least another day." She lowered the footplates and guided his feet onto them.

With a grimace, he glanced up at her. "You knew that would happen, didn't you?"

She stifled a laugh and raised her eyebrows. "Happens every time with you he-men. Although I hoped you'd be steady on your feet this time. That's one nasty lump on your head. Second time you've almost passed out on us. Sit back and enjoy the ride. Or do I need to strap you in?" She snickered. *Men.* "Do all men imagine themselves indestructible?"

"Do all nurses threaten their patients the way you do?"

She patted the top of his head and rolled him through the doorway.

"So, is Kim awake now? How's she doing?"

Lynne wheeled him toward the elevators. "She's still unconscious, but Dr. White hopes she'll respond to your voice. You only had a serious concussion and water in your ear from your dip in the bay, obviously still making you unstable on your feet. Kim had a more serious wound to her head and shoulder. But she's been resting peacefully."

Loring's hands fisted. "I hope I can help."

"Loring, have you tasted any more blood since you were admitted to the floor?"

"No, that's gone. Sure wish this headache was."

"Bump on the head, remember? You'll have a nice goose egg for a while. You're fortunate a headache is all you have. Aside from the dizziness, you've had no other symptoms that raise a red flag. Maybe the lump and the pain will subside by tomorrow."

"It's nice to hear you say something positive for a change instead of just bossing me around."

"And it's nice that your sense of humor is intact, as well, Mr. Trent."

He chuckled.

Lynne and Loring nodded to the CCU nurse after they passed through the sliding glass doors to the unit. The nursing station surrounded by monitors and several open-ended enclosures with curtains instead of doors was quiet with only two other patients. An officer sat at the door of Kim's room.

Her pale skin made little contrast to the white pillowcase beneath her head. A large bandage circled her head from where the bullet had grazed near the temple. The thick dressing on her shoulder bulged beneath the mint green material of her hospital gown.

Kim's breathing was shallow but steady, her eyes closed. The monitor next to her sent out a steady beep, and an IV dripped from a suspended bag into the tube attached to her left arm.

Lynne rolled Loring to the side of the bed, and she took the seat next to it.

With misty eyes, he reached for Kim's right hand, which lay on the top of the sheet. As he held her long fingers in his large palm, he took a deep breath. "She's always so full of life." A tear slid over his lower lashes. He brushed it away with the back of his free hand.

"We'll only have a couple of minutes." Lynne stood and touched his shoulder. "Go ahead and talk to her. I'll wait outside the door." She stepped through the opening, facing the nursing desk.

Loring's shaky voice drifted to Lynne's ears. "Kim?"

Kim moaned.

Lynne's head whipped around to gaze at Kim. Her eyelids fluttered but didn't open. Loring kissed Kim's hand.

He lowered his forehead to the edge of the bed. "I was so afraid I'd lost you. I love you, Kim. All this time—I've been such a fool not to tell you how much you mean to me."

Kim's lashes fluttered again. Her eyes slowly opened. She turned to Loring, and a faint smile came to her lips.

"You're awake." He brought her hand to his lips again. "Thank God, you're awake."

Lynne rushed to his side. Tears flooded her eyes. "Praise God." She should leave them alone, but— "We've been so worried. Sorry for the interruption, Loring. I'm just so happy Kim's awake. I'll go back outside." She patted Kim's hand and left them.

As she stepped to the hall, the CCU nurse hurried in. They might never get another moment's privacy until Kim's recovered. Lynne clamped her lips together to keep from voicing her thoughts. She peered into the room.

"Welcome back, Miss Travis." The nurse beamed as she checked Kim's vitals. "You've had a lot of people worried."

"I'll say." Loring grinned at Kim.

When the nurse finished, she returned to the station and picked up the phone receiver. Lynne fought the urge to join Loring and Kim.

She watched as Kim reached out a hand and ran her fingertips down one side of Loring's face. He had to be ready to burst with joy. Lynne recalled the first time a tingle ran through her at Nick's touch. She glanced at her watch. It was almost time for him to pick her up. The anticipation filled her with excitement.

"You need a shave," Kim said in a raspy voice. "And your eyes tell me you need sleep."

"I only need you." Loring smiled, then glanced at Lynne and back to Kim.

Awww. Lynne's heart leaped for joy. If only he could stay with Kim longer, but she had to return him to his room. She came up behind him. "Loring, I'm afraid we have to leave now. Kim, I'm so happy you're okay, and—everything." She pressed her lips together again.

Color filled Kim's white cheeks.

"We'll check back with you later. I'll take this character back to his room and make sure he rests up for his next visit."

"Thanks, Lynne," Kim whispered.

Loring braced himself on the edge of her bed and rose. He leaned forward and lowered his lips to hers.

Dr. White's tall frame hurried through the door. "I heard our patient is awake. Good job, Mr. Trent. Now I need to examine her, and you need to get back to *your* bed."

Lynne helped Loring back into the chair and turned him toward the door. "We're on our way, Doctor."

Loring twisted in the chair to gaze at Kim as he and Lynne left the room. The nurse reentered, and the privacy curtain scraped along its track as she drew it around the bed. He faced forward and expelled a long breath of air. "I want to stay with her."

"I know. But at least you had a special moment. She's awake, and you talked to her. Plus—" She rested her hand on his shoulder as they waited for the elevator. "I'm sure you can come back later this evening. In the meantime, you need to rest."

The door dinged open, and they entered the car. Lynne pressed the fourth-floor button.

She grinned as the door closed. It was time something positive happened. *Can't wait to tell Nick the good news.*

Back in Loring's room, Lynne helped him into bed. "Loring, the attack on you and Kim. It has to do with the reason you were sent here, doesn't it?"

"I'm almost sure it does." He leaned back on the pillow. "I've spoken to the Pensacola FBI office. They're investigating." He focused his eyes on her. "Lynne, be careful. You're in another situation that involves that fiend, Hamelin."

She nodded and bit her lip. "I had hoped he was past history."

"Hard to understand why this is happening, but God's in charge. He has His reasons, even if we never find out what they are. Just trust Him. It's all any of us can do until we catch Hamelin."

She pulled the sheet up covering Loring's legs and handed him the water cup he'd reached for. "I'll hold onto hope that God brings this to an end soon. The sheriff's department is providing protection for me until it's over, so I'm more worried about you and Kim."

"They got the drop on us once, but we'll get them before too long." Loring yawned.

She returned the cup to the bed table. "I'll check on you later. Try to go to sleep. The guard is right outside your door, and you have your call button in case you need us."

He nodded, lay back on the pillow, and closed his eyes.

As Lynne slipped out the room, her adrenaline surged. The details of Kim and Loring's close call revisited her thoughts all the way back to the nursing station.

The question wasn't if the next attack would come, but when. And on whom?

Chapter Thirty-Three

Two days later, Lynne entered Loring's room before the evening shift change. "Still doing okay?"

"All my equipment seems to function fine, the headache's gone, and there's been no taste of blood. I can even use the restroom under my own power." Loring chuckled. "Guess I have a harder head than even you or Kim thought."

"At the risk of repeating myself, it's a good thing you didn't smash *through* that windshield." They both came too close to being gator bait.

"Agreed. May I dress now?" Loring glanced at the pile of clean, folded clothes with a pair of new sandals lying on top of a chair in the corner. "One of our local agents kindly purchased these for me since our suitcases had sunk to the bottom of the bay before the sheriff's deputies could retrieve them. Not sure if anything we had is salvageable from that swim or not." His face wrinkled as if he could smell the mildew that would surely have formed by now.

"Your clothes should be fine after a couple of washings. Go ahead." She pointed to the folded garments. "Sorry you didn't have anything to change into earlier. I should have thought to call Nick. You're about the same size, and he would have brought something for you." She headed for the door. "Dr. White will be along any minute. He'll give you a final check and discharge you. He's running way behind today. My shift ends in a few minutes, so I'll say goodnight now. Sam and I want to have you and Kim over one evening for dinner before you return to Washington. Hopefully soon. The dinner, I mean." She laughed.

"That would be nice. Have a great night." He gathered his new clothes and disappeared behind the restroom door.

After leaving the happy agent, she joined Sam at the nursing station. "Loring says he's still fine. The only thing pounding now is his heart for Kim. Of course, he didn't say that last part. I'm so happy for them, Sam."

"Me too."

A second shift nurse stepped off the elevator.

Lynne grinned at Sam. "Time to leave. Sure wish Nick hadn't left town again, even if it *is* a mere two days this time. He's the guest preacher in another small country church. That man loves to preach." And she loved that he was doing what God called him to do. The only problem, she missed him.

"He sure seems to be a popular preacher. Do you think you can handle being a minister's wife someday?"

Lynne rolled her eyes. "Sam, you beat all. Nick and I haven't known each other long enough for a leap like that." Although it had crossed her mind more than once. Better change the subject before

Sam started teasing. "I just worry about his traveling with the weather so unstable. And so close to New Orleans. I've heard it floods a lot."

The second nurse to relieve the girls rushed out the elevator and hurried to the desk. "Sorry I'm late. Traffic's a bear."

Sam checked the time on the computer. "You're not really late. Few minutes only. And girl, we're not even into rush hour yet. I'm glad we don't work nine to five."

"Whew! I hate not getting here early. It took me longer today than normal. The car clock is broken. I forgot to put on my watch. I hate being late." She plunked herself into a desk chair.

While Sam prepared to leave, Lynne discussed morning shift details with both second shift nurses. "Mr. Trent, in room four sixty-seven, will no doubt be discharged whenever Dr. White shows up." They nodded.

Lynne retrieved her purse from the bottom drawer and joined Sam at the elevator.

Sam focused on her roommate's face. "I understand your concern over Nick with what's happened around here, apart from the weather. I'm anxious about Russ too. Since he went on that stakeout the other night, I haven't heard a word from him." She shook her head. "This criminal at large is to blame for everyone's anxiety."

The door dinged open, and the girls entered the car. As the door closed, Lynne laid her hand on Sam's shoulder. "Let's go home to a nice quiet evening. Play a board game or something. Now that the rain has let up again, it's one less worry. This is the strangest weather. More like spring than fall with the pop-up storms." She hit the ground floor button.

Sam lowered her brows. "Did you hear the weather report? Radar has detected yet another storm south of Puerto Rico. Our weather isn't usually all that bad. Pensacola must have a target painted on it this year. I hope the new storm blows over as fast as the last one. We've had enough problems with rising water."

Lynne's brows furrowed as she nodded. *Hope Nick isn't affected by any rising water. And all our other problems blow themselves out too.*

After two sleepless nights, how could she study? Lynne pushed the booklet for her upcoming advanced cardiac life-support renewal test to the side and drummed her fingers on the nursing station desk. Nick hadn't made it back yet from Louisiana as planned.

The early morning news had reported so many roads closed across the South because of floods caused by the nearing storm.

"Lynnz?" Sam nudged her. "Your phone's ringing." She pointed to the drawer where Lynne kept her purse.

Lynne opened the drawer and dove her hand in. She retrieved the cell from the bottom of her bag, but the call had already gone to voicemail. *Nick.* She sighed and listened to the message.

"Hey, Lynne. Thought I'd better let you know, I'm still stuck here in Louisiana because of rising water. But I just found out I-fifty-five north is open, or so they say. While I'm so near, I'll make a call on a former church member who moved into the Mississippi backcountry. She's a long-time friend of my aunt. I want to be sure she's okay and has everything she needs should this storm get worse. She lives over the state line in a small community. Reception may be nonexistent there. If the roads further north are open, I'll try to make it back to

Pensacola after the visit. Talk to you when I'm home."

She stashed the phone back in her purse and closed the drawer as she bit her lip. "Great. He's going into the backcountry to check on his aunt's old friend. And he may not be able to make a call there. He said he'll try to find a clear road and make his way home after the visit."

Sam glanced at Lynne. "Don't worry so. It's just a storm, and he's a southern boy. It's not as if he's never gone through this before. Relax. He'll be okay. He won't put himself in danger." She left the desk and began to set up medications for morning rounds.

Yeah sure. Sam had tried too hard to convince her. *Don't worry about the storm?* But Sam was accurate about one thing. He'd lived in the South his entire life. "I guess you're right. My nerves *are* frayed. And the news report last night about those missing kids hasn't helped any."

"Do you think it involves that Piper guy?"

"I'm sure it does." Lynne pressed her lips together.

"Are you worried he might slip past hospital security?" She scanned the area.

Lynne shrugged. Now she'd made Sam uptight.

With a hand less steady than normal, Sam organized the medicine cups according to patient rooms. "Why do you suppose they recalled Loring to Washington before they've caught this guy? The doctors haven't discharged Agent Travis yet, so she can't work on the case. I thought he was the expert on that criminal."

Lynne leaned back in the desk chair and closed her eyes. Not another headache. Just what she needed. "I'm sure they have their reasons."

Her phone chirped. She yanked the drawer open and reached into her purse for the cell. After two rings, it went silent. "Nick again?" No message. "He must have just passed into the dead zone he told me about."

At least Sam and Teri were around to talk to. It helped to voice her fears. But talking to Nick would help more. With Kim admitted to their floor, she could spend time with her on breaks. Lynne rose. "I'll check on Kim for a few minutes before I start rounds. If that's all right with you."

"Okay." Sam smiled and resumed filling medicine cups. "I'll call you if anything comes up."

"Thanks." Lynne hurried down the hall and entered Kim's room. She appeared to be asleep. Her breathing had a stable, rhythmic pattern. Lynne turned to leave.

"Don't go."

Lynne settled into the chair next to Kim's bed. "I'm sorry I woke you."

"It's okay. I haven't slept soundly since Loring was discharged, joined the sheriff department's stakeout right away, and then got called back to Washington. Every noise or movement wakes me." She stared out the window and sighed.

"Most people are that way in the hospital. Unfamiliar surroundings." She had to say something to snap Kim out of her depression. "But at least you and Loring spent some *quality* time together before he left. And boy did he make up for lost time." Lynne grinned.

Kim's lips stretched into a smile. "Loring told me he loves me, Lynne. He finally told me. I melted."

"I heard him. After we came to CCU the first time, I stepped outside the enclosure…but not far enough to avoid being the proverbial fly on the wall. I'm happy for you two." Should she ask Kim why he was called away? She'd already mentioned it. "Kim, why was Loring called back to D.C.?"

"Can't answer that one. When he stopped in before he left, he said it puzzled him." She reached for the water glass on the bed table but winced, and her hand shot up to her shoulder.

Lynne slid the table out from over the end of the bed and pulled it closer to Kim.

"Thanks." Kim sipped from the straw. "Loring had told me some time ago he suspected a leak somewhere in the bureau. He expressed his concern to our boss again yesterday, and the next thing he knew, he received a message from him insisting on Loring's return. No explanation as to why. Since the sheriff's department already had a lead on Hamelin, Loring thought it might be they felt he wasn't needed." Kim's eyes narrowed. "Or, it might have something to do with the leak."

Chapter Thirty-Four

*H*amelin viewed teens spread out over wet turf at a rave site he'd arranged. Good thing the storm stopped, or he'd have had to postpone the event. Along with his plans. That wouldn't have been a good thing.

"Good find, Appleby. Huge metal building on a darkened road surrounded by nothing but thick woods. And miles outside the city. You did well this time." This guy might be worth keeping around.

From their vantage point on the edge of the open grass area, Hamelin grinned. The kids gyrated through frenzied twists and turns to the thumping beat from giant amplifiers mounted on the building's walls. "They're showing signs of the drugs. Get ready."

"Look at that chick sloshing around in the wet grass, boss." Appleby pointed to a girl in a green luminescent wig, glitter makeup, and sequined top. He chuckled. "Get a load of those hip-hugging pants and neon-green fur legwarmers over the boots, covered in mud. Looks like a leprechaun…but she's shapely. S*he'd* bring a good price."

Hamelin gritted his teeth. "She's a cop, you idiot. Sizing up the situation. Bet she's wired too." He glared at Appleby. "Warn the others, and get the kids we've already collected out of here. This place will be crawling with cops in no time. I'll take care of her."

Appleby and the two thugs standing beside him pulled out their phones. As they shouted instructions to the rest of the crew, Hamelin headed toward the young woman. She followed the erratic moves of a gawky teenage boy, smiling and flirting with him. *You may have him fooled, Missy. But this will be your last dance.*

The boy backed away as Hamelin sidled up to her. The teen turned and made tracks for another grassy area used as a parking lot. Hamelin sneered. "Hello, little lady. Want to make some money?"

Her eyes widened. She sucked in her bottom lip but didn't move away. The multi-colored strobe lights turned her face sparkling green, purple, and yellow. "What'cha got in mind, mister?" An impish smile bordered on impertinence.

She was good. He'd give her that. But not good enough. He could spot a plant anywhere. Appleby was right. She'd bring him a pretty penny. Feisty. She'd regret trying to fool The Piper.

The girl's eyes avoided his gaze. She watched his hands and feet as if intrigued by them. Sizing him up, no doubt. Did the fool really think her petite frame adequate to take him on?

Hamelin took a step closer. He lunged at her throat with his huge hands, but a green blur sidestepped his thrust, and they closed on empty air. The petite cop's split-second response didn't miss. She stomped his instep, and as she spun, the heel of her boot caught him in the groin. He bellowed in pain.

When he straightened, he spotted Appleby a few feet away,

watching. *"Get her."* Hamelin hobbled toward his black Range Rover.

With Appleby yards behind her, the cop sprinted across the field. She yelled, *"Now."*

Patrol cars converged on the field from every direction, their blue lights flashing and sirens wailing. The panic-stricken teens scattered. Hamelin's dealers scurried like roaches for their vehicles.

Before he ducked into the black SUV, Hamelin glanced back at the slim, green-haired figure heading for a sheriff's patrol car. He brought the Rover's engine to life as the cruiser skidded to a halt beside her. She climbed into the rear seat. He'd have to pass on the pleasure of dealing with her...for now. His vehicle leaped forward.

He drove across the field toward the back road that led away from the rave, then stopped short of it and pulled the vehicle under thick, low branches in the shadows on the edge of the woods. From there, he could observe. But someone had to leave with the van parked behind the building, or the whole thing would be a bust.

The cruiser the female cop had jumped into pursued Appleby. It drew level with him and stopped. Two male officers sprang from the front seat. One vaulted over the hood and pulled Appleby to the ground in front of the vehicle. The other took off after another from Hamelin's crew.

Appleby fought like a cornered Pitbull, lashing out with feet and fists. Too bad he hadn't been such a scrapper with those agents that got away. He landed blows to the officer's face and legs.

With a well-placed uppercut to Appleby's chin, the muscle-bound deputy flattened Hamelin's henchman and shoved him face down in the wet turf, then straddled and cuffed him. The officer hauled the captive to his feet and propelled him toward the cruiser. The second deputy dragged the other dealer in the same direction.

Other officers had left their vehicles to gather up the rest of Hamelin's crew. One of his drug dealers eluded the cops and fled to the back of the building. Moments later, Hamelin spotted the black van racing past the far side of the metal structure and down another back country road. Well, at least that one got away. And with the merchandise. He'd earned his bonus.

This was all Appleby's fault. He'd messed up again. Otherwise, the cops wouldn't have known anything about this place. *You imbecile. Don't worry, they won't take you anywhere.*

Hamelin jerked the wheel and aimed the vehicle straight at Appleby. This was his chance while the officers were out of their vehicles. The Range Rover bolted forward. He'd take out that idiot, the cops, and the rest of the dealers, tying up loose ends. Then he'd take care of Miss Psychedelic. When he finished with her, she'd wish she'd chosen any career but the law.

The vehicle bore down on the deputy that held Appleby. The psychedelic-clad cop jumped into the front seat of the cruiser. She honked and screamed out the open window while she pointed to Hamelin's Rover coming up behind her partners.

Hamelin laughed. "They can't hear you, Sweetheart. Not with that rock music blaring."

A shotgun appeared out the cruiser's window. The glass of the Rover's back passenger window burst. Hamelin kept his foot to the floor and headed for Appleby.

When Appleby turned toward the Rover, he jolted away from the officer and ran. Hamelin flicked on the vehicle's bright lights. The deputy who had caught Appleby glanced toward Hamelin and threw his arms up to block the glare.

Appleby was only fifty feet away, caught in the powerful headlamp beams. He screamed. The officer jumped out of the way of the Rover.

A satisfying thump sounded from the front end of the vehicle as it slammed into Appleby. His body bounced over the top and rolled off the back end.

The Rover received a second shotgun blast through the back window, sending safety glass pellets everywhere. Hamelin accelerated. He'd at least get the second dealer and the cop before he got out of there.

The dealer lurched free of his captor's grip, pushed him to the ground, and ran for the woods. The deputy rolled across the turf to the cruiser. Hamelin's vehicle veered after the fugitive. "Forget the cop."

The Rover caught up to its stocky victim and smashed into him. The man flipped several feet into the air like a discarded rag doll, then dropped lifeless to the grass. Hamelin sniggered as he raced away from the cruisers. No way he'd get to that female cop now. He'd address her at a later date.

Officers jumped into their vehicles. In the descending darkness, Hamelin killed the lights, ran through low brush at the end of a line of trees, and plowed his way back to the dirt road. He jerked the Rover onto a second dirt road and backed the vehicle under low-hanging branches in a clump of trees.

Seconds later, cruisers flew by with lights flashing and sirens blaring in hot pursuit. He'd had enough of a head start. They'd be well down the road before they realized he'd taken another route. It paid to memorize the back roads. He smirked.

Now to regroup. The community would pay for fouling tonight's plans.

Lynne stared at the food she and Sam had prepared for a late dinner. It had been a good way to keep busy instead of worrying. But what would they do with all this food? "Sam. We've been cooking the entire evening and outdone ourselves. But the leftovers we'll have won't fit in our little freezer. We'll be eating Mexican food all week. Teri hasn't been home for two days. And with Nick still not back, and Russ—" She glanced up at Sam's frowning expression. "Anyway, who'll eat this stuff?"

The doorbell rang. Sam flew to the intercom. "Who's there?"

"It's me, Russ."

She twirled to Lynne, a huge grin on her face. "Reinforcements." She pressed the buzzer, opened the door, and ran into the hall.

"Well, at least Sam's happy." Lynne sighed, then chuckled and took out another plate from the cabinet.

As they sat down to eat, Russ explained why he hadn't called while on the stakeout. "I'm sorry I worried you, Sam. Since we've been undermanned, I've had to put in long hours and have been bushed. All I could do was get to the apartment and crash for a few hours before I had to go back. And we were under strict orders not to breathe a word to anyone about what was going on. The walls seem to have ears where this Hamelin guy is concerned. And I figured I'd spill the beans if I talked to you. You're so chatty with everyone." He shrugged. "Well, sorry."

"You're right. I can't keep my mouth shut. It's okay." She patted his hand. "You're here now. That's what matters."

His eyes grew as he eyed the food on the table. "Mexican. I've died and gone to heaven." He breathed in deeply.

Lynne chuckled again. "We've smelled these spices all evening. Plus the aromas from the desserts we made. Let's pray and dig in."

While they ate, Russ told them what happened at the rave, and how Derek died. "The coroner removed the bodies from the field, and the officer in charge dealt with the guy who owns the place. He's got a lot to answer for."

Sam placed her hands on her hips. "I'll say. What a horrible thing to do. Those poor kids."

Russ nodded. "I had Appleby right in my grip and lost him. That guy could have given us information."

Poor Steph. Lynne furrowed her brows. "I'm sure one of the other dealers you caught can tell you something." Or would they take the blame and let Hamelin off free the way his stooges in Chicago did? "Was Teri there?"

After he swallowed a mouthful of Spanish rice and beans, generously covered with shredded cheese and sour cream, Russ shook his head. "No. She's working on local problems because of the series of storms we've had. Another female officer named Caitlyn Delaney was with us. You should have seen her in her teenybopper getup pretending to be one of the kids." He snickered. "She fit in so well with these crazy teens. Tiny as can be, but boy, don't get on her Irish side."

Lynne covered her mouth to keep from losing a mouthful of cola.

"I've met Cat."

Sam didn't laugh. "So she was undercover with you?" A strange, worried expression came over her as she crunched into her taco.

"Nooo." Russ smiled at her. "Not undercover *with* us. She infiltrated the group of teens we were watching. Hamelin spotted her, somehow."

Sam and Lynne both exclaimed, "Oh, no."

Lynne lowered her forkful of enchilada to the plate. "Is she okay?"

"She's fine." Russ filled in the details while they finished dinner.

When they'd removed the dishes, Sam brought out a chocolate cake with cream cheese frosting. Russ's eyes widened. "Sure have missed your cooking, Sam." He grinned.

As she took out dessert plates and forks, the left corner of Lynne's mouth rose. "Okay, Sam. Why don't we have dessert in the living room so he can relax while he has his fill of *your* chocolate cake?"

Sam giggled. "Lynnz made the cake. This time."

He clamped his lips with his teeth for a moment, and his face flushed. "I'll bet it's terrific."

With their plates of cake in hand, he and Sam toddled off to the next room. Lynne filled a carafe with coffee and prepared a tray, then joined them. "You have no idea where Hamelin went?"

"Not for sure, but before we left the site, a commotion from an area where officers were holding teen participants of the rave caught my attention. One boy ranted at an arresting officer. Then he saw Cat without her wig on. He had danced with her, thinking she was a girl his age. He told her he'd witnessed dealers stashing kids in a van."

Russ put a large forkful of chocolate cake in his mouth and collapsed onto the back of the sofa. "Hmmm. Haven't had chocolate cake in a long time. This is great, Lynne."

He took a sip of coffee. "That boy kept yelling, 'You've gotta listen,' and 'You've gotta do something.' He was really upset. Part of the time he babbled incoherently, then he'd make sense again. He said he thought they drugged the kids. But he was sure the kidnappers had gagged, tied them up, and shoved them into a black van. One was the kid's young cousin. The teen rambled on again about some house on the beach one of the kidnappers mentioned, but the boy wasn't making much sense. And then he said an adult from the rave took off in the van while we rounded up the suspects."

"That poor kid." Lynne sat back in the armchair and shook her head. "He probably brought his cousin there. Now he has to live with it."

"Yeah. From his hiding place, the kid watched them load the gagged teens into the van. He didn't know what to do."

Russ finished his cake and coffee. He leaned back on the couch with a long exhale. His eyelids drooped. "Dispatch contacted the Feds." He yawned. His eyes drifted shut, and within minutes, he was snoring.

Sam pressed her lips together and smiled. "Poor guy." She brushed a crumb from his stubbly chin.

Lynne grinned. "Let him sleep. He's exhausted." She picked up the coffee tray and headed for the kitchen.

After the girls cleaned up and crammed the leftovers into the refrigerator and freezer, they sat at the table, so they wouldn't disturb Russ.

"Sam, let's leave him a note and take a ride to the hospital. I want to visit Kim. We know the roads are clear between here and there, and it hasn't been raining for hours. I have to talk to her about something that's crossed my mind. It may be nothing. But then again—"

"Should we call the sheriff's office for an escort? I'd hate to wake Russ."

"We'll be fine. No one would expect me to leave the apartment now. Hamelin's got bigger problems to worry about."

Chapter Thirty-Five

When Lynne and Sam entered the hospital lobby, Lynne headed for the elevator. *Sure hope Kim could remember.*

Sam turned toward the hallway leading to the ER. "I'll see if Steph's on duty while you're upstairs. She may not have heard about Derek yet and might need more cheering up than Kim. I'll meet you in the cafeteria, okay?"

"That's fine. I'm sure Steph will appreciate your stopping by. And hearing the news from you might soften the blow. Even if she had decided he wasn't the right man, she had feelings for him. I won't be long with Kim. Don't want to tire her out."

The door dinged open, and Lynne stepped in. On the fourth floor, she waved to the evening nurses and hurried straight to Kim's room. Her friend reclined in bed, TV tuned to the news.

Lynne entered. "So this is how you relax? Watching mayhem from this evening's rave and drug bust?"

Kim switched off the TV and smiled at Lynne. "Not much else to do here other than surf the channels. You don't have any good books on you, do you?"

"Sorry, Kim. I should have thought to bring you some reading material. I'll bring a book and a couple of magazines tomorrow." She pulled out the chair next to the bed and angled it to face Kim, then sat. "I have a fantastic novel in mind. No crime. A love story."

"Thanks. That'd be wonderful." She sat up straighter. "So what brings you to the hospital this late at night? You didn't come to fill me in on the rave events, did you? It's all over the news. They said a couple of suspects escaped. Shall I venture to guess one was Hamelin?"

"Yep. Deputy Highland stopped by the apartment after he left the rave. He told us Hamelin got away, along with another from his gang. But I think Russ really came to be with Sam." She grinned. "They've been an item for a month now. He ate dinner with us and promptly fell asleep on the couch after dessert." Lynne chuckled. "Poor guy was so fatigued from the hours he put in at that stakeout. Plus he chased down and subdued the main henchman."

"Loring mentioned the sheriff's department was undermanned."

"Teri said they're stretched thin, and these storms haven't helped matters. But I came to see you for a reason. Tonight, my mind wandered back to the interrogation I watched in Chicago."

Kim's brows furrowed. "I hope someday you can forget that horrible time in your life."

"It's not easy. Unlike you and Loring, I don't deal with murder on a regular basis. And, speaking of Loring, did he mention any leads on where The Piper might hold his human trafficking victims? Or is that classified?" Lynne grimaced. "Teens were taken from the rave tonight."

"I heard." Kim searched the wall as if it held clues. "Loring did mention abandoned houses not yet repaired from the storms that plagued the Florida Panhandle a few years ago. But there have to be tons of places like that stretching from Panama City to Pensacola. Since the summer tourist season is over, he could be using a rental."

Lynne knit her brows. "That's what I thought. But I recalled a comment you made during the interrogations. You told me about a beach house that the snake of a crooked lawyer Pemberton owned."

Kim jolted upright, then grabbed her bandaged shoulder. "Oww." Her eyes pressed shut. "I've got to stop doing that." She took a deep breath, slowly let it out, and opened her eyes. "Where was that place?" She lowered her head into her hands, rubbing her forehead just under the bandage. "Give me a second."

Her eyes shot open. "That's it. I remember now. It must be where that scumbucket is holed up and has those kids. It's somewhere near Pensacola…by the water."

Lynne jumped from the chair and rushed to the door. "Be right back." She sprinted through the hall to the nursing station, grabbed a pencil from the cup on the desk, a pad of paper, and bolted away before the on-duty nurse had a chance to ask questions.

Back in the room, Lynne handed the notepad and pencil to Kim. "Do you remember anything about the house? You're the sketch artist. Can you draw a picture from what you recall, like you do when people describe faces?" Lynne bit her lip.

"We had nothing specific on file." Kim frowned. "It was never part of our inquiry. And Pemberton destroyed his files when he found out we were investigating Hamelin." She scowled. "Word had it, Pemberton hosted some pretty sketchy parties at that house. Involving under-aged female *guests*." She gritted her teeth.

Her brows lifted. "But, I did see a photo of the place once in an article in the Boston Globe. A high-profile case involving Pemberton's firm."

Kim grinned. "At the beginning of the story, they called the home his summer mansion." She pressed her eyes closed again. "I can envision it. Big...by itself on a long strip of sand." She gazed at Lynne. "The photographer had taken the picture from a boat offshore."

Lynne retook her seat. "Can you draw it?"

"Hand me the goods, sister." Kim extended both hands. "But I can only give you a drawing of the back."

As Kim drew the rear of the large beach dwelling and its surroundings, Lynne stared in amazement. Kim had such talent. If the criminals only knew. Better they didn't.

A few minutes later, Kim showed Lynne the sketch. "I can't remember any more. Kind of rough." She shrugged. "Hope it's useful."

"I'm sure it will be." Such detail. And drawn from a picture Kim had seen so long ago. A rambling two-story home built on pylons surrounded by sand dunes. "Looks like one of those expensive Pensacola residences, but no neighbors. I wonder if it's still standing. Sam told me Hurricane Ivan destroyed so many houses in two-thousand, four."

"Yeah. It's pretty exposed. It would have been vulnerable, even with those pylons. But Pemberton had the money to have it built well.

He may also have had a property manager here in Florida. And after the louse committed suicide when his crimes caught up with him a couple of years ago, they'd have made repairs in order to sell the place. Don't think he had any family."

Kim glanced toward her room window. "Oh dear, our reprieve is over." Huge drops drummed against the pane. "I sure wouldn't want to spend the night on the beach. Not in one of these storms."

More rain. Lynne shook her head. Just what they needed. "You're safe here, Kim. From what Sam's told me, this hospital has weathered many a storm, including Hurricane Ivan."

Kim pointed at the picture on her lap. "Wish I could give you the location, but I don't remember reading that detail or if the department ever had it."

"It's okay. You did great with the sketch." Lynne took the pad and pencil from Kim and settled her covers. "The sheriff's department probably knows where it is, and they can contact the FBI." She fluffed Kim's pillow. "You've done your part. If the authorities can't identify the location, Nick might. He's a native Pensacolean. And he has a friend who knows every nook and cranny of the shoreline."

She smiled and lowered the head of the bed for Kim. "Time for you to get your rest. No more scary news reports."

"I agree." Kim placed her hand over her mouth and yawned.

"I'll send this to the sheriff's department. Sleep well." Lynne switched off the light and slipped out of Kim's room.

After a nod to the guard in the hallway, Lynne hurried to the elevator. She descended to the ground floor and rushed to the cafeteria. Her mind raced.

As Lynne approached Sam's table near a window, a large branch flew into the glass. She and Sam both jumped. The branch slid down the glass with a screech and fell to the ground.

Lynne clutched the edge of the table and laid her hand on her chest as she gazed at Sam. "I thought for sure that was coming through the window. What did you say the other day about not worrying about the storm? Here we go again."

Sam stared back. "Almost fell off my chair. Is Kim okay?" Her roommate's forehead wrinkled. "You were up there a long time."

"She's fine. And Steph?"

"She's okay too. Steph only felt sorry for Derek because he died. She's pretty sure he was a lost soul. He didn't get saved after Nick's devotional, and she doubts he ever did."

Lynne winced. A wave of sadness washed through her heart. "As much as I disliked him, I hate the thought of anyone spending an eternity in hell. Derek was in deep with Hamelin."

She sat at the table. "I have to send this to Teri." Lynne held Kim's sketch out.

"A picture?"

"Kim drew it. I'll explain in a minute."

Lynne photographed the drawing with her phone and sent the image to Teri. Then she dialed her number. Voicemail kicked in. "Drat!"

"Hi, Teri, it's Lynne. Just sent you a picture of a sketch Kim Travis drew a few minutes ago. It's a house somewhere on Pensacola Beach. Kim didn't know the exact location. A Chicago attorney by the name of Radcliffe Pemberton owned it before he died. Apparently, there was a connection between Pemberton and Hamelin."

She gulped in a breath of air and continued. "I remembered Kim mentioning this place and asked her to sketch it. Thought it might be where Hamelin's holding the abducted kids. Give me a call when you get this message. If your department doesn't know where it is, I may know someone who does. Bye. Stay safe."

Sam slid the cup of coffee she'd gotten for Lynne in front of her as the call ended. Her eyes widened. "You think that's where he's keeping the kids?"

"Thanks." Lynne took a sip. "Not sure. I thought it'd be worth checking out."

She tapped the number for the sheriff's office. This information had to get to Teri or another officer. "Busy signal." She tried a couple more times and then gave up. *This dratted weather.*

"They must be swamped with emergency calls because of the storm." Lynne took another sip of coffee as rain lashed the windows. Guess she'd have to wait until Teri got her message. "I sure hope Zack and his dad can help locate this place if Teri and her crew don't know where it is."

From above eye-level, Lynne followed a thin trickle of water down the glass until it joined others and became a stream. When would *this* bout of rain stop? She hoped Nick could find a way home soon too. She finished her coffee.

Sam rose from the table. "We'd better get home."

"You're right." Lynne followed Sam out of the cafeteria and into the hospital lobby. Should she try to find the house herself before the storm worsened? Someone had to do something. She rubbed an index finger over her lips. It wouldn't be hard to find such a large home, by itself, on an expanse of Pensacola Beach. She could check if anyone was there. After all, she was Navy trained and knew basic reconnaissance. But she'd have to borrow Sam's car.

Chapter Thirty-Six

Two hours before the end of Lynne's shift the next day, her call finally connected to the sheriff's office dispatch.

"I'll relay your message to Deputy Coleraine, Miss Temple. She and everyone else are out since the storm regained strength. We have one officer holding the fort here, and it's all I can do under the circumstances. But I'm sure she'll call in and then get back to you soon."

"Thank you." As she hung up, Lynne stared out the floor-to-ceiling windows next to the elevator. The rain hadn't stopped the entire night. Intermittent gale-force winds threatened to blow flying debris right through the glass. She should have checked out that house yesterday.

Repeated crashes of thunder followed by flashes of forked lightning lit up the darkened sky. Only one in the afternoon, and it seemed more like midnight. A sound, as if a large piece of sheet metal had been shaken, echoed through four-north. *Weird thunder.* The lights flashed off and on for a second.

Sam returned to the nursing station. "The patients are restless."

"I don't blame them. This storm makes me nervous too."

Sam's cell signaled a text. "Oh good. It's Russ. He wants to know if his little rebel gal is okay." She giggled.

Lynne peeked as Sam tapped back a message.

Fine, CU ASAP YankEboy.

She sent the message then frowned. "Little? As in short? Who's he calling little? Wait'll I catch up with that bluecoat!"

Lynne smiled. She was happy Sam and Russ had hit it off. *Wish Nick would call, even if only to tease her.*

The desk phone rang. "Four-north, Samantha Rease speaking." Her brows furrowed as she listened. "Okay...Don't worry...We'll cover until you can get here. See you in a while." She hung up. "I hope."

Sam blew at her bangs. "Lauren. She and Melissa carpooled to avoid adding another car to the roads. Now they're both stuck on Three Mile Bridge because of an accident. They'll relieve us as soon as possible."

Lynne closed her eyes. "What a place to be stuck in a storm." She opened them again, rose from the chair, and prepared patient snacks in the kitchenette for afternoon rounds.

By four o'clock, she and Sam had resigned themselves to pulling a double shift. The elevator door opened. Melissa and Lauren exited, dripping wet. They waved at Lynne and Sam, then ran toward the locker room. Right behind them, Nick stepped out and strode to the nursing station.

"Nick!" Lynne's heart jumped, and her pulse sped into overdrive. "I was so worried."

As he came near, his grin stretched from one ear to the other. "I'm the one who worried. About you. The closer I got to Pensacola, the worse the storm got. I drove by the hospital and saw Sam's car in the lot. I'd have called, but phone service is acting weird. Are you ready to leave, or are you working the evening shift?" The corners of his mouth turned down.

"We'll be ready to leave as soon as our relief changes into dry clothes. That was them who rushed out of the elevator before you. Their car has been stuck in traffic for the last three hours."

"I feel for them. Traffic is horrendous, but I think it's dying down now." He turned and waved his hand toward the elevator. "They left a puddle on the floor in there."

Lynne chuckled as she pointed a finger to the water in the hall. "Yeah, and a trail on the floor too. I'd better alert maintenance. Wouldn't want anyone to slip."

Several minutes later, Lauren ensconced herself behind the counter. "Thanks for being so understanding."

Melissa scooted in place right after her. "Yes, thank you."

After saying their goodnights, Lynne and Sam joined Nick in the waiting elevator as he held the door open. They descended to the ground floor.

In the hospital foyer, Nick reached into a plastic bag hanging from his arm. He pulled out two pink rain ponchos and handed one to each of them. "Here. I bought these in Mississippi before I left. Couldn't believe they had pink. I picked up the khaki one for myself."

Lynne laughed. "You've got to be kidding. They're great." She gave him a peck on the cheek. "You're always so thoughtful."

Sam held hers in front of her. "I love pink. Thanks, Nick."

When all three had donned the rain gear over their jackets, Sam headed for the door.

Nick stopped her. "I'll bring the truck under the covered entrance. We can drop you off at your car." He dashed out the doors.

Sam glanced at Lynne. "We sure found a couple of keepers, didn't we?"

"I'll say."

Several minutes later, Sam's vehicle followed Nick's truck out of the parking lot heading for the apartment building. Nick looked at Lynne. "Where's the sheriff's escort?"

"Guess they haven't been able to spare anyone with all the storm-related problems going on and being shorthanded." Lynne gazed at Nick's wrinkled brows. "What's wrong?"

"After my last call to you on Thursday, it was impossible to get through. My aunt's friend doesn't have internet." He shrugged.

"It's okay. You're home now."

"And on the way from Alabama, I heard a report on the car radio about the missing kids. I recognized two names."

"Oh, no. From the youth group?"

He nodded. "Kids who haven't attended for some time."

As they waited at a red light, Lynne extracted Kim's sketch from her handbag and showed it to him. "You've been out on the boat with Zack and his dad a lot. You must be familiar with the shoreline. Do you recognize this place?"

The light turned green, and Nick shifted into gear. "It's too dark to see. Wait until there's better light." Even with a raging storm outside, he couldn't wait to spend an evening with Lynne after five days apart. Was she out sketching pictures in this weather while he was gone?

Moments later, he pulled into the parking space and shut off the engine. Nick took a quick glimpse of the drawing Lynne held out for him. "Still can't see it clearly. Let's go in. Then I can take a good look."

He sprinted around the front of the truck and opened the passenger door. Lynne jumped out, and they ran for the entrance. Inside, they flipped off the ponchos, shook them on the front mat, and headed upstairs.

Sam opened the apartment door as they approached. "Told you I'd beat you home. I'll start a pot of coffee. That'll take the chill off."

"Home-brewed coffee instead of the vending machine stuff I've had all the way back to Pensacola. Sounds heavenly." He sat on the couch with Lynne. "Okay, let's take a gander at that picture."

Lynne pulled the sketch out of her purse and handed it to him.

"Sure, I recognize this place. It's on the way to Fort Pickens, less than an hour's drive from here. Good sketch. Zack always goes by the house when we're on the boat. He says, if he had the money, he'd buy the monstrosity and live right on the island." Nick gazed at her. "I keep telling him he's crazy. We all live close enough to the Gulf as it is. Why do you ask?" He laid the paper on the coffee table.

Lynne gaped at him. "Are you saying we went right by there during the boating party?"

"No…well, yes…but we were too far from shore to notice."

"Can you give me directions?" She dug her phone from the purse.

"Sure, but why? This is no day for sightseeing." He held his hand out to display the storm. Lynne paid no attention.

"Where is it?"

He wrote down the most direct route on the back of the sketch. What was she up to?

"Thanks. Excuse me a minute." She rose, then punched a number on her cell as she paced the living room. "Why hasn't Teri returned my calls? Nooo. Voicemail again." Lynne tapped in another number. "Busy signal." She sent a text message, dropped the phone back into her bag, and sat next to Nick.

"Lynne, what's going on?"

"Kim drew this for me last night. We think it's where Hamelin has those kids."

"Then we need to get the information to the sheriff's department."

"I've tried. I sent the picture to Teri's phone and left a message. But she hasn't responded. I don't know if she got it or the directions I just sent. I need to check the place out to see if someone's there."

"Lynne…are you out of your mind? Hamelin kills people." He loved her bravery, but no way would he let her get near that devil.

"You're right, the man is dangerous. But I can't stand the thought that he might escape with these kids. The Piper may be using this house as a hideout. He had a connection to the lawyer who used to own it."

Nick glanced at the sketch on the table while Lynne sent another message. Could it be possible? Were the kids there?

Sam brought in coffee and set the tray on the table in front of them. She took a seat in the chair next to the couch. Her forehead wrinkled. "Nick, is she trying to borrow your truck? I wouldn't let her have the car last night to go off on a crazy quest, looking for a house, having no idea where she was going."

"Thank you, Sam." He rubbed his forehead. *Thank You, Lord.*

When Lynne finished her text, she dropped the cell into her purse again. "I re-sent the location you gave me. I sure hope Teri gets the message. Dispatch said they're busy with storm-related emergencies the last time I was able to reach them."

Sam lowered her cup to the tray. "I haven't heard from Russ since he was here last night either, except for the thank you note he left before we got back from the hospital."

"Figures they'd be busy with this wind wreaking havoc." Nick sipped his coffee. He lifted the drawing. "Last time I saw this house up close was a few months ago. Boards covered the top floor windows."

Lynne grabbed his arm. "So Hamelin could easily use the place to hide in."

"I guess." Nick pursed his lips. "No houses nearby." He folded the sketch and shoved it in his pocket. A rush of adrenaline went through him. "I'll take a drive and check whether there's any sign that it's occupied. Then I'll go to the sheriff's office and tell them what I find."

"Oh no, you don't." Lynne stood. "You're not going alone."

Sam jumped from her chair. "Are both of you crazy, going out in this?" She motioned toward the window.

Lynne pulled a dry windbreaker from the coat tree and flipped it over her shoulders. She removed her identification and phone from her bag and stuffed them into a pocket. She faced Sam. "We're going to investigate this house."

Sam's jaw dropped open. "But, Lynnz—"

"You can't talk me out of it this time. The lives of these kids may be at stake."

Nick wrapped his arm around Lynne. "You're determined, aren't you?"

She nodded. "I'm a Navy girl, remember? I can do this."

Sam shook her head.

As Lynne and Nick started to leave, she turned to Sam. "If you hear Teri come home, tell her where we've gone and to check her messages. Keep trying to reach her at the sheriff's department. And if Russ shows up, tell him. And pray for us."

Sam sucked in her bottom lip. "All right." Her brows pinched together.

Nick and Lynne hurried out the door, down the stairs, and into the driving rain.

Chapter Thirty-Seven

As the sheets of rain pounded against the windshield, Nick held both hands clamped to the wheel to keep the vehicle from straying off the road. His hands ached as he tightened his grip. "Man, that last gust of wind almost threw the truck onto the shoulder." Not a good thing. He'd never get it out of that soft sand.

In the distance, he spotted the faint outline of a roof. "There's the place up ahead." He drove onto a gravel patch a few yards from the driveway leading to the beach house and parked on the other side of a long row of tall shrubs. A high sand dune covered with sea oats hugged the passenger side. "Good thing they put in this gravel, or there'd be no place to park other than the driveway. Probably put it in for those parties you mentioned. The dune between us and the beach will keep the truck hidden from even the top floor of the house. But you can't open your door. You'll have to come out on my side."

Lynne nodded and bit her lip. "Are you sure no one will see the truck from the road?"

"Nah. Those bushes between us and the pavement are too thick. And the gravel leaves no tire tracks." He held out his hand to her. "We'd better pray before we set off on this adventure."

They bowed their heads. "Father, we need Your guidance. If those kids are in that house, show us a sign of it. Keep us safe. Then help us get out of here without being seen. In Christ's name, I pray."

Nick let go of Lynne's hand and reached into the back seat of the extended cab to grab his new poncho and another jacket. He handed the poncho to Lynne. "Better leave the pink one. I'll use this rain jacket."

They slipped the rainwear on top of their windbreakers, and Nick laid his hand on the door handle. "Ready?"

"Ready."

He glanced at the sand-flecked rain peppering the windshield and then thrust open the door. The squall seemed determined to push him back into the truck, but he squeezed out and held the door for Lynne.

She hoisted herself over the console, grabbed Nick's hand, and slid out onto the graveled surface. As he locked the doors, she huddled beside him. He dropped the key into his pants pocket.

Low-hanging clouds scudded over them. Nick glanced upward. Would the weather continue to worsen? It'd be dark soon. Lynne's hand grasped his, and they traversed the tangled brush as they searched for a good view of the beach house. Rain stung his face and neck like liquid darts.

Nick leaned toward her. "We can get a look at the house through the brush. The thicket should cover us."

Lynne stayed flush against his side. "Those shrubs might break the force of the wind too. Wait. I'd better turn my cell on vibrate." She fumbled for the phone. "The sooner Teri calls me back, the better I'll feel."

"Right. Watch for flying debris." He switched his phone to vibrate as well. The sooner they got out of there, the better *he'd* feel.

A jagged, white object hurtled over their heads. Nick dove to protect Lynne. His arms wrapped around her. "That must have come from somebody's carport awning."

"Wow." Lynne's eyes widened like saucers.

They climbed up and down small dunes until they reached a larger mound of sand. At the top, sea oats swayed in the wind. A half-demolished stone wall came into view a few yards to their left.

As they stood and peered through the sea oats, Nick held Lynne's hand to keep her from slipping in the soft sand. He pulled her near. "Wind must be about thirty knots."

They shielded their eyes with cupped hands against the persistent sand flurries while they scrutinized the house. He tightened his collar. "No signs of life. If someone *is* there, they might have a vehicle hidden in the garage." He pointed to the far side of the house. "The roof is damaged. Rain must be pouring in."

Lynne spoke into Nick's ear. "Let's get closer. If we don't see anyone, we'll leave, and I'll text Teri again."

"Let's go."

They descended the dune and followed a meandering path flanked on both sides by more grass-strewn slopes. Occasional thick-stemmed scraggly bushes dotted the area. Short dips between the mounds of sand allowed a clear view of the house.

The wind suddenly curbed its angry charge. Nick smiled at Lynne. "Praise God. Maybe the storm's blown itself out." He gazed through a break in the dunes. "We have to hug these shrubs in case someone's watching out the window. This path should come out near the driveway. From there, we can check the front side and get to the garage."

When they had inched their way to a stone gatepost, Lynne nudged his arm. "It appears no one has taken care of this place for a long time." She pointed to the rusty, broken hinges and the remains of an iron gate.

From behind them, a gruff, staccato voice said, "Now what do we have here?"

Nick and Lynne spun to face a hefty man in jeans, T-shirt, and open windbreaker, soaked from the rain. He glared at them, a .45 caliber revolver half-covered by the sleeve of his jacket, pointed in their direction. The man advanced to within a few feet. "Get your hands up."

As the gunman glowered, Lynne's mind raced. They'd better do something quick. *Father, help.* An idea popped into her head. *Lord, give me good aim, in Jesus' name.*

"Turn around and walk." Using the gun to indicate the direction, he shouted, "Keep those hands where I can see them."

Lynne and Nick turned their backs to him.

Nick peeked at Lynne. "Look, fella, there's no need for this. We were just walking by and noticed this cool house. We didn't mean to trespass." He grimaced.

Really, Nick? Lynne glanced at him. *You expect him to buy that, in a storm?* She pressed her lips together. Had to admire the man for trying though.

"Out for a walk, my foot." The heavy man jabbed the gun into Lynne's back. "Now shut up and move."

Lynne stumbled and fell to one knee. "Oww. Oh, no." She reached and clutched at her ankle with both hands. Nick knelt next to her.

"Back off." The gunman shoved the pistol into Nick's side, then pointed it at Lynne. "Get up."

Lynne feigned a painful look on her face as Nick rose. She grabbed his arm with her right hand. "I can't. My ankle's twisted." She crouched forward and dug her left hand into the sand, then turned her head to check the position of their captor.

With his weapon still trained on her, the thug let out a string of obscenities. "You'd better get up or—" The big man reached for Lynne's elbow.

Before he could touch her, Lynne shoved Nick out of the way and drove her right leg back as hard as she could. She slammed her heel into the gunman's right leg above his knee. *Crack!* She threw the sand from her left hand in his face.

The burly man screamed and staggered backward on his left leg, dropping his weapon. Nick leaped onto the man and knocked him to the ground. Then he clenched his fist and rammed it into the thug's jaw, causing another bone-cracking sound.

Lynne retrieved the fallen gun from a patch of wet sand, engaged the safety, and dropped it into an empty pocket of her windbreaker. She zipped the pocket and helped Nick drag the unconscious man to a nearby stand of brush.

After Nick frisked him for more weapons, he grinned at Lynne.

She punched his upper arm. "Great going, Marine, even if you aren't one."

"Thanks, Lieutenant. Twisted ankle, huh?" Nick raised his brows and smiled. "Quick thinking."

"It pays to play the damsel in distress. Besides, I had to think of something other than *sightseeing* in a storm." She snickered.

"Touché." Nick stripped their former captor of his shoelaces and the cord from his jacket. He tied the man's hands to the thick stem of the middle bush. "These are deep-rooted and with the canopy several feet across, he'll be well-hidden. He won't go anywhere with that broken knee...until the sheriff's department arrives."

Lynne took the phone which Nick had extracted from the gunman's pocket and turned off the power. She dropped it into another pocket of her windbreaker and wiped rainwater from her face with her sleeve. "With the broken jaw you've given him, he won't be able to call for help either when he comes to. Guess we can assume *nothing good's* going on at that house."

"Yes, but what *is*? Sure wish Teri would call you."

"Me too. I'd better update her with what we ran into. Then I'll clean up this gun." She pulled back the hood of her windbreaker and gazed at the sky. "Hey, the rain stopped. But for how long?"

Lynne called the sheriff's office first. This time she got a rapid busy signal. After she'd typed a text to Teri and cleaned the sand-caked pistol, she and Nick skirted the driveway. They slipped around the gateposts into the front yard but didn't get far before Nick stopped her with his hand.

"Get down." He tugged Lynne beneath the shoulder of a small dune. They peered through a tall clump of grass at the top.

Lynne whispered. "What?"

Nick pointed.

Binoculars protruded from a half-boarded-up window. They were aimed at the dunes where Nick and Lynne had hidden the gunman. He whispered in her ear. "Must be searching for his buddy, but I doubt he saw us." At least he hoped whoever it was hadn't. The binocs disappeared.

A minute later, the front door opened. A thin, bald man holding a handgun stood on the dilapidated raised front porch. His only attire, a baggy muscle T-shirt and cut-offs. He scurried over the stairs to the footpath.

Nick and Lynne crouched behind the clump of sand.

As the man drew closer to the path, Nick kept him in sight. The second man lumbered toward his cohort still out cold under the bush.

From his hiding place, Nick crept up behind the second thug, tackled him, and hurled him between two dunes. The man's gun discharged and flew into the air. Nick leaped onto his opponent and plunged his fist into the man's abdomen. The thug gasped as his breath left him. When a second blow struck the side of the miscreant's face, he slumped to the ground unconscious.

Lynne scrambled for the discarded gun. "Here it is, stuck in a bush. At least this one I don't have to clean." She turned to Nick. "Way to go. Did you get his phone?"

Nick held it up, turned it off, and slipped it into his windbreaker pocket.

She handed the second firearm to Nick, who slid the thumb lever forward to engage the safety and stuck the gun into his belt at his back.

"You know how to use that?"

One corner of his mouth rose. "I have skills." He grasped the unconscious man's wrists. "Okay, you remember the routine, Lieutenant."

"Aye aye, Sir. And there's another waiting bush next to his buddy." She produced a scarf from her windbreaker pocket and handed it to Nick. "This one's jaw is intact."

"Good idea." Nick secured the scarf around the man's mouth.

After they had secured the second thug, Nick and Lynne dashed through the crumbling stone wall that surrounded the house and up to a patch of withered palm trees. Nick gazed at the once-imposing front of the beach house. "I don't hear anything, do you? Those two had to be the only ones. I'm sure someone else would have run out with that gun going off like it did." He swallowed hard. Should they find out if the kids were inside or wait for help?

Lynne smiled.

Was she enjoying this? Her military training must have kicked in. She was ready for action. He was neither a police officer…nor a Marine. Nick stared at the boarded windows on the second floor. Still, he wasn't about to let something happen to the kids if they were in there.

He sat back on the sand and laid one hand on Lynne's arm. "You need to get help. I'll keep an eye on this place until you get back." He pulled out his keys to the truck.

"*No,* Nick. If Teri hasn't called by now, they haven't gotten word. I'd have no clue where to go for help on this island. If you're staying…so am I."

"All right, Navy Girl. Fortunately, I *do* know how to handle a gun." He took it from his belt. "And since we can protect ourselves, let's see if the kids are in the house."

Lynne withdrew the gun from her jacket pocket. She retrieved her phone, turned it on, and left yet another text for Teri. Then she replaced the cell in her pocket.

The couple bolted from their cover and sprinted across the front yard, then tore up the stairs to the porch. Nick tried the front door. It opened with a slight creak.

Chapter Thirty-Eight

As Lynne and Nick stepped into the gloomy interior of Pemberton's once elaborate beach house, the wind picked up outside, but the house was still. Lynne tried not to gag. Odors of stale cigarette smoke, mildew, and old coffee assailed her nose. *Phew.* How could anyone stay in this place?

Nick pulled a penlight from his pocket, adjusted it to the widest illumination, and shone the light up and down the foyer and hallway. They checked the first room on the right. Must have been a living room. An impressive stone fireplace covered one wall, its mangled black screen on the hearth. Ornate wrought iron tools hung in their holder next to a matching grate piled high with wood. Beside the front window, a spindly wooden chair leaned against the wall, and another lay almost flattened on the floor. One oversized armchair with shredded material on the seat and back sat near the entrance. The rest of the room was empty.

Lynne tiptoed back to the front entrance, peered outside for any sign of movement, and closed the door.

Nick led her to the empty room on the other side of the foyer. She took his hand. What a creepy place. Wouldn't surprise her if they heard a howl and rattling chains. She shuddered.

They moved further through the hall to another expansive room with bare bookshelves. From what Sam had told her, properties like this all over the coast had met the same fate from past storms. Smaller houses in town had been completely demolished. Some never rebuilt or repaired. Sad. Possibly from lack of money or insurance on the owner's part. Or in this case, money tied up in court because of Pemberton's criminal past. She frowned.

Without a word spoken, Lynne and Nick came to the kitchen. Rusted appliances. No table or chairs. Nothing to show that anyone had lived there for a long time.

The last room they entered faced the back of the house and appeared to have been the dining room, judging by what was left of a French Provincial Buffet against the wall. Long narrow windows looked out to the deserted beach where waves crashed angrily onto the sand. The storm was renewing its strength.

They retraced their steps to the hallway and paused at the foot of a grand stairway which curved upward to the second floor. Nick stepped onto the first stair, turned to Lynne, and raised a finger to his lips. He whispered, "Keep watch from here. I'll check the upstairs rooms."

Her pulse quickened. "You've got another think coming, mister. You're not leaving me here…alone…and in the dark. The feature on my cell doesn't light up much."

He shook his head, then grimaced. They ascended the stairs with caution.

An eerie sound breathed in the upper floor of the house. Had to be the wind. Torn wallpaper along the wall of the staircase flapped as if waving them away. They stepped into the second-floor hall. *Wow.* At least twelve feet wide. Six rooms lined the hallway, three on each side. The first five doors stood open. Dark double doors at the far end of the passage were closed, as was the last single door on the left.

The room across the hall from the only closed single door had obviously been occupied by the two gunmen. Nick's penlight showed items of discarded clothing and newspapers strewn around the floor. A camp bed, wooden chair, and round table with a hurricane lamp in the center were the only furnishings. An open door led the way out to a balcony facing the dunes they had crossed. Crushed McDonald's bags lay on top of an open map on the table.

Lynne leaned close to Nick. "How long had they been here?"

He shrugged and then pointed to a padlock on the door across from them. They crossed the hall, and each put an ear to the door.

"I thought I heard something," Lynne whispered.

Nick held the lock. "This lock and bracket are brand new."

Lynne bit her lip. "Why padlock a room unless you want no one to get in...or out?"

"Shhh, we still have to check in there." He eyed the doors at the end of the hallway.

They inched across the final few yards of wet, shredded carpet to the double-doored suite. Nick turned the brass handle and swung one heavy door open, then flashed the penlight into every corner. On one side, rumpled linens covered a king-size bed. The ceiling showed no water damage, and the bedroom furniture looked like something Pemberton might have owned.

"Someone's been staying here." Lynne gazed at Nick. "Probably Hamelin."

Nick entered the room and checked the closet and attached bathroom. "No one's here now. Let's check that locked door."

They hurried to the secured room. Nick leaned next to the frame. "Is anyone in there? Ashley? Kevin?"

"Pastor Nick?" A faint female voice came from inside.

"Is that you, Ashley?"

"Yes, Sir. Can you get us out?"

A whimper from inside broke Lynne's heart. What kind of monsters would do this to children? She clenched her teeth.

Someone rushed to the door. "We're locked in, Pastor."

"It's Kevin." Nick backed up. "Kevin, I need you kids to huddle into the corner away from this entrance and turn your faces. Tell me when you're there."

Inside the room, the sound of scuffling feet scrambled away from the door. "We're in the corner, Pastor," the boy called.

Nick took aim. "I'll shoot the lock off. Stand still and cover your ears."

While they backed away from the door, Lynne held the penlight for Nick. She turned her weapon toward the staircase. *Lord, please don't let anyone else be here.* She listened.

A loud roll of thunder accompanied the report as Nick blasted the padlock. The noise echoed in the passageway, and the lock clattered to the floor. He kicked the door open.

Lynne pocketed her gun and slipped into the room while Nick kept watch in the hallway.

The four teens still huddled together in the corner. A few empty plastic water bottles and crumpled sandwich wrappers revealed the meager rations they'd received since yesterday. A makeshift privy stood in one corner of the room and gave off a horrible stench.

Someone had boarded the broken windows from the inside. Only narrow slits between the outside and inside boards would have admitted any light. Sand had blown through the gaps and covered the floor like sawdust. Puddles of water lay everywhere.

Lynne's eyes filled with tears. Two boys and two girls had spent the last twenty-four hours in semi-darkness, with no privacy, except what nighttime afforded them. Again, she clenched her teeth, then her fists.

The girls rushed to Lynne and threw their arms around her, sobbing. The boys ran to Nick and clustered as if they were five-year-olds in a strange school.

Nick gathered everyone into the hall. "We've got to move fast, without a sound." Another clap of thunder sounded.

With Nick in the lead, they started for the staircase.

Lynne's phone rang. The group halted, and five widened sets of eyes looked at her. She grabbed for the cell. "Must be Teri. I forgot to turn it off last time I sent a text."

"At last." Nick resumed their trek to the stairway.

Lynne held the cell to her ear as she followed the children. "Teri?"

"Lynne! I got your messages a second ago. The phones finally started working again. Where are you?"

"We're in that house I sent a sketch and directions for. We're okay. We found the kids."

"Got it. Already on our way. Were they alone?"

"We took care of the two goons who had them."

Before Nick was halfway down the stairs, the sound of heavy feet on the front porch echoed upward toward them. He hustled everyone back up the stairs and narrowed the beam from the penlight.

Lynne whispered into the phone, "Gotta go. We have company. Please hurry." She disconnected.

Nick thrust his truck keys into her hand. "I saw a set of back stairs to the right of the master bedroom. Take the kids and go."

Tears burned her eyes as she pressed the flashlight feature on the cell. She looked into his gray eyes and saw his determination. He was right. She had to get the kids out.

Lynne gave him a fast kiss on his lips and then shepherded the four teenagers toward the back stairs. "Try to be as quiet as you can." None of the kids wore shoes. The jerks must have taken them to keep them quiet.

As the group began their descent of the back stairs, Lynne took one last glance at Nick. He'd positioned himself in the darkest part of the doorway nearest the front staircase and doused the penlight. Faint light from a large hole in the roof outlined the weapon grasped in both hands. *God, help him.*

Nick fixed his gaze on the point where the intruder would first appear, while Lynne ushered the kids down the back stairwell, and hopefully, out the back door in the kitchen. The rolling thunder should cover the sound of their escape. He aimed the gun and held it steady.

Had to be thunder that blotted out the approach of a vehicle. *Too soon to be the deputies.*

Nick prayed it was a lone visitor. *And please let help arrive in time.* Now that Teri had contacted Lynne, the deputies would get here fast.

His eyes remained glued to the stairs. A shiver slithered up his spine. *Please help, Lord.*

Hamelin fumed as he entered the house. A long string of curses spewed from his mouth. Why hadn't these guys answered his calls? Lazy bums must be sacked out. *Can't see a thing in this place.* He swore, pulled out his cell, and aimed the light toward the stairs.

As he reached the staircase, he tapped in a message to the henchman he had stationed at the yacht.

Join me @ house soon as boat ready 2 embark.

He disconnected without waiting for an answer and started up the staircase.

Time was an issue. They had to leave Pensacola that night, storm or no storm. Risky on the water with those waves, but they had no choice. He'd miss his deadline, and the cargo would have to be permanently disposed of if they didn't get out of here before the weather got worse. But the captain had weathered many storms.

He slowed his climb and held the rail, his groin still in pain. Too bad he couldn't have gotten that little witch of a cop.

At a loud clap of thunder, the hair on Hamelin's neck stood on end.

Once those stupid kids were aboard the yacht, he'd have no more use for these two incompetents. Hamelin patted his sheathed Bowie knife and licked his lips. He grinned at a mental image of their paled faces as he brought about their demise. The Gulf would take care of the evidence.

As Hamelin reached the top step, a darkened male figure stepped from the first doorway. A flash of lightning lit the preacher's face and revealed a weapon pointed at Hamelin's chest. "Stop right there."

That preacher. Hamelin peered down the hallway into the darkness. Where were those two idiots he left in charge of the kids?

Hamelin's hand still rested on the knife fastened to the belt of his jeans. *Little did this Bible-thumper know the trouble he was in, even if he did have a gun.* It'd be no match for this baby. He stroked the knife with his thumb and smiled again. "Looks like ya got me, *Preacher-boy.*" He'd slit the guy's throat from ear to ear first chance he got.

"Pull off that belt and let the knife drop…slowly."

As Hamelin unbuckled the belt and lowered it to the steps, the preacher moved sideways, next to the railing.

"Now put both hands on top of your head and turn around."

Hamelin sneered. "You seem kind of nervous, *Preacher-boy.* You should be. I'll slice you into pieces…along with your girlfriend."

"Shut up. Start down those stairs. Slow."

Chapter Thirty-Nine

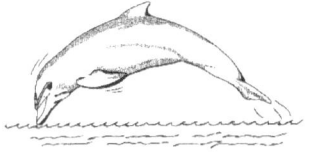

ynne and her four charges fled out the back door and followed a sandy trail through the dunes away from the house, her saturated clothes sticking to her like a second skin despite the windbreaker and poncho. "Come on, keep together, kids. We have to get help."

She pulled the cell from her pocket and punched Teri's number. *Busy. Not again.* "Pray, kids. Pray as you've never prayed before." She sucked in a breath of air. *Have to keep to the sand. It'd be easier on their bare feet.* "Pray Pastor Nick stays safe."

Tears and raindrops mingled on her face. Lynne kept the gun in her right hand in case they encountered more of Hamelin's men. She'd use it if necessary, but she sure hoped it wouldn't be. How far was Nick's truck? They had to get to it. Were they even going in the right direction? *God, please help.*

The four teenagers stumbled along behind her.

Between two large dunes, Lynne finally spotted the road and the tall shrubs Nick had parked next to. "Get down and stay here until I come back for you." The kids dropped onto the sand without a word. They must be scared out of their wits. She sprinted ahead.

After creeping to the road and checking for parked vehicles or lurkers, Lynne ran to the teens. They scrambled to the truck. She unlocked the doors, and all four kids climbed into the back seat, pressed together.

"Kevin, hop into the front."

She jumped into the driver's seat and with a trembling hand brought the engine to life as the boy squeezed over the front seat and middle console. Lynne pulled away from the gravel shoulder. After a jolting one-eighty degree turn, she headed the truck toward town.

Leaving Nick behind gnawed at her. But he'd want these kids away from danger, no matter his fate. God held him in His hands. And Nick was capable. He'd already proved that. But against The Piper? It had to be him. She swiped at the tears that blurred her eyes.

As the storm continued its assault on the island, Lynne turned the wipers on high. They couldn't keep up with the torrent. Eyes focused on the road ahead, she searched for headlights. Where were the deputies? Nick needed help now.

The teens were silent, except for an occasional whimper from the younger girl. Lynne slowed the truck, glanced back for a second, and patted the girl's knee. "You're okay now." Ashley wrapped her arm around the wisp of a girl.

Lynne turned her eyes to the road again. Flashing lights appeared in the distance. She swerved the truck to the side of the blacktop. "Thank God."

As soon as she turned on the truck's emergency flashers, she jumped out. Waving her arms, she bolted into the road.

The speeding patrol car skidded away from her. One front wheel sank into soggy sand on the shoulder.

Lynne rushed to the vehicle, as Teri lowered the driver's window. Russ had the radio to his lips and yelled, "We found Lynne Temple."

Seconds later, two other vehicles halted on the side of the road opposite Nick's truck.

As Teri and Russ exited the cruiser, Lynne clutched Teri's jacket arm. "Nick needs help."

"Where is he?" Teri glanced at the truck. "Are those the teens?"

Lynne's lip trembled as she nodded. "He's back there." She pointed. "At the house. He told me to get the kids to safety. It may be The Piper who came. Before we could leave. I don't know. Nick has a gun."

Russ and Teri exchanged glances. He asked, "Is anyone else with Hamelin?"

"I don't know. We heard footsteps. On the front porch." Lynne's heart beat like a jackhammer. "Nick told me to go with the teens. He hid in a doorway. Second floor. I don't know. I just don't know."

Tears coursed down her face as she reached into her pocket. "Here. Take this." She handed Teri the gun. "Nick needs help. Now."

Teri clasped the gun in her hand and put her arm around Lynne's shoulders. "We'll take it from here. One unit will wait here with you and the kids. The paramedics should be here soon."

"No. I need to get to Nick."

"Lynne, we'll get him. You're shivering. You all need attention."

"I'll get help when I'm sure he's safe."

"In that case, you can show us the turnoff. But when we get there, you *will* stay in the vehicle."

Lynne nodded and got into the back seat of the cruiser.

Russ turned off the flashers, and Teri pulled back on the road.

Nick let out a relieved sigh as he followed Hamelin down the staircase, the gun pointed at the center of the Goliath's back. Lynne and the kids would be safe. A few more steps and they'd reach the bottom. Cold fury snaked up his back as he thought of the threat Hamelin had made against Lynne. But he dared not show any emotion. "Keep going, nice and slow. Don't move those hands from your head."

Hamelin hobbled as he descended the stairs.

The kick from the female deputy Russ mentioned must have been as good as Lynne's.

At the bottom of the stairs, the giant stopped. "Where to now, *Preacher-boy?*"

"In the room to your left. Sit in that armchair."

"It's soaked." The big man sneered.

"I really don't care. Sit."

Hamelin eased his bulk into the chair and adopted a relaxed position, his hands still clasped on his head as if he'd leaned back to take a nap.

Nick crossed the foyer and opened the front door. He peered at the rain.

"Looking for a rescue party, preacher? I doubt anyone's out there in this deluge. Tell you what. You let me go, and we'll forget this misunderstanding."

Rain and sand swept over the threshold. Nick crossed the room to the fireplace and grabbed the one intact wooden chair. He brought it to the door and propped the back under the knob. He stood behind the chair. "We'll see who comes. And *I* won't forget *anything*."

Hamelin's serpent eyes glared. He spewed another string of vile words and threats.

Rage surged through Nick at the killer's words. The cell phone in Nick's pocket vibrated. He glanced down.

In an instant, Hamelin sprang from the chair, seized its arms with both hands, and hurled it as if the armchair weighed no more than a stool. It flew straight at Nick.

As he raised his arms in front of him, the thick leg of the chair slammed into his forearm. The gun slipped from Nick's grasp. Chair and weapon clattered to the floor on either side of him. Hamelin charged like a raging bull.

Pain shot through Nick's arm, but a surge of adrenaline hit him. He lashed out with his right leg. The edge of the shoe hacked into the base of Hamelin's knee. The big man bellowed and stumbled forward. Nick drove the palm of his left hand upward to Hamelin's nose, scooped the pistol from the floor, and slammed it into the side of Goliath's face.

"There it is," Lynne shouted and pointed to the driveway of the beach house as rain poured over the windshield. *Please let us be in time, Lord.*

Teri made a sharp right turn and sped down the driveway into the front yard, the second cruiser right behind. Before officers could exit their vehicles, a dark, shadowy figure staggered from the doorway several yards ahead and stumbled onto the stairs.

Russ and Teri rushed out of the car and sprinted toward the house.

Lynne's hands gripped the back of the front seat. Was that Nick? Or Hamelin?

The rain stopped as if someone had opened an umbrella and covered the island. She stared toward the house. The figure sat on the top step of the porch. *It's Nick.* She breathed a heavy sigh of relief and collapsed back onto the seat.

An officer from the second cruiser walked close to the car. "Let me out," Lynne shouted as she banged on the window. "Please." He ignored her and strode for the house.

Nick stood as Teri and Russ reached the bottom step. His right arm hung limp, while his left hand held the gun.

He was hurt, but alive. Even as her heart hammered in her chest, a smile took over, and happy tears slid down her cheeks. Nick handed the gun to Teri. He pointed to the house and then lifted the windbreaker with his left hand. Lynne's eyes widened, and her jaw dropped as Teri extracted a huge knife from his belt.

As another officer approached them, Russ spoke to him and aimed an index finger toward Lynne. The officer retraced his steps and opened the car door for her.

She leaped from the seat and headed for Nick as Russ and Teri entered the house. "Nick, are you okay?"

Nick shot his left hand out. "Wait." She halted inches in front of him. He laid his left hand on his right forearm. "I think it's broken." He sat on the stairs.

Her heart ached and flooded with love at the same time. "Oh, Nick." She lowered herself onto the step at his left and laid her hand on his shoulder. "Are you all right otherwise? What happened? Was it The Piper? Where is he? Did he do this to you?"

Nick gazed at Lynne and quirked his mouth. "Yes, it was him, and yes, I'm good other than my arm. He threw a chair at me, and I blocked it. Are the kids okay?"

"Nick, I was so scared." She rested her head on his shoulder. "The kids are with another officer waiting for the paramedics. They'll be taken to the hospital."

Russ stepped out the front door and halfway down the stairs with a big grin on his face. He motioned for the sergeant who had just arrived to follow him back into the house. Teri came through the door, weapons in her arms.

Lynne rose and helped Nick stand. They trudged their way to the vehicle with his good arm around her shoulders and hers around his waist. He gingerly slid into the back seat. When he winced in pain as he lifted his right arm by the sleeve of his jacket and lowered it to his lap, she leaned against the open door. Tears clouded her vision.

An ambulance technician hurried to the car to address Nick's injury. He immobilized the arm using an inflatable cylinder which became rigid with pressurized air.

Nick glanced at Lynne. She smiled. "It's called an air splint. They use it to stabilize your injury until you can get to the hospital."

Russ strode up to them. "What did you do to that hulk in there, buddy?" He snickered, then faced the EMT and nodded toward the house. "The guy's gonna need a gurney. Hope you brought a big one." He turned back to Nick and grinned.

Teri marched up. "Nick, Lynne had said you took care of two others. We didn't find anyone else in there."

Nick and Lynne grinned at each other. Lynne shook her head. "You'll find them tied up somewhere in those dunes." She waved in the direction where they had subdued the two men.

"Hey, Russ." Teri held her arm and an index finger out to where Lynne had indicated. "Look over there." She lowered her head to see Nick. "We'll give you a ride to the hospital instead of sticking you in the ambulance. You've kept company with these perps long enough tonight."

"Thanks, Teri. It'll be a joy if I never see them again."

Teri headed down the path Russ had taken.

The captain stopped at the cruiser. "Great job, Son. You too, Miss. But we don't recommend actions like this from the public under normal circumstances."

Nick nodded. "Neither do we, Sir. But sometimes you have no choice."

Before the captain could respond, the sergeant appeared at his side. "The house is clear, and we've collected the other two, Sir."

"Okay, Sergeant. Bring the dogs in and see what they find."

He returned his gaze to Nick and Lynne. "We'll get statements from you two later." The captain turned to go but spun back to them with a chuckle. "If either of you decides to change professions, call me." With a wink, he strode to the house.

Lynne took a deep breath. "I don't think so. Give me a nice safe, boring hospital floor any day." She slipped into the back seat of the cruiser next to Nick. "Now tell me what happened after I left with the kids."

"It'll have to wait until later. Looks like we're ready to leave."

She pursed her lips. *How could he leave her hanging like this? The stinker.*

Chapter Forty

$\mathcal{L}$ ynne parked Nick's truck in front of her apartment building and dashed upstairs. She had to change out of her wet clothes before she got sick from the cool night air.

As she closed the door behind her, PJ-clad Sam burst into the living room from her bedroom. "Lynnz! What happened? You're soaked to the skin. Where's Nick? I've been so worried about you two. I was just about to try calling Teri again."

"Nick's got a broken arm. No time to fill you in. I have to get to the hospital." She rushed across the room. "Need to change before I catch my death. Call Russ. He was there. I'm sure he'll tell you everything." She ran into her bedroom, shut the door, and changed. If only she had some of Jeff's or Jim's clothes to take to Nick.

As the clock struck twelve, Lynne arrived at the ER. Dressed in dry clothing, Nick lay on a gurney inside a cubicle, his arm in a cast. "You're dry. I mean, you're dressed. In dry clothes. I expected to see you in a hospital gown. Let me guess. You called your aunt and uncle, and they brought you a change of clothes."

"*Reluctantly.* I called on the way here. Didn't think Aunt Gwen would ever stop scolding after she wheedled the story from me." He pursed his lips, then smiled. "I told them you had my truck and would drive me to my place, so they went home."

"No doubt they'll give me a good scolding next time I see them since I'm the one who got you into this mess." Tears filled Lynne's eyes, and she hugged Nick. "I'm so sorry."

"Hey. I volunteered. We were rescuing those kids, remember? We had no choice under the circumstances."

After grabbing a tissue from the nursing station, she dried her eyes and reentered the cubicle. She sat in a chair next to the gurney. "Now, Big Guy. What happened after you made me leave with the kids?"

He chuckled. "Not much."

She slapped his leg.

Nick snickered. He explained how he'd followed Hamelin to the first floor and about the phone call that distracted him. "The chair leg must have hit my forearm. I was pretty sure it broke. But when that bruiser came at me, adrenaline kicked in. I swung my leg out as hard as I could. It connected right under his knee. Dislocated the joint. Or broke it."

Lynne chewed her lower lip then smiled. "I shouldn't be happy over someone's pain, but I can't help it in Hamelin's case."

Nick nodded. "I admit it. I enjoyed seeing him go down. He bellowed. I mean, *bellowed*. When he stumbled forward, I smashed his nose with the palm of my hand, did a spin you'd be proud of, and grabbed the pistol off the floor. I brought it up in a wide swing that hit Hamelin on the side of the head. He crashed to the floor."

"Thank God you came out of this with only a broken arm. You could have been killed if you hadn't put him out of commission." She popped out of the chair, hugged him again, and hopped onto the gurney next to him. "So you knocked him out."

"I wasn't sure. But I wasn't taking any chances. Do you remember the huge antique coat rack with the mirror and shelves in the foyer?"

"The wooden one with a seat?"

Nick nodded. "Since Hamelin could have been faking, and he was on the floor in front of it, I yanked it forward. It fell on him. Kept him from going anywhere."

Lynne blew a long breath between her lips. "So who called and interrupted your concentration? It wasn't me."

"I never checked." Nick pulled the cell from the windbreaker pocket. He tapped the option for missed calls. "It's Ashley's parents' number. I'm sure they've heard their daughter's safe by now. Although, I doubt they'll allow Ashley out after dark again until she's at least thirty-five." He chuckled. "But maybe that's a good thing."

She loved his humor. "Poor Ashley." Lynne shook her head. "I hope those teens learned a lesson."

"I hope they've learned something too. Maybe they'll come back to church after this."

Lynne bent to gaze into Nick's eyes. "Where did you learn the knee kick?"

"From Chris, Kathy's brother. We used to spar whenever he was on leave. He'd visit Kathy, but spend time with me while she was in class. Taught me what he'd learned in the Marines. We kicked a lot of trees in Escambia County."

Lynne giggled.

He searched her face. "What a beautiful sound. You giggling, I mean."

"I haven't giggled for a long time. Thank you."

Nick wrapped his good arm around her and pulled her to his side. His lips found hers, and a tingle coursed through her. *What a man.* Not your average junior pastor. *Hmmm…I wonder.*

She leaned sideways to give him a piercing stare. "Nick, you're not hiding a double life from me, are you? Like…undercover agent or something?"

Nick couldn't help but grin at Lynne. What should he tell her?

Teri Coleraine stepped into the cubicle. "They told me you were done. I'm here to take your statement and give you the good news." She halted. "Amm…I interrupting something?" Her brows rose.

As Nick's arm dropped to his side, Lynne scooted away from him. Her face turned a deep shade of rose.

Nick glanced from her to Teri. "Yes, Ma'am. But we can continue our *discussion* later." He smiled. "We'd welcome good news tonight. What do you have?"

Her mouth quirked as she sat in the chair Lynne had vacated. "Before the last two units left the scene tonight, a car raced into the driveway. In the dark, he must not have noticed the sheriff's department vehicles. No flashing lights. Didn't react until he was on top of us. Spun the car in the driveway and tried to escape. Without success, of course."

Nick's brows pinched. "Who was it? You already had The Piper, right? The hulk I knocked out?"

"We sure did. This new guy wouldn't talk, but an officer found incriminating evidence in his car when he checked the console. He was another of Hamelin's henchman, come to pick up the captives and take them to a yacht they planned to use for their getaway. Two units were sent to the dock and arrested the captain, searched the boat, and found more trafficking victims. The captain spilled his guts in exchange for a deal."

Nick gazed into Lynne's big, round eyes and circled her waist with his good arm. He glanced back at Teri. "Does that tie up everything? Or are there still gang members out there, somewhere?"

Teri brought out her pad and pen as she smiled. "For us, yes. Thanks to the information the captain supplied, we rounded up what was left of the gang." She looked at Lynne. "And your friend, Agent Trent, called before I headed to the hospital. He said they found their mole—actually, two of them. When Trent returned to Washington, he was told the order to bring him back must have been a miscommunication. It struck him as odd. He initiated his own investigation to ferret out the source of leaks and, in the process, they found one in the Jackson office, feeding information to Hamelin, and a second in their own department in D.C."

"No wonder Kim and Loring were attacked en route to Pensacola." Lynne grimaced.

"Yep. But now, this gang is history. Their human trafficking and drug business days are done. Hamelin will no doubt spend the rest of his life in the slammer. However long that may be. Even inside, convicts don't look kindly on human trafficking. He and his gang face very uncomfortable lives."

Nick squeezed Lynne. "This means no more peeking over your shoulder."

Lynne exhaled as if she'd been holding her breath since Teri walked in. "Thank God. And thank you for telling us."

"Thought it would make your evening. Now let me take your statements. I'll start with you, Lynne."

Teri took Lynne's account of the trek to the beach house, encounters with the thugs, finding the teens, and their escape. Then Nick gave his statement.

Half an hour later, Teri rose from the chair. "Okay, you two, try to rest. You've earned it."

Lynne stood from the gurney. "I'll say."

Nick slid off onto his feet and faced Lynne. "Shall we go, Navy Girl?"

She giggled again as Teri left the cubicle. "First...you didn't answer my question from earlier, Big Guy." She pinned him with her eyes. "*Do* you have a secret double life of which I should be aware?"

Nick slipped his hand onto the back of her neck and pulled her into a deep kiss that warmed him to his toes. When the moment ended, he gazed into her glistening hazel eyes and smiled. "My only double life is keeping you out of trouble, Miss Temple." He planted his lips on hers again. His fingers, still on the back of her neck, caressed her soft hair. Could she feel the love he had for her?

Chapter Forty-One

$\mathcal{L}$ynne's life spun into high gear for the new few months, caught up in a flurry of events during the holidays and through the New Year. Had it only been last August when she and Nick started dating? And yet, it felt as though they'd been together for years with all that had happened to them since summer. He'd even met her family at Christmas and fit right in. How long would it be before he'd be an official part of the Temple clan? Or she...a Livingston...she should say? "There you go again, Lynne, rushing things."

"What did you say?" Sam stuck her head through the doorway of Lynne's bedroom.

"Oh, nothing. We'd better hurry. Our fellas will be here soon. Don't want to be late for Kathy's wedding."

"I know. And I'm taking notes for my own big day this spring, even if it isn't a double wedding like Kathy's and Beth's. Although it might be if you and Nick could just get your acts together." Sam winked at Lynne, waltzed into the room, and checked her makeup in Lynne's dresser mirror. "I still can't believe Russ asked me to marry him last night. He's in so much trouble." She giggled.

Lynne stifled a laugh. This girl was such a trip.

"I'm engaged!" She waved her ring under Lynne's nose. "Me. Soon to be Mrs. Russ Highland."

Lynne hugged her friend. "I'm so happy for you, Sam." *I'd be even happier if...stop it.*

The doorbell rang, and Sam ran to the intercom.

Lynne's cell rang. *Teri?* She puckered her brows. Things had been so quiet since the arrest of The Piper and his gang. But the sheriff's department had kept the investigation open, just in case. Lynne pressed the green receiver icon. "Teri, what's happened?"

"Nothing. Girl, you really need to relax now that everything has settled down in your life."

"Settled down? I've been hopping ever since Kathy Kendall asked me to be her bridesmaid. So, what's going on? Why did you call? You'll be at the wedding, won't you? Nothing happened with the case against The Piper, has it?"

A chuckle came through the phone. "The only thing that's happened is the final member of Hamelin's gang has been sentenced. It's over, Lynne. I called to set your mind at rest."

A light, airy sensation fluttered through Lynne as if the last fear of running into one of Hamelin's men had just flown away. "Thank you so much for that wonderful news. Now, I hate to rush you, but—"

"It's okay. I know. I'm just walking out the door myself. Don't want to be late to the wedding."

Lynne disconnected and dropped her cell into her clutch bag. She made a final check of her violet, floor-length, flared hem bridesmaid dress, then pursed her lips. *Always the bridesmaid, never the bride.* "Oh, phooey. Where did that come from?" She needed an attitude adjustment. She would not spoil Kathy and Jacob's happy day. Lynne smiled. It was a happy day all around now.

What a surprise it had been when Kathy asked her to be a bridesmaid. They'd become good friends, probably because of Nick. How would he react when the couple exchanged vows?

"Come on, Lynnz. Russ and Nick are here. Time to leave."

A nosegay of deep purple and white violets in her hands, Lynne walked down the flower-adorned aisle of the church. She glanced at Nick, who stood next to Jacob as his best man. So handsome in his tux. Her insides quivered at the smile he gave her.

Someday. Someday soon. Please, Lord. I love him so much. What was that verse in Psalm? "...he shall strengthen your heart, all ye that hope in the Lord." *Yes, Lynne. There abideth hope for you.* Heat radiated in her chest as butterflies took flight. Had she really heard those words?

At the reception an hour later, the brides stood on the elevated balcony of the Barkley House at Pensacola Bay. They turned to throw bouquets over their shoulders to the single girls on the lawn. Lynne waited in the grass, far to the rear. Did this tradition hold any water? Did the one who caught the bouquet truly marry next? *Ha!*

The flowers took flight, and Lynne raised her arms. Both bouquets fell into them. *What?* She stared open-mouthed at Kathy and her sister, Beth, who doubled over with giggles. With her mouth still agape, Lynne glanced at Nick. He wore an undefinable expression on his face as if he held a secret, and it amused him.

"What are you snickering about, mister?"

"Nothing. Everything. The expression on your face." He chuckled.

Lynne walked up to him and punched his arm. He winced. She narrowed her eyes. "Oh, don't try pulling that injured arm bit on me again. You men. There's nothing wrong with your arm. Dr. White said you're fully healed."

He dropped his chin and pouted, then laughed.

After the guests left the reception, Nick took Lynne for a ride along the Gulf. What mild weather for February. And Valentine's Day was only a few days away. Could he wait that long? No.

She leaned back in the seat and closed her eyes.

He ached to hold her. *Was it too soon to expect her to make a commitment?*

Nick pulled into the first lot they came to along the Gulf and parked the truck. They got out, and Lynne removed her heeled sandals.

He led her along the surf without a word. He couldn't have asked for a more beautiful night. It seemed every star in the universe sparkled in the sky as gentle waves rolled to shore.

Lynne latched onto his arm. "Look." She pointed out to the water. "Dolphins swimming in the moonlight."

He circled her shoulders with one arm as they watched the bobbing creatures. "Do you remember the first time you saw dolphins here in Pensacola?"

She tittered. "I do. And I almost wound up swimming with them when I lost my balance on the pier. You saved me." Lynne gave him a peck on the cheek.

They continued their stroll.

A few minutes later, Nick stopped. He knelt in the sand on one knee as he took her hands in his. "I love you, Lynne. I've been in love with you since the first time we strolled on the beach in the moonlight."

She dropped to the sand with him.

He wrapped her in his embrace, and his lips met hers. When they parted, he pulled a box from his tux pocket and opened it.

When she glanced down at the emerald-cut diamond ring, Lynne's breath caught.

He slipped it on her finger and returned the box to his pocket. "Marry me, Miss Temple."

She threw her arms around his neck, and they toppled into the soft, sugary-white Pensacola Beach sand.

When their long, emotional kiss ended, they lay on their sides in sand-covered, formal attire. Nick took a deep breath and gazed into her sparkling eyes. "At least we didn't go swimming with the dolphins."

The  End

Be of good courage, and he shall strengthen your heart, all ye that hope in the Lord.

Psalm 31:24

About The Author

Raised in Illinois, Sharon attended most of her schooling through college in Chicago. She has also lived in Missouri, California, Florida, and Ohio. She is now a resident of Texas and retired from the clerical career world.

Her travels have also taken her to all but six states in the United States, plus Canada and Mexico.

Sharon K. Connell is a member of the American Christian Fiction Writers organization, the Houston Writers Guild, 2 Elizabeths Literary Magazine, and Christian Womens Writers Club (CWW). She runs a Facebook Group Forum for writers and readers, and puts out a monthly newsletter, Novel Thoughts, for everyone.

She is a graduate of the Pensacola Bible Institute in Florida and holds a certificate in fiction writing from the International Writing Program through the University of Iowa.

Stories Sharon writes are about people whose life experiences turn them to God and increase their faith.

She has written in other genres for short stories, but her genre is primarily Christian Romance Suspense.

Let the words of my mouth, and the meditation of my heart, be acceptable in thy sight, O Lord, my strength, and my redeemer.
Psalm 19:14

Links

Website: www.authorsharonkconnell.com

Amazon Author Page: http://www.amazon.com/author/sharonkconnell

Author's book page on Facebook:
https://www.facebook.com/averypresenthelpbook1

Author's Page on Facebook:
https://www.facebook.com/ChristianRomanceSuspense/

Group Forum on Facebook:
https://www.facebook.com/groups/ChristianWritersAndReadersGroup
Forum/

Twitter: https://twitter.com/SharonKConnell

Goodreads: https://www.goodreads.com/SharonKConnell

LinkedIn: https://www.linkedin.com/in/sharonkconnell

Pinterest: https://www.pinterest.com/rosecastle1/

Other Works
by Sharon K. Connell

A Very Present Help
Paths of Righteousness
His Perfect Love

~

Short Stories in Anthologies

Ding-A-Ling Holiday Blues
in Tales of Texas, Vol. 2

Spirit Lake
in Dark Visions

Thank you for Reading